SHATTERED ECHO

An Echo Branson Investigation: Book 1

Alex Westmore

Published by Inspired Quill: December 2018

Edition 1.5

Content Warning: This book contains themes of mental health and drug abuse.

Contact the author through their website: www.alexwestmore.net

Chief Editor: Sara-Jayne Slack
Cover Design: Deranged Doctor Design

Paperback ISBN: 978-1-908600-79-0
eBook ISBN: 978-1-908600-80-6
Print Edition

Printed in the United Kingdom

Printed in the United Kingdom
2 3 4 5 6 7 8 9 10

Inspired Quill Publishing, UK
Business Reg. No. 7592847
www.inspired-quill.com

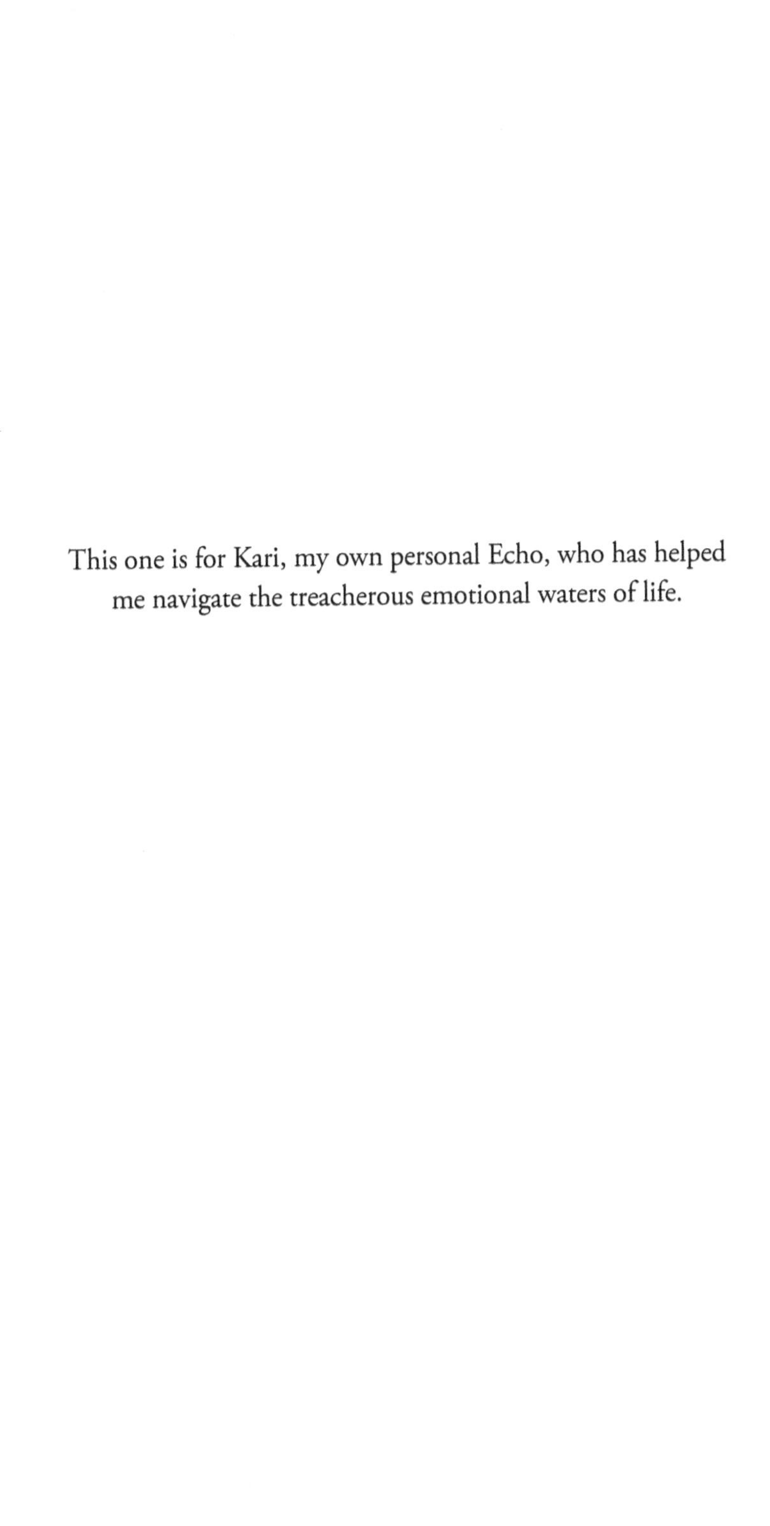

This one is for Kari, my own personal Echo, who has helped me navigate the treacherous emotional waters of life.

CHAPTER 1

I BECAME WHAT I am today at age fourteen, and it nearly drove me insane.

They say your teenage years are an insane time anyway, but mine were the real deal. Imagine coming into a paranormal power no one believes in and you didn't even know you possessed. Imagine being semi-normal one minute and supernatural the next. Imagine what would happen to your world if, suddenly, you knew what *everyone* around you was feeling.

That pivotal moment happened one chilly November afternoon of my freshman year in high school. High school had started out great for me: I'd been in a really nice foster home with two other non-foster kids for over a year and finally felt like I was getting a fair shake. The parents were cool, the kids didn't treat me like a stepchild, and life was good.

My best friend, Danica, and I were cutting through Mrs. Jorgensen's creek on our way home. It wasn't our usual route, but it was cold and we had things to do before the pep rally. Danica was a cheerleader and well-liked by everyone. We both attended a private school in Oakland, where most of the kids came from upper-middle-class white families. Our lack of social status was what brought us together. Danica didn't care that I was a kid with less than nothing because as a girl of mixed heritage, she found it hard enough to find *her* place. She was convinced that she'd never fully be accepted in either community whether she was one of *the haves* or not. If the black kids didn't like her, she just flipped them the bird. If the white kids didn't like her, she would just flip them two birds. That was the beauty of Danica. She didn't give a damn if you liked her or not.

Unfortunately, on this particular afternoon, someone liked her a bit too much.

That *someone* had followed us to the creek as we walked and chatted on our way home from school. I'd recently been feeling strange so I ignored the pinpricks on the back of my neck as we neared the hole some kids had cut into the cyclone fence.

As we neared the fence, those pinpricks changed into something I had never experienced. Like a blast of hot air on every nerve in my body, something warned me the person following us wasn't just using the shortcut; whoever it was intended to hurt one of us. I didn't know *how*, but I knew it as surely as if it had already happened.

Stopping just before the opening, I whirled around to face the cause of the tingling sensation: Todd Abrams, a linebacker on our football team.

"Hey," he said, leering at Danica. He never once looked my way. I was used to being invisible.

Blinking several times, I swallowed back a small pocket

of bile. The emotional blast radiated all the way to my fingertips and toes. It was almost as if I *were* Todd. I knew *exactly* what he wanted, and how he intended on getting his needs met. If I hadn't been so afraid of Todd, I would've been scared to death of what was happening *to me.* My heart raced, my palms were sweaty, my breathing became shallow, and I knew… I *knew* we were in trouble.

"Come on, Dani. We're going to be late," I said, never taking my eyes from Todd. My hands were shaking as I reached out to push Danica through the opening before he could get any closer. I sensed his intentions through every pore in my body, as if my soul kept jumping from my body to his. When my hand reached out to touch Danica, I suddenly felt *her* emotions as well. She was merely irritated by his interruption. She didn't know what he really wanted.

But *I* did.

"Beat it, Todd. I already told you I'm not interested." She was completely unaware of the danger; completely unaware Todd had come to get something he couldn't have.

"Jane," Todd said softly, looking over at me for the first time. He had shark eyes on either side of a putty nose. "Why don't you scoot along and let me walk Danica home?"

Yes, my real name – the name bestowed upon me at birth – is Jane. Jane Doe. I was born one of many Jane Does that year and actually remained one until my eighteenth birthday when I changed it to something more fitting; something more in line with who I turned out to be.

Something which was taking me over at that very moment.

Trying to ignore the weird feelings crawling beneath my skin like a bad drug, I inhaled deeply. Was I going crazy?

Was there something wrong with me? Could they tell? Danica, bless her heart, was staring at Todd as if *he* was nuts. Danica didn't appreciate *anybody* telling her what to do or assuming they knew what *she* wanted. If she had wanted him to walk her home, she would have asked him to. Apparently, she had already told him what she *didn't* want.

Todd's lust, anger, masculine arousal and something else I couldn't put my finger on felt palatable and tangible to me. I thought I was going to faint from the tornado-like sensations whirling through my mind, disorienting me. It took my breath away, and I had to fight to stay on my feet.

When I finally pushed the emotions away, I managed to say under my breath, "Danica. Please. *Go.*" This time, I shoved her with all my might, which wasn't easy. Danica was close to six feet tall; a good six inches taller than me.

Todd took a step toward the hole in the fence and I knew it was now or never. I knew it as if he'd whispered it in my ear; he wasn't taking no for an answer.

Swinging my heavy backpack at him, I hit him square on the side of the head, knocking him away from the opening and onto the ground. Then, with one final push, I shoved Danica completely through the hole before flinging myself on top of Todd.

"Run!" Glaring at Todd, who was lying on the ground holding his bloody head, I think I lost my mind. When my bag first hit him, half my books flew out, so I grabbed the nearest, heaviest one and continued my assault. I couldn't see where Danica went, but I felt her fear as I bashed Todd's head again and again with my five-pound math book. His lust transformed instantly to anger and rage. He wanted to kill me. He probably would have.

So I kept hitting him. And hitting him.

I don't know how long I smashed his forehead, but it was long enough for blood splatters to end up on my clothes. I probably would have kept hitting him until I crushed his head into a pancake, but Danica returned with Mr. Morgan, who pulled me off Todd.

"Jane!" Danica cried. I was still swinging my math book as Mr. Morgan dragged me off, and it took every ounce of strength Mr. Morgan had to keep me from going back.

Clearly, I had snapped.

Something had happened to me; something big and weird and scary. I was like a wild animal completely out of control. Mr. Morgan wouldn't take his arms from around me, even when I'd finally calmed down, which was wise. I kept glancing at the unmoving Todd, wondering if I'd killed him. I didn't think that was such a bad thing.

When the paramedics arrived for Todd, they came right behind the police. I was nearly incoherent by that time. Not because of what I'd done to Todd, but because my brain was frying from all the images and emotions I was getting from Danica, Mr. Morgan, the police, the paramedics, and even the bystanders who had wandered over from the park. I was a shore on which every emotion washed upon, and I just *knew* I was losing my mind.

Apparently, the police were pretty sure of it as well, and the next ambulance came for me. I remember being strapped down and given a shot of something. It finally calmed the whirlpool of emotions sucking me under.

"Be cool, Jane. Everything's gonna be okay."

As my eyes got heavy, the emotional noises of the crowd began to dissipate, leaving me with a question repeating through my mind like a skipping record:

Was I going crazy?

CHAPTER 2

EIGHT YEARS LATER, I was asking myself the same question. It wasn't like me to give someone a second chance to bury yet another dagger between my shoulder blades while I wasn't looking. So what was I doing here? Curiosity maybe? Wasn't the road to Hell paved with the bodies of dead cats, or was I mixing my metaphors? I grinned to myself at the image. Okay, so I *was* a little curious.

A week previously, my boss, Wes Bentley, as snooty as his name suggests, fired me from my lowly peon position as a stringer for the Police Beat section of the *San Francisco Chronicle*. I know, I know, how hard could it be to report on the numerous criminal activities in a place like the City by the Bay? Well, I wasn't fired for incompetency. I was fired for suggesting a well-known CEO was lying to our top investigative reporter during an interview. Lying through his ten-thousand-dollar DaVinci veneers.

Okay, so maybe I should have waited before blurting it out right in front of this prominent citizen, but I just couldn't help it. I had a foster parent once who told me my biggest problem was I lacked stoplights between by brain and my mouth. She was right about me not having stoplights, but wrong about that being my *biggest* problem. My greatest problem was also my biggest gift: the double-edged sword I wielded daily. When someone's lies are so huge and so powerful that they virtually knock me over, I have a tendency of contracting foot-in-mouth disease almost immediately. I can't help it.

I'm an empath.

I was born with the unique ability to "read" the emotions of those around me. Everyone *thinks* they want the truth, but that's until they get it. Then, all bets are off. It's not a fun place to be when someone says they love you when you *know* they really don't.

Like my ability to write and my fear of heights, being empathic is an innate component of my personality; as much a part of my genetic make-up as any other gene, only it kicked in when I least expected, but most needed it to. It has gotten me both into and out of trouble, and I knew the moment Mr. Bentley walked into the office which it would be that time.

Oh, I don't make a habit of reading the emotional state of others; first off, it's exhausting. Secondly, I have enough problems with my *own* emotions, thank you very much. I tend to use it only as a last resort, or whenever I think it justified. At that moment, in my ex-boss' office, it felt justified.

I knew Mr. Bentley didn't want to fire me that dark day, but his star reporter, Carter Ellsworth, had demanded my head on a rusty platter. Apparently, I had humiliated Carter in front of this lying, scheming, embezzling CEO, and that was the one thing that Carter Ellsworth could not abide: being embarrassed.

It wasn't my fault, really. I'd just returned from the police station and was walking by my favorite fountain at the front of our building. I have a thing for running water because it blocks out extraneous emotions.

Anyway, I was looking at the fountain, not realizing Carter was conducting his interview on the other side of it. I suppose the sound of the water also distorted any potentially damaging soundbites should the liar be illegally taped. It was a smart move on Carter's part, but he hadn't counted on me wandering by and pointing the finger like some tattling five-year-old.

As I started by them, I was slammed with a huge wave of deceit, dishonesty, and dissembling. Normally, I have mental shields up to protect me from inadvertent readings. Like I said, dealing with everyone else's emotions is an exhausting endeavor. You can only imagine what happens to empaths who are incapable of filtering out all the emotions that come at them every hour of every day. Unless a person is unconscious, emotions ooze from them like sweat from their pores; there's no smell, but they certainly have a physicality that only empaths can feel.

On that day, I felt them like a baseball bat to the back of my legs. The CEO's emotional darkness hit me with such force that I couldn't stop myself from muttering, "What a crock of shit," as I strolled by. It jumped right out of my potty mouth and landed on a pink slip with my name on it. It didn't matter that I was right, because as an empath, I was in the closet. I couldn't say, "Here's why I *know* he's a lying piece of crap." A world that can't fully handle homosexuals or biracial marriages sure as hell isn't ready for the likes of me.

Anyway, Carter got what he wanted, and I was let go.

So why did I go back?

Carter Ellsworth was the kind of guy who would ask to see the manager at a restaurant and demand the waiter be fired for some minor transgression, and he was pretty damn quick to pull the trigger and shoot my burgeoning journalism career right out of the sky. I knew plenty of people who despised him, and not one person who believed he had *any* redeeming qualities other than that damn Pulitzer. Hell, he probably slept with it.

When Wes walked in, I did a quick read and decided against raising my shields. Raising and lowering psychic energy forces is a little like the regular Joe putting his hands over his ears to keep from hearing someone. The only thing missing was the "Lalalalala."

"Thank you so much for coming, Echo. I wasn't sure… well, never mind. It was good of you to come." Wes Bentley stood in front of me and extended his well-manicured hand. Wes always wore that tanning booth glow; a little too much George Hamilton meets Bob Barker. I shook his hand and took note of his new Christian Dior suit and thousand-dollar hand-painted tie. Wes was one of the best-dressed men in the city and commanded attention wherever he went. At that moment, however, all pretense of command had been replaced by something I had never seen or felt from Wes in the seven months I'd been at the paper: contriteness. Yes, the man who cut me loose with the weak explanation that "if Carter wants you gone, you're gone," was standing there with his hat in his hand.

Now wasn't *this* an interesting turn of events?

Carter Ellsworth wielded power because he'd won a Pulitzer for work he did during the Iraq War that pretty much gave him *carte blanche* to destroy the nobodies of the world. Like me. Pulitzer winners are a rare breed, and the majority of them, from what I gather, prefer to keep their fame and fortune on the East Coast, in places like New York. For whatever reason, Carter preferred foggy San Francisco; probably because the frequent mist hid his ugly demeanor.

Wes moved to the other side of his desk. What is it with people who feel the need to conduct business with an enormous desk between them and others? I made a mental note that that topic would make an interesting article someday. You know, take a look at fifty successful men and women and examine the size of their desks compared to the size of their ego. It would be an interesting little psycho-sociological survey.

"Well, Ms. Branson, I appreciate your time, so let me get down to brass tacks. Have you found another job yet?"

Oh, how I wanted to lie; to say, yeah, the *New Yorke*r picked me up and offered me my own column and I'm moving there tomorrow. But the sad truth was, I couldn't even get an interview with any of the smaller papers in the area and was working part time at Luigi's, the bakery directly below my tiny apartment. Poor Luigi took pity on me when I told him I'd been canned, so he offered to help me out until I got a real job. Luigi was an angel walking among mortals, and everyone in the neighborhood and surrounding vicinity knew and adored him.

"I'm still looking for something in my field, yes." I read a sense of relief from him. He wanted something from me. This was getting more interesting every second.

"I see." West folded his overly tanned hands on the desk and leaned forward. "I'm going to be straight up with you, Branson. Tomorrow, you're going to be reading Carter's retraction of the Glasco's embezzlement story." He eyed me carefully as if trying to read *me*. Wes could look all he wanted, he would never *know* how I was feeling. Looking into his light blue eyes, I understood that he was trolling; feeling me out before laying the rest of his cards out on the table. There really was no need to since I was pretty sure I could see what was coming. A retraction for the editor-in-chief of a big newspaper is a little bit like getting caught with your hand in the cookie jar. It means that you didn't fully do your job. Whenever a story suffers a retraction, *everybody* looks bad, and worse… amateurish. Well, the only amateur who had been fired over this story was me. Apparently, the truth had come out and now both Carter and Wes were eating crow.

I wondered what crow tasted like and if you served it with white wine.

"So, he *was* lying." I knew it was a fact, but Wes had cut me off so quickly there had been no time to prove it; someone else had obviously done the job for me. I would have bet my last dollar that Jennifer Ridge, one of the best fact-checkers on the staff, was the one who found out the truth about the lying CEO.

"Near as I can tell, the man has no idea what the truth looks like." Wes shook his head sadly. He hated retractions. He hated *anything* that made him look bad.

"Jennifer?"

Wes nodded. "It took her longer than Carter wanted, so he pressured her to sign off on his story. You know how Carter can be."

I nodded. Jennifer was so good at her job that if an editor was unsure of the fact, they would write AJ in the margin; an editorial mark which had been created to simply mean 'Ask Jennifer'. "Actually, Wes, all I know of Carter Ellsworth is that he's an ass who struts around like the only rooster in the hen house."

Wes tried to hide his grin. The grin he could hide, the emotions behind it, not a chance. As a reporter, Wes Bentley held the truth in the highest regard. At this moment, he appreciated mine. And why shouldn't he? I had nothing to lose by being honest and he was so used to having someone's lips attached to his ass that my honesty must have been refreshing.

"Well, ahem, yes, Carter does have a tendency to take himself a little too seriously."

"Or something."

"I don't know what you've heard about me, Branson, but I am a man who owns his mistakes. It's not easy, mind you, but you don't get to be in a position of power without taking responsibility for both the good decisions and the bad. Under the circumstances, I was wrong to fire you. I assumed Carter's story had checked out and you had not only been unprofessional, but had made him look bad. Wrong on both counts. I would like to right those wrongs."

"What did you have in mind?"

"I would like to offer you your job back."

The beauty of my gift is that emotional subtleties peek

around the obvious, and I get a clearer picture of what's going on with the person I'm reading. Wes was offering me my job back, hoping I would accept it without playing hardball.

Unfortunately for him, I did not grow up in a warm and loving environment with a soft, cushy life. I grew up moving from one home to another in the ghettos of Oakland, California. You don't last there as a white kid if you can't hit a fastball, and I was one hell of a hardball player. I knew I'd been unjustly fired, but the problem with my power is that it's impossible to explain without uncovering exactly *what* I am. I wasn't about to unveil that part of me to anyone other than my closest friends. So no, I wasn't going to make this easy on him. "I appreciate your offer, Wes, but the police beat isn't really for me. I came here with the idea of being a journalist. I have the drive, the talent, and the instincts for it. I think I would rather wait until a real offer comes along." I rose and extended my hand. "But thank you. I do appreciate knowing that I was right about Glasco." One thing I'd learned from a dozen or so foster brothers was the importance of a good curveball, and I had just fired one right past Wes Bentley.

Wes quickly rose and scooted around the enormous desk. "Well then, consider yourself offered a real position here. I like your style, Echo. You don't miss a beat and you don't mince your words. All of those are essential ingredients for being a top-notch reporter."

The swing and a miss sound you heard was *my* bat whiffing at the curveball Wes just threw past me. I was so stunned, I barely knew what to say. "Reporter?"

Wes nodded. "Liz Pensky is going to the *Post*, so I need

a new IR. The job is yours if you want a shot at it."

Now *that* was a job offer… and one that I wasn't expecting. I could tell by the look in his eyes he enjoyed the surprise. I blinked several times and thought carefully about my response. I knew that, given the chance, I *could* be a good investigative reporter; a *really* good one. I wanted to use my expensive Mills College education for something other than running around collecting short pieces for the Police Beat. This was my chance; my big chance. The question was did I want to take a job from a guy who fired me at the whim of the Golden Boy reporter?

Hell yes I did.

"What about Carter? Won't he have something to say about this?" I didn't care that my question rankled Wes. Don't throw a carrot in front of me if it's dirty or rotten, 'cause I'll throw it right back.

"*I* run this paper and *I* make the decisions around here. I gave him what he wanted when I thought he was right. Obviously, he wasn't. Do you want the job or not?"

"I accept." I reached out and shook his hand. "When do I start?"

"How does tomorrow morning sound?"

"I'll be here."

"Excellent. Then stop by HR before I saddle you with a pro. You'll be working with someone until you get the hang of it."

Nodding, I opened the door to his office. "I appreciate the opportunity, Wes. I swear, you won't regret it."

Wes stepped so close to me I could smell the coffee he'd had for breakfast. "I just have one question before you go. How did you *know*?"

"That Glasco was lying?"

"Yes. Carter said that you sounded so cocksure of yourself. How could you have been so sure?"

Grinning, I stood on tiptoe and whispered, "Like you said, I have great instincts."

Wes pulled away and eyed me once again. "That's it? No source?"

Smiling even wider, I started out the door. "That's it. Well, and maybe just a teeny bit of voodoo magic."

WHEN I GOT out of Ladybug, my red 1965 VW Bug, Luigi was waiting at the front of the bakery with his arms akimbo.

"I can tell by the look on your face…" Luigi Tarabini was wildly gesticulating as I walked through the door.

"Now don't get your panties in a wad, Lou."

Luigi threw his head back and laughed. He'd come from Italy to the United States with his parents when he was a young boy; not that anyone could tell by his accent that he'd been here for over fifty years. Growing up in Little Italy will do that to you, I suppose.

"So… what happen'?"

"He offered me a job."

Luigi's pretend mad face softened. "A good one or a bad one?"

"A great one. A *real* one. He wants to train me as an Investigative Reporter." I walked to Luigi and hugged him. "Thank you for letting me work here… again. I owe you."

"Not another wor'. You know you can always work here."

"And you can always be counted on. How come you're still single?"

"Always turning the tables on Luigi, eh? You go on now an' leave an ol' man to make a living."

I smiled warmly into his brown eyes and lightly brushed some flour of his very full, very Italian mustache. "You sure you don't need my help down here?"

"I got some day-olds you can take, and maybe you can help me with the dishes later."

"Is the dishwasher out again? I'm going to give that plumber a piece of my mind." Luigi had a heart of gold and didn't deserve to get the screwgie from disreputable repairmen. I made a mental note to revisit my plan to dig up the sewer dwellers who made their living by taking advantage of good, hard-working folks like Luigi.

"It's not working so good, no."

"Will you let *me* make the call this time? I'm sure our consumer experts at the paper can recommend a reliable plumber who can get the job done right the first time."

"You worry too much."

"And you get ripped off too often. I'm going upstairs to get my things ready for tomorrow, then I'm coming down here to help you. *Capiche?*"

Luigi rolled his eyes at me. "Two years and still no accent!" Throwing his flour-covered hands in the air, he left me to tend to Mrs. Malone, or, as we called her in secret, The Widow. Mrs. Malone was the poster girl for octogenarian flirting. I thought it was really cute. Luigi felt otherwise.

When I finished up with Mrs. Malone, I grabbed the day-olds and took a hard left to the stairway leading up to my apartment, situated over the shop.

Luigi's Bakery had been in the same place for sixty years. His father, Luigi Sr., opened it shortly after landing in San Francisco, when Luigi was about eight. I managed to get the apartment when Luigi's mother passed away and he inherited her house on Nob Hill. He rented it to me for a song because he didn't need the money and because I do errands for him. I also cover whenever he needs a break to go to the bank or the store. Anyone who thinks running a bakery sounds easy is a fool. It's a physically demanding labor of love. Since I moved in two years ago, shortly after my graduation from Mills, Luigi and I had looked after each other. Oh, and my Italian accent? It's quite good, really, but I love pushing his buttons.

Opening my front door, I was greeted, as I always am, by my Siamese cat, Tripod.

"Hey Cutie," I said, kneeling down to scritch his ears. Yes, that's *scritch*. You scratch an itch or a dog's back, but if you attempt to apply that maneuver to a cat, you'll find its claws embedded in your hand. Cats prefer scritching, and if you own one, you know exactly what I mean.

I rose and checked my messages. There was one from Danica, still my best friend, and two from telemarketers. As I erased the messages, Tripod rubbed up against my legs as best he could. I had found him on the bakery doorsteps, cold, wet, and dehydrated one foggy morning. Luigi said I could keep him if I had him checked out by a vet. So, I bundled him up and took him to Dr. Elaine for a full battery of tests, which revealed a rare cancer present in his left front leg.

Two years later, Tripod is cancer free and manages quite

nicely with three legs. As a result of keeping him alive, he's been the best pet in the world.

I picked up my phone and called Danica's office. Her secretary put me right through, as she always does.

"Hey there unemployed chick. How's the job-hunting going? Any bites?"

"I bagged one; a really good one, too."

"Excellent! Do tell."

So I did, much to Danica's delight. Danica and I had been best friends since the eighth grade and had shared all of the ups and downs, trials and tribulations that college had to offer. After five years together at Mills, we both decided the Bay Area was where we'd make our fortunes. Unfortunately for me, Danica was the only one who'd made any.

After graduating with a degree in computer science, she'd created a program that instantly alerted a company whenever someone was trying to break through a firewall or other security system. Unlike other programs, hers alerted via audio as well as video, before slamming a wall around all files and locating the thief. The program was aptly named The Echo, after me, but not because I was her best friend; she'd gotten the idea back in high school when I finally learned how to shield myself from the onslaught of emotions from people near me. The Echo was patented, Danica made a bundle, and now she was the sole owner and CEO of Savvy Software, an up-and-coming company beginning to be noticed by the other big players in the space. Silicon Valley was keeping a *close* eye on them.

"I can't believe old man Bentley admitted to making a mistake," Danica said, crunching something in my ear.

"Carrot?"

"Bingo."

"Diet?" Danica had tried every diet on record, not because she needed to, but because her Geek Squad of computer programmers were working on a dietary software program even the biggest yo-yo dieter could get results with.

"Not this time. Baby's got back and looks like she's gonna keep it. So, when do you go to work, Clark?"

I grinned. Danica had been calling me Clark Kent since I was the editor of the Mills newspaper. She had always called my gift my *superpower*. What a geek. She was one of the very few people who knew about me, and the only *natural* who knew. My supernatural friends and I prefer the term paranormal; it's less arrogant.

"Tomorrow morning. They'll apprentice me with a seasoned veteran until I learn the ropes. I am *totally* excited."

"It's what you've always wanted, Clark, though it's beyond me what you get out of digging around in people's dirty laundry. Quite frankly, I've never really understood the pull."

"You just don't have any appreciation for the press."

Danica made a few derisive noises. "If I want the truth, the *real* truth, I sure as hell won't get it from the news. Anyway, let's not go there. Congratulations on your ladder climbing. It's about time your superpowers gave you a leg up on the competition."

"Hey, the last time I used my ability I got fired."

"You got fired because Carter Ellsworth is a dick. Uh oh, my red lights are blinking. I better scoot along. A boss's work is never done. The Boys are all excited about our first role-playing game and they keep bombarding me with questions. You know how they are. I want them to focus on the diet program, and all they can talk about is some dumb hack and slash."

The Boys were a trio of Berkeley graduates who had been rejected by a number of top firms because they wanted to be hired as a package deal; unheard-of in the over-saturated computer nerd market of Silicon Valley. After being turned away by just about every major software company, they arrived on Danica's doorstep. She took one look at their résumés and hired all three on the spot. In a way, they were to Danica what Tripod was to me; grateful for a chance, and they rewarded Savvy Software with some of the best programs on the market, making Danica even richer.

Now, the three of them shared an enormous office where they spent far more than the requisite 40 hours developing programs to put Savvy Software on a bigger technological map. Their office, nicknamed The Batcave, was a technological and electronic marvel filled with all the latest gadgets and geek-ware.

"Then you better get moving. You can't leave those boys alone for a second."

"Isn't that the truth? Let's have dinner after your big day so you can tell me what it's like to finally be on the A team."

"How about Aliotto's?"

"You're on. Damn, now Heidi is buzzing me. Gotta go. See you tomorrow, six-ish."

After hanging up, I opened a can of cat food and fed Tripod before picking out my outfit and shoes for my big day. Tripod picked out the slick number for me. He has impeccable taste in clothes. I knew when he liked something just like I knew that that CEO was lying. Not all empaths can read animals, and I can't read all of them, but I can and have always been able to read Tripod. That's why I couldn't let the vet put him down. His will to survive was just too strong. He *wanted* to live and here he was; living high on the hog, eating canned tuna. But he lived for catnip. My cat was addicted, but it was the only thing that perked him up after he lost his leg. Animals like Tripod appreciate the second chance to live. I think we all need second chances, and sometimes even thirds and fourths.

After my fourth foster home, I was pretty aware of the importance of second chances. In a foster home, second chances are as rare as blue diamonds. As a foster kid you are, by nature, incredibly expendable, so if you blow it, if you make any irreconcilable mistakes, you'll find yourself right back in the care of social services.

By the time middle school started, I'd been in nine different homes. It wasn't that I was a bad kid; I just wasn't going to be anyone's Cinderella. If you're lucky enough to have missed out on the foster care system, count your blessings. In California, a foster child can bring in $1200 a month. Add four foster kids to a house and that brings you an income of almost $5,000 a month, or $57,000 a year. For many, not *all* mind you, but for many, being a foster parent was a job; a high-paying, stay-at-home job. That meant we children were little more than dollar signs who cooked, cleaned, washed cars, did yard work, you know... basic Cinderella chores.

Well, I was *nobody's* indentured servant, no siree, and that attitude got me kicked out of more than one foster home. When I wasn't at a foster home, I was being educated in the game of Life by Britt Bevelaqua, senior orphan at the children's home. Senior orphan was Britt's self-described *nom de plume.* She was three years older and lightyears wiser than me, and was my first idol. I thought she totally rocked. Britt smoked, she wanted a tattoo, and, most importantly, she refused to be pushed around by anyone. For whatever reason, Britt took me under her wing and educated me on the ins and outs of the Californian childcare system. I learned that we were worth money; that that money was seldom used toward our care, and that without love and kindness, there was no need to accept our Cinderella status. So, like my idol, I was in and out of homes for being "disrespectful, irresponsible, incorrigible, blah, blah, blah."

The second to last time that I saw Britt, she had slipped me two $20 bills and told me to use them only when I needed to get out for good. At the time, I was just 13 and preparing for what would hopefully be my final foster home. Britt was 16 and preparing for her freedom. She was through being part of such a flawed system. For Britt it was time to run.

And she did.

I lay there every night for two weeks, wishing I had asked her to come back for me. But Britt knew I wasn't ready to run, and she wasn't going to drag around excess baggage.

What Britt *didn't* know, what she *couldn't* have known was just how soon I would be following in her footsteps. In less than a year I would find myself coming face-to-face with the onset of my gift.

And I wasn't the least bit prepared for where it would take me.

CHAPTER 3

WHEN I GOT to work my first real day of being a reporter, I waited outside Wes Bentley's office with my eyes closed, meditating. Sometimes stress interferes with our ability to properly maintain both the shield and our general health and wellbeing, and meditation was one way to reduce that stress.

I was feeling pretty good when Wes called me in, but the moment I walked into his office and saw who was sitting in the other chair, I felt my shield rattle a little.

"Echo, have you ever been formerly introduced to Carter Ellsworth?"

Carter turned to meet me, his face dropping the moment he heard my name. "But... I thought you—"

"I did fire her," Wes said, grinning like a wolf, as if this was his own personal joke. "Before I realized that *she* was the only one who understood that your man was a liar. I don't fire people who have good instincts, Carter, and so I've hired her back. Now, if you have a problem with that—"

Tired of being invisible, I extended my hand to Carter.

"No, we haven't been formally introduced. I'm Echo Branson."

Carter turned from my outstretched hand to Wes. "Is this a joke?"

I retracted my hand and sighed. What an asshole.

"Don't be rude, Carter," Wes said. "When a lady extends her hand, show some respect and shake it. I will not have Neanderthals in my office."

Carter turned to me and extended his hand. I wondered if Neanderthal behavior applied to women as well. I decided not to test it and shook his hand. His disdain filled the room, and I felt it even with my shield up.

"Good," Wes said. "Now, let's get down to business." Wes moved to the other side of the desk and motioned for me to sit down, so I did.

"Carter, you know how much retractions chap my hide. We've been through all of this. But Echo, here, shows promise and I'm putting you in charge of showing her the tricks of the trade." Wes held his hand up to stop Carter from saying something he'd regret. "It's been my experience in thirty plus years of journalism that all good reporters, at some point, need a reminder of the basics… you know… go back to the roots of what makes a reporter stand out from the others. I am giving you the opportunity to teach someone what you know as well as remind you about the principles of *good* reporting. This assignment serves a dual purpose for both of you." Wes turned to me. "Echo, my gut tells me you have what it takes to be a great reporter. Not a good reporter, not a famous reporter, but a *great* one. Good reporters are a dime a dozen. Everyone who can dot an i or press the spell check button thinks they can write, but it takes someone really special to do what Carter does. Because I am a man of some worth and integrity, I'm going to make up for firing you by offering you the chance to learn from the best in the business." Leaning back in his five-thousand-dollar leather chair, Wes laced his hands behind his head. "Do either of you have any questions?"

With the anger fairly oozing out of Carter, it was pretty clear how *he* felt about this whole thing. It felt unjustly punitive to him. Had I been in his position, I might have felt that way too, but I wasn't. Wes wasn't kidding around. He honestly believed I had something special and he wanted me trained by the best reporter he had. Who was I to look a gift horse and his jackass in the mouth?

"I really appreciate the opportunity, Wes, and I'll do everything in my power to make you proud."

A slight grin twitched at the corners of Wes' mouth. "Excellent. Then unless either of you have any questions, I suggest you get started right away."

I rose and thanked him for his time and waited for Carter. I didn't have to wait long. When Wes Bentley issued a directive, you moved your butt. Carter's was moving so quickly, I practically had to run to keep up.

Without saying a word, he grabbed his car keys and headed for the elevator. I wasn't about to let him treat me like some homeless dog, and I was about to say as much when he stopped at the elevator door and turned on me.

"Look, I know you probably think this whole thing was quite a coup, but—"

"You don't know *jack*. Don't presume to know what I think about *anything*. We can either continue spinning out about something that's over, or we can move beyond it."

Carter's blue eyes burned into mine. "Beginner's luck isn't something to crow about, Branson." He shook his head. If Carter wasn't so enamored with himself, he'd be good looking. Wavy black hair, deeply set blue eyes, and a cleft chin, he looked the perfect role for a news anchor. He was slightly over six feet tall, but carried himself like he was much taller. One thing I can say about Carter: he was an impeccable dresser. His navy-blue mock turtleneck contrasted with his eyes, and his black blazer had to have been tailored to fit his body so perfectly.

"Luck? If that was beginner's luck, what do you call *your* move? Advanced Mistake?" I held his gaze. I could feel his anger simmering. One point for me. "So, what's on the docket for today?"

"Docket?"

"Never mind. Look, you don't have to like me to train me, and I don't have to like you to learn from you. We're both professionals here, aren't we?"

Carter laughed derisively. "No, *I'm* a professional, Branson. You're—"

"Careful, Carter," I said, unsmiling. "Don't lower yourself into the gutter. If this is that hard for you, then why don't you just march back in there and explain it to Wes."

"I might just do that."

I motioned to the door.

Carter glared at me. "You think I want to drag a rookie, and that's overstating the situation, around with me because some asshole lied and we printed it? It happens all the time; only Wes seems to think it's some egregious error that never happens. Well, it does. So, don't think you're going to *help* me, Branson. I don't know how long old man Bentley is going to ride his white charger, but until he comes to his senses and throws you back into the little pond you crawled out of, stay out of my way."

Little pond? Ouch. I turned and grabbed his arm before he could get away. "All I want is a chance."

"And all I want is a place on the French Riviera. Grow up, Branson. Real life doesn't work the way you think it does."

Just then, Wes poked his head outside. My guess was that his secretary told him what was going on and he decided to check it out for himself. "Still here? Get a move on, Carter, and be sure you show Branson something she can use. Every day, I want her to be able to tell me one thing she learned from you. Got it?"

Carter shook his head in disgust. "Yeah. Sure."

"Carter, don't make me regret giving you a second chance as well. Understand?"

Carter fairly glowered over at me. "Fine. I'll be at 1215 Lamarr on Russian Hill. You can follow in your own car." Then he turned to me. "You *do* have a car, right?"

I didn't reply. This was going to be a lot harder than I thought.

IT TOOK LESS than twenty minutes to reach the beautiful lavender Victorian with white trim. The house was palatial by Victorian standards, and someone had dropped a pretty penny fixing it up. That's one thing about San Francisco homes; no one can beat our Victorians. No one.

When I got there, I found Carter leaning against his silver Lexus, punching something into his phone while continuing his conversation via his headphones. He didn't bother to look up when I approached. I waited, good little puppy that I was, until he finished his conversation, and then I asked him what it was we were here to dig up.

"Okay, here's the gig," Carter said, pocketing his phone. "We're getting an exclusive here, so please just sit still and be quiet. Don't act like you're a reporter, don't even act like you're interested. Just. Sit. Still. What's the number one rule?"

I shook my head. "I don't—"

"Rule number one: stay out of my way. Think you can handle that?"

I glared at him. "Gee, let me think. I don't really know. It's so tough." I started up the stairs.

"I'm not screwing around here, Branson! Can't you just watch and learn?"

"I could. Who knows? Are you coming?"

He pushed past me on his way to the door. Loathing would be too polite a term for what he was feeling for me at that moment. "You're impossible."

"Maybe, but I happen to think you're pretty good at what you do."

He whirled around. "Pretty good? A Pulitzer only ranks as pretty good in your book?"

"I'll admit it's impressive, but what have you done lately? You can't ride that pony forever, Carter. Haven't you heard that you're only as good as your last book?"

"Interesting you mention that. I'm writing my memoirs."

Of course he was. "Memoirs? How old are you, anyway?"

"Thirty-seven."

I shook my head. "People under fifty should wait to write their memoirs."

"Why is that?"

"You haven't really lived life by your mid-thirties. I mean, I know you've had some life experiences and stuff, but come on."

Carter got to the top of the stairs and shook his head. "Are you always so Goddamned opinionated?"

I nodded. "Always."

"Figures." Reaching for the doorbell, Carter sighed. "Silence is golden, remember?"

"So is the truth. Try finding it while we're in there."

When we entered the house, I tried not to stare at the gorgeous antiques filling the entranceway. The hallway floor was a light marble with gold veins. Even the paintings on the wall were antiques, or at least, great reproductions of them. My guess was the former. Whoever owned this place could afford the real thing.

"Mrs. Galloway will see you now," the maid said.

Maid? Who had maids complete with old-style maid uniform in San Francisco? It made me nauseous. I disliked this woman immediately. "Mrs. Galloway? Of—"

Carter shot me a look. "Be *quiet*. Don't make me send you to the car."

"You wouldn't." But I knew he would.

When we entered the enormous sitting area, Mrs. Galloway sat straight-backed in a red and green Queen Anne chair. She had a petite teacup and saucer in her lap with the teabag string hanging over the side. I estimated her age to be close to sixty. She wore her hair like Grace Kelly and was wearing a Donna Karan teal pants suit. Not that I know my fashion very well, but DK is Danica's designer of choice.

We were following up on the story that Mr. Galloway had gone missing. He'd vanished a week previously, leaving behind his wife and daughter, his very lucrative financier business, and everything in between. The cops had found his car at the Oakland airport, and didn't suspect foul play because Mrs. Galloway had mentioned her husband had recently suffered a bout of depression. We'd run one or two articles about his disappearance, but without foul play, the story faded by day three. Carter obviously felt there was more to the disappearance than the cops believed, or we wouldn't be here.

"Mrs. Galloway, it's so nice to meet you at last." Carter's charm entered the room before he did, and I could see why he was so good at getting people to open up. His smile, his demeanor, and everything else about him warmed up the room. Well, everything except Mrs. Galloway. The only warmth emanating from that old woman was sitting in her lap.

"Mr. Ellsworth," she said, extending a left hand that sported the sister to the Hope Diamond. How she could even move that hand was beyond me. "Please, do have a seat." Her eyes locked onto mine and I immediately read a wariness directed at me. I wondered if it was because I was a female or because I didn't have Carter's credentials. I figured it was a little of both. I'm an empath, not a telepath.

"I didn't realize you would be bringing your assistant."

"My…? Oh, yes well, it's an important story. I want to make sure I get it right."

Mrs. Galloway looked dubious as she motioned for me to take a seat. Innocent people don't tend to be suspicious, but Mrs. Galloway was filled with it.

SITTING DOWN, I watched Carter work his magic. He was smooth, relaxed, and very patient with her. I was most impressed with his listening skills. He was a master fisherman; letting the line out slowly, effectively keeping her talking. His questions were delivered slowly and deliberately, allowing Mrs. Galloway plenty of time to answer. I had to mentally congratulate him. He was very good.

There was only one problem with this interview.

She was lying.

I wasn't trying to read her. I mean, I didn't go into the interview with any agenda other than to watch *a pro* at work. Carter is a Grade-A jerk, but I can separate my personal feelings from my professional duty. My duty was to learn from one of the best. Unfortunately, my abilities often supersede my desires to do the right thing and kick in at the most bizarre moments.

Like now.

Suddenly, without warning, Mrs. Galloway reached over and touched my arm. I was so busy trying to scribble my notes down that I didn't see her reach for me.

Some emotions strike chords louder than others and in my empathic world, dishonesty was one such note. Different empaths have different abilities. Not all of us can read animals. Most of us feel positive emotions more than negative ones. Some of us have additional abilities that complement our empathic skills, or a smattering of other psychic abilities as well, but for those of us still sane, we are aware that the strength of our shields determines the longevity of our sanity. My lowest shield had just been corrupted, and that meant one thing: I sensed every emotion in the room whether I wanted to or not.

I winced at the power of her deceit. I didn't want it, I hadn't tried to read it, and now, I just wanted it to go away.

What was I supposed to do now? Raise my hand and point to Mrs. Galloway and shout out *liar, liar, pants on fire*? I had already screwed Carter once with my "opinion". How in the hell was I going to tell him yet another big story was slipping sideways on him?

Clearly, I wasn't.

Suddenly, all of the notes I'd taken had a different ring to them. Everything was becoming much clearer to me. We were here because Mrs. Galloway had called Carter to offer him an exclusive. Mrs. Galloway acted like she didn't know where her husband was, but the emotional read filtering through my system said otherwise. Why would she call us here only to lie to us? What could she possibly have to gain from this charade? And perhaps the better question was; what in the hell could I possibly do to get Carter to see that, for some reason, Mrs. Galloway was manipulating him? Of course, I couldn't *prove* any of this. Not yet. Not now. I would have to start the game pretty quickly before Carter started writing yet another story written on a foundation of lies.

But what could I do? If I didn't say something and this was another print and retraction, my career would sputter and stammer before it ever got a chance to sprout wings and fly. I would go down with him. If I *did* say something, Carter would demand proof. I would have to do some real investigative digging before I opened my mouth and sealed my fate. And while I relished the idea of doing that, I didn't look forward to telling Carter my suspicions. This time, I showed some restraint. I merely looked up at Mrs. Galloway and forced a grin. Yeah, she was lying, all right, and she was a pretty smooth liar at that. For whatever reason, she had constructed an elaborate story focusing on Mr. Galloway's depression. She'd intimated quite a few times she never really knew what was going on in his life; she just knew he was popping Zoloft like candy.

"I CAN'T BELIEVE it," Carter said as he stepped over a newspaper lying on the sidewalk.

"Can't believe what?"

"That you actually kept your mouth shut the entire time. I'll give you a point or two for that."

"So what did you think?"

"About your self-restraint?"

"About her story. What did you think of *her*?"

Carter fingered the cleft of his chin as he leaned against his Lexus. "Something didn't ring true, but I can't put my finger on it."

I nearly leapt up and down. "Really?"

"Yeah. Too pat. She was awfully calm for a woman whose husband was missing. It felt like she didn't care one way or the other if he showed up. She also seemed to lean a little too hard on the antidepressant issue; like she wanted to make sure we got it."

I nodded. This was a moment where I had to play my cards right. "You think she might know where her husband is?"

Carter inhaled slowly. "She knows *something*."

"What makes you think she's not on the up and up?

What were you looking for?"

Carter grinned; his first genuinely warm moment with me. "I've interviewed a lot of people in my life, Branson. You learn to watch for subtle nuances; eyes shifting or closing, body language that just doesn't jive with the words. You even start paying attention to breathing patterns. I'm a very astute people reader. Unfortunately, that's not something I can teach you. You either have it or you don't. If you do, then you learn to hone it like a chef's knife until you're really, really sharp."

"Wow. So she gave you all kinds of nonverbal cues."

Carter had a faraway look in his eyes, as if he had just performed some sort of hypnotism on Mrs. Galloway. I had to hand it to him; he was playing his mentor card with a great deal of vigor. "Nonverbal cues as well as verbal. Her voice had a flat quality to it; almost as if the whole thing bored her."

Okay, so Carter wasn't a complete noodle. I was a little impressed by his observational skills because he'd been right about Mrs. Galloway's voice. She *did* sound bored, or uncaring of the fact that her husband was missing. She went on for a bit too long about his depression, and mentioned he never used the Oakland airport because he hated having to cross the bridge. She also said he seldom withdrew more than $200 at a time. All of this was mentioned without inflection. The woman was an iceberg.

"So, where do we go from here?"

Carter pulled his cell from his pocket and started typing on the screen. "How are your computer skills?"

I thought about the Boys. "Pretty good."

"Let's see what you can dig up that hasn't already been

dug up about Mr. Galloway; find something we don't already know. Dig hard, deep, and fast. We need to find him before the body surfaces."

"Body? You think he's dead?"

Carter looked at me. "Don't you?"

I didn't. Mrs. Galloway not only knew where her husband was, she knew what had happened to him. "I definitely think she knows something, if not a whole lot more than something."

"And how do you know this, Branson?" He folded his arms across his chest in a *prove it to me* attitude.

What could I say? *The same way I knew the first time?* "She mentioned a couple of things I thought odd."

"Such as?"

"The dog. There were three pictures of Glen and the dog, but there was no dog."

"So?"

"Carter, there *was* no dog. Not anymore." I watched him watch me. He wasn't getting it.

"Branson, what on earth are you talking about?"

"When we walked by the front of the house, I noticed two matching dog dishes on top of the trash can in the side yard." That was only part of the truth. When we entered the Galloway home, I'd sensed only two bundles of emotional energy: Mrs. Galloway's and the maid's. There were no other creatures in that house.

"Good eye, Branson. What else did you notice?"

I flipped my pad open. "Twice, she referred to her husband's mental state as being somewhat shaky. She also said – let me find it here – oh, here it is. She said that if he were going away, he would surely have taken his meds."

"And?"

"She was leading us. It felt incredibly rehearsed and manipulative." I shrugged. "It just felt really insincere."

"She was trying to lead the entire time. When you get an exclusive that goes like that one just did, you have to ask why. *Why* would she practically beg for an interview and then try to guide it in the direction *she* wanted it to go? Why did she keep suggesting he'd been kidnapped? Twice she referred to waiting for a ransom note. If that were the case, where are the police? Why aren't they here tapping her phones?" Carter pocketed his cell.

"What now?"

"Now we get down and dirty. I'm going to check out the cops' paper trail and see if they can't help me fill in the blanks. Was their life insurance policy paid? Is there a suspicious will?"

"A mistress?"

Carter cocked his head at me. "Where did *that* come from?"

"There was only one photo of Mr. and Mrs. and it was their wedding photo. There was one of their daughter and grandkids, but there were two of Glen and a dog. People who've been married that long usually have way more photos than that. And if you looked at the ledge the photos sat on, there was more than half the space left, as if someone had taken the other frames."

"Not bad, but I'm sure the cops have covered the mistress angle already."

"So what, exactly, am *I* looking for?"

"Anything that rings alarm bells. You know, when things just don't *feel* right?"

I grinned. Oh, if only he knew. "Yep."

"That's what we're looking for. *That* moment. Take tomorrow to fiddle around online. Here's my cell number if you find anything." Carter handed me a fancy business card with his photo on it.

"Tomorrow? What about the rest of today?"

"I've got a lot of work to do. Boring, tedious stuff that you wouldn't be interested in. Meet me at the paper tomorrow around nine. Bring coffee and doughnuts and we'll see if we've gotten any bites." Without further ado, he turned on a dime, got in his car and roared off, leaving me standing there. How was I going to learn anything like this? I knew busy work when I saw it.

My only real choice was to find the evidence proving Mrs. Galloway was not only lying, but also that she knew what had happened to her husband. I needed *irrefutable* proof. And if Carter wanted me to dive into cyberspace to find that proof, then so be it. I knew three Cybernauts who could get around the internet as easily as I could walk to the park.

I dialed Danica's office.

"Hey Heidi, it's Echo. No, I'm not really needing to talk to the boss right now. I was wondering if the boys were in. They are? Cool. Will you please tell them that I'm on my way? I need their help."

Help.

The "boys" were more than the cavalry. They were the big guns… and right now, I *needed* big guns.

ENTERING THE BATCAVE was a little like entering the bedroom of triplets. There were electronic and digital toys everywhere, and there were three of everything; three remote-controlled cars, three robots, three of each major gaming system, three laptops, three computers, three plasma screen TVs. There were even three virtual-reality stations complete with goggles and headphones. If it was electronic and had bright lights, they owned it. That was one of the reasons why their workweek was well over 60 hours; the emphasis wasn't ever on the work. The boys got their best ideas when they were either playing on the foosball table or beating each other up in some video game.

For her part, Danica left them alone because they were well worth the hefty salaries she paid them.

"Hey, guys, Princess is here!" Roger said when I opened the door. They had no secretary, no reception area, nothing. They preferred to deal solely with their incredibly lenient boss, and unless otherwise bothered, they seldom left the Batcave.

"Hi Roger," I said, shaking his clammy hand. Roger was the coolest of the geeks. He wore his brown hair in a ponytail and subsisted mainly on corn nuts and diet Coke. There was a warmth about Roger that drew women to him, but he was incredibly uncomfortable around most females. I was an exception because I wasn't just Danica's best friend, I was the Princess to her Queen, and that's what they called me. Princess.

How cute is that?

Franklin set the controls to his Xbox down in order to greet me. "Hi, Princess. What brings you to the Batcave?" Franklin pushed his black-rimmed glasses back up the bridge of his long nose. He'd been wearing the same style of glasses since he was seven years old because they didn't pinch his nose. I could only surmise how many times he'd been beaten up as a kid.

"Here on business, Franklin, and I could use your help."

"Fun business or adult business?" This came from Carl, who was still playing on the computer. His mop of red curly hair always looked like an oversized wig. When he rose, he unfolded like a cartoon paper doll. Carl ate all day long and never put an ounce on his six-foot-four-inch frame.

"I'm afraid this is going to be dull adult business, guys."

The three of them looked at each other. The word adult was like swearing to them. "What do you need?"

As I explained my story, all three jumped behind their computers, fingers flying at breakneck speed over their respective keyboards. "Give us as much information as you have on the guy. Names are good, addresses, social, that sort of thing."

I gave them everything I had, which didn't feel like much, but Carl explained that information was like a snowball; once they started it rolling, it not only picked up speed, but grew proportionately to what was out there.

"Give us a few, Princess. Go bother the boss." Carl said.

Turning to leave, I was almost out the door when Franklin called me back.

"You want emails, too?"

I turned slowly. "You can do that?"

All three of them grinned. "Not legally, no, but that's the fun of it."

"To go where no man has gone before," Roger added.

"Knock yourselves out, guys. I'll be back in half an

hour."

I left the Batcave and made my way to Heidi's desk.

"Oh, Echo. She's in a meeting right now."

"I'll just leave a message then. I just wanted to let her know that I'm borrowing the boys for a little research project."

Heidi grinned. She reminded me of every high school cheerleader I had ever met: all legs and teeth and perfect hair. She'd been a great secretary to Danica, who was not an easy boss by any book. "You mean they're actually *working*?" Heidi laughed. She wasn't very enamored with technology. At thirty-three years old, and a single mother of two, she had her own juggling act down pat. Good multi-taskers were hard to find these days, but Danica managed to surround herself with plenty.

"Well, just tell her that they're screwing around for me."

She nodded and checked her schedule. "Are you two still on for dinner?"

I nodded.

Heidi's phone beeped. "The boys beckon."

The boys had already begun compiling over a hundred printed pages of emails, bank information, credit applications, and other forms Galloway had filled out. They completed their task before I could read through the first stack of papers. Danica's guys were the best in the business, but it never ceased to amaze me how thorough they were. They scooped out far more data than I needed.

"I'm not going to ask how you got your grubby little techno-hands on this stuff. I'm sure it was illegal… or magical… or something else incredible." Hefting the stack of papers, I smiled. "Just don't get busted."

Carl shook his head as he pulled more paper from the printer. "Don't forget who we are. *We* are the reason the Boss created the The Echo in the first place: besides, it's fun."

I took more paper from Carl. "This is *fun* for you."

"Absolutely," they all said in unison.

"We can get through anything."

"What about The Echo? Can you breach that?"

Franklin nodded. "Breach it, yes. Get *away* with breaching it, nope. The Boss designed a secondary program that leaves hackers' fingerprints, so-to-speak. Unless we tossed our machines, we'd be busted for sure. That's the beauty of her program."

"So what's your interest with this guy, anyway?" Roger asked. "He's not the kind of guy you want to get hooked up with."

"Why not?"

The boys looked at each other. "Let's just say he gets what he wants. The man's amassed a fortune."

"So… what's the deal?" Roger asked.

I told them about my new job, for which they were all genuinely happy.

"Be careful," Carl admonished. "This guy's no innocent little banker." He pulled more paper from the printer and handed it to me. "He moves money around like he might be trying to hide it."

Franklin nodded. "I'm thinking fraud or embezzlement."

"Really?" I glanced down at the paper.

"The guy has a lot to lose, Princess. *A lot.* You check all those papers carefully, then burn them."

"Yeah. We'd be up shitola creek if those ever got out. We really like our jobs."

"And our freedom."

I nodded. "Gotcha." Straightening my papers, I started for the door. "This is great. I owe you guys."

Carl jumped up to get the door. Danica thought his crush on me was cute. "The Boss has been telling us ever since you got hired at the paper that you're going to be a star reporter someday, even before your promotion. Anything we can do to help that along – we're here."

"Want us to keep digging? See if any bodies come up?"

"I think you better get some real work done. Aren't you developing a game or something?"

"Games, plural. Roger is working on a more accurate voice-to-text program that's better than anything on the market. Franklin is working on an accounting program, and I am *this* close to finishing my latest RPG."

"Aren't there plenty of voice-to-text programs out there already?"

"Sure, but the Boss wants one that's voice activated for folks with disabilities."

Franklin nodded. "Yeah, she wants to give the program away to peeps with disabilities, the elderly, people with MS and other limiting conditions, you name it. It's easy to set up and easier to use and will make it much more stress-free for them to email and write. Pretty cool, huh?"

I warmed all over, happy to have someone like Danica Johnson as my dearest friend. Our time at Mills had drilled into us the importance of giving back, and Danica took that to heart. She gave oodles of money to charities all over the Bay Area. "She never said anything."

"Because it's not done. When it's finished, she'll be crowing about it to anyone who'll listen."

"Thanks, again, for all the work. You really do rock."

As I took my bundle of facts out to Ladybug, I realized I had yet to deliver Luigi's day-olds. There they were, still sitting in the back of my car. I felt slightly ashamed. Danica was making technology accessible to everyone, and I couldn't even remember to deliver bread to the homeless.

Once in Ladybug, I headed for the Mission District where I knew the little extra staleness wouldn't bother anyone.

As I drove through the crowded streets, I wondered what Carter was doing. Sending me off to do busy work was his way of keeping me out of the story. I wasn't stupid. I was going to comb through every single printed page until I found something, *anything*, that could prove what I'd felt inside that Victorian.

And for an empath, what we intrinsically felt was every bit as real as what we knew intellectually.

All I had to do was prove it.

CHAPTER 4

WHEN I CAME to after beating Todd's brains in with my math book, I found myself strapped to a white bed in a white room under white sheets, with a dark cloud hovering somewhere inside my skull. Whatever drug they'd shot into me had given me a horrible headache and a metallic taste in my mouth.

If you've never woken up after being drugged, and found yourself strapped to a bed, count your blessings. It was the worst thing in the world; a nightmare of gigantic proportions, and when the haze finally drifted from my head, I realized my wrists were strapped with thick leather restraints. Just like on TV. My legs were no freer.

One minute, I was walking home with my best friend and talking about Homecoming, and the next minute… here I was.

Alone.

To wake up and know you cannot move, cannot scratch your nose, cannot do a thing for yourself is the absolute scariest feeling in the world, and even though I was trying really hard not to, I did the only thing anyone would have done in my position.

I panicked.

Yep. I started thrashing about like some wild woman; yelling, kicking, fighting against the restraints which weren't going to budge. I don't know how long I flailed around before an enormous black orderly entered the room. With his appearance came this weird calming effect I felt to the marrow of my bones.

"You gotta calm down, Sweetpea," he said, reaching over to touch my arm. I stopped fighting, mostly because I was just so glad I wasn't alone anymore. I think that was the scariest part; to feel so utterly abandoned.

"Where am I?" I asked, my heart beating madly. The sound pounded through my head, like an echo. Calm strength from the hulking man peering down washed over me like a warm blanket, helping me relax. "Who are you? Where am I? What's going on? Why am I tied up?"

"One question at a time, Sweetpea. I'm George and we're in the psych ward of Alta Bates Hospital. Do you remember anything that happened before they brought you in here?"

It took a second for me to remember; not because of the actual memory, but because of the lingering emotions from my first empathic episode and the drugs still in my system. My throat was killing me and that horrible taste lingered in my mouth. "Can I *please* have some water?"

George poured some into a plastic cup and bent the straw to my lips. "You aren't gonna spit it at me, are you?"

I frowned. "Uh, no. I think I'd rather just swallow it." As I sipped the water, I knew the emotions calming me were not mine. I wasn't sure how I could tell the difference between my own emotions and someone else's, but I could. I was tied to a bed, for God's sake; what was there to be calm about?

"Thatta girl." George put the water on the bedside unit. "How you doin' now?"

"Can you unlock me?"

He shook his head. "Only when a doctor gives the okay. You gotta stay calm, like you are now, and they'll cut you loose quicker. Okay? No more thrashin' about."

"How's Todd?"

"Is that the boy whose head you caved in?"

Sighing, I nodded. "Is he… is he dead?"

"Don't know about that. You want me to find out?"

"Would you? I'd really appreciate it. I-I didn't mean to—"

"I'm sure you didn't."

"Thank you for the water."

George smiled kindly. "You got manners. I'll give you that much. If I go get the doctor, will you promise to stay calm?"

"I promise."

"Okay, then. I'll check on that boy and let the doctor know you're awake. Stay calm, Sweetpea. I won't let anything happen to you." George leaned over and peered hard into my eyes as if searching for something. "Be cooperative and you'll be outta those in no time. Trust me. No one wants to see a young gal like you tied down."

I nodded as two tears rolled down my temples. "Where are my foster parents? Do they know I'm here?"

"The doctors can tell you all that."

"I don't know what happened."

"Shh. That's okay. We're gonna get you the help you need." George pulled a small packet of tissues out of his pocket and wiped the sides of my face.

"Thank you."

"I'll be back in a jiff. I know it's hard, but just take deep breaths and don't panic. I promise I'll be right back."

"You swear?"

"I give you my word. You do some deep breathin' exercises, okay?"

I nodded and watched him leave the room, taking his calm with him and leaving me with panic rising in my throat. There's a sound a door makes when it's locked from the outside and it's far louder than when you lock it yourself. Big. Scary. Click.

Closing my eyes, I inhaled slowly and deeply as George had recommended. It really helped. I was finally calming down again when George returned with the doctor.

"Hi, Jane. I'm Dr. Knowles. How are you doing?" Dr. Knowles was a petite woman in her forties.

George stood at the foot of the bed and winked at me as the doctor finished her examination.

"Well, I'm in a nut house tied to a bed for bashing a guy's head in with my math book. It's not more complicated than that…"

Dr. Knowles grinned. "I'm sure." She took out a penlight and shined it near my eyes. "Headache?"

"Pounding. I'll bet Todd's is far worse than mine. I didn't kill him, did I? Please tell me I didn't kill him." This last was directed to George.

"I got a call in. We'll let you know as soon as they call

back."

I licked my parched lips. "Thank you." I could feel Dr. Knowles studying me; assessing my stability. I felt like a lab rat caught in a maze.

"George seems to think if we unlock you, you'll be cooperative. What do you think?"

I nodded and licked my lips again. "I'm not really a violent person. I mean… I know it kinda looks that way right now, but I'm not."

She smiled and motioned for George to leave. He did. "Then what happened, Jane? It says here," she opened up a file with my name on it. "You were repeatedly striking a young man in the head with your math book. Is that true?"

I nodded.

"Can you tell me why?"

Blinking several times, I exhaled. "He was following us home and I-I thought—" what *had* I thought when I hit him with my bag? It wasn't a thought, really. It had been more; so much more, but I had no name for it. I just knew what I knew; that I didn't know *how* to explain it without sounding like a nut case, and I wanted out of these shackles.

"You thought what?"

"I thought he was going to hurt us."

"Did he do something or say something that led you to believe this?"

Before I could answer, George reentered with two other orderlies who were just as big as he was.

"Jane?" Dr. Knowles prodded.

"Honestly? I don't know. It was just a feeling I had. It was a really, really bad feeling, and it scared me."

Dr. Knowles never took her eyes from mine. "I see. Do

you get these bad feelings often?"

I shook my head. "Not really. I mean – not ever."

"Interesting. Well, here's what's going to happen. George is going to take your restraints off. You and I will chat for a few more minutes and then he'll take you to your room where we will observe you for the next forty-eight hours. We'll prepare a report for the police should Todd's family press charges. Do you understand what I've said?"

I nodded. "Do my foster parents know where I am?"

"Yes. They will be able to see you at the end of our observation." Dr. Knowles stepped back while the orderlies started unlocking me. My heart was still pounding. A flood of emotions started pouring over me; boredom, concern, care, even hunger. Someone in this room was hungry and it wasn't me.

"Just relax," George said from the foot of the bed. "Let the guys get you out and then we'll show you where you are and go over what's going to happen in the next twenty-four hours."

I nodded and lay there, trying to block out the confusing mixture of emotions. When they were through unlocking me, the other two orderlies left, but George stayed at the foot of my bed. "There. Better?"

Rubbing my wrists, I sat up and reached for the water, downing it all from one pull on the straw. "Much better. So, we're going to see if I'm nuts. Does that about sum it up?"

Dr. Knowles grinned and pulled up the chair. "We're going to assess your mental health, that's all. I'm going to ask you some questions just to see what you were thinking and feeling and to try to get a better idea of your general state of mind. Your foster parents are sending us your medical records so we can put all of the puzzle pieces together to find out what happened today."

Looking up at George, I nodded. "Is my friend Danica okay?"

Dr. Knowles glanced over at George, who nodded. "She wanted to go with you in the ambulance, but couldn't."

I nodded. "She's my best friend."

Dr. Knowles nodded. "Those are always good to have. Are you ready?"

About a half an hour later, when the doctor was finished asking me a battery of questions, George escorted me down the hallway. I had never been in a psych ward before, but I'd seen plenty on television. Let's just say that Hollywood usually got it right. There were all sorts of noises coming from people I couldn't see, but could definitely feel. It was almost like being on a sound stage, with horrendous sounds coming from every nook and cranny of the ward. I swear to God, human beings aren't supposed to be capable of making such sounds. It was awful.

The only thing worse than hearing those horrific cries was seeing myself in the metallic mirror. My wavy brown hair looked like perennial bed head. My face looked like I'd used some of Gene Simmon's white face paint, and the bite mark on my forehead was redder than ever before. A dog bit me on my forehead when I was a kid; at least, that was what I was told. I can only remember bits and pieces of my life after I turned six, and nothing before that. I don't even remember who told me that the dog bit me, but the scar looked like six little teeth marks in a half moon shape, and had an annoying habit of throbbing whenever I was stressed out. It throbbed now.

"This place is pretty scary your first night here, Sweetpea. There are all sorts noises and sounds that you've never heard before. Don't let it get to you. Just breathe through it and stay relaxed. That's key here. Stay relaxed. Stay calm. And remember that all of this is temporary." George opened a door to a room not unlike the one I came from. There was a bed, a bare toilet, and a camera high up in the corner of the room. That was it. At least there weren't any shackles.

"Thank you for being so kind to me."

He stood at the doorway as I sat on the bed. "I get off at eleven, so if you need anything after that, Tony will be on. He can help you get somethin' if you can't sleep." George smiled kindly.

I held my hands up. "No more drugs. I've had my fill for the rest of my life."

"Good. Now, what did I tell you to do?"

"Relax. Breathe deeply. Stay calm."

"Thatta girl."

"George?"

"Yeah?"

"Am I going to jail?"

He stepped back into the room. "I wish I knew, but you can't be worryin' about that right now. Whatever happened to you today needs to be taken care of. Focus on that."

And so I did. When the door closed and locked with its big, ominous click, I took several deep breaths as I climbed onto the hard bed. Relaxing was harder done than said. What was happening to me? What had I done to Todd? Where was Danica? What did my foster parents think? And, more importantly, was I going insane?

These questions and more banged around in my tired mind as I closed my eyes. I was still feeling the residuals of the drug they'd pushed into me, so it didn't take long for sleep to claim me even in the midst of cries that continued to haunt me for the rest of my life.

CHAPTER 5

I READ AN article once that said many of the homeless beggars on the streets of San Francisco earned an average of $30,000 a year. I remember scoffing at that figure until my professor pointed out that many of the panhandlers were out on the streets 14 to 17 hours a day, seven days a week, 365 days a year. She estimated that a panhandler needed to pull in a little over four dollars an hour to meet that mark; a goal which was quite attainable, especially during feel-good holidays like Valentines, Thanksgiving, Mother's Day, and Christmas. Of course, money is a moot point if you spend it on alcohol or an addiction of another sort, as many homeless do. I know because one such homeless person was a friend of mine.

Bob and I had been in the same foster home in the seventh grade; he was a year older than me, but had missed a lot of school because of family hopping. Like me, Bob had been in and out of home after home. Unlike me, he struggled in school and those struggles led to some behavioral issues that made him hard to deal with.

I helped him as much as I could, but poor Bob could barely sit still. Our foster parents didn't believe in medicating children, so they refused any sort of help for his hyperactivity. My foster dad had remarked, "ADD and ADHD need two more letters: BS."

So he continued acting out in class, getting multiple detentions, and usually failing every course except PE. Bob wasn't stupid like many in the foster care circus; he just needed help that wasn't going to come.

Eventually, our foster parents sent Bob back. They sent me packing about three months later for "acting out." Some people just shouldn't have children; not even the 1,200 dollars a month kind.

I didn't see Bob again until I moved into the city and took Luigi's day-olds to the Mission District for the first time. I was fighting with this enormous bag of pumpkin bagels that hadn't gone over very well, when I nearly knocked Bob over. He immediately recognized me, but it took me a couple of moments to see through his long hair and ratty beard. He was too thin and had aged considerably. Bob had opted to live on the streets rather than endure another failure in a foster home. In a way, I couldn't blame him. A kid can only take so many rejections and beatings before the grime of the streets becomes an acceptable option.

I DIDN'T HAVE much money on me, but the ten dollars I offered him wasn't accepted. Bobby didn't want my money, but he *did* want my bag of bagels. He said the guys he hung out with needed the food more than the booze. I'd been delivering Luigi's day-old bagels to him ever since.

"Hey, Jane, you're late." Bob waved at me as I handed

him the plastic bag.

"Haven't you heard? Beggars can't be choosers."

Bob tossed his head back and guffawed. "You slay me, Jane." Opening the bag, Bob peered in as he always did. "Damn. Raisins. You like raisins, Jane?"

I shook my head. "I don't."

"In the day-olds, raisins are like little stones." Bob closed the bag and smiled at me. "But don't worry, *this* beggar is not an ingrate. Thank you. You have no idea how much the guys 'preciate these. It's somethin' we look forward to."

Bob was a little like the panhandler Pied Piper. His constituents loved him. The business owners liked him. He may have been a drunk, but he wasn't a nutcase and he didn't steal. He was just a good guy who had gotten lost in the shuffle as a kid and never found his way out.

"How are you doing today, Bob?" I already knew, of course, but an empath can easily appear disconnected from the people around her if she doesn't at least inquire about them. It was one of the many lessons I'd learned from my mentor.

Bob looked down the street both ways before pulling me into the nearest alley, taking me by surprise. I wasn't afraid of him. It was just a really strange thing to do.

"A friend of mine's missing," he said so softly I almost didn't hear him, but when Bob spoke in his delicate whisper I felt fear.

"What do you mean?" I wondered how a homeless person could be considered *missing*. Lost, I understood, but missing?

"His name is Rusty and he plays chess at the park every day. Every single day. But he hasn't shown up in the last two days and we're worried. All of us."

I'd never seen Bob worried. I lowered my shield. He was neither drunk nor mentally unstable; just really scared. "Nobody has seen him?"

Bob shook his head. "Not a soul. The last person to see him was Oreo, and that was at the liquor store two days ago. As long as I've known him, Jane, he has *never* missed a day of chess. The guy lives for the game."

"You don't think he's just sleeping off a drunk?"

Bob shook his head. "Rusty drinks before he sleeps, but never during the day. He takes his chess seriously and alcohol clouds his thinking. Can you check the hospitals in the area? Maybe he got rolled."

"I can do that. I'll check with the SFPD as well." I handed my card to Bob and patted his back. "Be sure to call me if he shows up. I've got this new job and I'm really busy running around trying to impress people."

"Oh yeah? What's the gig?"

"Investigative reporter. It's going to take a lot of time to get where I want to be in my career, and this is my first real break."

Bob's face lit up. "Oh wow. Good for you, Jane. You deserve it. Nobody I've ever met works harder than you." Bob had never warmed up to my new name. When we were kids, he used to laugh and say that I would always be his plain Jane.

"If I find anything, I'll come down here looking for you, so make sure your people know to expect me. I'll get on it this evening and see what I can see."

"I really 'preciate it. Nobody's saying nothing, but we're all a little jumpy down here. I don't know – I've been sleeping with one eye open because somethin' don't feel right."

Some things never changed. Bob slept with one eye open when we were kids. "You stay safe, okay? I'll see what I can find out. Do you have a last name for him? Maybe a description?"

"We don't do last names, but he has long red hair, freckles, and wears his 'Nam dog tags."

I jotted this information down. "Got it. If you remember anything else, call me." We said our goodbyes and when I returned to Ladybug, I had to shake off Bob's nervousness; Rusty's disappearance had really spooked him.

With a couple of hours to kill before my dinner with Danica, I returned to the office to make some calls to the hospitals in the area. When I arrived on our floor, I caught the end of one of Carter's workplace-stopping stories, starring none other than me.

"Can you even believe that? She thinks thrown away dog dishes are some sort of clue! Like she's Nancy Drew or something. Old man Bentley's paired me up with Inspector Clouseau! Or is it Inspector Clue*less*?"

The three lackeys who were listening to his story laughed as if they were watching the Comedy Channel. Then one of them saw me and his eyes grew so wide that the others, including Carter, turned to see what he was staring at.

"Go on, Carter," I said. "Finish your character assassination."

The three suddenly uncomfortable audience members bowed their heads and slunk away with their tails between their legs. Served them right.

"Oh come on, Branson. Have a sense of humor. You have to admit—"

"You. Are. An. Asshole." I said, stepping up to him. The room became incredibly quiet and thick with tension. "Is this how *big* people with tiny minds spend their time?"

Carter pulled himself up to his full height, hoping to intimidate me into silence. No such luck. I hadn't been this pissed off in a long time. "I believe you would do well to note the manner in which you speak to me, Branson. After all, I am a man of—"

"Little integrity? No class? Foot-in-mouth disease? Stop me when I hit a wrong answer."

Carter looked over my shoulder at the people watching our show. Public confrontation made him uncomfortable, and I was pretty sure he wasn't used to anyone taking him on face-to-face. He needed to know that I wasn't *just* anyone, so I did something I immediately regretted. I couldn't stop myself. Some things never changed no matter how much I wanted them to or how hard I tried.

"Look, you arrogant ass, Mrs. Galloway was jerking your chain the entire time. She played you for the fool you are. Yet again, you interview someone who lied *right to your face* and you were just too stupid and too arrogant to know it."

Carter's eyes narrowed and he lowered his head like a bull getting ready to charge. "You got lucky with your little parlor trick once, Branson. It won't work this time. *This* time, you'll actually have to prove it. Think you can do that? Think you can actually *prove* that Mrs. Galloway was lying because of some damn doggie dishes? I'm willing to put *my* money where *your* mouth is."

"I, uh—"

He shook his head in disgust. "It figures."

And then, I did something I never thought I would do. "My car."

"Excuse me?"

"I'll put up my '65 bug."

"You're kidding, right?"

"I'll put up my 1965 bug."

"Against my Lexus? Are you insane?"

"It's a collector's car. It's a classic. It's a—"

"Volkswagen!"

Shrugging, I pushed past him. "Coward."

"You can put up your *classic* bug for my Lexus, but you'll have to do more than that. You have one week to prove Mrs. Galloway is hiding something. After that—"

"I didn't say she was hiding something. I said she was *lying.* Right to your face."

"So here's the deal. You have one week. If you can't prove it, I get your red car *and* your pink slip."

Now *that* was unexpected. "You want my resignation?"

"Absolutely. You're a thorn in my side who doesn't know shit about journalism. If you can't produce the goods, I want you out of here. Go make someone else's life miserable."

Well, I'd pretty much asked for that, hadn't I? What could I do? Back out and apologize? Pretend like I never said it?

"You're on."

CHAPTER 6

"I CAN'T BELIEVE you painted yourself into such a damn tight corner." Danica pushed her salad around on her plate until she found the croutons she was looking for. "What in the hell were you thinking?"

"I wasn't. I was just so ticked off that he was making fun of me in front of everyone I just popped off."

"And now you've got to put up or shut up. I cannot believe you bet Ladybug. You love that car."

"I'd love to keep my job even more." Shaking my head, I sighed. "He's just such an ass."

"Be that as it may, you've really done yourself in this time. I don't doubt the boys were able to come up with information. The question is can you use any of it to your advantage?"

"I've gone through about half of it. So far, I've figured out that Mr. Galloway was having an internet affair with some woman in Ashland, Oregon."

"That thickens the plot a bit, doesn't it?"

"It gets better. Just before he disappeared, he withdrew

over a hundred thousand dollars."

She whistled. "And the cops don't seem to think there's a problem here? What's up with that? I mean, if this guy was such a big wig, how come the FBI hasn't been called in, know what I mean? There's a lot that isn't making any sense."

"Well, I spoke with a Sergeant Finn about it when I called about Rusty."

"Rusty? Who in the hell is Rusty?"

"He's one of Bob's homeless buddies. Rusty is missing. I told Bob I would check out the hospitals and see if the cops knew anything."

"And do they?"

I shook my head. "No on both counts. Without a last name, no one was very cooperative. No one remembered a long-haired, redheaded guy with dog tags from Vietnam."

"Kinda hard to locate a missing person who's probably been missing for five or ten years, don't you think?"

"I know, but I couldn't say no to Bob. Anyway, while I was talking to Sergeant Finn, I asked him about the Galloway case. Know what he said? He said that there *is* no case. No foul play, no case. End of the story."

"Uh oh."

I shook my head. "I read Mrs. Galloway's deceit like the Sunday paper. There's something not right. I wouldn't have bet Ladybug unless I was *sure* something hinky was going on."

"Hinky? One day as an investigative reporter and already you've got a whole new lingo? You've known me for what, eleven years, and I can't even get one *girl fren'* out of you?" Danica laughed before finishing the rest of the croutons in her salad. "You going to follow the internet affair angle?"

"I don't know if that will lead anywhere. Hell, who *isn't* having an internet affair these days?"

"No kidding. Seems like everyone is pretending to be someone they aren't. It's too weird. What happened to going to a club and meeting someone and getting laid?"

I grinned. "And this from a computer maven."

"Hey, only a fool would get involved with someone online. Me? I prefer flesh-to-flesh contact."

"Of course you do."

"What are you going to do to keep your car and your job?"

"I need to *prove* Mrs. Galloway was not only lying to Carter, but that she knows where her husband is."

"You really think she knows?"

I nodded. "Positive."

Danica leaned forward. "You could try bluffing her. You know – tell her *you* know that *she* knows. Something like that."

"Not a bad idea, but I need proof this time. My career depends on it. If Carter has his way, he'll destroy me, and I can't let him do that."

"Well, the boys are at your disposal if you need anything. If there's any evidence in cyberspace, they *can* and *will* find it for you. Just consider them your own personal research team."

We ate our dinner and chatted about our lives. Danica was a power dater. She only dated powerful men and even then, the rule was they couldn't stay the night. Since I had known her, no one had *ever* stayed the night and seldom did her bedsheet entanglements last longer than a month or two. We weren't sure if she had commitment issues, but no man had ever managed to be enough for Danica Johnson.

I, on the other hand, had a handful of failed relationships to my credit. I had yet to find a man I trusted enough with my secret, which made a real relationship almost impossible to pull off. Even with my guards and shields up, I knew when a guy just wasn't my emotional match. There's no getting around that fact when you're an empath. It was a little like having x-ray vision; sometimes you see things you just don't want to see.

So, there we were, discussing the lack of love in our lives, when someone sent over an incredibly expensive bottle of champagne.

"For you," the waiter said, motioning to me.

"What? Who?" Men seldom gave me a second glance when Danica was in the room. I was a pale five-foot-four brunette whose most outstanding feature was the bite mark on my forehead. I was as average as they come, and next to Danica, I was nearly invisible.

"The gentleman at the bar sent it."

Before I could say anything, Danica wheeled around. "Oh, Clark, he's a cute one."

"He's the asshole," I muttered under my breath as I handed the champagne bottle back to the waiter. "Tell him I'm not interested."

Danica turned back to me. "That's Carter?"

I nodded as I shooed the waiter away. "Send it back, please."

"Excuse me?" he stood there, I'm sure, wondering what woman sends back a bottle of Dom, but that wasn't *my* problem. "Send. It. Back."

To my surprise, Danica plucked the bottle out of the waiter's hand and poured herself a flute. "Never let a bottle of good Dom go to waste. Why not accept it and enjoy? Look at this as your last meal." Danica turned her flute to Carter and tipped it toward him. "Maybe it's a peace offering."

"Like a cannon ball was—"

"Oh goodie! Here he comes. He's hunky. I love cleft-chinned men. It's so virile, so—"

"He's a jerk."

She shrugged. "Nobody's perfect."

I groaned. "Please don't do this to me. Not now. Not tonight when I've already suffered a humiliation at the hands of that jackass."

"Do what? You better not be reading me."

"I don't have to read you to know when you're up to no good. I can tell by that look in your—"

"Good evening, ladies," Carter said *ladies,* but he was staring into Danica's green eyes. I'd become invisible once again.

"Are you following me?"

Carter finally turned to me, his eyes sparkling with every flicker of the candle sitting in the middle of our table. "That a tad self-absorbed, don't you think? Believe it or not, Branson, I'm not the least bit interested in either you or your puny little life." He turned to Danica and grinned like the wolf from Little Red Riding Hood. "Unless of course *you* would like me to."

Now I just felt plain foolish.

"Introduce me to your lovely dinner companion,

Branson."

Lovely? What real man ever uses the word lovely? "Carter Ellsworth, the Grand PoohBah of Assholes, this is my best friend, Danica Johnson. There. You've met. Now go away."

He was unmoved and unmoving. "It's a pleasure." Carter extended his hand, but Danica merely looked at it in that way that says *you're kidding me, right?*

Danica had tried to teach me *the look*, but I had never been able to master it.

Retracting his hand, Carter was undaunted. "Don't believe everything Branson says about me. She's biased."

Danica sipped her champagne and gave me the signal. The signal was something we invented in high school when she wanted to be read. We'd started it as something fun to do at a boring party. Guys hit on her *a lot*. A lot. Lots of guys. All the time. Even weird guys who were out of their league. She has these exotic green eyes and this beautiful caramel colored complexion that draws men like moths to the proverbial flame. Although I'm pretty sure moths have a better chance against the flame than most men have against Danica. She was brutal where men were concerned. So, to prevent any unnecessary lingerers from hanging on too long, she would signal me with the twitch of one eyebrow. Then, I would read her and either swoop in for the save or find my own way home. With Danica, it was six of one, a half dozen of the other.

A quick shield lower and I could see she didn't care for Carter. She was enjoying toying with him and sizing him up. I had seen, firsthand, what the high school girls in Oakland would do to a brother who did one of them wrong, and it wasn't pretty. Danica had this unique ability to knock people off their pedestals like no other. Carter was now dangling from his.

"Mr. Ellsworth," Danica started. "Her best friend is mixed race. She belongs to every environmental group on the West Coast, and she volunteers at the shelter. She doesn't have a *biased* bone in her body. If she's decided you're worthy of her disdain, she would make that decision all by herself."

Carter looked at me. "Are all of your friends this fiery?"

"You have fiery and loyal confused," Danica retorted. "Thank you for the Dom and for allowing me to meet the jerkoff who talks shit about someone as good as Echo behind her back. Now, be off with you. You're blocking my light." She made a shooing motion with her hands.

Carter was unfazed. "Talking shit implies I wasn't telling the truth about her. It was a funny story. Branson simply didn't think so."

"Know what I think?" Danica leaned forward. "I think you're a bully with an undeserved superiority complex. And if I were a man half your size, I would kick your balls so hard, you'd become a hunchback."

Carter laughed. He actually laughed! "Would you now? You meet me and come to this conclusion in what? Thirty seconds?"

"It takes less than two seconds to call a dog a dog." Danica finished her champagne and handed Carter the empty flute. "And I'll tell you this much: Echo is going to kick your sorry ass all over the place with this Galloway story. You might want to wear protection."

"Oh, really? Would *you* like to make a friendly wager on

that?"

"Friendly wagers are for friends, and *we* are most definitely not that."

"Then how about an unfriendly one?"

Danica cut her eyes over to me. I knew enough to keep my mouth shut. She needed no help from my corner to handle the Carter Ellsworths of the world.

"An unfriendly wager with a snake? What do you have in mind?"

Carter grinned. "You really think she's going to cash in on the Galloway story based on a couple of dog dishes? Get real. Or are you living in the same alternate universe as she is?"

"I am and I do."

"Then make your wager."

Danica's aura fairly glowed. "When she smokes you, and she will, I want my company on the front page of the business section on a Sunday."

"The company you work for?"

"Come out of your cave once in a while, paperboy. The company I *own*. I've been trying to get on that cover section of yours forever."

"What's the company?"

"Savvy Software."

Carter was surprised. "You *own* Savvy Software?"

She didn't even twitch. "Is it because I'm black or because I'm a woman that surprises you so much?" Danica snapped her fingers. "Oh, I know… it's because I'm a black woman."

"I'm not surprised. I just—"

"That's what *I* want when I win, paperboy. Now, what's

your wager? What do you want if a miracle occurs?"

He chuckled. "A miracle, huh? You have that much faith in the nubile Branson?"

A slight grin formed on her lips. "Absolutely."

"Enough to risk going on a six-hour date including dinner, dancing, and delicious dessert with me?"

"Six hours? That's not a date. That's a marriage."

Shrugging, Carter grinned. "You want the cover; I want six hours to change your mind about me. It's your call."

Danica held her hand out and shook his. "Deal."

Carter took her hand and stepped closer. Like most men who looked into her eyes, Carter was riveted. If it wasn't so pathetic it might have been enjoyable.

"Branson must *prove* Mrs. Galloway was lying to me about knowing where her husband is. *Tangible* proof."

"Correct. And when she does, she gets the byline, I get the front cover and you get lost."

"Of course. But I must warn you—"

Danica held her hand up. "Don't underestimate my best friend, paperboy. The last guy who did that—" Danica shrugged as she looked away, extricating her hand from Carter's.

"I will look forward to our date, then."

Danica grinned a grin she usually reserved for the Oakland ghettos. "You'll be looking a long time. Thanks again for the bubbly. Now, if you don't mind." She gave him the shooing motion once more.

As Carter turned away, she called him back. "Yo, paperboy."

"Yes?"

"And the word is *neophyte*, not nubile. Unless you find

Echo young, desirable, and marriageable, I'm pretty sure the sixty-four-cent word you were looking for was neophyte. If you're going to toss out grown-up words, at least know what the hell they mean."

Once Carter was gone, Danica leaned back and poured herself more champagne in my glass. "I want that front page, Clark."

"I know you do."

"Can you do it?"

I swallowed hard, thinking of the pages and pages of computer printouts back at my place. "In a week? I don't know. I think so."

"Excellent. I want you to kick his ass all over the court."

I grinned. "I'm pretty sure you just did."

AFTER DINNER, I pored over every printout the boys had given to me, astounded by the depth of the information they'd managed to come by in such a short amount of time. Now, it was up to me to put it all together and see if I could find out what it was Mrs. Galloway was up to.

The emails bordered on pornographic. It reminded me of phone sex. It was always with the same screen name: Belly Dancer. Their emails were long, detailed, and painted a picture of two people who had met through a bulletin board about belly dancing.

The conversations progressed quite quickly from innocent discussion about the nature of belly dancing to belly dancers, to small flirtations, and then full blown, all out *inamorata.*

Ugh.

I felt like a peeping Tom or weird voyeur as I read their private and considerably intimate discussions. This was not a happily married man playing around in his mid-life crisis playground. This was a man who enjoyed his internet romance enough to want to take it one step further.

It had been going on for nearly six months before they agreed to meet. A timeline would help me separate events and get a better idea of what had been going on in the last year or so.

During the first three months, their emails were sporadic at best. In month four, something happened to make Mr. Galloway come out of his shell and begin flirting shamelessly, wanting to know when they could talk on the phone. By the fifth month, they had taken their relationship to the cellular-phone level, but still emailed all day long talking about the great phone sex they'd had the day before. In month six, Mr. Galloway met up with Belly Dancer in Redding, California, a few hours' drive north of the Bay Area. I knew this not just from the emails and phone records the boys had hacked into, but from a credit card receipt for a hotel room for two nights for the date indicated on the emails. The receipt wasn't signed, and I found that strange.

"So… no foul play, eh?" I reached for my mint tea and sipped it. Something wasn't clicking here. How was it I had all this information, but the police were claiming no foul play? Internet romances went awry all the time. How could they have passed this up?

Pushing my nagging doubts aside, I continued working on my timeline. After Redding, Mr. Galloway purchased a couple of expensive pieces of jewelry in Danville, a small town in the East Bay. I wondered if this guy ever used cash. The receipts for his credit card use were extensive; the man liked his plastic, to be sure, but I thought it strange that he didn't seem very careful in hiding his paper trail. For an astute businessman, he seemed very reckless with his personal affairs. That didn't add up, either. I made a note of it.

After their Redding rendezvous, they started getting serious. He brought up going away for a week together, maybe going to Catalina in a sailboat or renting a houseboat on Lake Shasta. He claimed his wife was talking about divorce.

As I was staring at my timeline, Tripod hobbled by, purring loudly. I was reminded about the photo of Glen and the dog as well as the dog dishes. Where *was* the dog? I made a note to check. "I know. You want some catnip, don't you? Not now. Maybe later." My cat was in love with catnip and I was his pusher. I was a bad cat owner.

With paper strewn everywhere, I rose and stretched. I was missing something. What about his car being left at the airport? Had he left it there intentionally? Had he taken a flight? Surely, that information would easily be found, but I had nothing showing any purchase for a plane ticket or that he'd gotten on a flight. Wouldn't he have used his credit card?

I picked up the phone and called Sergeant Finn. He was out, so I left a message for him to call me.

"Maybe I need to interview Mrs. Galloway myself," I said, pulling out a little patch of catnip for Tripod. "I'll bet I could get to the bottom of this if I did. Maybe she'd crack. What do you think?"

Just as I was going to give it a rest, my phone rang. Caller ID said it was SFPD.

"Hello?"

"Echo Branson, please. This is Sergeant Finn."

"Hi there, Sergeant Finn. Thank you for getting back to me so quickly."

"No problem. You say this is about the Galloway case? I thought I'd made it clear—"

"I know what you said, but I think there may be more."

"Funny you should call. His car's been moved, Miss Branson. Is that what you're calling about?"

"Echo. You can call me Echo."

"Okay, Echo. Look, I don't want to see you wasting your time on this non-story. Whatever is going on between the Galloways is not criminal or even newsworthy. He's probably just having a little fling and she's pissed off about it."

"Where was the car moved?"

"It's at the Berkeley Marina."

"The Berk—"

"I don't want to be rude, but it's my dinner time and I just wanted to call and let you know there isn't anything going on with the Galloways as far as the San Francisco Police Department is concerned."

"Oh. I'm sorry." I looked at the clock. It was almost 11:30. Cops' hours must suck if they have to eat dinner at midnight. "Would you mind meeting me for dinner? I promise I won't bother you after that – it's just – this is my first big story. I need a break."

The line was quiet for a moment. "I wish this was a better story for you then, because, quite frankly, no crime has been committed."

Inhaling deeply, I took a huge chance and told Officer Finn my predicament. When I finished, I heard him chuckle. "So, Carter Ellsworth has you in a headlock, does he? Do you have any idea how much we *hate* that guy's guts?"

I didn't. "Who doesn't? He's such an ass."

"On that point, we all agree. Look, I'll be eating at the Del Mar Cafe in about fifteen minutes. I can't promise I have any answers for you, but I'd hate to see you go down without a fight. That guy's a Grade-A jerk."

"Thank you so much. I'll be there in ten minutes."

"Excellent. See you there."

After snatching the remaining catnip out of the paws of my stoner cat, I grabbed my keys and headed downstairs.

Did I mention that Sergeant Walt Finn is really cute?

CHAPTER 7

Eleven minutes later, I walked into the Del Mar and waved to Sergeant Finn who was sitting alone in a booth. He rose as I neared the table, a huge grin on his face as if we were old friends. I'd seen him on several of my Police Beat runs and always thought he was remarkably cute in a studly cop sort of way. He was a rectangle of a man with broad shoulders, an equally broad chest, and a flat stomach. His tight-fitting uniform shirt looked painted on and I could see the creases from his bulletproof vest.

"Sergeant Finn."

"If I call you Echo, would you call me Finn? I hate Sergeant and I hate Walter. Walter is my dad's name, my grandfather's name, my great-grandfather's name, and—"

"Your son's?" I sat down when he motioned at the booth.

"Hell no. I made a promise to myself in high school that I would be the last in a long line of Walters. There are so many great names to choose from, like yours."

I fished around a little bit more. Men can be so obtuse.

"And what does your wife think about this?"

"I'm not married. And if I ever do, that's a deal breaker. I am going to spare some sweet little boy the weight of Walter." He grinned. "So, just Finn will do."

"Fair enough."

"Would you like something to eat? I know it's late and all—"

"How's the pie here?"

His grin returned, and this time two deep dimples appeared on his cheeks. A man with dimples slays me. "I like that in a woman. Their dessert is the mint at the door. They have excellent pie here. I recommend the apple pie."

When the waitress approached, I ordered apple pie a la mode. I watched him order a bacon cheeseburger with a side salad and Coke. His skin was dark olive, and his sandy brown hair was cut close to his head. It wasn't a buzz cut, but short enough not to get in his way. There were slight curls at the end, like little commas all over his head. His deep, chocolate brown eyes took in the whole room in hawk-like fashion. I had no doubt that Sergeant Finn knew exactly who was in the cafe and how long they had been there.

When he finished ordering, he turned those eyes on me. "Normally, I'm the one assessing a room."

I smiled and poured sugar in my coffee. "You're not listening. I'm not normal."

He laughed at this. "Something tells me you're probably not kidding." Leaning forward, he lowered his voice. "Have you interviewed Mrs. Galloway yet?"

I nodded. "Carter did."

"Did she tell you that this isn't the first time she's

reported her husband missing?"

"Oh. No. When was the first time?"

"About four months ago."

"What happened?"

"He went away for the weekend. Apparently, he needed some alone time or something. Who can say with these rich guys?"

Now, I leaned forward. "So, there's no crime? None?"

"Not that I know of. Misplacing your husband isn't really a crime. Your hubby taking a time out from you isn't a crime. Hell, having an affair isn't a crime."

"No missing person's report?"

"She wouldn't file one because she said this was so much more than that." Finn shrugged. "I know this is important to you, but to be honest, there are real crimes happening out there to regular folks. We don't have time to hold the eccentric rich folks' hands during their self-induced dramas."

I sighed. "Then why am I sitting here?"

"I'm going to be honest with you here, Echo. There's no love lost between Carter Ellsworth and me. He's gotten into the department's way more times than I can count. I don't like him, and I really don't like it when he calls the station asking us to make sure that we give any Galloway information to him and not to any of his *subordinates*." Finn looked me hard in the eyes. "Subordinate, Echo. And it was more of a demand than a request. I know he may be some bigwig in your circle, but he's just a pain in the ass in mine."

I felt a chill crawl up my spine and lodge near my heart.

"Apparently, you pose a threat to the old boy, and anyone who's a threat to that jerk is a friend of mine. Believe me, he has no friends at SFPD. That's why you're sitting here."

A lump of something dark formed in my stomach.

"Is he an old flame or something? He sure has it out for you."

I shook my head. "I embarrassed him once. He'd love nothing more than to see me get fired a second time around."

"As much as I would hate to see you get fired, I don't know I can be of much help. There just isn't any big whodunit here. We've moved on."

"Really?" I told him about the emails, the jewelry purchases, and the internet affair. He had a wonderful poker face and gave nothing away. His only response was to shrug his shoulders and say that having an adulterous affair wasn't against the law. Still, he was slightly intrigued even though he didn't realize I knew it.

"Even with all of that, we can't prove a crime has been committed. Now, if you can give me something that shows some sort of foul play, I'll move heaven and earth to help you."

I sighed. This was going to be harder than I thought. What in the hell was I going to do without my car?

"If anything comes up, you'll be the first to know. I would really love to help you get a drop on that wiener."

I laughed out loud. Danica used to call boys wieners. "Thanks."

"No, I mean it. You know, cops aren't very fond of reporters. We never get a fair shake from you folks no matter how much blood is spilled on the streets. We can never do it right enough, never get there fast enough, never be fair enough. Guys like Ellsworth get off on rubbing our noses in some story he cracked before we did; as if he could do so without an inside in the department." Finn shook his head sadly.

"Well, just as long as you don't put me in the same category."

He grinned. "Hardly. I'd just like to see the department get a fair shake every now and then, but with guys like that dirt bag Ellsworth, well, you get the picture."

I smiled. Finn was one of the good guys. Integrity and loyalty were as vital to him as eating and drinking. I liked him already. "Maybe I can help paint a different picture. Of reporters, I mean."

He grinned and those dimples jumped out at me. "Here's my cell number. I don't have to tell you it's frowned upon for us to be talking to reporters."

I reached for the card. "I understand. Here's mine." I slid it across the table discreetly. "Because you know – it's frowned upon for us to be seen eating doughnuts with men in blue."

Finn threw his head back and laughed a rich, sincere laugh that made me like him even more.

We finished the rest of dinner on more personal notes. He was twenty-nine and had been a cop for almost eight years. He was the oldest of eight kids in a typically Irish Catholic family. He loved his job, lived alone off of Market, and confessed to being somewhat of a movie buff. He was close to his parents, loved the city, and wasn't addicted to anything.

So why was he still single?

What I liked most about him was that he was a great conversationalist; there was a give and take to our exchange, a nice ebb and flow, as if we were old friends. So many men I'd met blathered on about themselves, but he asked questions and listened attentively. It was really quite enjoyable, and I didn't want it to end.

Neither did he. When his pager when off, he sighed. "Well, I'm up. I've had a really good time."

"I'm glad. Oh. Wait." I rose and put a five on the table. "Have you heard anything about a missing homeless guy?"

"You're kidding me."

"I wish I were. I know it sounds ridiculous, but—"

"*That* is an understatement. Do you have any idea how many homeless people there are in the city?"

"I know. It's just – a good friend of mine said a friend of his from the streets is missing. I told him I would see what I could find out."

"You have homeless friends?" His eyes softened as he said this. "I'm not sure I've ever met anyone who has homeless friends."

I flashed him my best grin. "I told you, I am not normal. I have all sorts of friends – including men in uniform."

"I see that. Well, Echo Branson, I'm glad you include one SFPD sergeant among them."

"Oh, I do, Sergeant Finn. I certainly do."

CHAPTER 8

WHEN I GOT back from my visit with the charming Sergeant Finn, I dove back into the massive paperwork mountain growing inside my little apartment. Thanks to the doped-up Tripod, my papers were scattered everywhere. He turns into Speed Racer after ingesting the evil weed and races around my apartment until he crashes and burns.

Luckily for me, his little scattering routine pointed me toward something I hadn't noticed before. As I was straightening up my piles, I noticed a laptop purchase at approximately the same time the affair began. A laptop? That was interesting. Was this where Mr. Galloway kept his email correspondences? Would Mrs. Galloway let me take *her* computer to see what was really on there?

I went to bed with my mind swimming with data, and my heart a little hurt at the prospect that I'd done exactly what Danica said I had; I had painted myself into a very dark, very bleak corner, and unless I came up with something pretty quickly, my shot at the big leagues was going to blow up in my face, and I'd be walking to new job interviews and trying to find a new best friend.

But that's not what woke me.

I'm in the one percent of adults who suffer from night terrors. No, not nightmares. Night *terrors*. Night terrors occur at a very different point in the sleep cycle than nightmares. I've had them ever since I was a teenager, but they became worse as my skills grew. I'd seen several therapists when I was in college, but most of them wanted to prescribe sleeping pills or some other drugs, which I can never take. So, I put off sleep until I'm totally exhausted and then I go to bed in the hopes I can sleep through the night. Sleeping through the night happens only twice a week on average. I usually wake up with these horrible cold sweats that soak the bed.

My first cold sweat happened the first time I was in the Johnson unit. I'd been there a couple of days and did little more than eat, sleep, and answer question upon question. As kind as George was to me, I just didn't have anything left to give. He was always trying to get me to go out into the day room, but one nanosecond in there and I thought I would go insane. Can you possibly imagine what it would be like to feel *all* of the emotions of a room full of mentally ill people? I could have fallen down the rabbit hole forever.

Instead, I stayed in my room and slept until it was time to talk to a doctor or eat.

THE FIRST MORNING I was there, George reported that Todd had a concussion, but he would live. Except for his bruised reputation, he had come out of this with just a few stitches. No one was pressing charges because they were all pretty clear I had lost my mind and might never get it back. My foster parents had already kicked me to the curb. By noon, I was once again a ward of the state. I didn't blame them, of course. Foster children were hard enough as it was. To know that one of your foster children was capable of such violence meant only one thing: get back in line, little girl.

"What about Danica? She's my best friend. Has she come or called?"

"She's called a dozen times, Sweetpea. If you want to see her, you're gonna have to cooperate with the doctors more. They're just trying to help."

Nodding, I sighed. My head pounded, as it had since I arrived. I was exhausted from the night terrors, and I couldn't stop feeling emotions which obviously were not my own. I knew I was sliding into the mental abyss, but was too afraid to share it with anyone. After being shackled to a bed, I'd pull off my own ears to keep from experiencing that again.

"I'm trying. I don't know what she wants from me."

"The truth. Always the truth."

That *sounded* easy enough, but I didn't know what the truth was. Was I insane and didn't know it? Had something happened in my brain chemistry that made me susceptible to other people's emotions? What was I supposed to say to her? *Hey doc, I know what you're feeling. You're bored, you hate your job, and you wish you were anywhere but here.* Yeah… that might work – if I wanted to be locked away forever.

"I just don't know what truth she wants."

George cocked his head and leaned against the wall. "You sure you don't want to talk about it? I don't judge people."

I looked away and nodded. "Thank you, but right now, I don't have any truths for you or for the doctors. I wish I did."

He left me alone that morning pondering my fate with my door open and my mind closed. I'm pretty sure he meant for me to go through it, not for someone else to slip on in, but that's what happened.

"Yo. You the newest nut on the block?"

Opening my eyes, I was staring at a girl about my age with fuchsia hair sticking up like little spikes from her head. Her head reminded me of a flower. "Excuse me?" I quickly sat up; her energy was practically knocking me off the bed.

"I'm the welcome wagon for incoming psychos. I'm Celeste. I'm a carver."

"A what?"

"I'm here for carving up my body like a fucking turkey. And you are?"

"Jane."

"Jane? Super boring name. I always wished I had a cool name, but my parents named me after my grandmother, which wouldn't be so bad if she had one remotely nice bone in her body. What a bitch." Celeste took a deep breath before continuing. "What brings you to our humble abode?"

"I beat up a football player with my geometry book."

Celeste's eyebrows rose and she took a step back. "No shit? Cool. I know a few football players I'd like to take a math book to. Why did you do that? You got violent tendencies? Tourette's? Schizo? Manic depression?"

"I thought he was going to hurt us."

"Oh." She stepped back into the room. "Cool. Get to

them before they get to you, I say. So, did you kill him?"

"No."

"You going downtown?"

"Downtown?"

"Yeah. You know – jail. They get you for an A and B?"

I shook my head. Her energy made my head hurt, and the way she spoke made my stomach churn although I didn't fully understand why.

"So, how come you don't come out? Scared of all the cuckoos out there?"

"Not really. I keep having these horrible headaches and I just don't feel like visiting."

Her eyes were almost midnight blue, and they were looking at me with a great deal of sincerity. Either that or I was *feeling* it very clearly. I didn't know any more.

"How come you cut yourself?"

"My version or theirs?"

"Yours."

"My girlfriend wouldn't come out so she dumped me. According to my shrinks, to cover up my broken heart I cut myself. You know, one pain replaces the other, and *voilà*, here I am. Wanna see?" Before I could say no thank you, she had her wrists and forearms in my face.

"Looks like it hurt."

"It hurt like hell. That's the point."

"You said you had a girlfriend?"

"Yeah, but don't think I'm all, you know, hittin' on you or something. I just liked her, that's all." She shrugged, but I knew differently. Her heart got broken big time.

I nodded. "Okay."

Celeste squinted as she studied me. "You're kind of

normal, aren't you?"

Forty-eight hours ago I might have said yes. "I guess that depends on what abnormal looks like to you."

"Bummer for you, then. You know what happens to normal kids in psych wards? They go crazy. If you weren't a whack job when you got here, you sure as shit will be when you leave."

"Is there any way out?"

"Out?" Celeste grinned. "Now you're talking. I don't know if there's a way out, but it might be worth looking into. You stay in here, and you'll be drooling and twitching in no time. Take my advice and whatever you do, do *not* take any of the meds they give you. Here." Celeste pulled a button off her shirt and handed it to me. "They always look under the tongue, but they never check between your cheek and gum. Practice putting the button there in case they start drugging you. Once the drugging starts happening, kiddo, it's game over. So practice, okay?"

I took the button and nodded. "I will. Thank you."

"Cooperate, Jane, and things will go much better for you. If you aren't going to cooperate, then at least pretend to."

She sounded just like George, so how bad could she be?

AS I LAY there working the button around my mouth with my tongue, I turned Celeste's words over in my mind. Sane people go crazy in the psych ward? That, I could believe. This place was unlike anything I had ever experienced in any nightmare.

Little did I know my nightmare was just beginning.

CHAPTER 9

A S I WAS unlocking Ladybug, I suddenly felt the weight of my big mouth and stupid bet. I loved this car. It was a present to myself when I graduated from Mills, and was the perfect car for getting around a city like San Francisco. I could park her anywhere.

"Goddamn it," I growled, leaning against the car.

"Bad morning?"

Whirling around, I saw Bob. "You're far from home. Are you lost, little boy?"

Bob shook his head. "Came by to see you. Someone else has gone missing, Jane. Gone without a trace."

"Are you sure?"

Bob nodded. I could smell stale beer on his breath. "Positive. Donnie has a wife and she said he went to get something to eat and never returned. She's worried sick, Jane. She said this isn't like him at all. I have to agree. Donnie's crazy about her. He would never want her to worry."

"And no one else has seen him?"

Bob shook his head slowly, and then I heard his stomach rumble. "No one. We've checked everywhere. I swear." His stomach roared once more.

"Come on. Let's see if Luigi's got a little something to quiet that belly of yours." I locked my car back up and walked into the tiny bakery. Luigi was in the back as he always was until about nine. His brother, Franko, waited on customers and handled the counter in the morning. He was a good baker, but not in the same league as Luigi.

"Hey Frank!"

"Good morning! Louie tells me you got a job."

I grinned. "I did. Well, I have one for the moment. Whether I keep it remains to be seen."

"The moment is all we have, so enjoy. What will you have this morning?"

I ordered a coffee and bagel with cream cheese, and Bob ordered a coffee with a bear claw. I tried to get him to order more, but he wouldn't.

"What's really going on down there?"

"That's just it. Nobody knows. No one has a clue, but we're all feeling it. It's freaky."

"And no one has seen or heard anything?"

"That's the problem. If you want to know what's going on in San Francisco, ask a homeless guy. But Jane, none of us have seen a Goddamned thing.

We're everywhere. You can be in a crowd of uptight businessmen on Market Street and we see you. We see everything that happens in this city. So to *not* see two of our own go missing, well, it's rattling our cages."

"I've already checked the hospitals. I've even talked to SFPD, but—"

"Try the morgue."

I blinked several times before replying. "The morgue. You want me to check out the morgue? I don't even know what these guys look like."

"You don't have to. I can guarantee you that any medical examiner will be able to tell you if the body on the slab is a homeless guy. It's one thing if one of us gets rolled by a bunch of punks, but it's a whole different ball game if someone is targeting us for some kind of sick fun. At least if we know we aren't getting killed, we might be able to rest a little easier at night. It's not a good thing when drunks start carrying knives and razor blades because we're afraid."

Rest easier. What an odd concept for a street dweller. "I'll check it out, but Bob, without real first and last names, I'm just spitting in the wind. You have to get me more than just nicknames."

Reaching his dirty fingers into his jacket pocket, Bob carefully extracted a folded bar napkin. "I did a lot of asking around and found out Rusty's last name was… is Van Pelt." He handed the napkin to me with only a slight tremble.

I looked at the scrawled writing on the napkin. "And Donnie's last name is Jack? His *last* name is Jack?"

Bob shrugged. "We all called him Donnie, but I suppose his name could be Jack Donnie. I just don't know."

I put it in my notebook. "I'll look into it today. In the meantime, why don't you spend the next few nights at the shelter? You look awful."

He grinned and nodded his thanks to Frank. "I'm a little tired is all. We spent most of the night looking for Donnie." Bob shook his head. "His woman is out of her head with worry, Jane, or I would have waited until DOD."

DOD was the street acronym for day-old day. The day they gave away the day-old breads. *My* day.

"It's not a problem, Bob, really. I've got a lot of running around to do today, so one more stop isn't going to hurt me. Is his wife around so I can talk to her?"

"She won't talk to strangers, Jane, but if anything else comes up, I'll let you know."

"If I find anything out, I'll come by."

"And if you don't?"

"Consider that the good news."

He nodded and took a bite from his bear claw. "How's your new job so far?"

"Could be better. Could be much worse. If there's something weird happening to your community, it might make a really interesting story. Maybe it would put a fire under the Mayor's butt to open another shelter. You know how things get done in an election year."

Bob chewed slowly. "Real estate is priceless in this city, Jane. You know that. Mayor Lee can't afford to give up a prime piece of real estate for more homeless services. We're not that important."

"You're probably right. It doesn't mean we can't still try."

"I'm not probably right, Jane, I *am* right. Mayor Lee's a decent enough guy, but nobody wants to see another shelter go up in the neighborhood. You know how it is; it's that 'not in my backyard' syndrome."

"You don't think the cops would be interested at all?"

He shook his head sadly. "Jane, hookers get the shit beat out of them every night. Do you see cops out there trying to protect them or solving those crimes? We're even lower on the food chain than prostitutes. We're expendable. In the eyes of the law, we barely even exist. We're just invisible fleas on the back of a dog."

It was as bad as it was true.

"Then we're on our own."

"Some things never change, huh, Jane?"

AFTER BREAKFAST, I dropped Bob back in the Mission District before calling Mrs. Galloway and asking her if I could stop by for a few follow-up questions. To my surprise, she heartily agreed, and forty minutes later I was back in the Victorian sitting across from her.

Nothing had changed about her as I read her energy and observed her aura. She wasn't suspicious or the least bit leery, which I found a little odd. Maybe it was because I was another woman and she could lower her guard.

"Thank you for seeing me on such short notice."

"Anything that will help find my husband."

I nodded, but didn't grin. I didn't like Mrs. Galloway as she sat there draped in her deceit. This was a ruse and she was playing a role. "I'm sure the police told you Mr. Galloway's car has been moved. Kind of makes you wonder if he's really missing at all."

She nodded and folded her hands in her lap. She was wearing a light pink shirt with white slacks. Her hair was perfectly coifed and her makeup looked professionally applied. "I found that very disconcerting. Who would do such a thing? And why?"

I asked the obvious. "You don't think your husband moved it?"

"My husband? Don't be absurd. If he was capable of

moving his car, he would have called me. He would have come home."

I stared at her. There wasn't a sliver of truth coming from her mouth. I didn't get the feeling Mr. Galloway was dead. People who have lost loved ones, no matter what the circumstances, have a specific feel about them; that void is easily read by an empath like me. It's an intense loss they can't cover up or hide.

"Okay, let's back up a second." I had decided on the way over I was going to try a different tact to Carter. "Mrs. Galloway, do you have internet access in the house?"

"Of course. Glen did most of his bill paying and correspondence over the internet."

I noted her use of the past tense. Now, why on earth would she use past tense when she *knew* he was still alive?

And Mrs. Galloway knew, alright. Finn was right about there not really being a crime, but if there was no crime, what game was she playing?

"Would you mind if I took a look at your computer?" I felt her energy shift. It was one thing to weave her elaborate lies into the fabric of our conversation; it was another thing for her to put those lies into action.

"My computer? Of course not. Follow me."

When we entered Glen's office, it reminded me of a library I'd seen in a Sherlock Holmes movie. Cherry bookshelves wrapped around expensive hardback books with gold print on the spines. His desk was impeccably clean and in the left-hand corner sat a photo of Glen and the dog in a golf cart. *How odd*, I thought, and walked over to one bookshelf to peruse the titles. You can tell a lot about a person by the books they read. What I learned about Glen

Galloway was that the entire bookshelf had faux books. You know the kind; you see them in model homes and at home improvement stores. They aren't real, but groups of hollow books that *appear* to be leather classics.

I wondered what else was fake.

"What, specifically, are we looking for?" Mrs. Galloway asked as she sat at the computer and looked around. The computer was a desktop; not a laptop like I had expected.

After watching her not even know how to turn it on, I reached over and pressed the little half-moon button that put the computer in sleep mode. "Is this the only computer in the house?"

"Oh, yes. This is Glen's office. He worked on his computer all day long. I never knew what he found so interesting, but he was in here all the time. I imagine he was checking stock quotes and sports scores. I'm afraid I don't know much about computers."

This speech was stilted and rehearsed. She felt manipulative. Yes. That was the overwhelming feeling hammering at me. She *wanted* me to dig into this computer. She was almost relieved that someone had finally decided to look at it. Her hand on the mouse was practically all-aflutter, just waiting to go to work. This whole thing was truly bizarre, and I let her lead me where she wanted me to go.

"That's okay. I just wanted to see what his workspace looked like." His monitor had a screen saver of a lily field on it, so I jiggled the mouse and got to his desktop. "Have the police looked at any of this?"

"No. That's why I called the paper. The police just don't care. They didn't do any of the kind of investigating you see on television."

"Yeah, well, maybe they'll be back. Do you know any of his passwords?" I wanted to get into that email account and see if the man had been foolish enough to play with his little belly dancer from the comfort of his own office.

"You think we might find some clues?"

Oh brother. *Clues?* Who did she think I was, Joe Friday? She *wanted* me snooping around. She was practically giddy at the thought, and before I knew what was happening, the stoplights between my brain and my mouth stopped functioning. "Mrs. Galloway, where is your husband?"

She slowly turned to me. "Excuse me?" Her voice was a frozen stalagmite.

There was no backstroking out of this one, so I forged ahead. "I think you know where your husband is. I just can't figure out your angle. Even the cops don't think a crime has been committed. What the hell is going on here?"

The blood drained from her face. "Is this your idea of a sick joke?"

I shook my head and pressed on. "Where's your dog?"

"Get out! I thought you were going to help, but you're just like those stupid cops! You cannot come into my home and—"

"If the dog isn't with Glen, Mrs. Galloway, where is it?"

"Get out! I'm calling your supervisor. Carter Ellsworth would *never* treat me like this! My husband is missing and Mr. Ellsworth is the *only one* who cares." She rose and power-walked to the front door, flinging it open dramatically. And the Oscar goes to...

"Mrs. Galloway, please hear me out."

"I've heard enough of your twisted suspicions. Now go."

As I started for the door, I threw down my last gauntlet.

"Fraud is punishable by jail time, Mrs. Galloway. Jail time. And I'm not talking Martha Stewart's jail time, either. You might want to think about that if you're going to continue down this path of lies."

"Path of… get out!"

I did and she slammed the door so hard I thought one of the windowpanes broke. This would not bode well for me at the paper. I had just pushed Mrs. Galloway into the same corner I was in. Desperate people do desperate deeds, and now I would just sit back and see what this desperate woman was going to do.

AFTER I GOT home, I taped my timeline to the wall and made a few phone calls. The morgue was a big zero, which was a good thing, I suppose. They hadn't had any homeless people in over a month, and certainly no one by Rusty's description.

I was poring over my paperwork for a third time when the phone rang. It was Sergeant Finn. "Why hello there, my new friend Sergeant Finn. To what do I owe this pleasure?"

"Hi there wannabe-reporter. I spoke to the Chief about your homeless guy. Apparently, he's not the first to have been reported missing."

"What?" I quickly grabbed my pen and paper.

"Two or three days ago, some drunk guy stumbled in with the same story you told. I guess his buddy was missing, but we blew it off. Nobody thought much about it until I brought it up. One missing homeless guy is nothing to write home about, but two makes—"

"It's three now. My friend Bob came to see me this morning. The guy's name is either Donnie Jack or Jack Donnie. He's been missing since last night."

"You sure?"

"Bob's a pretty reliable source. He doesn't exaggerate or engage in melodrama. He's got nothing to gain by being dishonest."

"I can't promise anything, mind you, but I'll do my best to see if we can't get some kind of investigation opened here."

"I appreciate that, Finn, really, and not because it's a possible story for me. Bob is really scared of whatever's going on out there. I don't know how much you know about the homeless culture in this city, but it takes a lot to scare them."

"I'm sure it does. I make no promises about anyone caring about this. I just wanted you to know that I gave it my best shot."

"I understand. Thank you so much for calling – and for trying. That means a lot."

"No problem. Anything more on the Galloway piece?"

"Not anything I can prove. You said his car was left at the Berkeley Marina."

"In the parking lot."

"Isn't it possible someone else might have moved it?"

Finn sighed. "I don't know what game Mrs. Galloway is playing with you and Ellsworth, but I wouldn't waste too much more of your time with her."

"I wish it were that easy. Thank you so much, Finn." Hanging up, I smiled. He was a really nice guy. At least when I talked to Bob I'd be able to tell him that the cops were on it.

Returning to my printouts, I kept coming back to the laptop and the dog. I also kept coming back to the fact that his car had moved. Moved? Wait. Weren't there cameras in airport parking lots? I made a note to call both the Oakland Airport and the Berkeley Marina to check. I was looking up the numbers when my phone rang again.

"Hello?"

"What in the hell did you say to Mrs. Galloway, Branson? Never mind. I don't want to know. Whatever it was, she's spitting mad! She says you come anywhere near her, and she will have you arrested on the spot. Way to go, Branson. Way to alienate our only connection to this story. Could you be any more unprofessional? Do you have *any* journalistic skills to speak of?"

"Is there something you need, Carter? I don't have the time to sit here while you bust my chops."

"How about an apology or something?"

"You're right. I'm sorry you're such an ass." I hung up. He sounded so angry I expected him to call me back. He did.

"What?" I barked when I picked up the phone.

"Do you have *any* idea what you're doing?"

"Yeah. I'm building a garage for the Lexus I'm going to own. Now piss off!"

"Branson!"

I hung up again. It felt like being clawed by a cornered cat. Mrs. Galloway had come out swinging. I must have really rattled her cage for her to want me to stay away. I'd hit too close to home and now she'd gone on the offensive.

This spoke to something I hadn't put much thought into; she had opened her doors to us not once, but twice.

She even took me to Glen's computer as if she had *wanted* me to actually find something. She *wanted* a story, but why?

I worked a little longer, trying to put more pieces together. Where was the dog? I jotted on my To Do list, which was growing exponentially every five minutes, to contact the animal shelters in the area. I'd seen a lot of dogs like that one before. What kind of dog was it? A quick trip to the internet told me it was a Jack Russell.

So, what did I have? I had a missing dog, a belly dancing girlfriend, an online romance, a mysteriously moving car, and a wife who was the only one who knew what in the hell it all meant.

CHAPTER 10

"**S**O, I'M BACK to being a ward of the state again." I was sitting across from Dr. Knowles on my fourth day in the psych ward when she told me what I already knew.

"And how do you feel about that?"

I shrugged. "Who could blame them? I beat a kid to a bloody pulp. I'd get rid of me, too."

"How are you sleeping?" Dr. Knowles liked to change subjects quickly. I had a teacher who used to do that because she felt our responses were more sincere.

"I'm having nightmares or something. I'm kinda living in one during the day, so I shouldn't be surprised that I have them at night."

"I've studied your tapes, Jane, and what you're experiencing isn't a nightmare. They're called night terrors."

"What's the difference?"

"Nightmares and night terrors can be differentiated both biologically and psychologically. Nightmares occur largely in REM sleep in the second half of the night. Night terrors usually occur in the first hours of sleep, and the sleeper typically doesn't remember the episode. Night terrors occur during non-REM sleep and don't occur during the dream cycle. They're often accompanied by physical manifestations of the terror."

"Physical manifestation?"

"You're fighting something or someone in every episode."

"Are you sure?"

"It's on the tape, Jane. Every night. Is this news to you?"

"Gee, Doc, I don't know. I've never had twenty-four-hour surveillance in my bedroom." It bothered me to hear I was doing something I couldn't remember. Apparently I was losing my mind in *both* the daytime as well as the nighttime.

"You have no memory of your episodes?"

I wished she would stop calling it that. "Nope."

"Well, I've prescribed you a sleeping pill. You must be exhausted."

The truth was I felt pretty good and even well-rested. I didn't need a sleeping pill, and was thankful Celeste had given me the button idea. I was pretty sure I could hide a cereal bowl in my mouth, I had practiced so much.

As if on cue, Dr. Knowles brought up Celeste. "I understand you and Celeste have become friends."

I shrugged. "The only friend I have has come by every day and still I haven't gotten to see her. I would clean every bathroom in here with a toothbrush if I could see Danica for just five minutes. Why can't I see her?"

"It's complicated, Jane, really. You'll get to see her soon, though. I promise. Now, let's talk about your last foster parents."

For the next half-hour, we talked about all my foster

parents and how it made me feel to be unwanted. It's funny; I'd never really *felt* unwanted. I felt more uninterested than anything else. Unwanted was for sissies who sat around feeling sorry for themselves because they hadn't been adopted. I never had time to feel sorry for myself. I was too busy surviving.

My session over, I was heading back to my room when a huge commotion broke out in the day room. Normally, I'd ignore the hourly outbursts, but today, something drew me closer, like the pull of an accident that just happened in front of you.

Orderlies were yelling, people were scattering, and someone ran by me with shackles. It was the shackles that drew me closer. I hated those things more than anything on the planet, but whoever they were intended for actually *feared* them. *That* emotion came through loud and clear and rang in my head like one of those stupid canned horns people use at football games. The feeling was so loud, I didn't even notice when Celeste approached me.

"Come on, J, let's DD outta here." Celeste grabbed my arm.

"Wait."

"For what? The Mute's gone bad, man. She's gonna blow and you don't wanna be there when she does."

"The Mute?"

"You need to get out more. Yeah, The Mute. She's gonna do something stupid. Come on. I'd rather not watch her stab someone with scissors or something."

I pulled my arm away and started back to the day room.

"What's the matter with you, J? Have you lost your mind?"

"Probably." When I got to the day room, George, Tall Tommy, and Sal were all cornering the girl known as The Mute. To my horror, she held a pair of scissors to her own neck.

She wasn't bluffing.

"Get back, Jane!" One of the nurses ordered.

"Stop!" I yelled over them in a voice not my own. I don't think I had ever raised my voice like that. All three orderlies turned to me. When George saw it was me shouting, he muttered something to the other orderlies before approaching me. "Let her through."

The nurses let me go.

I swallowed hard. I could barely function in here with the emotional noise battering my brain, but I remained focused and calm. "She's not bluffing, George. Please. If you guys get any closer, she *will* shove those scissors into her neck."

George looked hard at me and whispered, "How do you know this, girl?"

"I-I don't know." I lowered my voice. "I just do. You have to believe me, she's not kidding."

George peered into my eyes so long, it made me uncomfortable. Finally, he turned back to the day room. "Hang on a sec', guys. Back off and give her a little breathin' room."

One of the younger doctors pushed through the crowd. "What's going on here? I thought I said to sedate her. Can't the three of you handle her? She's just a girl." The doctor was a smallish Asian man who weighed all of 100 pounds, ninety of which were nothing but ego.

George cut his eyes over to me. "Sweetpea?"

Making my way over to her, I was nearly knocked down by the fear coming from The Mute. "What's her real name?" I whispered to George as I walked by.

"Mary. Her name is Mary."

Dr. Ego shook his head. "What in the hell is going on here? I told you how I wanted this handled. Sedate her!" The little doctor was getting irritated that nobody was listening to him.

"Jane can help us out here, sir."

"Don't be ridiculous. She's just a child."

I ignored the remainder of their conversation and focused on Mary The Mute. Her fear wasn't just because of the shackles, which she hated, but of what she was willing to do to herself. She was terrified she was about to end her own life.

"I know you're really scared," I said softly as I approached her.

Her eyes were on fire and she looked at me like a trapped feral animal. I had stopped questioning why or how I felt every emotion she was experiencing. Neither were important in this moment. Mary was going to kill herself if someone didn't do something. "I know you're not kidding about using those." I motioned to the scissors. "I had the same thoughts when they had me all trussed up, too. It's the shackles, isn't it?"

Mary swallowed hard and then barely nodded. The scissor tip remained pressed against her throat, but I felt some of her fear ebb slowly away.

"Will someone please do their job and get this room under control?" The doctor demanded. His frustration bounced off me as if he'd thrown a pebble at my head.

"Give Jane a second, please." George said. "Unless you want to be responsible for whatever Mary does with those scissors." George returned his attention to me and Mary. "Go on," he whispered.

I nodded and stepped closer to her. She blinked several times, but made no move to step away or to use the scissors. "You don't need to be so scared. I don't trust anyone here, either, except George. You can trust him. I swear." I watched Mary's eyes move over my shoulder to George. "And you can trust me. I'm not a loon or a nut job. I'm afraid, too. See, I get these feelings from people, and I'm getting them from you now. Someone else used to tie you up when you were a kid, huh? That must have royally sucked."

Mary lowered the scissors a little. It was so very strange. I felt like I could hear her through her emotions. She couldn't speak – she didn't have to; not to me. I was hearing her loud and clear.

"I've spent my whole life restrained. I'm scared shitless because I have no place to go from here. I have no family, no home, nothing. There's nothing for me to go back to. There's only one person who cares if I even make it out of here." I sighed. "Do you have a family?"

Mary nodded.

"Lucky you. I know – none of us in here are very lucky. I mean, we're in *this* horrible place, but at least *you* have some place to go when this nightmare is over. But you know what? Eventually, nightmares end. They all do. This one will, too. For all of us. And when it does, don't you want to be around?"

Mary hesitated before lowering the scissors some more.

She trusted me – trusted my words.

I turned to George. "Can you *please* put those shackles away? She doesn't need them. Please don't rush her."

George nodded and signaled the other orderlies to back away. Then he said something to the doctor, who stepped aside. "Go ahead."

I sat down at a table near Mary and patted the tabletop. "Come sit, Mary. Leave the scissors there and come sit with me awhile."

Sitting next to me, she held the scissors in her lap. Her fear was much less now that the shackles were out of sight, and I felt her exhaustion more than anything else. She was weary from the panic that someone was going to bind her up once more. She'd had a lifetime of being tied up. My heart hurt from the pain of a childhood even worse than mine.

"I'm Jane," I said softly. "I'm here because I beat a kid up with my math book."

She grinned slightly and I realized she was a little younger than I was.

"And you're here because—" I closed my eyes and there it was. She wasn't born this way. "Oh. You suddenly stopped talking, huh?"

Her eyes grew wide. She looked as surprised as I felt. Nodding, she blinked back her tears.

"Nobody would listen to you about being tied up by your stepdad, so you just stopped talking." I shook my head sadly. "That's messed up, Mary. Someone should have listened to you, huh?"

She nodded.

Slowly, I reached over and took the scissors from her and leaned closer. "Some dude once said that living well is the best revenge. I've always believed that. It's what I want to do when I get older to prove to everyone that I was worth the time and energy they didn't give me." I took her cold hand in mine and smiled softly at her. "Grow up to live well, Mary. Grow up to show everyone how wrong they were. I'll bet when that day comes, we'll both be sipping champagne from our yachts and laughing at all the little people in our lives. Doesn't that sound like fun?"

She smiled and nodded.

I suddenly felt emotions from someone behind me. "You go with George now, okay? He's a good guy and he'll make sure no one puts those shackles on you anymore. Okay?"

She nodded and then looked down at her wrists. It was the first time I noticed the scars.

"You know what they say – suicide is a permanent solution to a temporary problem. Remember that, okay? All of this is temporary."

Mary nodded again as she rose.

"Go with George." I rose.

Mary stood, and nodded as she started past me. Just as we were side-by-side, she whispered so softly I almost missed it. "Thank you." Something changed for me at that moment; something really huge: *I* stopped being afraid. Even if I really *was* going nuts, it wasn't so scary anymore.

When I got back to my room, I lay on the bed and wondered if Danica had given up coming to see me. I missed her so much. Locked away in here, it was as if the world outside wasn't real anymore. You knew it was out there, you knew it went on without you, but every day you were gone you became less and less a part of it, less and less real –

almost like you were evaporating or slowly fading away.

I was almost asleep when there was a slight knock on my door. It was George.

"How is she?" I asked, sitting up.

"Better."

"No shackles or drugs?"

"Nope. Neither. Whatever you said to her really helped."

I nodded and looked away. George had come to my room seeking answers. I didn't know the specific questions, but I had a pretty good idea of what he was looking for. "That's good. You know, you guys need to ditch those shackles."

George pulled up the chair. His eyes were riveted to mine. "We need to talk, Sweetpea. I saw what you did out there and I need you to hear that you're not going crazy."

I nodded and swallowed hard. "How do *you* know?"

George leaned closer and whispered, "I know what's happening to you. I know what you are."

What I was?

Oh, that was just grand. If I hadn't fallen all the way down the rabbit hole before now, I sure as hell was about to.

CHAPTER 11

"WE GOT A new hit with the credit card." It was Carl. I switched ears with the phone.

"Where?"

"At the marina. The dude laid down a pretty penny to rent a boat."

"When?"

"Early this morning. If this guy is on the run, he isn't doing anything to hide it."

I jammed my feet into my shoes and ran a comb through my hair. "And you're sure?"

"Absolutely. Of course, the card could have been stolen, but it was used. That's not all. There was an e-mail to him confirming a meeting in Oakland."

"Belly Dancer!"

"Oh yeah."

"Can you read it to me?"

"Sure. It says *confirming meeting point in Oakland or surrounding. Can't wait. Finally.*"

"That's it?"

"For now. I'll let you know if we get more later, okay?"

"Okay. Thanks so much, Carl. This could really be the break I need."

"Be careful, Princess."

I had dressed and was on my way to the marina in under ten minutes. Tripod was sound asleep when I left, no doubt still nursing a hangover.

When I got to Berkeley, I told the guys at the marina that I was doing a story on tourism and the number of water vehicles rented every day. They were incredibly helpful and even though the registration sheet was upside down, I could very clearly see Glen Galloway's signature. Apparently, he'd come alone.

"Does everyone have to sign your registration form?"

"Oh yes. We have insurance forms and complete registration forms that must be filled out. No one goes without one."

I jotted down some notes, but was curious about the fact that Glen Galloway had used his own name.

This was getting stranger by the minute. When I was done, I walked along the marina thinking about how this all looked. Was Finn right about this being a non-story and a big fat waste of time?

First off, Glen Galloway wasn't missing. Secondly, no crime seemed to have been committed other than the questionably ethical one by him via the internet. Thirdly, only Mrs. Galloway's insistence suggested there was any foul play.

I turned and headed back to the marina.

"Need more info?" The young man asked when I returned.

"Just a couple more questions. Do people take their pets with them when they go out onto the water?"

"Sure. Just this morning, a guy went out with his dog."

Bingo.

"Really? Must have been a big dog to guard for sharks or something, eh?" I grinned, winking back at him.

"Naw. It was one of them rat terrier things. A Jack Russell maybe?"

I grinned. "Thank you."

"No problem."

As I got to Ladybug, I inhaled deeply. So, Glen Galloway *had* taken the dog. I knew it!

I sat there with my mind reeling. I couldn't tell Carter. Normally, I'd call Danica, but I was afraid I would worry her about losing the bet. She didn't like to lose. Maybe that was because she seldom did. But if she thought I was going to send her on a six-hour date with a jerk like Carter, well… she might just kick my ass.

I knew I could talk to the boys. Those guys would eat this up with a spoon. But I couldn't really sort things out with them. They liked to grab it and run, leaving you slightly breathless and a little bit out of the loop. That's not what I needed right now. I needed someone who would listen, ask a few questions, and then let me straighten out my thoughts.

There was one person I always turned to when I needed advice, or just needed to be heard. We all crave that special person who really knows and understands us; whether we speak every day or every other month, just knowing that they're there makes all the difference in the world.

I needed that difference right now. I desperately wanted

someone to listen, to know me, to remind me of who I am and what I can do. Danica was my best friend, but I needed the only person in my life who could give me what I needed.

I needed Melika.

CHAPTER 12

"WHAT… WHAT DO you mean you know *what* I am?" I stared at George. He *knew*! I could see it in his eyes. "Be honest with me. Am I nuts?"

George smiled. "Not even remotely. What you got is a gift." George put his hand out and I put mine in his. He led me out into the hall, where we walked a ways until we came to the small quad outside. It was enclosed with a twelve-foot-tall fence.

"A gift? You're kidding me, right?"

He smiled and slowly shook his head. "If you are what I think you are, it might feel like a curse, but you gotta believe me, it's a gift. You knew what Mary was feeling without her ever saying a word, didn't you?"

I nodded, feeling enormous relief. "What's happening to me? All of a sudden—"

"You feel all these emotions from everyone around?"

My jaw dropped. "Yes! That's exactly what it feels like! It comes in waves. Sometimes knocking the wind out of me. Sometimes, I feel it in my head, like I can actually *hear* their feelings in my brain. What's wrong with me?"

George patted my leg. "Nothing's wrong with you, Sweetpea. Trust me. You're so special, God gave you a rare and precious gift." He held his hand up to stop me. "But it's only a gift if you know how to use it, otherwise, I know it feels like you're losing your mind. But you have to trust me. I know what I'm talking about."

"I can barely trust myself, George. You have no idea."

George leaned closer. "Actually… I do."

"Are you—"

"No, but my mother is."

I blinked several times. "She feels things, too?"

He nodded. "More than most. What you are, Sweetpea, is an empath… and probably more. We won't know what all you have until you're checked out."

"An empath?"

"Yeah. You're a feeler. I've only met a couple in my life, but I'm pretty sure you're one."

"You mean there are… others?"

"Sure. Some are quite powerful. Not all are empaths. Some are telepaths, some clairvoyants. You, little one, are in a select group of individuals known as paranormals or, as my mother likes to call them, supers… for supernaturals. The key is learning how to control it."

"Control it? I don't even understand it."

"I know, I know. First thing we have to do is get you out of here."

"Excuse me?"

"What you have, Sweetpea, we can't help you with here. Conventional medicine doesn't even recognize what we're talking about. All we'll do is talk at you or drug you up, and neither of those will protect you."

"Protect me? Protect me from what?"

"From all those emotions hammering away at you. You gotta learn about your skill; know how to harness your power, how to protect yourself, how to understand who and what you are. You're well beyond the scope of what our doctors can do. You haven't mentioned any of this to Doctor Knowles, have you?"

"Are you kidding? Even if I wanted to, which I don't, I wouldn't even know where to begin." There was an incredible sense of relief knowing that George understood. He *actually* understood. I would have cried, but I didn't have time. I was overflowing with questions. "There are so many things I want to know. Oh my God. All this time, I thought I was going crazy."

George ran his big hand over his head. "I'd like to answer your questions, Sweetpea, but you need answers from someone who has all of them."

"Your mom?"

He nodded. "Melika. She's the real deal. I'm just a spotter."

"A spotter?"

"It's my job to help find those like you who don't know what they are yet and get to them before… well… before they do something stupid."

"Like kill themselves?"

He nodded.

And so it turned out that George's mother wasn't just an empath, but a very powerful woman who spent her time teaching people new to the world of psionics how to adjust to and utilize their abilities; telepaths, clairvoyants, empaths, and telekinetics came to her from all over the world *if* they were caught in time. The majority of us were not, and usually ended up in a rubber room or worse.

"Will she come see me?" I asked.

George shook his head. "Can't. She lives in New Orleans."

"New Orleans?" I whispered. "Louisiana?"

He nodded. "She's the best there is. If you're going to live with this and be sane, you need someone to show you how. You *need* help and Melika can give it to you. She may be the only person who can."

"But how? Can she call me here?"

George slowly shook his head. "This isn't something you can learn about in an hour or a day or even a month. We're going to have to get you out of here. I can get you off the floor and out of the hospital, but we're going to need some help getting you from here to New Orleans, especially since you're only fourteen. Is there someone who can help? Do you have any of your own money?"

Yes and yes. There were two people I knew who would help: Danica and Britt Bevelaqua. I hadn't heard from Britt since she ran, but I still had the forty dollars she'd given me. No, it wasn't enough for airfare, but it was a start. "My best friend Danica can help."

"Okay. You give me the number and let me see what I can do. We've got a lot to do and not much time to do it in." George held my hand tightly as he outlined his plan. When he finished, I sighed.

"But George, won't they just release me back to the state pretty soon? Can't we just wait until then instead of sneaking out and risking your job?"

He rose and motioned for me to follow. "You beat that boy up because of something you felt, didn't you?"

I nodded as I followed. "I knew as sure as if he'd said it. He wanted Danica and there was nothing that was going to stop him. I've never felt that kind of emotion in my life. Then, after I hit him, I felt his anger and rage turn toward me. He was going to really hurt me, so I just kept hitting him so he wouldn't have that chance. I think I would have killed him if Mr. Morgan hadn't grabbed me."

"And what about Mary? You *knew* what was going on with her, huh?"

"She's scared of the shackles and being tied down. She can talk, you know?"

"Can, but won't."

"Won't but does. Where are we going?" George was taking me down a locked hallway forbidden to the rest of us.

"You'll see."

We took a couple of squeaky turns down hallways filled with moaners, screamers, chatter bugs, and singers. I knew where we were now. We were in the J ward; where the hopelessly insane awaited removal to some other treatment facility where they would, most likely, live out the remainder of their sad and incomplete lives.

When George finally stopped, he peered into a small glass window in the door. "Look in here."

I had to stand on tiptoe to see, and when I did, I recoiled. A poor, demented young girl was rocking back and forth, mouth hanging open with a foot-long string of drool hanging from her chin. She looked no more than fifteen or sixteen. "What's wrong with her?" I turned from the window, feeling goosebumps on my arms. "She's so…"

"Unstable?"

"So young to be crazy."

"She wasn't always, Sweetpea. As a matter of fact, her mental health was fine when she got here."

I remembered Celeste's words about this place making people crazy. "Did bringing her here make her go like this?" I asked.

George sadly shook his head. "No, it's not where she is that made her ill, Sweetpea. It's *what* she is that did that to her. You see… that sad little girl in there is an empath. She came in here for the same reasons you did, but I couldn't get her out in time. I couldn't get her to Melika in time."

CHAPTER 13

"**H**I, MEL. IT'S me."

"Echo! How are you, girl? You've been creeping into my thoughts a lot this past week. You all right?"

"I'm good. It's just... well... I have the chance to get this investigator's job and I'm having a hard time with what I think I'm seeing."

"Ah. Well then, that explains the confusion I'm getting from you. The first thing you need to do is clear the fog surrounding you. Your spirit cannot clearly see those things you're feeling from others. You know as well as I do that it is not the presence of facts that quells confusion, but the willingness to see all possibilities. Tell me what you think you know."

So I did.

"You read her twice?" Melika asked when I finished my tale.

"Yes ma'am. Both times, I knew that she knew where her husband was, all while claiming that he was missing. The police didn't even open the case because they don't believe there's been a crime committed."

"What do *you* believe?"

"That's just it. I don't know."

"Yes, you do. If you believe that something is amiss… then consider yourself correct."

"But I don't even know which way to turn. This is my big chance, Mel, and I'm afraid I've really put myself on the short stick."

"No, you haven't. My dear, you spent four years with me, constantly wanting me to clear the way for you and give you answers you already had." Mel chuckled. "Some things never change, child."

I grinned. "They need to change, though, don't they?"

"Growing up is never easy… especially for us."

"I can't interview Mrs. Galloway again."

"You don't need to. Seems to me she's already shown you what you need to know. My guess is, *she* is not the key to the puzzle, but the directions on the box."

I sighed, thinking about the piling evidence… but evidence to what? "If not her… who?"

"Not who, my dear. *What.* Who, as you've discovered, tend to say one thing while meaning another. You need to meditate on *what* you know. Open your mind and see what comes to you."

"Meditate."

"Yes. Your skills allow you to pick up energies you may not have been searching for. Remember my dear, keep your mind open to all possibilities. If you do that, the answers will come like fish to a light."

I grinned. Melika was the wisest person I'd ever met; not

just as an empath of incredible abilities, but as a person. I had learned more from her in four years than I had in the rest of my life put together.

"I'll do that, Mel. Thanks."

"It's what I'm here for. Have you spoken to that son of mine lately?"

"We spoke last week. He's doing a lot of overtime because of the nurses' strike, why?"

"Next time you see him, tell him to come home soon. His grandmother thinks she's not going to be around much longer and wants to spend some time with him."

I felt something seize my heart. "Is there something wrong with Bishop?"

"Wrong? Oh no, there's nothing to be concerned about yet. She's just been playing with a necromancer who has her convinced that she'd like it better on the other side."

I chuckled. Bishop was the most colorful woman I had ever met. Born in Haiti, she was brought to New Orleans by a wealthy landowner when she predicted he would suffer a great fall if he attempted to sail to the United States within the next month. He did anyway, nearly dying in the process. His ship sunk off the Haitian coast, but his servants had managed to drag him to shore, with not one but two broken legs. He spent the next three months searching for "that little dark girl with the big green eyes," in the hopes of bringing her to the United States with him. When he finally found her, he offered to bring her entire family to the new plantation he was having built, but no one except Bishop wanted to go. After considerable dickering and haggling, Bishop boarded a ship bound for America.

"Why are necros so incredibly bizarre?"

Melika chuckled softly into the phone. "I reckon being able to talk to those who have passed would tend to make one a tad batty, don't you? I keep telling her to stay away from that one, but you know how Bishop can be; nobody can tell her a damn thing."

"I'll be sure to tell George the next time I see him. You don't think she—"

"Hon, I never know what to think where that old woman is concerned. This could just be another play to see her grandson. Who knows?"

"I appreciate your wisdom, as usual, Mel. Thank you."

"Perhaps, in the future, you won't shoot your mouth off and put yourself in such a bind."

"I know. I got cocky. I guess I just wanted to show this turd up."

"That's never been our way, child. Whenever we step onto a path that is not true to our calling, our way becomes hazy, as yours is now. You need to remedy that. Once you do, your way will become clear. Now… who's the young man?"

"Young man?"

Melika's soft laughter floated through the airwaves. "Oh child, we empaths spend so much time guarding against other people's emotions we forget to both feel and examine our own. There's a fella you got soft spot for."

"There's no fella." I knew better than to lie, but it wouldn't be any fun for her if I gave in so quickly. It was a silly game we had been playing for years.

She chuckled again. "Oh… I think there is. But never mind. You've got plenty on your plate. It's no wonder I was thinking of you so much. You remember what I told you.

You'll find your answers once you have clarity. Seek clarity always."

"I will. Thank you."

"And keep me informed."

"As if I had a choice. Please tell Bishop that she has to stay on this side until I have a chance to say goodbye to her."

"Oh, you little devil, you. I'll tell her, but don't be surprised if you receive a summons. You know how crazy that old woman is about you."

I agreed to come if I was summoned and then we signed off. I hung up feeling better than I had in days. Melika had a way of doing that, and had been doing so for over a decade. All through college, she had been there for me, listening to my stories about my classes and my professors. She was more than my friend and mentor. She had saved my life. When someone does that for you, you tend to listen to their advice.

What I needed to do was clear my mind of all the factual clutter I'd absorbed. My empath ability extended well beyond my mental capabilities to handle it all.

Closing my eyes, I started one of the many meditation techniques Melika had shown me over my four-year stay in the bayou. Inhaling deeply, slowly, I felt my body relax and the noise in my mind settle. As my head cleared, I realized how much it felt as if I'd been listening to music through static, and once the station was clear I could actually start to define the lyrics.

In and out, slow and rhythmic I breathed until my mind was finally quieted. Gone were all the facts from the printouts, the data from the notes, the copious amounts of information I'd been poring over and absorbing. Gone was the static and the noise from my mental energy field. And as each noise dissipated, I came closer and closer to the clarity Melika had spoken of.

Clarity: the ability to see, hear and feel things as they truly are. Melika used to lecture me on the importance of clarity all the time. As a teenager, when I first arrived on her doorstep, clarity was the last thing I thought I needed. I didn't *want* to see things clearly. I knew what it looked like, and it hadn't been pretty.

But Melika has a way of breaking through even the thickest walls and she did so in order to show me the error of my ways. Clarity is the key to so many things; successful communication, decision-making, life choices, you name it. She taught me how vital it is to keep the mental and emotional clutter out of my life so that I can see things how they truly are.

I think I was so caught up in delivering concrete proof to support my empathic skills that I strayed very far off my path and created the haze I was floundering in.

With the static gone, I let my mind and spirit take me where it would. I saw the computer sitting on the table. There were hands on it… a woman's hands, complete with gaudy diamond. It was Mrs. Galloway at the keyboard, typing away. I could see her hands as they flew across the letters. She was quite an adept typist for a woman who acted like she didn't know a cord from a USB.

I wasn't being clairvoyant or telepathic; I do not possess those skills in my psionic repertoire. What I do possess is the ability to recall the emotions of someone who has touched me, such as Mrs. Galloway. When things are clear, then images contribute to the overall picture behind the emotions. I hadn't been able to *see* any of this earlier because

I had done a fine job of cluttering myself. What I was seeing now was Mrs. Galloway on a laptop.

Wait. A laptop?

Yes. There it was, much clearer now. She was using a laptop.

Inhaling deeply to release the image, I saw something else; something even stranger that almost made me open my eyes. Mrs. Galloway was petting a Jack Russell Terrier before handing the dog over to a man. I knew it was a man by the hands. It was a sad moment for Mrs. Galloway. She actually liked the dog.

Why was the dog so key to me? Why was… I was going deeper into my meditation when the phone rang.

I opened my eyes and blew out a breath. "Damn it." I tried not to growl into the phone as I picked it up.

"Echo, it's Finn. I hope I'm not bothering you."

"Oh. Hi. No. I was… I was just meditating."

"Really? Oh. Well… I…"

"It's okay, really. I'm done. I'm as relaxed as I need to be. What's up?"

"I just thought you'd want to know… that non-crime, non-story you're working on has become both."

My stomach did a little twist. "Don't tell me you found him."

"Not exactly. We found the boat he rented. Just the boat."

"Where was it?"

"In the middle of the bay."

My hand went to my mouth. "Oh no."

"Yeah. Oh no is right. There wasn't anyone in the boat. Galloway was gone."

"Gone?"

"We're thinking suicide because he left a note and there was a bunch of sand and rocks piled in the corner of the boat."

Suicide? Well, *that* sure came out of nowhere. "You're telling me you think he committed suicide by jumping into the Bay?"

"That's what homicide's got down so far. No sign of any foul play yet. They've impounded the boat, but at this point, our not-so-missing person appears to be walking among the fish. I wanted you to know first in case you heard it from some other source. It doesn't look like we're going much beyond what we've done."

"Thanks, Finn. I appreciate it. Looks like I'll be writing that pink slip of mine in a couple of days, so if you hear of any openings…"

"Yeah, your nemesis was already down at the docks, which is why I called you. A buddy of mine for OPD hates Ellsworth with a passion. I asked him to keep me posted if he shows up."

"And he showed up."

"Yeah, getting in everyone's way. As usual."

I grinned. "When I get my walking papers, Sergeant Finn, can I buy you dinner for all you've done?"

"Dinner? Hell, Echo, this wasn't even worth a warm beer."

"Maybe so, but you've done so much already. I like to pay my debts to society."

"Okay, but to tell you the truth, I'd rather you kept your job."

"Thanks."

"I'm not kidding. Good reporters are hard to come by. There was a time when journalists just reported the news. Now, they're practically manufacturing it. No offense."

"None taken." It was true, though. Journalists were now making headlines instead of writing about it. A couple of big shot reporters got busted for cooking stories, who sold their stories to book publishers, and who demanded the same seats as Congress folk in DC's finer restaurants. Fame, and the quest for it, has not bypassed my chosen profession.

"True. But what makes you think I'm any different?"

"I've been doing this job long enough to spot quality folks, Echo. You're not at all like your colleagues."

"Well, let's just hope that I still *have* my colleagues once this is all over. Carter will run a story about the suicide and then put this to bed."

"I wish I had better news for you. I'll let you know if there's anything else worth knowing."

"I mean it about dinner."

"And I mean it about your job. Do what you must to keep it, short of going against your own moral code. Gotta run. Good luck."

I hung up feeling sad, angry, bummed out, and slightly confused. Suicide? Nothing in my notes indicated that he was despondent. After all…

My phone rang again. I assumed it was Carter calling to gloat. "Yes?"

"Princess, this is Franklin. We got an email that came through this morning. From Belly dancer to our guy."

"What does it say?"

"It's short and sweet. It just says *I love you, but I can't do it. Go back to your wife.*"

"Does it have the time sent?"

"Sure. One o'clock this morning. Well, a few minutes after. Does this help?"

"I'm not sure."

"If we get any more hits, I'll let you know."

"Thank you."

"Oh, and Princess? The boss is spitting nails right now. Apparently, she's about to lose a bet. You know how competitive she is…"

"Indeed I do, Franklin. Maybe I'll stop by to see her today and see if I can't rub her sore spot."

"No need."

My doorbell rang followed by three hard pounds.

"That would be her." Franklin snickered. "See ya."

Hanging up, I answered the door to a whirlwind who blew right by me. "Be straight with me, Clark. I'm going to have to go out with that dick, aren't I? I would rather eat a turd."

Closing the door, I marveled at her gorgeous silk Dior pantsuit. Her shoes were Jimmy Choo and the color matched perfectly. Long ago, Danica had tried to groom me where fashion was concerned, but we determined I wasn't built for designer anything. I would always be a fashion don't.

"Hold onto that turd thought. I'm not out of this game yet."

She turned on me, eyes ablaze. "Don't toy with me. Ellsworth called to let me know they found an empty boat and the suicide note. That jerk off was practically orgasmic."

I could imagine. "Hold on…"

"Which is the only orgasm he'll ever have around me! I

swear to God, Clark…"

"Down girl. We're not done yet."

"No? Do you have *any* proof to back up your read of that old cow? Anything at all?"

"I have proof that something isn't as it seems. I just don't know what it is yet."

"Oh, that's just great. You're throwing me to the wolves here."

Sighing, I ran my hand through my hair. "There's something hovering around the periphery of my vision, but I haven't been able to grasp it completely. I was just meditating before you blew in. You *do* realize that you blew in here, right?"

Danica opened my refrigerator and pulled out the pack of peanut M&Ms. "You know how I hate to lose, and I *really* don't want to lose to that guy. You deserve this job, Clark. You're a great writer, you have the nose for it, and you never know when to give up. Seems to me, this is the perfect job for you. So don't give up now." Danica walked over to my timeline and examined it. "Damn, you've really put a lot of time into this. Look at this. You practically have their lives down hour by hour."

"I'm trying to be a real reporter. There's a lot of legwork and a lot of tracking leads."

"Looks like my boys have been busy helping you with that end of it."

"They have. Of course, for them, it takes no time to gather info that'd take me days."

"Then what's your plan?"

"Mrs. Galloway won't see me again, but I'm pretty sure she would see another reporter… or someone posing as a reporter."

Danica turned and cocked her head. "Me?"

"Yes. Think you could be a reporter for an hour?"

"I'd do almost anything for an hour if it meant winning this bet."

"Good. Here's what I want to do."

CHAPTER 14

LIFE IS FILLED with unlikely heroes and mine is no exception.

After George dropped his big bomb about my tenuous future, we got down to planning my escape. He could help me escape at night, but what then? I had really grown to care about the big guy and I wouldn't hear about him risking his job. All he needed to do was get me off the floor and the rest was up to me.

Or so I thought.

When I finally got the chance to talk to Danica, I had very little time to tell her what I needed. "There's forty bucks in my backpack in the inner pocket. I need you to get me a fake ID. Just use my student body photograph when you go."

"A fake ID? Are you nuts?"

"I will be if you don't get me out of here." So I explained to her our plan.

"What about money?"

"George is loaning me cash for a ticket, but I need an

ID that says I'm eighteen."

"Same name? I mean… Jane Doe already looks like a fake ID, know what I mean?"

I thought about my recently discovered powers. "Echo. I want my name to be Echo."

"You're kidding?"

"No. Echo is perfect. It… suits my new… life. Trust me on this. I am so much more of an Echo than I ever was a Jane."

"Fine. Echo it is. And your last name?"

I thought about the only girl who had ever been nice to me in the foster homes I was in. "Branson."

"Echo Branson?"

I laughed. "Why not? I'm going to be starting a new life."

"Are you ever going to tell me what really happened?"

I had written her several letters trying to explain to her why I tried to crush Todd's head in. I wanted her to know what I was, but it's hard to explain something you barely understand yourself.

"But why New Orleans? Why so far away?"

"There's a… school there that specializes in my… issues…"

"What issues?"

"I'll tell you as soon as I can explain it better. I'm still adjusting to the idea that I *have* these issues that are really creeping me out. You've got to get me out of here."

"Of course I will. What will happen if we get caught?"

"They'll lock me down and pump me full of drugs that will probably make me go insane."

"So… no pressure."

"None at all."

"And there's forty bucks in your backpack."

"Inside the small zipper pocket. Britt gave it to me before she left. She told me to spend it only when I was ready to run. I'm ready to run. Really, really fast."

Our time was up and I hung up knowing that she would do everything she could to make that run possible. I didn't know that she would have as much help as she did, but then, Danica knew how to get things done. That was why she was so successful in college and after; nothing stopped her once she set her mind to something.

Escape was easier than I thought. Once George was able to get me off the floor undetected and wearing regular street clothes, I was able to walk casually out of the hospital as if I was just a visitor.

When I reached the parking lot, I looked around for Danica, but couldn't find her. I started to panic a little, but then I saw a black Trans Am screech into the parking lot. I felt a familiar presence, but since I had no experience with my "gift," I couldn't pinpoint it.

"Need a lift?" someone asked from the car. I knew the voice as soon as I heard it.

"Britt?"

"Get in, goofus! You trying to get us busted or what? Come on, girl, we don't have all day."

The passenger side opened and Danica stuck her head out and waved me over. "Come on!"

Scooting around to the other side, I hopped in next to Danica and Britt peeled away even before I could close the door.

"Parking lot cameras," Britt muttered as an explanation

for why she had floored it. "Don't worry. We'll be ditching this ride in a few."

And so we did. Hotwiring cars was something Britt had learned from her time on the street and she was very good at it.

"Okay ladies, Oakland airport, here we come."

I turned to Danica, but before I could ask my question, she answered me.

"Britt put her cell number on the bills she gave you in big, red letters. I called her and…"

"Told me you'd finally wised up and decided to run. So, here I am." She cut her eyes over to me. "You look ready to run." Britt flipped her wallet open and pushed my fake ID out with her thumb. I took it and grinned.

"Echo Branson, eh, Jane?" Britt grinned as she drove. "Cool name. It suits you."

Danica threw her arm around me. "We couldn't have done any of this without Britt. She took care of everything."

I looked over at Britt. The streets had aged her. She was seventeen going on thirty. Her short hair was blonder than I remembered, but her eyes were as blue as ever. She was wearing faded jeans with designer holes in the knees and a gray SFSU sweatshirt. I'd never been happier to see anyone than I was her. "Thank you so much, Britt."

"Hey, we orphan Annies gotta stick together, you know? I'm just glad I could help."

"You got money?" Danica asked.

I nodded. "A paperless ticket. Melika bought it for me."

"Who's that?" Britt asked.

I thought for a minute. "She's the woman who's going to save my life."

Britt smiled. "Then you're all set to go."

And so I was.

Less than twenty-four hours later, I stepped off the plane and into a brand-new life of supernaturals.

FOR A KID who grew up in California, New Orleans was another country. Everything about it was unlike anything I had ever experienced; the smells, the sounds, the energy, *everything* was so… foreign.

As I made my way through the airport, I found a kid standing at the baggage claim with a sign that read Echo Branson. I nearly walked by, but he caught my eye and stopped me in my tracks. The emotions from a plane full of people had given me an enormous headache.

"Echo?" The boy said. He had the darkest skin I had ever seen. He wore shorts, black Nike high tops and a red t-shirt that said something about Alligator Adventures. He looked all of twelve.

"Oh. Yes. I'm sorry. That *is* me."

He grinned with teeth whiter than white. "I know. Come."

We got into a silver car that was waiting for us.

"I'm Jacob," the boy said, extending his hand.

I shook it. "Where's Melika?"

"Oh, she hardly ever comes to town."

"Town? Where does she live? George said she lives in New Orleans."

Jacob kept grinning. "She does. She lives down in the bayou."

"The what?"

Jacob groaned. "Ah, man. You don't know what the

bayou is?"

"No. Do you know what the Tenderloin is?"

"Uh… no."

"Then we're even."

Jacob sighed and shook his head. "George shoulda warned you. I mean… the bayou is… well… it's not like any place on earth. You'll see."

We drove in silence through streets lined with homes that rivaled the Victorians in San Francisco. People were everywhere and many of the areas reminded me of San Francisco, only older. I mean, this place was *old*. You could smell it in the air. It was like I'd been transported back in time. I was mesmerized by the color of everything. What a charming and wild little place this was. I loved it immediately.

"Pretty cool, eh?"

I nodded, looking out the window. It appeared that people here were into things like voodoo and palm reading, not to mention food, food, and more food. There was a restaurant every other building, and each was packed.

"Melika wanted you to see it because she said it would be a long time before you'd see it again. You have a lot of work to do and the city distracts from all that. In the bayou, there aren't nearly as many folks around to bother the process."

"The process?"

"That's what we call it."

"We?"

"You'll stay in the bayou with Melika and the rest of us while she teaches you what you need to know."

I nodded and leaned back. His somber tone reminded

me that this wasn't a vacation. I was actually a kid on the lam. "How come I don't feel any emotions from you?"

"I'm blocking. Don't worry. Melika will show you how, too."

Sighing, I watched the landscape go by. This was my new life, my new beginning, and I was already realizing that I couldn't have been more out of my element if I'd been on the moon.

"Don't worry if you're feeling overwhelmed. We all felt that way when we first got here."

Watching a new world fly by, I thought about my last couple of days at the hospital. They had been pure torture, and I understood, all too clearly, why that poor drooling girl had cracked.

So here I was, coming to empathic boot camp where I would, hopefully, learn to block out the noises threatening my sanity. This was serious; not a frivolous moment to be squandered. Yes, New Orleans was a most incredible place, but it was so much more than that to me. It was the keeper of a mysterious woman I knew little about, but who offered to teach me how to live with what had historically driven people mad. And as we left New Orleans proper and started to wind our way to the bayou, I looked forward to meeting this woman who was going to save my life.

An hour later, we pulled up to a tiny cinderblock house precariously perched on a sliver of land. It looked like a shed behind one of the more dilapidated houses in the Oakland ghetto.

"She lives *here*?"

Jacob shook his head. "Nope. Bones lives here. He's the boatman."

"Boatman? We need to take a boat?"

This seemed to amuse Jacob. "You really don't know much, do you? Where have you been? In a cave?"

"Actually, I've been in a psych ward," I replied, leveling my gaze at him. "Sorry I didn't have time to bone up on my geography."

"Oh. Gee. I'm sorry."

"Ya gonna stan' there yakkin' all day, boy?" a tall man asked. He looked like a skeleton with a black plastic bag pulled over his bones. He spoke with an accent I hadn't heard before.

"Hold your horses, Bones. She's one of Melika's newbies and she's new to the whole bayou thing."

Bones hobbled over to me as I shut the car door. Bending down, he peered into my eyes. "Ain't nothin' to fear out here unless you goes in the water."

"What's in the water?"

"Death." Bones said, shaking his head and grinning. He had maybe half his teeth. Maybe.

"Stop scaring her, Bones, you old bag. You know Melika doesn't like it when you panic them."

"Then don't tell her, boy." Bones straightened and sent a warning glare over to Jacob. "You too old to be a tattler, Jacob Marley."

Jacob Marley? Wasn't he a character in the Dickens story?

"I won't tell her, but stop scaring the girl. It's hard enough."

"Fine den. Come on, missy. Get in the boat." He pronounced it *boot*.

I looked over at "the boat." It looked like a cartoon boat

that had been shot at by Elmer Fudd. "You want *me* to get in *that*?"

"It's the only way," Jacob said.

"Get on in, missy," Bones said, tossing two oars to Jacob before grabbing a really long pole. "Gator getter," he said, grinning.

Tentatively, I stepped into the rickety raft, my eyes scanning the water for alligators.

"They ain't none near here," Bones said, chuckling under his breath.

"Then what's the stick for?"

"Um… just what he said. In case a 'gator gets curious, then he just pushes them away."

I scooted to the very center. They had no right calling this piece of Swiss cheese a boat. "With a Goddamned stick? Don't you have a machete or a shotgun or something?"

Bones was chuckling as he pushed away from the shore. "We don't kill somethin' that lets us live on its land. We're the trespassers here, missy. We leave 'em be. It all works out." It was then that I noticed the crappy boat actually had a motor. I wondered if it even worked.

"You gotta respect the bayou," Bones said softly. The only other sounds I could hear were insect noises and other wild sounds I knew nothing of. Our wildlife in Oakland were gang members howling at the moon during drive-bys.

I was a long way from home.

"Well, Jacob Marley, educate the girl."

Jacob sighed and nodded. "bayou comes from the French word meaning small stream and is used when talking about the delta of the Mississippi. It's not a swamp, though folks call it that."

I nodded. Swamp, delta, bayou, it was all the same to me.

"The water's got the creatures in it that'll kill you; 'gators and snakes mostly. Stay outta the water and you'll be fine."

"Um… don't *gators* and snakes come to land?"

"Sure, but not to get you. They come to land for other reasons, but if you go in the water, you're in *their* home and could end up as *their* dinner."

I looked down at the brackish water and cringed. It looked filthy. At least if an alligator was going to get you, you'd never see it coming. "What's the green stuff hanging from the trees?"

"Spanish moss. The Cajuns used to use it to stuff their mattresses with." Jacob looked at me and sighed. "Don't know what a Cajun is, either, I 'spose."

I looked away, suddenly feeling very small… or was it just that the world had suddenly got bigger?

"Cajuns were the French speakers who came here from Nova Scotia and preferred the bayou over the city. Cajun is also a type of cooking. You'll see that a lot here."

"Then what's Creole?" I'd seen plenty of signs in town about authentic Creole cooking.

"Creole means different things to different people. Creoles down here were born in the West Indies or came from French descent. You *do* know that Louisiana is French, right?"

I knew that something was French about it, but not exactly. "Yes, I know."

"Creole is a language, a way of cooking and a people. Melika is Creole. Her family is from Haiti." He looked hard at me and shook his head. "There are tons of definitions for both words. Whatever you do, don't confuse a Creole with a Cajun. That really pisses 'em off." Jacob nodded to Bones. "He's Creole. Call him a Cajun and he'll dump you in the water."

Nodding, I ducked my head as we passed under a long strand of Spanish moss. "What are you?"

Bones and Jacob both laughed. "Me? I'm from the Bronx."

"New York?"

Jacob nodded. "Finally, something you *do* know. I've been here since I was eight. Not sure I want to go back to a city."

I nodded, understanding exactly what he meant. "Can you tell me anything about Melika?"

Jacob shook his head. "She's not like anyone you'll ever meet, but that's all I'm gonna say about her. She hates being discussed. And trust me… she'll know."

Nodding once more, I put my hands in my lap just as I heard something *kerplunk* into the water. "What was that?"

"'Gator. Get used to the sound."

"Is it coming toward us?" I saw every nature horror movie flash through my head.

"Nope. Relax, missy. I ain't never lost one a Melika's students, 'specially wid Jacob Marley on board."

I looked over at Jacob, who grinned. "He's not kidding."

I spent the remainder of the time in awe of the human beings I saw living on the bayou. There were some shacks that made Bones' house look palatial. Each shack had a short wooden dock and a boat even more rickety than the last. As we floated on, the shacks became fewer and fewer and I realized there were no electrical lines.

"How do they get electricity out here?"

"Dey don't."

"No electricity. No plumbing. Nothing like you're used to," Jacob said.

Oh, now I *knew* I was out of my league… maybe even out of my planet. "Please tell me you're just messing with me."

"Look around you. You see any telephone poles out here? The bayou is as primitive and as wild as it gets. You don't come out here for luxury or even rest. Tourists get the nickel ride to see a few 'gators, but the livin' out here is hard." Jacob looked hard into my eyes. "You're here to learn, and you'll learn from the best. Trust me. You'll be really glad you came."

I sat in silence. I could handle alligators, poisonous snakes, mosquitoes, and crawdads better than I could the thought of turning into that drooling, rocking nightmare of a girl back at the psych ward. My greatest fear of being burned alive had been replaced by the fear of turning into *that*.

The remainder of the trip was spent in silence, with only the lapping water communicating to us. Bones never used the small engine or the oars, preferring the big pole like those guys in Italy. Occasionally, Jacob would row a bit, but not often.

I was missing Danica already. When she asked me when we would see each other again, I honestly didn't know. At fourteen, your friends are your life and I had left both behind. I couldn't think about her going on without me.

She swore we would be best friends forever, and I knew all fourteen-year-olds believed in those immature possibilities. But me? I *had* to believe it. She was all I had.

"We're here," Jacob announced.

Looking up, I saw a tiny woman standing on the end of a dock that looked newer than the other docks we had passed. "That's her?"

Jacob nodded. "She always comes to the boat to greet the newbies. She'll get a feel for you right away."

We approached the dock and the older woman waiting for us. She was wearing a black sundress with big black galoshes. In her right hand was a walking stick. Though I knew she was George's mama, she didn't look a day over forty, and I knew that he was twenty-five. Her hair had no grey in it and hung like a black sheet down to her shoulders in a single, thick braid. Even as the boat pulled alongside the dock, eyes like two big emeralds locked intently onto mine. Like Jacob, I felt nothing from her and realized that this was the first time in days that I hadn't had to deal with any emotional onslaughts.

"Afternoon, Madame," Bones said when the boat came to rest at her feet.

Melika smiled knowingly as she reached into the front pocket of her dress. She withdrew a little baggie and handed it to Bones. "Try this on it and make sure you heat it up nice and good, you hear?"

I looked at Jacob and started to ask a question, but Jacob shook his head at me.

"Now, Jacob, just 'cause we have a pretty one doesn't mean you can go and forget your manners." She turned her smile at me and warmth ran from the top of my head to all my extremities. Whether it was from me or her, I couldn't tell. "I'm Melika, dear. You must be Echo."

Jacob scurried off the boat and helped me to clamber out.

"Yes, I am. It's a pleasure to meet you."

Melika reached for my hand and held it tightly as she gazed deep into my eyes. It felt like we were standing there forever. "Oh my," she said softly.

"What?"

"It appears that George got to you not a moment too soon." Melika continued looking into my eyes, holding my hand, searching for something. I could barely feel it.

"You can barely feel it, my dear, because I am virtually unreadable to any but the strongest of us. Try as you may, you will *never* know what I am feeling, just as a telepath will *never* know what I am thinking." Melika released me and took my chin in her hand. She smelled of mint and oranges. "But you *do* have a great gift, to be sure."

"It feels more like a curse."

Smiling, she released my chin. "Every gift can become a curse and every curse, a gift. It is how we choose to use it that makes the difference."

And so, without taking another step, lessons began that would change the course of my life.

CHAPTER 15

I REALLY DIDN'T want to go back to the paper and face Carter, but I needed to see what, if any, information he had that I might have missed. It wasn't my idea of a great time, but I had no choice.

"I've got your pink slip all filled out for you," Carter said from his computer.

"Game's not over yet, turdball."

"Oh come on, Branson, give it up. The guy sunk to the bottom of the bay with stones in his pocket and rocks in his head. Goodbye cruel world. *Hasta la vista,* baby. Same to you, Branson. You're toast. There's no story, no lie, nothing. Nada. Nicht. Nil. The big goose egg. It's o-v-e-r and the fat lady is singing."

"But our deal was—"

"Our deal was that you had to prove she was lying. Can't do that now, can you?"

"What did the suicide note say?"

"My source says that old man Galloway was brokenhearted and couldn't go on living."

"That's it? That's the best your source can do?"

Carter turned away from his computer. I saw he was already writing the article, and moving on to bigger and better things. Yeah, you're only as good as your last story, and it appeared that Carter had just written his.

"So, that's it? Story over?"

"There *is* no story. What's the matter with you? You need to go back to Journalism 101. When a story is over, it's over. There are no leads, there are no great mysteries here; just one sad ending."

"Why would a successful businessman with the life that Galloway had, commit suicide? And why in the bay? And why out on the Berkeley Marina?" I would have asked and why with his dog, but I think I would have lost some credibility.

"The better question is… who cares? It's a suicide, plain and simple. I've done some fact checking, and his finances are in great shape, he—"

"There was a hundred grand withdrawn a few—"

Carter held up his hand. "A grand for a man like him is like a buck to slobs like us. Let it go, Branson. You lost. You'll be too busy looking for another job to worry about the Galloways of the world."

I stood there a minute wondering what it would be like for Danica to go on a six-hour date with him. It might be the end of a lovely friendship if I failed her, not to mention the loss of my Ladybug. "I have until Sunday and I'm going to take it."

"Come on, Branson, don't be pathetic."

"Run that story at your own peril, Ellsworth. Back-to-back retractions won't look good on your résumé; might even diminish some of your cock-of-the-walk attitude."

"You're joking. There won't be a retraction. It's a simple cut and dried story. Or is that sunk and died? Now, I've got to finish this story, so if you don't mind—"

"Who's your next target?"

"I've got bigger fish, Branson. Stop pestering me. You would be better off spending this time preparing your ultra-thin résumé. I hear they're hiring at Burger King."

Turning on my heel, I started for Wes Bentley's office.

"Is he in?"

"Yes, but he's leaving for lunch."

"See if he'll see me for one minute."

One minute later, I was walking with Wes to his car. "I'm just saying, wait to print that story or you'll be printing another retraction."

Wes stopped at his car and leaned on the fender. "You're telling me that my main guy is about to make *another* mistake going to press too early with the story? What are you? Psychic?"

I shrugged. "There's more to this story, Wes. I guarantee it."

"You're asking a tall order, Ms. Branson. For me to tell my number one that he's going to have to wait because some rookie thinks there's more to this story… well… that's just not good business."

"And two retractions on major stories is?"

I could see him thinking about it. "How sure are you?"

Inhaling deeply, I licked my lips and took the plunge. "Ninety five percent sure there's more to this story, but I'm only 50-50 that I can get proof to back my supposition right now."

"Fifty-fifty is not good odds, Ms. Branson."

"No, it isn't, but I'm ninety-nine percent sure if you print Carter's story you're going to eat it."

Wes stared out over the city from his parking spot at the top of the garage. I felt him weighing whose wrath he would rather incur: Carter's or his own. "I've been a successful businessman by listening to my gut, and though my brain is screaming inside my skull right now, I'm going to go with you on this. Something tells me you might just know what you're talking about. If you don't, you better plan on moving to the East Coast when Carter gets through with you."

"Thank you, sir. You won't regret it."

"Make sure that I don't, Ms. Branson, or you will be cleaning out your desk."

I watched Wes drive away, feeling a huge clock ticking in my head. I unlocked my cell and called Danica. "Did you set it up?"

"Absolutely. You know, Clark, I don't have your superpowers, but I swear to God that lady was chomping at the bit to talk to another reporter."

"Where did you say you were from?"

"The LA Times."

"Why so far away?"

"They have a Danica who works there. I figured if she called to check…"

"Damn, those boys are good."

"Yeah, I ought to pay them more. Anyway, we're covered for two o'clock. Are you sure you want to go through with this? People like Mrs. Galloway sue people like us for pretending to be someone we're not."

"Then let's make sure she never finds out. I'll see you at two." After hanging up, I called Sergeant Finn's cell phone. "Hi. It's Echo."

"Hey. What's up?"

"Quick question. When the investigators boarded the boat, was there a dog on board?"

"A dog?"

"Yeah. Have your guys check at the dock to see if they can confirm that Mr. Galloway brought his dog on aboard."

"His dog? Are you sure? I can hear the guys now, laughing in my face."

"Stay with me here. Just do me the favor."

"What do I get in return?"

"What do you want?"

"To take you to lunch some day soon."

Heart be still! "You drive a hard bargain."

He chuckled. "Am I that boring?"

"Not even remotely."

"Great, I'm on it. Just sit tight."

I didn't have to wait long. Finn called me right back.

"No dog on board. No sign of a dog."

"Really? Are you sure? Did you tell them to check with the rental guy? Doesn't forensics vacuum and…"

"That's CSI bullsh– crap, Echo. Suicides are low on our priority."

"Look, Glen Galloway had his dog with him when he rented the boat. Are you telling me he committed suicide with *his dog*? What did he do? Strap his little dog body to him? Or do you think he weighed the dog down with rocks as well? Who commits suicide with their dog? A dog *Mrs.* Galloway is pretending doesn't exist."

"Are you sure about this dog thing?"

"Yes. I spoke to the harbor guy myself. He remembers Galloway having a Jack Russell terrier with him. The same dog whose photo is sitting on Galloway's desk."

"Okay, okay. I'll check it out, but if there's nothing, will you promise to let this go?"

"No."

Finn laughed. "Did I mention that I find women who don't know when to give up semi attractive?"

"Only semi?"

"I have my standards."

"I appreciate that."

"Well, I want you to keep your new job for my own personal reasons."

"Don't go getting all sweet on me, Sergeant Finn. I'm not crazy about cops, remember?"

"That's okay. I don't like reporters, remember?"

"Lunch is on you then, when you find out about the dog."

"Okay, but where are you going with this dog piece anyway?"

"Think about it. And think about the yummy lunch you're going to owe me."

"Not a bad debt."

I hung up, smiling. He was a really good guy who was about to discover that he would soon owe me more than lunch.

WHEN I GOT to Mrs. Galloway's neighborhood, I parked far

away and walked. Ladybug was just too obvious. I'd been regretting putting her up for the bet. The bane of my existence was my impulsive nature. It had never done anything but get me in trouble.

Now as I walked toward Mrs. Galloway's, I prayed that something would crack this story open for me. I needed a real break or I was going to be without a job, without wheels, and with a very pissed off best friend who was, at this moment, committing fraud by acting as a reporter.

You had to love her.

Standing just outside the house, I closed my eyes and centered my energy. All I needed was just one quick read, just one piece of Mrs. Galloway's energy that would enable me to see if anything had changed within her. She'd already been told about her husband's suicide; if she believed it, I would feel it.

Melika had taught me that life is all about the choices we make; how important it is to be sure, to go slow and steady before committing to a plan of action. I wasn't a hundred percent positive about this particular plan, but it was all I had. If Mrs. Galloway's emotional energy had changed and displayed a true sense of loss, I would drive Ladybug to the office, sign my pink slip, and start over. I would concede.

Opening my eyes, I stood on the curb and stared through the window at Mrs. Galloway as she spoke with Danica. Danica moved closer to the window to examine the photos, and Mrs. Galloway followed, gesturing to the frame Danica held onto. It didn't even take my best or strongest powers to feel that she had not suffered a deep loss. None. Even if she had hated her husband, I would have felt *something.* Loss and grief are two of the strongest human emotions. Even if what you lost wasn't that important or that special to you, you still felt it and it still changed your energy field. As Danica interviewed her, there was nothing in that woman except secrecy and deceit. Though I saw her pull a tissue out, it was all for Danica's benefit because I detected not one hint of sadness.

So… Glen Galloway wasn't dead. Every time she answered one of Danica's questions, there was a slight flicker to her aura that belied her true answers. The grieving widow was not her best angle, but I'm sure she'd pulled that role off to everyone else who knew her. She'd probably fooled everyone but me.

And so what?

Again, I had proof of nothing.

I left the window and waited back at my car.

"What did you think of her?" I asked Danica when we got back to her car.

"She must have used a dozen tissues."

"Overkill?"

"Oh, hell yeah. She was going for an Oscar, to be sure. It was weird. She kept trying to get a peek at what I was writing down."

"What *were* you writing down?"

"I was making a list of all the antiques in the room."

I smiled. "She didn't see it?"

"Hey, what do you take me for? An amateur? I can commit fraud with the best of them." Danica sighed. "Now what? You have less than forty-eight hours to prove what only you know. I may have my suspicions about her, but I didn't come out of there with anything concrete. Sorry,

Clark."

I sighed along with her. "She didn't say *anything* about why he might have committed suicide, or the dog?"

"Just that he seemed depressed but didn't know why." Danica crossed her arms and looked at me. I knew what she was about to say, but I couldn't stop her in time. "Know what you need?"

"Don't say it."

"You need Tomas."

"I said don't say it."

"Clark, he's the best telepath you know. If he—"

"No. You know how I feel about him and the way he uses his powers. No way. I am *not* that desperate."

"Umm… yes you are… and so am I. Six hours? I'd rather eat yellow snow."

"Hush."

"You are always so stubborn where he's concerned. He'd be here in a heartbeat."

"I don't care. No way. End of story. I do not want or need him back in my life."

"He could help."

"No thanks."

"Stubborn jackass."

I shook my head. "He's never done anything but turn my life upside down. I would rather sentence you to a torrid six-hour orgy with Carter and a gorilla than to let Tomas interfere. Not now. Not when I'm just getting started."

Danica shook her head. "Ewww. That's gross."

"And eating yellow snow isn't?"

"If I have to go out with Carter, you are going to owe me until the day you die."

"I know."

Sighing, Danica patted my shoulder. "Then get out there and get your proof. And if there's anything the boys can get you, don't hesitate to pick up that phone."

I picked up the phone all right. I called Rupert James, a local Necromancer who owned one of the nicest yachts in the Berkeley Marina. Rupert and I had met during my junior year in college, when there had been a haunting of a local boy. Melika had sent us to put a lid on the situation and see if the boy was also a necromancer. Turned out, he was being haunted by a kid he'd killed during a gang fight in Oakland. That's what a necromancer does… they talk to the dead.

And I thought *I* was cursed.

I'd enjoyed working with Rupert and he said I could call him any time for a nice sail out on the bay. I needed a nice sail right about now, but unfortunately, I got a voicemail that said he was in Catalina and would be returning in a few days. I didn't have a few days. Hell, I barely had a few minutes.

I started off toward my car, trying to push Tomas from my mind. He was the last thing I needed in right now. Tomas had never been anything more than a good-looking complication in my life. Like most telepaths, he felt superior to the rest of us. He always had. It pissed me off back then, and it pissed me off now.

Me, need Tomas?

Never.

CHAPTER 16

I MET TOMAS Redhawk my first day in the bayou. He was sitting on the steps to Melika's porch. Unlike so many of the other shacks lining the bayou that were made out of thin pieces of wood and sheet metal, this cottage was made out of stone. A small wisp of white smoke curled from the chimney, and I wondered if there was a trail of breadcrumbs somewhere. A deck wrapped around the front of the house and had a wooden swing hanging at one end and a set of wooden Adirondack chairs at the other. Quaint.

That was when I noticed Tomas sitting on the stairs with his arm draped around a bloodhound. I was immediately struck by his looks. Unlike the folks I'd met or seen so far, Tomas' complexion was Native American. His hair was black tar that hung well past his shoulders. His light hazel eyes looked at me with such intensity, I had to look away. He was at least twenty… maybe older. It was hard to tell.

"Stop it, Tomas," Melika admonished. "Please bring her things to the blue room, Jacob. Tomas, please take Zeus for a walk, will you? I don't need you underfoot right now."

Tomas rose and seemed to keep rising for several seconds. He was enormous; legs like the trunks of some of the trees we had passed, a chest that stretched his shirt to tearing point, and arms that said he did a lot of heavy lifting, all made him quite an imposing figure. "I thought—"

"I know what you thought, Tomas, but not now. Can't you see she's a fish out of water? Scoot. Come back when you can be useful."

"Yes, ma'am." Tomas and the wrinkly dog strode away, leaving tree branches and leaves bending in their wake.

"Don't pay him any mind for right now. You'll be working with him later, but this trip has made you weary. Jacob will take you to your room. Take a little nap before dinner and get your energy back up. What we have to do needs to begin immediately. My son explained what happened to you in the hospital, but I'll need to hear every detail of your life from the first moment you felt that that boy was going to harm you. So, rest, my girl. We have a lot of work to do."

Nodding, I took two steps and then just started bawling. I'm not talking crying and sniffling; I mean an all-out meltdown. I sobbed uncontrollably until Melika put her arms around me and pulled me closer. She was right about me being exhausted. The horror of the hospital, the fear of the escape, the awful goodbye to the only person who loved me, not knowing when I would see her again. Add to that feeling all the emotions of every person on the plane and entering a land as foreign as Ethiopia, and I was ready to collapse.

Okay… so I *was* collapsing.

By the time I got to the blue room, I was more than ready for a nap. And I did. For nearly twenty-one hours.

When I awoke the next day, it was slightly after two in the afternoon.

"Welcome back," came Jacob's voice from a rocking chair in the corner of the small room.

"What time is it?"

"Two fifteen."

I frowned, trying to remember how the times changed from one time zone to the next.

"Of the next day," Jacob said, smiling. "You've been asleep almost twenty-four hours."

"What?" Sitting up, I looked out the window at the bright sunlight. "It's tomorrow?"

"That's one way of looking at it. Melika has lunch on the table."

Inhaling deeply, I rose and stretched. I hadn't slept that well in ages, but nearly twenty-four hours? Sheesh. "I didn't know I was so tired."

"Everyone does it when they first get here. For some, it's the first good sleep they've had in a long time."

"Is that how she knew I needed a nap?"

"Melika knows everything about us."

"Us?" I looked at him curiously.

"That's all I can say right now. Melika will start your lessons after lunch. Be smart and listen carefully to everything she says. When I say she knows everything, I'm not kidding. She can give you your life back. No one else can."

I followed Jacob down the stairs, smelling this incredible aroma with every step. At the bottom, sitting at a small picnic table, were Melika and Tomas. A huge pot of something had steam rising off the top. It smelled so good; I couldn't stop salivating.

"I trust you slept well," Melika said, dipping her ladle into the reddish stew, as Tomas cut a piece of corn bread out of the pan and set it on the table. My stomach made its embarrassing announcement that it was hungry. "Have a seat and eat up. There's plenty."

"I'm sorry I slept so long. It's sort of rude."

"Always listen to your body, my girl. Let that be your first lesson. Your body will always tell you what you need, where you need to go, what to do, if only you'll let it. Primitive man relied more heavily on his body than his mind. He ate when he was hungry, not because someone or some social rules told him it was time for dinner."

I sat at the picnic table across from scary Tomas, who never took his eyes from me. He was sort of creeping me out.

"I'm Tomas," he said, extending a hand. "We haven't formally met."

I reached across the table and shook his hand. "Echo."

"Interesting name."

I shrugged, retrieving my hand. "It fits."

Tomas motioned with his chin over to Jacob. "As fitting as Jacob Marley?"

I started to ask what he meant, but my stomach continued to make itself known. My plate was loaded down with yummy red stew and a chunk of corn bread. There was a crab-like thing in the stew that I had never eaten before.

"Crawdads," Tomas said.

"We eat crawdads the way your people eat chicken.

Tomas, show her how."

He picked up one of the crawdads, popped his thumb under the head and then pulled it off and sucked it before removing the meat from the shell. "Sucking his brains out is a Cajun thing, but don't do it if you don't feel up to it."

As I would later discover, there are a lot of Cajun ways and Creole ways and Southern ways and Louisianan ways of doing things. I had never seen so many customs in my life. But no matter whose way was right, they all had one thing in common: an appreciation for fine food. I never ate so well in my entire life before or since.

I dug in with a gusto that almost scared me.

"Always keep your body well-nourished, which is very different from well-fed. Eating well does not mean eating a lot. Treat your body like you would an expensive automobile; give it only the best." Melika sipped her coffee and smiled at me.

"And so it begins," Tomas said under his breath.

Melika swatted his arm. "Hush, you. Unless you want to spend your days with Zeus."

"No, I'm good." Tomas held his hands in surrender.

"So, my girl, tell me what happened that day and don't leave a single detail out."

Tomas turned to me. "You'll find that Mel is quite detailed-oriented, so the sooner you get used to sharing the details, the better."

Nodding, I finished my meal and started my story. I wouldn't get three sentences out before Melika would stop with a question or five. Tomas wasn't kidding when he said she liked details. She didn't just like them... they were demanded.

When I finally finished telling her every single thing that had transpired since I whacked Todd in the head, it was nearly five o'clock; three hours in the telling.

"Very good. Now, I have a clearer picture of how you came to be. What we *don't* know is how you came to be *what you are*." Melika motioned to Jacob, who rose and started clearing the table. "Come."

I followed her outside to the porch. We sat in the Adirondacks while Tomas took the steps with Zeus.

"What do you mean how I became what I am?"

"Most of us are born one way or the other, Echo. Very few of us come to it in the middle of our lives. It is difficult when that happens because we are incapable of understanding what is happening to us until, more often than not, it's too late."

I looked over at Tomas, who was petting Zeus. "Him?"

"Born."

"Jacob?"

"Born."

"You?"

She grinned. "Born. Like I said, very few are like you. As you learn and grow here, perhaps we'll discover what it is that brought it out in you."

"George said I'm an empath. Is that true?"

"That remains to be seen. At first glance, you appear to be clairempathic; you feel the emotional energies of others. You can read their auras until it becomes a part of you. You can experience their emotions, and sometimes be overrun by them."

I nodded. "But... I must have lost it or something because I can't feel anything from any of you. Jacob mentioned something about blocking, but I don't…"

"Blocking means we have erected a psychic shield that prevents our energies from leaking to you, and you can't read us because we won't let you. That's what blocking does; it protects all of us from each other."

"Really? You can actually do that?"

"So can you. At least, you will when I'm done with you."

"So… you're all empaths, too?"

Tomas threw his head back and laughed. It was a sound I would hear repeatedly for the next four years of my life.

CHAPTER 17

L UIGI NABBED ME as I made my way up the stairs. "I got two bags o' day-olds, Echo."

"Two bags? What happened?"

"Some bastar' order two dozen pumpkin spice and then never pick up."

"Sure. I'll drop these off with Bob. You need any help around here?"

"I'm good. You go now while they're still warm."

When I got to the Mission, Bob was nowhere to be seen, so I started asking around. No one had seen him. Now, I'm not one to sound the alarm prematurely, but Bob could *always* be found.

Ditching my day-olds, I headed deeper into the Tenderloin. Everyone I stopped to ask about Bob were either too drunk, too strung out, or too oblivious to even know who Bob was. I had been on the streets for over an hour before someone finally remembered seeing him.

"Bob? Saw him early last night. He was talking to some guy in a van."

"A van? What color van?"

"White? Light blue? How the hell should I know? I was drunk as a skunk, it was dark, and we mind our own business out here. You a cop or somethin'?"

"Could it have been yellow?"

"Coulda. Like I said… it was dark."

"Okay… do you happen to remember where you were?"

"I dunno. I was pretty messed up."

"Then how sure are you that it was Bob at all?"

He seemed to think it over. "Fifty-fifty, maybe?" He scratched his nine o'clock shadowed chin. "Wait. Yeah. I remember… he was wearing them really cool hiking boots some do-gooder gave him. Columbus or something. Bob really loved them boots. Always yammering about them and the friend who gave them to him."

I sighed. *I* was that do-gooder and he did love those boots. "Your name is…"

"Leroy. Leroy Brown. You probably heard of me. I'm the baddest guy in the whole damn town."

I wrote his *nom de plume* down, lowered my shield, and knew, of course, that he was lying. It's not uncommon for street folk to make up names, or, as was more common, have them foisted upon them by someone else. I imagined that, at some point in time, Leroy here probably *was* a bad ass.

"Thank you, Leroy. Look, if anything comes up, here's my card. Call me any time day or night."

Leroy nodded, took my card, and started away. Then he stopped and turned back around. "You really want to know something, you oughtta ask Shirley. She knows everybody and everything that goes on down here."

"Where can I find her?"

"This time a day, she's napping in the park. Can't miss her. She got a white dog, a black cat, and a green bird. Be careful a them animals. If that dog growls at you, she won't talk to you. You gotta pass muster with them animals before she'll give you the time of day. So, if the dog barks, just keep goin'."

I thanked him and started for the park. Was Bob now among the missing? I pushed the thought out of my mind.

When I arrived at the park, I found Shirley and her menagerie sleeping on a bench. The white dog, which looked like a Dalmatian with one black spot right between his eyes, was curled up under the bench. The black cat was asleep on what appeared to be a pile of rags. Perched on the back of the bench was the green bird, a parrot of some sort. The parrot had a yellow head and eyes that were studying me. I can read many animals, but not birds.

I stood there remembering Leroy's cautionary words of advice, so I lowered my shield to allow the dog to sense my friendly emotions. Animals are incredibly empathic, which is why they're now employed as more than guide dogs. Some breeds of dog can sense seizures before they happen, and there were plenty of accounts of animals behaving weird prior to major seismological events, tornadoes, and other natural phenomena.

Kneeling, I stayed a good twenty-five feet away from the dog and waited. He slowly opened one eye, looked at me, and then opened the other. I smiled, feeling his friendly disposition wash over me. He liked me. What's not to like? I have a three-legged cat.

As if on cue, the cat raised its head and looked at me. She knew right away that I was friendly, and returned her head to her paws.

The dog, however, rose and ambled toward me. His nose was pink and his eyes were blue, and there wasn't an ounce of fat on his sleek frame. I put my hand out for him to sniff, which he did.

"Cotton doesn't usually warm up to strangers that quickly."

Looking up, I saw Shirley staring at me from her position on the bench. She was the pile of rags.

"He's gorgeous," I said, petting him under the chin.

"Don't say that too loud. You'll give him a big head."

I rose. "I'm Echo," I said.

Shirley slowly sat up. She looked a hundred and five years old; like one of those apple dolls with a thousand folds and wrinkles. She had a green kerchief in her hair, which was completely white and heavy like straw. Like most homeless along the Tenderloin, she was wearing different outfits. She had on a green dress, a purple skirt, red stockings with holes that showed blue leggings underneath, several white socks, a multi-colored macramé vest, and a pair of brown shoes. When she sat up, the cat rose and stretched before walking over to me and checking me out.

"And who are you?" I asked, scritching the cat.

"Her name is Midnight and she's a real bitch." Shirley stretched and yawned. She was only missing a few teeth. "Of course I say that lovingly. Cotton wouldn't know left from right without her. He's so foolish about that damn cat as to be stupid."

"She the boss of the bunch?"

"Ho, yes ma'am. Emerald here steers clear of her, but that dog…" Shirley shook her head and the bird hopped on her shoulder. "I'm Shirley, but you knew that already, didn't you?"

I moved closer.

"Come. Sit. It isn't every day we're visited by someone my animals like. Especially that one." Shirley tilted her head in the direction of Midnight.

As I sat on the bench, Midnight jumped up and immediately sat on my lap. Tripod would need a double dose of catnip once he got a whiff of Midnight. "I have a Siamese."

"I know. You came with a question, so I'll spare you the small talk. They call me the Teller. Short, of course, for Fortune Teller. But you didn't come here to get your fortune read. What can I do for you?"

I wasn't prepared for this. Turning to face her, I realized she had one blue eye and one green eye. I nearly fell over. One of two things was happening here; either she was one of my kind, or she possessed some other psychic ability because my shield was *always* up. Just to make sure, I put a wall around my mental energies as well. I was an empath, after all. My powers did not extend to telepathy, but Tomas and Melika insisted I learn how to protect myself from them. I was not a quick study but I did eventually learn, after long, tedious, and grueling hours of frustration, yelling, and even throwing things, how to perform the most rudimentary mental block.

Shirley grinned. "My. I don't see that move very often. Of course, it's not often I'm coherent enough to notice. Whoever sent you… did they tell you I'm a loon? A nut job? I fade in and out of sanity like the San Francisco fog. Mostly in. In. Sanity. You're getting me on a good upswing, but that could change at a moment's notice. I'm not kidding you, either. So, out with it."

I have to admit, I was a little unnerved. "I'm looking for my friend, Bob. He's a street person, too, and I think he's missing. I was told you knew everything that goes on down here."

"Hoo-haa." She blurted out, making the bird's wings flutter a bit. "That's a good one. A missing homeless person... honey, you must have too much time on your hands."

"Haven't you heard that three homeless guys have gone missing? Four, if you include Bob."

Shirley stroked Cotton's head. "Of course I've heard. We've all heard. Sad thing is, there's nothing anyone can do about it. Nobody cares about us nobodies. How can you claim someone is missing when no one goes by real names? Can you miss someone if no one knows who they are?"

"*I* know who Bob is, and I know he might be missing. I tried to get the cops involved, but..."

"Hoo-ha! That's rich. Honey, are you for real? We're the invisibles out here. If Bob is missing, you're probably the only person who gives a rat's ass. You can't make people give a shit about the invisibles."

"I'm not like other people."

Shirley chuckled. "Oh, honey, we *both* know you're not that, though just what *is* special about you, I can't quite tell."

"Do you know the others?"

She sighed loudly. "One of them was Rusty, eh?"

I nodded.

"I had hoped that maybe he had just wandered off. That

happens, you know. Guys get tired of being here, tired of the harsh life, and they just wander off and never return, like a cat that leaves to go off and die."

"And they're never found?"

"Invisibles are never found. We may show up in a body bag in the morgue, but without anyone to give a damn, we're buried without incident. The rest who keep living are busy struggling to survive. We don't have time to worry about those who failed." Shirley sighed as she patted Cotton's head.

"*Something* is happening out here and something has happened to my friend Bob. I'm going to find out what it is, because believe it or not, I *do* care." I rose and pulled a business card from my wallet and handed it to her. "You're not invisible to me, and I'm not going to stop until I find Bob." I looked hard into her eyes. "I was invisible once, Shirley. I know *exactly* how it feels, and I'm not just going to walk away from this without some answers. You can call me day or night if you find anything out or hear anything."

Shirley studied my card, turning it over in her hand. A slow smile spread across her face and I wondered if this was one of her out of sanity moments. "Ah... well... that certainly clears things up."

"What does?"

Shirley tucked my card in her sock. "I'll check around and see what I can find out. The missing guys are Rusty, Don, Jack and Bob?"

"I appreciate your time, Shirley, and your pets are very sweet."

She nodded. "Keeps me from being lonely."

"Good. Thanks for your help."

"Lord knows why you care so much, Echo, but I appreciate that you do. Be careful."

"Be careful?"

Shirley nodded. "There's evil afoot out here. That's all I know."

As I got back into Ladybug, a cold shiver ran down my arms and legs. Quickly looking around, I didn't see or feel anyone. Maybe the chills were just a response to what she had said as I left.

Evil afoot?

Just what was I getting into?

CHAPTER 18

MY FIRST WEEK with Melika was eye-opening, to say the least. It wasn't just the bizarre food or location in the swamp that was strange, but the lessons I learned from others like me. I had had no idea how close I came to losing my sanity... of coming to the edge of reason and falling off.

I was an empath. Unlike those born with the gift, I had come into mine in a moment of crisis; not uncommon for supernaturals, or supers, as Tomas referred to us. Because it came upon me so quickly and without notice, it had the potential of quickly consuming me and driving me mad. I owed my sanity as well as my life to George... I would end up owing my future to Melika.

"The first lesson is going to be the hardest one, yet the most important," Melika said my second day there. We'd loaded up a small boat with picnic items as she and I headed out to the bayou.

The bayou, like I said, was another world unto itself. Out here, there was no hustle or bustle of crowds or people too full of their own self-importance. Out here, there was just you and nature. You either learned to become part of the natural world or leave it behind on your way back. For me, there *was* no *back*, there *was* no home. There was only this moment, and I was, at this moment, staring at an enormous alligator basking in the sun on the banks of the bayou. I couldn't help but hear Linda Ronstadt, though there wasn't anything blue about it, really.

"You got all tensed up when you saw the 'gator. Do you know why?" Melika adjusted her large straw hat. Her black dress was similar to the one she was wearing when I arrived, and the rubber galoshes seemed to be her shoe of choice. Today, she had a shawl wrapped around her shoulders even though it was already over eighty degrees out.

"Because he could eat us."

Melika barely glanced at the beast. "Could. The question is, does it *want* to?"

I stared at the prehistoric creature as the boat glided silently by. Neither of us were rowing, but just floating down the river. I was pleased to see that this boat also had an outboard motor at the rear. No one seemed to use them on the bayou.

"Well… I guess it could, but…"

"Don't guess. Guessing is for naturals. *We're* not naturals, Echo. We're *super*naturals. We can do things they cannot. A natural would make all sorts of assumptions about that 'gator. I don't want you to assume. I want you to read it."

"Read it? You mean—"

"Look at it. Everything has a vibration, an energy, a frequency that others can tune into. Not everyone has the ability to tune into others, and not all empaths can read animals or the natural environment. I want to see if you can."

Nodding, I tried to put my fear of the ugly beast aside long enough to really focus in on it. Sure enough, I was immediately hit with a wave of bored energy from the alligator. He was more interested in napping than he was in eating us. "Oh my God! I did it!"

Melika smiled softly. "Very good. So much of what we're going to be doing for the next couple of weeks is just to determine the strength of your power. You must be patient during this process because we cannot proceed with the education until we know what you can do—"

"Wait a second. What do you mean? Are you saying there could actually be *more*?"

"Oh yes, my dear. Our gifts are as varied as our faces. Many empaths have additional sight as well as telepathy, clairvoyance—"

"Clair what?"

Melika continued to smile. "The ability to see past, present and future moments."

"You've got to be kidding me. People can really do that?"

Melika tilted her head and when the sunlight caught her face, she looked years younger. "There are all sorts of gifts, Echo; gifts that primitive man once used in order to survive. All of you who have come to me have always been dubious about the other gifts, even though you possess your own." Melika took her hat off and sighed. "Let me ask you this: do you think the idea of flight was impossible to the people of the Middle Ages? Or that fuel-powered cars seemed like just a silly dream? Do you think men and women of the Wild

West ever believed we could walk on the moon? They didn't even know about things like bacteria or germs.

"And what about the idea re-attaching cut off limbs, or transplanting organs? Don't you think there was a time when the majority of people thought these were merely fantastical ideas?"

I nodded.

"And what about computers? Television? Radio? The internet? Those used to be beyond the scope of man's ability, yet here they are. We can drive, fly, do microscopic surgery and even clone creatures now, but these things were once considered impossibilities."

I nodded, watching another 'gator slip into the water. "But they *weren't* impossible."

"Indeed, because they all happened. Now, we have pills that can keep us from getting pregnant, we can travel at the speed of sound, and even some forms of blindness can be cured. But isn't it funny that with all mankind can accept and do, we still do not believe in the power of the human mind that created all of this?" Melika put her hat back as I used the pole against a nearby bank.

"Just because society does not believe a thing exists does not mean that it doesn't. Everyone thought the Wright brothers were bonkers. We know now that they were not. They merely had a vision beyond the scope of their peers. This has been true of every great man and woman ever born. Do you know that DaVinci created the design for the first parachute hundreds of years before flight?"

"No way."

"It's true. Echo, people believed in the possibilities of witchcraft, of alchemy, of Merlin's power and the mental capabilities of the pagans. But science came along, Christianity grew powerful and soon, what couldn't be explained or proven became an impossibility. Those of us with supernatural powers were forced underground by the fear of being hunted and destroyed. People like you and me lived in fear of being found out."

"Are you telling me that… that witches are real?"

"And why wouldn't they be? Everything that *appears* impossible in our time has every chance of becoming possible one day. *We* are one such impossibility, Echo. Just because the people before your time say a thing can't be done doesn't mean it's true. It just means *it appears to be true in that moment in time*."

"I get it."

"Then, don't you find it interesting how many insane people who are locked up say they hear voices? In our time, the belief is that only unstable people hear voices. According to modern man and science, these voices must come from within that person. Because it is impossible *for science* to prove that we can do what we do, we've labeled those who actually can hear voices *insane*."

"But it *is* possible. We're proof of that."

"Oh, dear girl, only a small number of us know how very possible it is. It's funny; science tells us that animals communicate in any number of ways we can't. But we can only talk? Why, if we're so damn smart, can't we communicate much in the same way dolphins can?"

"Because we can?"

Melika nodded. "Exactly. And we have always been able to. You see, once we started using language, we actually evolved away from telepathic communication like the rest of the animal kingdom. But not all of us. Just as there are still some white Bengal tigers left in the world, there are those of us who can do what the rest cannot."

"We're the supernaturals."

Melika grinned. "Yes, we are. We, my dear, we *are* the living, breathing impossibilities of our time. In *our* time, that which can't be proven scientifically or held up by faith doesn't exist." She patted my leg. "If it was ever *proven* that we truly existed, we would still all be forced back into hiding. Do you know why?"

I shook my head.

"Because we would be reduced to being lab rats. Scientists would *use* us to see how to duplicate or replicate our gifts."

I was beginning to get it. "Because the government would want to exploit us."

Melika grinned slightly. "Absolutely. Think what it would do for a president to be able to have an aid who could read the minds of everyone in the room."

My stomach lurched at the thought. "Oh my God…" Bringing my hand up to my mouth, I shook my head slowly. "We would never be free."

"Never. If governments could tap into what we have, they would do it regardless of what it would mean to us or our freedom. Think about it. Unscrupulous people would want us to tell lottery numbers, to manipulate people in power, to become spies, to do all sorts of things that we might not want to do. We would be poked and prodded like—"

"Aliens?"

"Precisely. Our powers are as alien to the world as an

extraterrestrial being, and that puts us in danger. So, we must be careful in the real world not to bring too much attention to ourselves. Of course, there are those of us who are flashy and out there, but that's because they rely on the public not to believe that what they are seeing is *actually* happening."

"Oh wow. That's scary."

"Actually, what's scary is what happens to those of us who we can't get to in time."

I thought about the girl back in the psych ward. "I've seen it."

"You, my dear, are an incredibly powerful empath, and when we are done, it will be up to you to locate those who haven't yet lost their battle with insanity. You will, like my son, become a spotter in order to save those who need help. When you do, you will bring them here, to me, for the same help and guidance you're getting. That is the only deal on the table for you. In exchange for the semblance of a normal life, you must agree to help others like you."

"How will I find them?"

"You'll know. Some will be beyond help. Others won't want it. But for those who do, you must reach out to them in the same way George did for you."

I nodded and said nothing.

"You will, at times, see those who choose to make money from their gifts. Case in hand are two of those men on television who speak to the dead."

"No way. You mean—"

"What I mean, dear girl, is that we are everywhere. Those of us who don't go insane live relatively normal lives. But even in the living of those lives, we need to be able to help each other because no one else can or will."

Leaning back, I heaved a huge sigh. It was so much to take in.

"Yes, it is, which is why we are just chatting. Before we can even start helping you understand and utilize your powers, you must first understand the nature of the supernatural community to which you now belong."

"Supernatural is such a… weird word."

"I prefer super over paranormal. I try to excise the word normal out of my vocabulary. There is *nothing* normal about us. When we wake up every morning, we must create shields, deal with excessive energies, protect ourselves against psychic vampires, and try not to let our powers ruin our lives."

"Psychic vampires?"

"A crisis turned your powers on, so-to-speak. They were always there, lying dormant, waiting for the right chemicals to flip the switch. Your switch was flipped, my dear, and that's why you felt what that boy wanted from you."

I thought about poor Todd's head. "But I think I would have killed him."

"No, you wouldn't have. You would have felt his life ebbing away and come to your senses. You're no killer, Echo. You must believe that."

"Melika, you've just told me that witches exist, that people can talk to the dead, and that alligators can send vibes people can read. I'm pretty sure I can believe that."

She smiled. "You're going to be asked to believe a heck of a lot more than that in the weeks and months to come."

I bowed my head and tried to keep the tears from coming. Melika reached over and touched my knee. "You're not alone and you're no freak. You have a gift. But like all good things, there's a downside to it if you don't know how to handle it. My job is to give you the tools to master it all."

"But how did I *get* it?"

"Clairempaths come by their powers genetically. Somewhere in your family history there are others with similar powers."

"I wouldn't know. I'm an orphan. My birth name is—"

"Jane Doe. Yes, I know. I know a great deal more about you than you realize." She smiled. "I have a few powers of my own."

WE STAYED ON the water talking about life, about other supers she had taught and how each of them managed to find their own way. I told her about Danica and how much I missed her. To my surprise, Melika promised that I could talk to her tomorrow, when I got to go to town. This perked me up immediately. It was one thing to escape from the psych ward, but I felt so cut-off from the rest of the world out here on the bayou.

Of course, the best part was how calm I had become. Melika had called it stabilizing. She said it was important for me to clear out the energies from the psych ward and settle down from all the anxiety and fear I had been experiencing. I have to say that sleep really helped. I felt rested for the first time in forever.

When the bugs started eating us, Melika showed me how to start the motor so we could head back up the bayou more easily. Now, if you've never been in the Louisiana Bayou, the best way I can describe it is a water labyrinth. There are main thoroughfares, side streets, inlets, and assorted waterways, none of which were marked with any sort of sign. There was absolutely nothing to let you know where you were and it all looked the same. All of it.

But I quickly realized that, to the casual observer, it only appeared that way. As Melika started pointing out various trees and other landmarks, I started to see the bayou with different eyes. There were too many greens to name, various trees of all sizes, and scenery that was more stunning than any I had ever seen. I was beginning to understand why some people never left here.

When we finally returned to the cute little cottage, Jacob was waiting on the dock. "What is it, Jacob?"

"Another incoming, ma'am," Jacob said, holding up a cell phone. "TK."

Melika nodded solemnly. "I've been expecting him. Where is he?"

"Atlanta."

She nodded. "Tomas packed and ready?"

"Yes, ma'am."

"Thank you, Jacob." Melika took his hand as he helped her from the boat. When she got out, she turned to help me. "Tomorrow, we will discuss how to protect yourself, how to reserve your energy, how to make your powers work with your life. You need not ever be afraid here. You are safe. You aren't going crazy. I know that you have never had a real family, but I'd like you to consider all of us here your family."

I swallowed hard and nodded. "I'd like that. I'd like that a lot."

And with that, for the first time in my life, I had a family.

No wonder I had slept so well.

CHAPTER 19

M Y CELL PHONE had a message on it from Walt Finn, so I called him the moment I got to Ladybug.

"Echo! Thanks for calling back so quickly. I don't know how much longer we can go without pulling you in. You seem to know things no one else does."

"Why? Has something happened?"

"You were right about the dog. Detective Jardine is interviewing Mrs. Galloway in a couple of hours."

"Looking for what?"

"The whole dog thing bothers him. I'm calling you because if this goes south, I'm going to have to pull you in. I don't want to put you in an awkward position, but I think you've got some leads Jardine could use."

"What have I got to lose at this point? My time is running out and I'm fresh out of ideas. If I have to become part of the investigation, fine."

"Good. I just… well… I value our newly formed alliance and… I don't want you to feel used or anything like that."

"Put your mind at ease, Finn. I trust you." I turned right onto Van Ness and barely missed a cyclist.

He heaved a sigh. "Thank you. I'm glad. I'll let you know what, if anything, Jardine finds out from Mrs. Galloway."

"Thanks. I appreciate it."

"You sound worried."

"I am, but not about Mrs. Galloway and her wayward hubby. My homeless friend, Bob, is now missing. That makes four missing homeless in under a week. Isn't there anything we can do?"

"I wish I could offer some help in that department, but no one is biting. Maybe if you wrote an article."

"And say what? How SFPD won't help? I don't think so."

"No one is saying you have to lay blame. Tell you what. Maybe I can make a deal with Jardine. If we can throw him a bone about the Galloway case, maybe he'll put someone on the homeless case. Let me see what I can do. Gotta run. I'll keep you posted."

No sooner had I hung up than my phone rang again. "What the fuck have you done?" It was Carter.

"I've done a lot. I showered, I've eaten, I've played with my cat. Can you be a tad more specific?"

"You know what the hell I am talking about. Wes won't run my Galloway piece. He didn't say why, but I'm pretty damn sure you had something to do with it."

"So?"

"God. Damn. You. Branson! Who the hell do you think you are? You've got nothing! This is professional suicide! You can't make something out of nothing, and stopping me from going to print is an amateurish move at best."

"Apparently, whatever trash you wrote, Wes doesn't want or he'd take it to press."

"Being incompetent is one thing, but making an enemy of me is a foolish, foolish mistake."

"Carter, I was your enemy before Wes held your story."

"You're going to regret this, Branson. When this all comes out in the wash, you won't be able to get a job as a paperboy."

I hung up on him. Again. I didn't need his threats. The truth was, he was probably right. If I didn't come up with a real story, Carter had enough clout to make me invisible.

By the time I got home, I was mentally drained. Too much noise in my head exhausted me. I needed to meditate, to get centered, to quiet my spirit.

A huge Tupperware container filled with lasagna waited for me at the front door. I smiled. Luigi was the best.

After consuming most of the lasagna, I put the phone on silent to meditate. My belly full, my mind finally beginning to quiet, I quickly fell into a state where all those bad energies left me. I was there for a long, long time, regenerating my spiritual energy and just cleansing my soul.

When I was coming out of it, I could hear Franklin's voice saying something about seeing the obvious. Had I missed the obvious? Had I looked through it instead of *at* it?

Opening my eyes, I rose and stretched. Tripod sat in the window ignoring me.

"Come on; jealousy isn't becoming on you."

He wouldn't look at me. He had smelled Midnight on me and turned away on a dime. There was only one thing that was going to make him forgive me.

I would have to bring out the catnip.

"If you were my child, I'd be arrested for child abuse." I said, dropping catnip into his bowl.

Tripod leapt off the ledge and went straight for the bowl. He stopped to look up at me once to let me know that we were friends again.

"Blackmailer."

I watched him scarf it like the addict he was. Blackmail. I considered the word and then pulled out a fresh legal pad. I hadn't given motive enough thought, so I wrote MOTIVE at the top of the page and started down the list of possible motives for why Mrs. Galloway would lie.

The first thing I needed to figure out was if she knew where he was. She knew he was alive, so why would she go along with it? Blackmail? Extortion? I was pretty sure it wasn't a kidnapping. I don't think kidnappers take dogs. Was this a scheme *between* the Galloways? I wrote SCHEME at the top next to motive. Why would a husband and wife plan something like this? To what end?

Let's see… the internet affair was called off and so he made it look as though he had sent himself to a watery grave. This was what we were *supposed* to believe. Had Mrs. Galloway found out about the affair? Maybe *she* was blackmailing *him.*

How weird would that be?

So, where was he, and how did he get off the boat? And how… wait. Of course! Another boat! Duh! Someone had come out to get him and the dog. Who could that be? I picked up the phone and called the boys. "Hi guys, it's Echo. I have a question for you. Do the Galloways own a boat?"

"A boat? Like a sailboat?"

"Anything that floats will do. I need to know that and if so, where the sloop is."

"Slip. They're called slips. I can pull this up in a nano. So, you haven't cracked the case yet, Princess?"

"I wish. Time is really running out for me. I may be grasping at straws, but I'm not out of the game yet."

"Okay… here we go. It looks like they have a boat of some sort, yeah. You want me to see what we can find out about it?"

I stared down at my pad. "There's something bothering me about the affair, but I can't put my finger on it. Can you—"

"We'll double check the files and see if anything pops. I'll call you if we find something."

"Thanks." Hanging up, I went back to my timeline and notes. Now, someone could have picked him up or he could have brought one of those blow-up rafts. In the rocky bay, that would be dangerous, but not impossible. I wrote DIVORCE on the top as well. If he was "dead," who got the business? What did Mrs. Galloway stand to gain from it? Was this about love or money?

I shook my head and lay on the couch. The grains of sand were falling rapidly. I could feel it.

The phone rang and I got to it on the first half-ring. "Princess? It's Carl."

I quickly sat up and watched my cat lying on his back, spread eagle and enjoying his catnip hallucinations. I was going to have to do something about that. "Tell me this is good news."

"We shoulda hit it before, but we weren't looking in

that direction. First of all, the boat they own is in dry dock getting some repairs."

I crossed out the idea that Mrs. Galloway picked him up in their boat. "Okay."

"We went back through the emails and that's when it hit us. The woman is supposed to be in Oregon, right?"

"Ashland, yeah."

"She's not."

Now I was standing. "What do you mean?"

"Let's see if I can explain this in lay terms. Emails don't go directly from one computer to another. Generally speaking, they actually go through at least four. If you're online from home, it goes through your ISP's mail server. It's up to the mail server to deliver the message. It does this by finding the recipient's mail server, where it stays until the recipient logs on to pick it up. You with me so far?"

"I think so, yeah."

"All of this information is traceable and shows up in the header. There's from, to, date, and mailer. These headings get longer as the mail is processed. So the received emails provide a detailed history of the sent message. In the case of these emails, I can tell you that they were routed through the same server."

"Meaning?" My skin was prickling from excitement.

"What it means is, if there *is* a woman sending emails, she's doing it from San Fran, from the same internet provider as their home computer. It says so right here. See, unless you know how to forge addresses and route emails through other servers, your information is easy to read. You pick up the numbers, run them through a locator, and then you have it. That's why the cops always take the hard drive… there's plenty information on it even when you think you've deleted it all."

"So let me get this straight; the woman's emails are *not* from Oregon."

"Nope."

"They're from San Francisco."

"Not the same computer, though. Same ISP number means from the same area. They obviously didn't think they needed to cover their trail. Joe Normal Guy has no idea how emails are routed. He thinks just because they get a new address and send email from a different computer means they've covered their tracks. Let's say you pay for a service like Comcast in Berkeley. When you log in and send an email, it goes through that server."

"Even if I use a laptop?"

"Wouldn't matter. At this point, you have to wonder if there's a woman at all. I mean, why pretend to be in Ashland, when you can pretend to be in Rhode Island? Secondly, if there isn't a woman, there's no real romance…"

"And no reason to commit pretend suicide."

"Exactly."

"But we have hotel receipts for Redding."

"That's another thing; if you were really having this illicit affair, would you pay for anything with a credit card? I mean, how dumb is that? It's as if you were intentionally laying a huge paper trail."

"I had wondered that. You're my new hero, Carl, thank you so much."

"No problemo. Keep us in the loop. Until then, go get 'em."

I hung up, staring at my notes. I decided to rewrite my

notes in some order.

1) *Glen Galloway had pretended to have an online affair.*

2) *He pretended it was over.*

3) *He pretended to kill himself.*

4) *He laid the groundwork so that all of this was believable and easy to follow.*

5) *Mrs. G prompted an investigation and continued to press for one even when the police rejected the notion that a crime had happened. She wanted an investigation knowing there was a paper trail already in place.*

6) *She contacted the news because she wanted the hoax believed.*

Okay… now what? He is reported dead so he can… what? Start a new life? What about her? What does she get? *Everything.*

She was the widow of a Fortune 500 company's CEO. She gets the house, cars, everything. These people were rich. Still, even if he gets a new life… *she's* the real winner of this charade. She *really* gains. If that was true, then *she* must be the mastermind of it all. *She* was the key. Picking up the phone, I nudged Tripod with my toe to make sure he was still alive. He was, but he was seriously high. Then, I called Walt Finn.

"Finn, it's Echo. Do you think you can set up a meeting with Jardine?"

"Wow. Are you psychic or what? Jardine just asked the same thing. Well, actually, he wanted your number and I wouldn't give it to him. He wants to talk to you about that damn dog."

"When?"

"He's off at six... well... he has dinner at six. Can you meet him at Chuck's Rib Joint around then?"

"Absolutely."

"I gotta warn you... Jardine hates reporters. Big hate. But his bark is worse than his bite. Don't let him or his enormous size intimidate you."

"Don't worry. What does he look like?"

"Can't miss him. He'll be the biggest SOB in the joint. He's tall, dark, and ugly. He's an enormous Portuguese-Samoan with an overly-healthy appetite."

"Tell him I'll be there at six."

"Great. I've put a good word in for you, so behave."

"Behave?"

"Yes. I know you're under the gun, but Dicks are slow and methodical. They need processing time. Know what I mean?"

"I'll try."

"Thatta girl. Good luck to you."

"Thanks." I hung up and turned around to find my cat staring into space. He was sitting up, which was good, but he had that far-away stoned look. "Tripod, come here."

He didn't budge, so I walked over to pet him. He purred and blinked, finally snapping out of it. I needed to get him off the dope. No, what I *needed* was to get to the bottom of this damn story.

CHAPTER 20

AFTER I WAS well-rested and well-fed, it was time to get down to the real lessons. Tomas had gone off to Atlanta, leaving me and Jacob to tend to the many chores around the cottage. The weather was mild in the bayou, but without electricity, Melika cooked by a fire that was always burning. There was also a brick barbecue on the side that she used as well. Let me tell you, that woman could cook. I think I gained ten pounds the first ten minutes I was there. It was a good thing I had chores, or it would have been twenty.

It's weird to think that my bayou experience was the closest thing to a normal family that I'd ever had, but that was the truth. Jacob was the most respectful young man I had ever met, and abolished every notion I had ever had about kids from the Bronx. So I didn't know Cajun from Creole or Havana from Haiti; I *had* watched enough television to know where the Bronx was and what it was like, and he embodied none of those rough edges.

Melika was like a parent in that she had expectations to

fulfill. We had to rest, eat well, do our chores, and be respectful of each other and our environment. Once we finished with our morning chores, our first lesson started, and it wasn't at all what I thought it would be.

"The average stay with me is three or four years. I know it seems like a lot, but gaining complete control of your powers is a long and often complicated journey. It is not easy, and there are no shortcuts, but it *will* mean the difference between having a real life and possibly having none at all."

I gulped hard. I couldn't imagine being in the bayou a year, let alone four.

"There are two ways out of your power: suicide and insanity. Many choose the former, after long battles with the latter. To successfully master yourselves, you must invest fully in the process. Do you understand?"

I nodded.

"Good. Now, since Jacob has been here so long, he's in charge of this week's morning lessons. When you finish your work, he will take you out on the water and educate you about this new environment."

"Is that part of the process?"

Melika grinned. "Oh yes. You see, a super must always familiarize herself with her environment. It should be the first thing you do wherever you go. Knowing your environment keeps you safer. Always be aware of the hazards and pitfalls. That way, you can be prepared." Melika rose and walked out to the edge of the dock. "Were you prepared when Todd overtook you? Did you see anything in your surroundings you could have used as a weapon? Did you see any way out besides violence?

I shook my head. "No."

"You felt the threat and acted, correct?"

"Yes."

"Had you been more aware of your environment, you might have had other choices. A life without options is not a life worth living. The more you understand the bayou, the more you'll know about life. The bayou *is* life."

At first, I wondered if maybe this was a mistake. I didn't see how knowing about the bayou was going to help me. I thought maybe this was a big, fat waste of time.

I couldn't have been more wrong.

That day, Jacob opened my mind and my world. I saw a texture and layers to the world around me I never knew existed. In Oakland, a tree was a tree. Here, every tree served a purpose, every plant important to the whole. If we don't learn the interconnectedness of the universe, how can we ever truly be a part of it? How can you know a place if you don't know anything about it? How can you know *yourself* if you haven't combed the depths of your being?

You can't.

So when we got back, I felt full of life and energy that only nature can provide. I understood why Melika sent me out on a boat with Jacob, and I started looking forward to it every morning. He was a great teacher and I learned more about biology and life from him in one week than I learned from any teacher in any school.

After a snack, Melika took me out into the backwoods behind the cottage, where there was a fire pit with several stumps for sitting. It was to become one of my favorite places in the world.

"I come out here because we need to be away from any

potential emotional energies. What we have to do needs to be done undisturbed."

I nodded.

"The most important skill is called shielding. Shields help empaths keep out extra emotional energy from others so you aren't overwhelmed. But this shield does more than keep out unwanted energy. The edge of it works as a psychic alarm; when anyone psychically crosses it, the shield warns you that someone is near. It keeps us safe and protected. Under normal circumstances, a shield maintains itself for quite some time. The stronger you are, the better and longer the shield holds up. Now, there are many things that will quickly erode a shield. Stress is a big problem, and so are negative emotions from others. Lack of sleep is a culprit in the deterioration of a shield as well, which is why I want you to eat and sleep well. Anytime your physical body is out of balance, you are vulnerable to attack."

"Attack?"

"Yes. An attack can be from the wave of emotions coming in through your shield, or it can be an attack from another psionic being. Rest, time alone, and meditation are wise, so before I teach you how to create a shield, I'll need to show you how to meditate. Meditation is a huge key, but it must be done effectively. Many people don't know the correct way, and there is *definitely* a right way for our purpose."

Who would have thought it would take me two months; two long, grueling months just to learn how to meditate. For a while there, I thought I was actually incapable of it. Of course, I wasn't learning alone, either. After my first week, Tomas returned to the bayou from Atlanta with another student. His name was Zack and he had also just come into his powers.

Only, his powers were not empathic in nature at all. Zack was a TK, or a telekinetic. Tomas referred to him as a mover; someone who could move objects using the energy from his mind. Zack was a sixteen-year-old boy from Savannah, Georgia; a redhead with freckles and a bad haircut. Tall and lanky, you just knew kids teased him all the time.

Of course, that was when I realized it was a mistake to tease someone with out-of-control telekinetic abilities. A TK is a very powerful being indeed, and I saw how powerful he was the moment he arrived.

When Zack stepped off the Bones' boat, he was just like I had been: disoriented, exhausted, and on the edge. I could feel his tender emotions and fear as he got off the boat and looked around. As he started up the steps, he lost his balance, and when Tomas reached out to help him, Zack, out of fear, put his arm out straight toward Tomas and knocked him to the ground without ever touching him. It was the most amazing thing I had seen in my life. From then on, Tomas gave him a wide berth, and whenever Zack left a room, Tomas could be heard muttering under his breath, "Spoon bender."

I would find out later what that meant. In the meantime, I, too, gave Zack room to roam. That was the first I would see of a TK, and Zack, who would astound me on many occasions with such feats as the one I just witnessed, would become one of my best friends and remain with me in the bayou for the next four years.

CHAPTER 21

CHUCK'S RIB JOINT was just the kind of place you'd expect a cop to hang out; it was a gritty, old, not the least bit fancy, paper napkins and plastic cups kind of place. Cops and truck drivers always knew the best places to eat. I'd never eaten there, but had heard it had the best ribs in the city.

Pulling into the tiny, yet full parking lot, I gathered notes together and sat them on my lap before taking a few moments to meditate. This was my last draw of the cards and I needed an ace. I didn't have blathering time.

Five minutes later, I entered Chuck's and immediately spotted the enormous Samoan taking up an entire corner booth. In front of him was a plate of ribs reminiscent of those that tipped over the Flintstone's car. I swear to God, there was half a cow or a whole pig sitting on that plate.

Detective Jardine looked up from his plate. He had barbecue sauce on his chin. "You Finn's girl?"

"Excuse me?"

He held up the rib he was eating. "I'd shake your hand,

but… sit down. Want to order something?"

I shook my head. "No thank you. I'm good." I sat across from him and grinned.

"Vegetarian?" He said it as if he asked if I had leprosy.

"Carnivore."

He liked this. I could tell. Detective Jardine wasn't nearly as ugly as Finn had alluded. He was darker than I thought he would be, with black, wavy hair and chocolate brown eyes. He had an enormous face, like a cartoon face on silly putty that had been stretched. It was his smile that was disarming. When he grinned at me, his whole big face grinned. "Finn didn't tell me you'd be so cute. He trying to keep you all to himself?"

Why do men think that cute is a compliment? Cute applies to babies, puppies, and smart three-year-olds. "Hardly. I appreciate you taking the time to see me. Finn told me you're not crazy about reporters."

"Hate 'em, actually. Hate Ellsworth the most." Jardine set his picked-clean bone on his plate and wiped his hands-on numerous napkins. "Finn told me to check out the dog angle, and I have to say that it's bugging the crap outta me why a man would drown himself *and* his dog. I don't buy it."

I nodded. "Exactly. So… what happened to the dog?"

Jardine sighed and toyed with another rib. "I dunno, but I'm sure you got an idea or five."

"May I?" I pulled my file out and set it on the table.

"You talk. I'll eat."

"Okay. I don't think Glen killed himself. Yes, he left a note and yes, he wasn't on board the boat, but I think someone came to get him *and* his dog off that boat to make it look like a suicide."

He nodded while gnawing on his bone. "Interesting. How do you suppose?"

"Raft? Inflatable? I think he had help."

"They have a boat."

"Right. It's dry docked, but I'll bet you another plate of that cow that their emergency skiff is missing."

Jardine slowly looked up at me. Something changed in his eyes. "You're good. You sure you don't want something to eat?"

"I'm sure."

"We found a suitcase he brought with him. It was empty. I thought that was weird. They figured maybe he transported rocks or whatever he used to sink to the bottom."

"He didn't sink to the bottom, Jardine. I wish I could explain to you how I know that, but trust me, Glen Galloway is alive and well."

"But why? Why go through all of this?"

"Good question…"

Detective Jardine listened patiently as I explained to him about the online romance connections and how there really wasn't a woman in Ashland, Oregon, but someone was going to great lengths to make it look otherwise. Jardine was a great listener. I guess that's what made him a good detective. I decided then and there that I liked this big, scary guy.

When I finished the internet piece, I leaned back and sighed. "There's more, but let's just stick to the feigned romance for now. It certainly points to a deception of sorts, don't you think?"

Jardine pushed his plate aside and leaned on the table. "And if I take this to my techies… will they agree? Will they find the same things?"

"Depends on how good they are. *My* guys are the very best and I'd stake my life on any information coming out of their mouths."

He nodded. "Impressive. What else you got?"

That was a loaded question. "I'm sure your team has most of it."

He chuckled. "There's no *team*, Echo. I'm the only member on this *team*." Jardine signaled to the waitress, who took the plate away. "So, how can we help each other with this mess?"

Inhaling deeply, I sighed. "When you uncover the truth, I'd like the exclusive. I'd love it if you handed the story back to me."

"Anything else, hon?" The waitress asked. "Apple pie tonight, Darryl. À la mode or dry?"

Jardine chuckled. "Aren't you funny? Two pies, both à la mode, and be generous with that scoop of yours, Suzy Q. Last time, it was barely a teaspoon." He winked as she swatted him with her order pad before going back to the counter. "That's it? All you want is to be the first to hang Galloway in the court of public opinion?"

"The only thing I'm trying to do is keep my job." I told him about the bet. Again, he listened calmly, asking no questions until I had finished. It took longer than I expected to tell the story about Carter, but that was because the pie was so delicious.

"Best damn pie, eh?" Jardine asked when I finished my story. "You know, I hate Ellsworth. He's the kind of journalist who doesn't care who he hurts with that Goddamned poison pen of his." Jardine shook his head. "The guy's pond scum."

"Can I ask what he did that brought this on?"

"Just don't trust him, and don't ever turn your back on him. That guy is trouble, and if there's anything I can do to make his life miserable; you can count me in."

I nodded, remembering what Finn had said about not pushing. "My number's on the folder. Call day or night if there's anything I can do." I pushed the file over to him.

Jardine rubbed his chin. "I'll look through your stuff here and see if I can't pin the tail on the donkey." He took the file and smiled at me. "I understand that you're under the gun and that your job is on the line. I'll look through it all and see what I can see." He pulled a twenty out and tossed it on the table. I didn't think it was nearly enough and when he saw my eyes, he grinned. "They won't charge me here, so I leave her a good tip."

I smiled. I was liking him more and more. "Nice."

"Good service gets a good tip. Great pie gets a great tip." Jardine rose and put the file under his arm. He was enormous; almost twice the width of an already large man. "You need a ride anywhere?"

"I have a car, but thanks… and thanks for the pie and your ear. Solve this in less than a day and you'll be my new hero."

"Who's your old hero?"

"Would you believe me if I said a computer geek?"

"Thank God. I thought you were going to say Finn. The guy's a first-rate boob."

I held my hand up. "Stop right there. I think Finn's a

nice guy and a good fr—"

"Oh relax, Echo. I'm only bustin' his chops 'cause he's my cousin."

"Your cousin?"

Jardine started laughing. "Yeah. Did he call me an ugly Samoan?"

"I… uh…"

He was still laughing. "Never mind. I'll call you when I get a hit." Jardine walked me to my car. As I opened the door, he leaned closer. "Finn would kick my ass if I told you this, but he likes you, too. Good night, Echo."

I watched Jardine lumber away, my mouth hanging open.

He liked me?

CHAPTER 22

S HIELDING WAS, BY far, the hardest lesson. I don't know why I thought it was something I could learn in a day or so, especially when meditating had been so tough to master, but boy, was I wrong. This was the single most important skill Melika had to teach me. Without it, without being really efficient at erecting it, maintaining it, stabilizing it, and lowering it without incident, my chances to live out a semi-normal life were slim-to-none. I wanted a life. No, I wanted a *normal* life insomuch as I had never had one. I'd been in and out of so many foster homes, they'd installed a revolving door for me. I knew nothing about normal.

Until I came to the bayou.

Every day was different. The weather altered on an hourly basis, the creatures were unlike anything else I had ever seen, and the river itself seemed to change on a whim. I loved it. I never saw myself as a naturalist, never gave much thought to the world around me. Oh, I paid very close attention to *the people* around me. You did that when you lived in the ghetto. It was *ghetto* back then. We didn't pretty up its ugly nature with euphemisms like inner city or 'hood.

You can spray gold flecks on a dog turd and it would still be a turd. So, when I lived in turdville, I paid really close attention to gangs of every color, drug dealers of every race, prostitutes of every shape, and pimpmobiles of every make. For your physical safety in the ghetto, you paid attention or you paid a price.

Out in the bayou, you did the same for the same reasons. I learned to love the sound of the 'gators as they slid off the muddy banks. They made a distinctive sound in the water that no longer frightened me. There were hawks whose calls were music to my ears, and insects whose nightly serenade sent me to sleep.

And then there were the various characters who came and went, and that was always fun to see. There was the French-speaking woodcutter, a grocery delivery woman with only one eye, and a gardener of sorts who had a boa wrapped around his neck.

And then there was Bishop.

Bishop was Melika's very colorful mother, and it was her powers that eventually brought the family from the West Indies to the plantation. When she was finally able to free herself from the debts of her "boss," Bishop went straight to New Orleans, a city she loved, and opened up what was to become one of the most profitable tarot reading businesses in the state of Louisiana. Big wigs, CEOs, restauranteurs, and drag queens came to her for advice, solace, and a glimpse into their future. But Bishop wasn't a twenty dollar an hour shill pretending to read cards. Bishop had the sight; the pinnacle of all clairvoyant powers. She could see more clearly into the future than any other person Melika had ever met.

The first time I met her was my third week in the bayou. Melika and I were working on building a shield I could keep up for more than a minute, when Bishop and her boatman pulled up to our dock.

Melika and I walked out to the porch. "Oh Lordy," Melika said under her breath. "She's earlier than usual."

"Is that her?" I whispered. "Is that your mother?" Jacob had told me all about Bishop on one of our morning bayou trips. He told me that she was some big voodoo priestess who scared half the population of New Orleans. The other half lived and died by her readings, paying a small fortune to see what lay ahead.

What I saw in the boat was a very small woman draped in all black and wearing a hat. She must have stood less than four feet eight. Her boatman helped her out of the boat, but he remained there.

"Yes, dear girl, that's my mother. She comes to check out the new blood every blue moon. She always knows whenever there's a new one of us in town. It's her way. Now don't let her scare you. That's her way as well."

Zack joined me and Melika on the porch, and together the three of us started toward the dock. No wrinkled old hag, Bishop's skin seemed to defy time. As she walked up the pier toward us, she carried herself like a woman who owned the world, and though she was short in stature, she made up for it in attitude.

"You must be Echo," Bishop said before I could open my mouth to greet her. Like everyone else on this side of the bayou, she was blocking, so I couldn't read her at all. "My, my, Melika, what have we here?" Bishop had an accent unlike any I had heard in the bayou, but it wasn't her voice that mesmerized me, it was her eyes. Bishop's eyes were yellow. "Do you know what you have here?" she asked Melika without taking her eyes off of mine.

"I am well aware, mother."

Bishop released me from her gaze and looked up at Melika. "Nick of time. Good boy, my Georgie. He's a gem, that one."

Melika nodded once. "Indeed."

"How are her lessons going?"

"Well. She's bright and unafraid." Melika put her arm around my shoulders and pulled me closer.

"Excellent. Fear is a useless emotion for us. We need not fear a thing from those who cannot do as we do." Bishop looked over at Zack. "Ah… a mover. Tell me, boy, can you move my hat from my head?"

Zack stared at Melika, who, to my surprise, nodded.

"Take your best shot, boy."

Blinking a few times, Zack hesitated and Bishop held up her hand.

"Wait," she said, turning back to me. "Can you see it?"

I frowned. As far as I knew, my powers were emotional, not visual. I had never seen…

"Not true," Bishop replied, interrupting my thoughts. "You *think* your powers are merely emotive, but you're wrong. My daughter will, of course, show you how to better utilize *all* of your senses, but for the moment, I want you just to look carefully at Zachary."

I nodded and did as she asked.

"Now, relax your eyes. Don't focus on the physical being of Zachary, but on his image. If you see him but don't really see him, you'll notice something about him. Like those silly pictures you stare at until you see something else. What is it you see?"

Sure enough, as I relaxed my eyes, I could see a slight haze all around him, as if outlining him. "A haze... like a blur."

"All living things are creatures of energy, Echo, and for those with your gift, it is visible to the naked eye much in the same way night vision goggles zoom in on the heat from our bodies. You have the wonderful gift of being able to read people's auras. Now tell me what color it is."

"Umm... green?"

"Be specific. Is it olive, lime, emerald, forest—"

"Dark green. Like a forest green, yeah."

Bishop nodded and patted my shoulder. "Good girl. Dark green means mental stress, which is precisely what Zachary is feeling right about now. Isn't that right, Zachary?"

He nodded, but didn't move.

"Cool," I murmured, trying my new skill on Bishop.

"He's the only one you can read right now because he has not yet learned how to block. But keep your eyes on him and tell me what happens." To Zack, she said, "My hat, young man."

Zack rubbed his hands together before turning his palms toward Bishop. Nothing happened. Zack frowned and I felt him press harder. Still nothing.

"Color?"

"Orange."

"Meaning?"

"He's trying really hard."

"Good girl. Orange means strong motivation. Keep trying, Zack."

I watched him try, the color changing to more of a pumpkin color.

"Color?"

"Pumpkin."

"Ah, yes. Self-control. Well done. That's good, Zachary."

"But—"

"It's okay, my boy. I asked you to do something I would not let you do."

"*You* stopped me?"

Bishop smiled. "Of course." She stepped closer to him and smiled kindly into his face. "You must remember always, my boy, that no matter how strong you think you are, there's always someone stronger than yourself. Always. And because you can't identify other supers, you must never assume the people around you are not. Using your particular abilities in public could very well be the last thing you do."

Zack nodded. "Yes, ma'am, but how—"

Bishop held her hand up. "Not now. Later. Be a dear, Zachary, and get me a glass of Melika's lemonade, please."

Zack bolted into the house,

"Mother, stop scaring the boy."

"I'm not scaring him. The boy is a male, Melika. You know how dangerous male movers tend to be when they come into their powers." Bishop turned to me. "I don't go for all that fancy science fiction talk like telekinetics, pyrokinetics, etcetera. I've always preferred calling them as they are. While movers are the most physically powerful of us, they are also the most vulnerable because it takes just once for someone to see them use their gift, and everything could change in the blink of an eye. So you must be vigilant in how and when you use your gifts. Always vigilant. Do you understand?"

"Yes, ma'am."

"Good. What you are going to face is much more difficult than these last weeks. Always stay focused. Always be disciplined. Having power does not give you carte blanche to use it indiscriminately."

I nodded. "You sound so much like Melika."

Bishop chuckled. "Of course I do. Who do you think taught her everything she knows?"

And that was my first meeting with a woman I would come to love as a strict grandmother. I would learn so much about her powers, about mine, about life and my place in it. For a fourteen-year-old girl who had never belonged, this was just about the biggest gift anyone could give me.

And I wasn't going to waste it.

CHAPTER 23

WHEN I GOT home, I was exhausted. My hopes of keeping my dream job now lay in the hands of Detective Jardine. He believed me. That much I knew. But cops wanted hard evidence, and unless my information led him to that evidence, I was going to be shit out of luck.

Luigi was following me up the stairs. "Some ol' woman with a bunch of animals came by lookin' for you."

"What did she say?" I dusted some flour off his shoulder.

"Just that she has some news."

"Thanks, Luigi."

Once in my apartment, I checked my messages and found one from Danica, one from Finn and yet another blistering one from Carter, who told me in no uncertain terms to stay away from him, the office, and anything associated with the story, blah, blah, blah. He told me it was over and to accept defeat graciously… if I had any. Then he instructed me to leave the pink slip with the receptionist.

"Smug bastard," I muttered, pressing delete halfway

through his tirade. I didn't need this right now. Finn's message was to tell me that Jardine really enjoyed his meeting with me and that he was going to get right on it.

Danica's message was music to my ears. She complained of working too hard and wanting to get out for a drink.

WHEN I PICKED her up and announced I had a few errands to run beforehand, she didn't mind. Danica was always up for an adventure.

Half an hour later, we were in the Tenderloin.

"This is one of your errands? Jesus, Clark, you trying to get us killed?"

"You can stay in the car if you're afraid."

Danica reached into her purse and pulled out a small revolver. "I'm never afraid as long as I have my leetle fren'."

Danica's father had given her a gun shortly after I bashed Todd's head in. She didn't carry it until our sophomore year in college when there was a rape near campus. Mills College is one of the safer colleges on the West Coast, but it sits in a questionable neighborhood in Oakland. I wasn't surprised that she still carried it.

"So, what are we doing here this beautiful evening?"

"Looking for a woman named Shirley." We got out and started down the street. The Tenderloin reminded me a lot of the bayou: creepy, with dark alleyways and unfamiliar creatures, some of which were deadly. It was easy to get lost, there were freaky sounds you never wanted to hear again, and you had to watch where you walked.

"You sure this story is worth it?" Danica whispered.

"This isn't about the story anymore, Danica. It's about finding Bob."

"You're such a bleeding heart."

When we got to Geary, we heard Shirley before we saw her. Apparently, she was in one of her "in" moments of insanity because she was ranting at nothing.

"There she is."

Danica stopped. "*That's* your source?"

"Hush. She's... she's one of us."

Danica stared over at Shirley, disbelieving. "Oh God, is that..."

"*That's* what you and Britt saved me from becoming, yes."

"What is she? A Telepath?"

I shook my head. "Near as I can tell, she's a scryer."

"A what?"

"A scryer. The other day, I handed her my card and she said something like... *oh, now I understand* or something to that effect. I got a pretty decent aura read from her that indicates paranormal potential but I didn't get much of a read emotionally."

"Was she blocking?"

I nodded. "That told me all I needed to know. Other than you, I don't know too many regular folks who can do that." All normals can do minimal blocking if they're taught how. Danica had been a willing and quick study; far quicker than I.

"What's she raving about?"

"I have no idea."

"Think she'll remember who you are or should I have leetle fren' ready?"

"You pull that gun out and that big white dog will kill us both."

"What is it with homeless people and pets? If you can't feed yourself…" Danica shut up when I gave her a withering stare.

"Do I need to send you back to the car?"

"Are you kidding me? I'm not leaving you out here alone. I don't give a shit if she's Nostradamus, you need backup."

"Backup? Who are we? Starsky and Hutch?"

"More like Danny Glover and Mel Gibson, although I've always fancied myself a little like Foxy Brown and—"

"Are you through?"

She nodded. "Let's get this over with. I really want a drink in a nice, warm, seedy bar somewhere."

As we approached Shirley, I could hear her ranting something about Catholic priests and George W. with a little Rush Limbaugh thrown in for good measure. "No gun," I said between gritted teeth.

"Can I mace her?"

I didn't bother to respond. When Cotton spotted me, he sat up and wagged his tail. His thumping tail woke Midnight up, who was lying on a red scarf. When Shirley saw the dog's reaction to me, she stopped ranting and cocked her head at me. She was no longer blocking and I lowered my shields to feel every psychotic emotion she was experiencing. She didn't quite remember who I was and was perplexed as to her animals' response to me.

"Shirley, it's me, Echo. Remember?"

She squinted at me with her head still cocked to one side and then she turned to Cotton. "I don't, but my dog does. Seems to like you, too, which is odd. They don't like many people. You from the government?" She lowered her voice.

"CIA maybe?"

"Why CIA?" Danica blurted. I sent her another *shut up* glare.

"The CIA has been looking for me for a long time. If you're from the government, you can just move along because I'm not going with anyone ever again unless I'm in a Goddamn pine box, you hear me? The Group is never going to get me. Is that who sent you? The Group? Well? Are you or aren't you?"

"No, Shirley, we're not."

She looked me up and down. "Well, if you were, Cotton here woulda chased you away lickety split-like. He hates government nearly as much as I do. Hates cops, senators, mayors, anyone in a uniform and anyone who carries ID other than a driver's license." Shirley looked over at Danica. "You afraid?"

"Of you? No."

Shirley tossed her hair back and laughed like a lunatic. "Don't imagine you'd say that if you weren't packin' heat. You like heat, don'tcha?"

Danica looked over at me and I shook my head. You can take the girl out of the ghetto…

"Shirley, do you remember talking to me the other day about missing homeless guys?"

She scratched her head and then sighed. "I don't think I know you. Why are you asking me these questions? Are you from the government? Is that it? You want what I have? But you'll never get it from me. Never. I'll take your eye just like the last one, you son-of-a-bitch. You think I won't just 'cause you're a female?"

"Come on, Clark, we're wasting our time here. She's got

nothing." Danica turned back to the car, but I stayed.

"Check your sock, Shirley. I gave you a card and you put it in your sock. That sock," I said, pointing.

"Really?" Shirley reached into her pocket and came up empty. "Who sent you? The Secret Service? Oh yes, they're always looking under the wrong rocks. Do you know how many times I tried to warn them about 9/11? Then, when it happened, *then* they were finally interested, but it was too late." She chuckled. "They've been looking for me ever since."

Danica was suddenly back at my side. "You didn't say she was clairvoyant," she whispered.

"Hush," I said.

"We're all in danger, you know? *They're* not just after me. They *know* we exist. They just can't get their hands on many of us, but they keep tryin'. Lordy, how that group keeps on tryin'."

"Come on, Clark. Let's get out of here. Whatever it is you wanted; you're not going to find it here."

Sighing sadly, I had to agree. The lucid woman I met had been replaced by this ranting woman before us. "Damn."

Danica tugged my arm and Cotton responded by baring his teeth and letting out a low, threatening growl.

Shirley quieted Cotton. "He's taken a fancy to you, Echo." When she said my name, everything about her seemed to change. "Oh. We *did* speak, didn't we?"

I nodded. "About the missing guys from the street."

Closing her eyes, she breathed in slowly. "Yes. Yes, we did. As you can see, I'm not quite sane at the moment. I apologize." Her eyes transformed back to their earlier crazed stage. "Come tomorrow... I must have something to say to you... didn't I... don't you live in a bakery?"

I nodded, feeling her revert back to her insane self.

"I have something... did you know the CIA uses bakers all the time? It's the hours they keep... people don't get suspicious. You're suspicious, aren't you? Good. You *should* be. It's safer that way. Go on. Come back in the daylight when it's safer."

"Come on, Clark."

Danica was right. "Okay, Shirley. I'll come back later."

As we walked away, Danica let out a low whistle. "Wowee, Clark, you sure know how to pick 'em. All that crazy talk about the CIA."

"It's serious stuff, Danica. If they knew... I mean, what if they got their hands on me? What if they threatened to kill everyone I loved if I didn't point out the other supers I knew? What do you think I would do?"

Danica looked hard into my eyes. "You? You'd take your chances and throw me to the dogs."

"Danica!"

"Am I wrong? I'm not saying you don't love me, because I know you do. I *also* know that you're part of something larger than your own life, or mine for that matter. You'd have to protect those who protected you."

"*You* protected me!"

"Once, Clark. Look, it's no big deal. It wouldn't happen that way, would it? I mean, they wouldn't threaten the people you love, would they?"

I said nothing.

"Oh shit."

"I know you saw a loon back there, but *something* scares

her. I feel it and it's very real."

"Oh puhlease, are you saying you think the Goddamn CIA is after her?"

"I don't know. I just know that her fear is real; that doesn't mean that the threat is."

Danica groaned. "Does that mean you're going back there?"

"Not tonight. I'll drop by the park to see her tomorrow. She came by my place because she had *something* to tell me. She didn't just come by to visit and drink tea."

"Fine. Where are we off to now? The soup kitchen? Goodwill?"

"Very funny. No, we're going to where Bob used to hang out and see if anyone knows anything."

"I'm not going to get my drink for a really long time, am I?"

I looked over at her and slowly shook my head. "I'm afraid not."

CHAPTER 24

I HAD BEEN on the bayou for a little over six months when Melika announced that we were ready to finally "go into town."

"New Orleans. The Big Easy. The most colorful place in the country. I think you're both ready for the excesses of such a place. It's the perfect testing grounds for all the lessons you've learned so far."

New Orleans! I had heard so much about it from Tomas whenever he deigned to speak to us. He had an odd role at the cottage. He wasn't really a student, wasn't really a teacher, either. He was more like a handyman or substitute teacher/bus driver/school bully. I never got the feeling he liked us; me, in particular. Maybe it was our age difference or maybe he was just a jerk, but he seemed to enjoy teasing me more than anyone else.

I asked Melika one day after a lesson why he was with us and she told me that Tomas was a very powerful telepath who offered to help her take care of the newbies. She told me not to judge him, but to keep an open mind.

It was with an open mind that I learned that Tomas was an avid naturalist, a consummate chess player, and a royal pain in my ass. I tried everything to be nice to him, but he treated me like a bothersome little sister, and that pissed me off. I was glad to be getting away from him and his wisecracks.

"Bishop will pick you and Zack up at Bones' place," Tomas said, barely looking at me. "This is something the two of you have to do on your own. I'm not always going to be around to help you kids out. You're ready for this. You make sure you construct a strong shield and keep it up for a prolonged period of time with many people around."

"What will we do?" Zack asked.

I had come to love Zack like a brother. He was respectful toward the process, toward Melika, and toward me. He wasn't at all like the twelve-year-olds I'd grown up with in various foster homes; the kind of boys who pulled wings off of butterflies. Zack was kind and gentle, thoughtful before speaking and considerate of everyone's feelings. For a twelve-year-old, he was very bright and well aware of his surroundings. He didn't care much for Tomas, who had steered clear of him ever since their initial meeting.

"Do?" Melika grinned as she handed me a wad of twenties. "What else? Eat! Think of yourselves as two cows and the Big Easy as your pasture. Graze away. In New Orleans the topic of conversation at lunch is where you're going to eat for dinner. And in between eating, you can shop, shop, and shop some more. Oh, I'm sure you'll find quite a bit to do. You'll love it. I'm sure."

And boy was she right.

New Orleans was the most amazing place I had ever

seen, and now, I got the chance to get right up close.

After picking us up, Bishop showed us her place. It was just like the tarot reading parlors in Oakland, only with a more authentic feel. It was in the back of a voodoo shop, and when we arrived, there was a line waiting for her.

"Now, you know where I am. I shall be here until six and then we'll go grab a bite to eat at the Oyster House. Now, my daughter has a habit of coddling her students, but I don't share that affliction. The Oyster House is well known. Be there at six. Unless there is a dire emergency, I don't want to see your faces until then. I trust Melika gave you ample funds for a good time. Go enjoy yourselves."

We both nodded and started out of the voodoo shop when Bishop called me back and hooked me under the chin. "Large crowds like the ones you are going to encounter are filled with intense emotional energy. If you ever feel like your defenses are down, find an alley or a quiet place where you can rebuild. If that fails, you must return quickly to me here. Do you understand me?"

"Yes, ma'am."

"You are getting stronger every day, and my daughter believes in you… in your gift. She says you have powers you haven't even tapped into. Still, you are young and new to handling them. Be aware. Always aware."

"Yes, ma'am."

"Now go. Enjoy yourself, and take good care of Zack. It's always the boys who manage to find a way to screw up on their first time out."

I nodded and left.

"What did she say?" Zack asked when I returned to him on the street. There were hundreds… no, thousands of people milling about, most of them carrying beer or red punch in a plastic cup, and it wasn't even noon.

"She told me to make sure I keep my defenses up and to come back if I lose it and can't get it back up."

Zack giggled. "That's funny."

"Don't be a perv. Now, don't lose me, okay? We need to stay together."

"You're not scared, are you?"

Scared wasn't the right word. Apprehensive was more like it. Six months without a lot of people around was a blessing for me. No hassles, no emotions, no problems with foster parents or foster kids. I think I could have lived the rest of my life on the bayou.

"Not scared. Cautious."

"You ready?"

I grinned. "Let's do it."

And boy did we. We had so much fun looking in all the voodoo and tourist shops. There were so many little shops with cool things in them; everything from alligator heads to hot sauce, and we went into them all. Zack's favorite was the street performers. He couldn't stop staring at the jugglers and magicians. Maybe a little too much because when we walked away and into the next shop, he turned to me and said, "Think the juggler would be impressed with this?"

When I looked up from the map I was staring at, I saw him juggling three pieces of candy without his hands. The three pieces, manipulated by his mind, circled around each other. My mouth dropped open and I quickly looked around. "Stop!" I hissed.

That broke his concentration and the candy clattered to the floor. "What?"

Grabbing his arm, I pulled him out of the store. "What in the hell are you doing?"

"Nothing! I was just—"

"I *know* what you were you doing. Are you stupid? If Melika or Bishop ever found out, they'd kill you."

"Lighten up, Echo. I was just messin' around."

"Well, don't. She'll send you packing if she so much as suspects—"

"Okay, okay. I'm sorry. It won't happen again."

"Good. Now let's get out of here." As we turned to go, three twenty-something men stood in our way blocking the exit.

"Excuse us," I said, feeling my shield waver.

"How'd you do that, dude?" The biggest one asked. He was tall, bald, and had a tattoo of something on his neck.

"Do what?" I asked, trying to maneuver around them.

"You some sort of freak or something? We saw what you did. How'd you do it?" the shortest one took a step closer. I didn't need to lower my shield to know that this wasn't good.

"He's into magic, you know?" I said, pulling Zack closer to me. "He's not very good yet."

"Bullshit. I know what I saw."

I could feel Zack beginning to panic. That meant I was losing my shield. We were in deep dog shit and I had no idea what to do to get us out of it. If Zack panicked and used his powers, we'd really be screwed.

"I want to see you do it again. I bet Buster here twenty bucks it was real. He says it was an illusion."

Zack started to move, but I put my hand on his shoulder. If he made a move, we were never going to get out of this unscathed. I had to act before he did. "Leave us alone," I said, squeezing Zack's shoulder. *Oh God, someone help us*, I thought. I even called out for Bishop in my head. Somebody had to get us out of here before Zack did something foolish.

"Just show us what you did and you can go."

"Don't," I uttered to Zack, digging my fingers into his shoulder.

"Look, you're really beginning to piss me off," the larger one said. "Just fuckin' do it again."

That's when I felt him. That's when I released Zack's shoulder and stood a little straighter. That was when I stopped feeling afraid. We were *not* alone.

"So, which is it? The easy way or the hard way?" The short one asked.

"How about the *high*way, fellas."

Without turning around, I knew it was Tomas.

"Fuck off, Injun Joe."

Tomas put his arm around my shoulder and one around Zack's. I worked on rebuilding my shield, but I couldn't manage. I was feeling their anger, their agitation, their aggression. I could also feel Tomas' ire.

"I know it's hard to believe, gents, but the two kids here and I could drop you like that." Tomas snapped his fingers. "And not even get dirty."

The three thugs threw their heads back and laughed. "An injun, a girl and a freak could take us on? Are you fuckin' nuts?"

"You on drugs or somethin', Chief?"

To my surprise, Tomas chuckled. "Tell you what. I'm gonna give you *boys* a chance to turn around and walk away before we embarrass the hell out of you."

My heart was racing as the last remnants of my shield fell away. I had nothing to contribute to our defense and it was taking everything I had to keep up my own. I wondered what the hell Tomas was thinking by antagonizing these guys.

"You must be high, Chief, if you think—" the tallest one took one step toward us and then dropped to his knees grabbing his head in pain. The other two looked at each other before also taking a step toward us. They, too, dropped to their knees. Whatever Tomas was doing to them was causing them a whole lotta mental agony. All three were holding their heads.

"You boys oughtta lay off those Hurricanes. I hear they can give you a mighty big headache. Come on, kids. Let's get out of here. It stinks."

The three of us turned and walked away. At the corner, Tomas released us and turned to look back. "Hang on a sec."

Zack and I both turned back toward the three guys who were now attempting to get back on their feet.

"The tall guy," I said softly. I felt his intentions as clearly as if he had been holding a sign that said *I have a gun and I'm going to blow your head off with it.*

Normally, as a powerful telepath, Tomas would have been able to read his intentions far faster than I could have read his emotional state, but the attack on the three of them had obviously left Tomas weak.

"One shot, Zack," Tomas whispered. "That's all I'm giving you, and I will totally deny it to Melika if either of you snitch."

Zack looked up at Tomas, who nodded.

The big guy reached behind him and before he could move one more inch, Zack raised his arm as if he were holding a shot put, and thrust it forward. The guy flew backwards about ten feet, crashing into the side of the store. The other two looked at us, then at their friend, before deciding against pursuing any further action against us. They got up and ran, leaving their friend lying on the sidewalk.

"Nice shot," Tomas said. "Not one word about this. Don't talk to each other about it, don't even think about it. It never happened."

Zack and I could barely manage a nod. I was overwhelmed and unprepared for all of this and was beginning to lose my sense of balance. Emotions are one thing; drunken emotions fill you with this weird, hazy feeling. It's ugly and disconcerting, and I was having a real hard time focusing. "Tomas…"

"I know. Come on." Taking my arm, he pulled me into a hotel lobby. When we entered, Tomas knelt down and took my hands in his. It was the most intimate gesture we had shared.

"Can't get your shield back up?"

I shook my head, glad to be off the street and inside where there were fewer people. I was beginning to sweat from the attempt at keeping my shield up.

"No problemo. Take all the time you need." Rising, he slapped Zack on the back of the head. "You and I are going to have a little chat. Echo, you do what you've been taught to do."

"He was just—"

"Don't try to save his ass, kiddo. What he did back there put you both in danger. Not only that, if Melika found out, she'd send him packing so fast, he'd arrive home yesterday." To Zack, he said, "Showing off is *never* smart. You know better than that." To me he finished, "You get your defenses back up. Zack and I will be waiting for you over at Cafe DuMonde."

It took me about ten minutes. Then, I walked over to Cafe DuMonde and, after having my fill of the best beignets in the world, I was feeling more like myself again.

"Thank you, Tomas," I said at last.

He nodded as he sipped his coffee.

"Were you following us?"

He stuffed an entire beignet into his mouth and shook his head. "Not really. It's my job to make sure you're safe."

Zack looked over at Tomas and then at me. "He heard you. He heard you call for help. Cool, huh?"

I looked over at Tomas, who averted his gaze. "You did?"

Shrugging, he sipped more coffee. "You'd stopped blocking, so it was pretty easy to pick up your thoughts. I'm just glad I wasn't that far away. But don't worry, kiddo. Zack swears it'll never happen again, right Zack?"

Zack nodded contritely.

"Well, I'm glad you're here, Tomas. Thank you for saving us from ourselves."

Tomas rose and dropped a twenty on the table. "Next time, you might not be so lucky. Enjoy the rest of your day."

When Tomas was gone, Zack slumped down in his chair. "I coulda taken them. I didn't need *his* help."

"Once again, do you have any idea what you could have

done?"

"Yes, but—"

"But nothing. You don't have the *right* to put all of us at risk with your dumb male ego, you hear me? Haven't you heard a damn thing Melika has taught us about protecting each other? Damn it, Zack, you know better."

"All right, already. Jesus, don't you start lecturing me, too, Echo. Tomas totally busted my chops. I said I was sorry."

I finally had to just let it go and by six o'clock, we had eaten too much, shopped too much, and had too much fun. We'd even had our palms read by a woman who was no psychic, but we were curious about what she would say. My shields held up for the rest of the day, Zack finally stopped pouting, and my feet were killing me from all the walking.

My shields were still holding when I entered the Acme Oyster House, otherwise, I would have known what to expect when I walked in… but I didn't.

As I approached the table where Bishop was sitting, she looked up and gave me a little finger wave. She was talking to a woman whose back was to us. "Right on time!" Bishop said.

When the woman turned around to look at us, I stopped dead in my tracks.

It was Danica.

She had come to New Orleans.

CHAPTER 25

NO ONE HAD seen Bob or heard from him. Two more homeless were missing from the night before, but nobody trusted us enough to tell us anything more than they hadn't been heard from. That was the biggest problem with this story; a person could just go off, never to be heard from again, and be relatively safe… or they could be dead. No one knew.

Something was happening to the homeless in the Tenderloin.

The Tenderloin?

It dawned on me that maybe these disappearances weren't exclusive to the city. Maybe there were others missing from Oakland or Berkeley. *That's* what I needed to find out. Maybe if there were more elsewhere, I could get someone to listen to me. I made a mental note to check out the other places around the Bay Area that had high homeless populations.

When I woke up the next morning, it was time to face the music. I was going to lose my car, my job, and a lot of points with my best friend. Maybe if I just stayed in bed all day, no one would notice.

Two seconds later, someone noticed. I let the machine get it.

"Branson? Looks like your time is up. Bring that pink slip and the little red car by the office before noon, will you? And no hard feelings. Someone somewhere will hire you."

I groaned. Then I just lay there feeling sorry for myself for a couple of minutes before finally forcing myself out of bed.

The phone rang again. "Crap." Picking it up, I tried to sound cheery. "Good morning."

"Nice try with the voice, Echo. You okay?" It was Tomas.

"I'm fine. Please tell me you're not in town."

His answer was a slight chuckle. "You wish. Look, just tell me the truth and save us both a lot of trouble. What's going on?"

"I'm about to lose my job and my car because of a stupid bet."

"That's not what I've been picking up. There's something else."

I *hated* when he did this and he knew it. "Where are you?" It wasn't until after I left the bayou that I realized just how powerful a telepath Tomas truly was. Neither time nor distance diminished his powers if he was emotionally connected to you. No matter how strong your shield was, he was always strong enough to get around it.

"Well, yesterday, I was in upstate New York checking out a potential clairvoyant, and today, I'm in Los Angeles checking out a spoon bender. Young kid named Ryan.

Seems he's making a name for himself by performing."

"He for real?"

"Oh yeah. He's the real deal. Only problem is, he's starting to get big and people are paying attention to him."

"What are you going to do?"

"Don't know yet. He's pretty powerful."

"As strong as Zack?"

"No, but that's because he wasn't trained. If he was trained, this kid could probably be moving cars. But enough about me. You want me to catch a plane and come up there? I can be there by—"

"No. That's okay, really. I'm handling it."

"Not very well. Don't be so pigheaded."

"And don't tell me what to do." I felt as childish as I sounded. "I appreciate your concern, Tomas, but there isn't anything anyone can do for me."

"Not true. I can come up there and rattle some cages. Who's this Carter guy, anyway? Sounds like a real prick."

"Stop that."

"Well, if you won't tell me—"

"Look, I made a bet that I was right about this story, and it appears that I wasn't. So what you're getting from me is the stress about finding a new job without having a car."

"Now, that wasn't so hard, was it?"

I sighed. "Sorry. Old habits die hard." It was always the same old story with us… he wanted more than I could give, but too often tried to get it any way he could. "Are you staying in Los Angeles for a while?"

"Nope. I just came to check on the bender and report back to Mel. If you need my help, you'll have to get ahold of me the old-fashioned way."

He meant telepathically. "Why? Where are you off to?"

"Australia. I'm going on a walkabout with the Aboriginals. They have a lot to teach me and Melika thinks I deserve a vacation."

"And she thinks a walkabout is one of those?"

He chuckled again. "You know how she is."

"Well, have fun."

"If you need me—"

"I won't. But I appreciate the offer." I hung up, a little perturbed that just the sound of his voice had such a calming effect. I both loved and hated that he was always so patched into me, like some morbid eavesdropper, but nothing I had ever said to him could make him turn that part of me off in his brain. Most women would love to have a man know them as well as he knew me, but I'm not like most women and his way of knowing is simply too deep for my liking.

After showering and prettying myself up, I finally made it out of the house by fifteen after ten. Most homeless don't start moving around until well after nine, and I was determined to get to Shirley before she went back around the bend.

As I got into my car, perhaps for the last time, my cell rang. It was Jardine, and he wanted to know if I could drop by the station for a second. I agreed, since I had nothing but time anyway.

When I walked into SFPD, the place, as always, was a boundless ball of energy, but I got in to see Jardine right away. He led me to a conference room, where we sat across from each other. For a minute there, I felt like a suspect in a case. I could have read him to find out why he'd called me in, but I wouldn't. I didn't want to be like Tomas and go where I wasn't wanted. I felt people deserved my respect and their own privacy.

"I looked over your notes until four in the morning. I looked at them with a fine-toothed comb. You're right about your guys being good, because they're right on the money." Jardine slid open the folder about the bogus email. "These led me to the hotel receipts. The Redding hotel was booked over the phone. The sign-in sheet never showed anyone by that name arriving and signing in."

I nodded. "But if he never cancelled…"

"When you order from one of those online places, they charge your card then and there."

"And the email from Redding was another bogus email."

Jardine nodded. "We also ran the gas cards and none of the Galloway vehicles can make it there and back without filling up. Not one credit card receipt for anywhere near there."

"Cash?"

Jardine shrugged. "Could be, but I doubt it. This guy was heavy into the plastic and debit cards. Also, there were those emails about what a great time they had in Redding. Nothing adds up about this at all." He was shaking his head. "Not one damn thing. So… I did the only thing left open to me. I bluffed."

My heart skipped a beat. "Oh God… don't tell me."

A huge grin spread across Jardine's face. "Yep. Mrs. Galloway folded under the hostile pressure I put on her."

I almost came out of my seat. "She *confessed*?"

His grin grew. "I leaned on her pretty hard. Threw words around like fraud and prison. She sang like a canary. Poor thing. Had to be sedated shortly after the interview.

Well… er… I suppose it was more of an interrogation. I ate her lunch. Big time. By the time I got through with her, she thought I was telepathic or someth—"

I jumped up and ran to the other side of the table and hugged him. My arms got about halfway around. "Thank you so much!"

He laughed and his whole enormous body shook. "Okay, okay, everyone's looking. You want the rumor mill to start working overtime? Finn would kick my ass."

Pulling away, I straightened my clothes. "Can you tell me about it?"

"Hell, we had a deal, remember? You gave me the arrest and now I'm paying off my end of the deal. Have a seat."

I sat back down and started for my pad. My heart was going a million miles a second.

"Okay, after looking over your notes, which were great, by the way, I realized that it was time to take off the kid gloves. I buried her with a stream of information that let her know I held all the cards. She folded like a pup tent in a hurricane."

"What was the piece that nailed it?"

"The emergency raft was missing from their boat, and according to the boat guys, would have fit perfectly into the empty suitcase that was on board. She went white when I told her that we *knew* there had never been an affair and that I was going to subpoena her desktop, laptop, business files, bank records, the whole shebang. After laying out all of the charges I would be bringing against her, she coughed up the whole ugly story." He motioned to my pad. "And it's not only ugly, but movie-worthy."

I nodded and uncapped my pen. I was almost delirious.

Not only was I going to keep my car, my job, and my best friend, I was going to stick this story so far up Carter's ass, it would come out his ears. "I'm ready."

"Well, first off, there *was* an affair, but it wasn't with a woman and it wasn't online."

"He was gay?"

Jardine shrugged. "Apparently, he got tired of being in the closet, the Mrs. found out and was furious. Not about the affair, mind you, or even that it was with a man. She was furious because of how it would *look*. You know how these high society types are; more concerned with appearances than reality. Keeping the family name dirt free is what this was all about. Remember that big deal that was going down for the Galloway corporation? Well, it was with some Christian organization, and the Mrs. was worried that his little indiscretion would ruin it."

"Is it too obvious to ask why they didn't just get a divorce?"

"We'll never really understand how the super-rich operate, but Mrs. G. wasn't willing to let him smear the family name or botch the acquisition." Jardine leaned back and grinned. "But that's not the best part. The best part is that Glen Galloway was boinking the stepson of Ricardo Esteban." He waited until the name registered.

"The *son* of the President of Mexico? He was having an affair with *him*?"

Jardine nodded and leaned back. "From the looks of it, a pretty hot one, too."

Oh God, but this story was getting better and better. "I don't think I can write fast enough."

He laughed. "Apparently, they met in Mexico during a

business trip. They fell in love and continued their tryst over the phone until she found out."

"How did she find out?"

"Cell phone bill. The internet affair shit was all about paper trails. Apparently, Mr. G. bought a lot of cell phones off street kids in order to talk to his *amore,* but a couple of times, he slipped and used the cell phone from his car. I guess she discovered it by accident, and… well… the rest is history."

"So, she found out and then what?"

"Gave him no quarter. She wasn't going to be humiliated by having everyone know that her husband left her for a man. She wasn't going to have this lucrative deal fall through, and she wasn't going to allow a divorce. So… they concocted their plan to fake his death."

"And that's why there's a hundred grand missing from the account, right?"

Jardine nodded. "To start a new life in Mexico."

"I don't imagine President Esteban knows that his son is gay?"

"Bingo. She had old Galloway by the balls. Anyway, the plan was to start a paper trail, done solely by the Mrs., then fake his death, which he did. He got in the raft – with the dog, by the way – and was later picked up by Ricardo. They headed back to a life of anonymity in a small town in southern Mexico. That way, she could keep her pride, the lion's share of the money, and he got to keep his boyfriend and his beloved dog, Jack. I guess something happened when the old man fell in love, and he just wanted out. He was tired of business suits, tired of board meetings—"

"Midlife crisis, eh?" I was writing very fast and shaking

my head at the same time. What a great story this was… and it was all mine.

"Big time."

"So… she blackmailed her own husband?"

Jardine nodded. "That's what makes this story so damn good, don'tcha think?"

"I don't know what to think, Jardine. This has everything; international issues, sex, betrayal, blackmail, lies…"

"And you'll do the story justice, I'm sure." He glanced at his watch. "Look, this is gonna break soon, so you better get right on it. I'll try to keep the dogs off of it for as long as I can, but you know how that goes. I'd hate to see you scooped by Channel Seven."

I closed my pad and grinned. "So, what will happen to Mrs. Galloway?"

Jardine rose. "Hell if I know. That's entirely up to the DA. The rich live by very different rules than the rest of us, Echo. Maybe that's a follow up story you can do if she walks… which she will."

I nodded and rose also. "You don't *really* think she'll walk, do you?"

"What I think is immaterial, Echo, but off the record, my guess is she'll make a generous contribution to the Policemen's Fund, pay restitution for the wasted man hours, and weather the backlash she's going to receive from the press. Other than that, no harm, no foul."

"That's disgusting."

"That's the way it works, sport. The ultra-rich are this country's royalty."

"And what about Glen?"

"Oh, Glen will have his hands full dealing with Esteban if anyone there really cares about his gay son. I think the piece he'll have a hard time handling is the fact that he entered Mexico illegally with a fake passport. My guess is that he'll spend most of that hundred grand greasing the palms of government officials in order to escape Esteban's wrath. He'll lose some money, maybe even lose his boyfriend, but I doubt much harm will come to him."

"That's amazing."

"You've got your story, Echo."

"And then some. One last question. Why was she so fired up to get the press involved?"

"Ah, that's a good question. He couldn't simply vanish because then his board of directors couldn't appoint her the CEO for at least two years. They had to think that he was dead, because then she could step right in and take over." Jardine shook his head. "I think there's more to it than that, but her lawyer arrived and she went mute on me."

"And the dog?"

He laughed. "Is probably in love with a Chihuahua by now." Jardine grinned. "Just do me a favor, will you?"

I grinned. "The case was solved solely by you, Detective Jardine. No one needs know any differently."

He smiled the warmest smile at me. "Thank you. You have my number if you ever need anything. You're going to make a fine reporter, Echo. You did a helluva job on this case. I tip my detective's hat to you."

I started out the door, but then turned around to him once last time. "Thanks for believing in me, Darryl."

"Hey, truth be told, it wasn't me. It was that damn cousin of mine. He kept telling me to listen to you... that *he* believed in you. Those are high marks from that cop, Echo. He don't trust too many folks."

Smiling, I started out of the building and called Danica before I slid into the car I was going to keep. "Hey there."

"Just tell me this… did you hand him the pink slip or did you shove it up his ass?"

"Neither. Hold onto your hat, honey, because it doesn't get any better than this."

CHAPTER 26

I HAD NEVER been happier than I was to see Danica sitting at that table. We hugged each other tightly for a really long time. I felt like if I let go, she would vanish, so I held on until she whispered, "I can't… breathe."

Pulling away, I held her face in my hands and just stared into her eyes. "It really is you."

"Goddamn it, Jane, what have you been eating? You look fantastic!"

I laughed giddily. She laughed. We laughed together, and nothing ever felt as good as that moment. "Good food will do that to a girl."

"Ahem."

We turned, and I realized that I had completely forgotten my manners. "Oh. God. I'm sorry. Zack, this is my best friend in the world, Danica. Danica, my new buddy, Zack. I take it you've already met Bishop."

"Yep, and that big ass Native American dude who picked me up at the airport. Thomas?"

"Tomas," I corrected. I turned to Bishop. "How…" and

stopped when she raised a hand.

"*How* is hardly ever relevant or important, Echo. What matters is that Melika felt it was time for you to remember that there is a whole world outside the bayou and that you are still a member of that world. It becomes very easy to get lost down here… to become assimilated into our world. The bayou, which once felt foreign and frightening, now feels like home, but it isn't. Your home is back in California, where you will, one day, return to begin anew. We've brought your lovely friend to New Orleans to remind you of that."

"But… am I…"

Bishop motioned for us to sit. "Sit. Eat. You won't find a better po' boy anywhere in the world. Eat first, and then go to Jackson Square and find yourselves a park bench to sit on and catch up."

My eyes grew wide. "Catch up. You mean… on everything?"

Bishop leaned across the table and took my hand. "There comes a time in our lives when we must decide who to trust and who not to trust. You must always remember how vulnerable we are, as individuals and as a community. We are each responsible for the other and for the safety of both. This is your first test. Only *you* can decide if she's safe, loyal, and worthy to possess a secret that could damn us all. Only *you* know the truth about her heart."

Inhaling deeply, I looked over at Danica and nodded. She sat there, wide-eyed, wondering what in the hell we were talking about.

After six months with Melika, I knew the importance of keeping mum about our powers. As long as our gifts were still considered a thing of myth, we would remain safe. I understood that quite clearly. However, I also understood that someday, I would return to the life I had so quickly left and I would need someone who knew and understood what I was.

But at fifteen, was Danica that person? Were *we* mature enough to handle the truth of who I was and what I was becoming? At this moment, I didn't know, nor did I care. Danica had flown halfway across the country to see me, and that was all that mattered.

We ate our delicious po' boys and waved goodbye to Bishop and Zack before heading off to Jackson Square. We held hands and bounced along like sisters, barely stopping to take a breath.

"This place is *awesome*." Danica said as we walked to the Square.

"Yeah, it's pretty cool."

"Pretty cool? This place is so *way* better than any place I've ever been." Danica laughed as she threw her arms around my neck. "Damn, girl, I have missed you. You look so good, Jane... oops. I guess I should get used to calling you Echo, huh?" Danica sat down and took my hand. "Okay, *Echo*, what the fuckaroonie is going on here? Some humungous, and, might I add, gorgeous Native American dude picks me up at the airport and brings me to this old, super bizarre woman who talks in some kind of code about some kind of secret. What the hell?"

I threw my head back and laughed. "I have missed you so much!"

"No, you haven't. How could you? This place is so awesome. No wonder you've been too busy to call. I stopped waiting for you to get in touch two weeks after you left. Then, out of the blue, I get a call about coming here, and of course, I jump for it."

"Your parents?"

"Took some convincing, but they finally agreed to let me come take a look at Tulane and Xavier."

"Danica… I'm really sorry…"

"Hey, I wasn't pissed or anything. I mean, hell, you're here and I was there, and…"

"I have so much to tell you, but first, I just want to listen. Tell me all about school, about your life. Tell me everything."

I was so happy sitting there, in New Orleans, with my best friend gossiping about people as if I had never left. She told me about Todd having to get stitches, and how everyone teased him for weeks about getting his ass kicked by a girl. She told me who was dating whom and what teachers were bad. And as Danica kept talking, I tried to decide whether or not to tell her the truth. It was such a huge decision for me. I just didn't want to blow it. Melika trusted me, trusted all of us to be selective in who we told. I used to lie in bed at night wondering about the moment I revealed everything to her. Three months ago, I was sure I would tell her the first chance I got. Now… now I wasn't so sure.

"You gotta be sure, Echo."

I looked around for Tomas, but he was nowhere to be seen.

"Stop looking around, goofy girl. I'm not in Jackson Square."

"Where are you?" I thought. I have to tell you, the first

time you link up with a telepath, it feels a little schizophrenic. You can "hear" the voice in your head and it doesn't feel or sound like your own. It's quite bizarre, and though this wasn't the first time, I never quite got used to it.

"Not important. Look, if you're going to tell your friend, do it in a setting that will help her understand. She can't understand anything sitting here in New Orleans. Tell her on the bayou."

"When? How?"

"Meet Bones at his place tomorrow morning around nine. Take her to Du Monde and then take a cab to Bones' place. You'll know when you're out on the river whether it's the right time. Trust me, kiddo."

Trust him? He scared the crap out of me… out of all of us. And now, here he was, for the second time in a day popping up in my head, giving me unsolicited advice.

"Trust me, kiddo."

Turning all of my attention back to Danica, I listened attentively, asking all the right questions, wanting to be in the moment with her. She had lost weight and colored her hair. She looked really good.

We stayed up half the night cruising Bourbon Street and catching up. It was big fun and I discovered I could relax knowing that somewhere in New Orleans, Tomas was lurking, listening, reading, keeping tabs on Melika's students. I discovered that I could feel whenever he popped in and out of my mind. I decided then and there to learn more about the strengths of telepaths, because from what I'd seen on this trip, Tomas was, by far, the most powerful of all of us.

We were allowed to stay at Bishop's fine Victorian home

for the night, which was such a blast. We baked cookies and just sat and talked. She wanted to hear all about the psyche ward and the people who were now my family. We didn't get to sleep until four in the morning, and were back up at the crack of dawn to set out for Bones' place. We were never allowed to take anyone to Melika's, so I told Bones we just wanted to go out to the bayou.

"Ummm… Echo, are you serious about getting in that thing?" Danica stepped away from the boat as if it might bite her.

I chuckled. "It's okay, Dani, really. I thought exactly what you're thinking, but I know from experience that it floats. It'll take us where we want to go."

"Which is where? Where *are* we?"

"The bayou. I'm going to show you where I've really been for the last six months, and… well… to explain what's been going on with me."

Danica nodded. "Hey, I'm up for an adventure."

I grinned. "Oh, Danica, you have no idea what you're in for."

Turning to me, she grinned. "Oh yeah? Try me."

Ten minutes later, I did.

"You've been living all the way out here? You have got to be shitting me. No TV?"

I grinned. "Nope. That's why I wanted to come out here. You think I've been partying away in New Orleans, when the truth is, I've been living in a cottage out here."

"No. Damn. Way." Danica looked around the bayou all big eyed. "Here? Out here?"

"Further out, actually, but it's all the same after you get to a certain point."

"Holy shit. People can't live out here, can they?"

"Can and do. That's why I haven't called. This is the first time I've been to the city since I arrived."

"What in the hell have you been doing all this time? You can't…" and then she heard that familiar sound. "What in the hell was that?"

"Just a 'gator."

"A what? Don't screw with me, Jane! Are you telling me there are alligators in the water?"

I nodded. "But don't worry. They're not after us."

"How do you know? Maybe they're ready for breakfast." Danica was looking all around the boat.

This was the moment of truth. Since Danica trusted me enough to come out into this foreign land in this rickety boat, I needed to trust her enough with *my* truth. "I know because… because I'm not like everybody else, Dani. That's why I'm here; to learn how to handle my abilities."

"Abilities? What in the hell are you talking about?"

Inhaling deeply, I went for it. "I'm an empath, Dani. I feel people's emotions. That's what happened with Todd. It was the first time I had ever felt my—"

"Wait. You *feel* people's emotions? How cool is that?"

"Not so cool, sometimes. That's why I'm here; to learn how to use it, hide it, defend against all incoming emotions from people around me."

Danica looked around. "Are we on Candid Camera or something?"

"Dani this is serious. I have these—"

"Superpowers? You're sitting there telling me that you have the ability to feel other people's emotions? For real?"

"Yes. And Melika teaches us all out here so we can focus

on learning what we need to without going insane."

"So you go to school with Zack to learn how to be a superhero? What's the big guy?"

I didn't want to say. It was outside our code of conduct. "He's not an empath, if that's what you're asking."

"I don't really know what I'm asking, Jane. You bring me out into the middle of a fucking swamp and…" she stopped in mid-sentence and started looking frantically around. "Who the hell?"

I realized at once what was happening. *"Stop that!"* I ordered. *"You're scaring her!"*

"She'll never believe your words, kiddo, and unless you want Zack to kick her ass, there may be only one way to get her to believe."

I thought for a moment. *"Can I tell her?"*

"You're probably going to have to."

"Then let me, damn it." Reaching out, I held Danica's hand. "That voice in your head is Tomas."

Danica's mouth dropped open. "No way. That is so damn creepy."

I told Tomas to stop. He responded by telling me to call if I needed more help.

"He should be gone now."

She listened for a moment and then nodded. "Damn, Jane, what in the hell happened to you?"

"You ready to hear this now?"

She nodded. "That was so weird."

"It gets weirder, believe me. Me, Zack, and another kid called Jacob are all here to learn how to handle our powers. No, they're not superpowers like in a comic book. These are real powers genetically woven into who we are. My power allows me to pick up the emotions of others. The first time it happened was with Todd. I guess the crisis I felt coming triggered its recessive nature and I knew what he wanted."

Danica simply shook her head. "And this is no joke."

"I know this is a lot to take in, but I wanted you to know why I was here and why I hadn't been able to call you. I wanted to, but what could I say? *Hi, I know you're my best friend and all, and you saved me from going crazy, but I'm not the girl you think I am?* I'm here learning, not partying, not playing. Learning how to live a normal life… or at least semi-normal."

"So… you really *can* feel people's emotions?"

I nodded. "And apparently, lots of animals, as well, which is why I knew that 'gator had no interest in us."

"Holy shit, Jane… er… Echo. This is weird, but pretty damn cool at the same time."

"Well, that's why I'm out here in the wilderness with people I didn't know in a place that might as well have been the moon. I'm here trying to get my life together. I desperately want to be normal, Danica, and only Melika can show me how."

"Oh, this is rich. You have some sort of superpowers and now you want to be normal? Are you insane?"

We both looked at each other and laughed.

"This is serious, Dani."

"Oh, right. My best friend has just told me she knows what alligators are thinking, and I'm supposed to be serious? Come on, Jane! You have to give me a break."

"I just need you to know how serious all of this is, Dani, because telling other people would put our lives at stake. I trusted you with my life once, and now I'm trusting you with my future."

She looked over at me, her eyes locking onto mine. "If you can do what you say you can, then do it now. You'll know how much you can trust me."

I looked at her a long time before asking, "Are you sure?"

"Have I ever lied to you?"

"No."

"Ever let you down?"

"Never."

"Then do it."

So I did. I read her and knew that she would never tell, never betray me, never let me down.

She never did.

Not once.

CHAPTER 27

WHEN I FINISHED telling Carter and Wes about the outcome of my story, you could hear the proverbial pin drop. It took everything I had not to do the happy dance across Wes' desk. Instead, I maturely sat back and watched as Carter turned yellow then pale, and Wes turned red and then pink. They were a veritable rainbow. I needed no reading to know the emotions that were swirling in this room.

"Damn good work, Ms. Branson," Wes said, smiling with his mouth at me while glaring with his eyes at Carter.

"Thank you, sir."

"You've really shown me what you're made of and how damn tenacious you are. I can't begin to tell you how pleased I am that I did not have to print *another* retraction." He slowly turned to Carter, who was now green. I'm sure he was wishing that he was sitting on a cactus anywhere but here. "Carter?"

"Sir?"

"You and I will chat later about your proposed article on

the Galloways, but at this moment, I'd really like to hear you congratulate Ms. Branson's ability on her first real assignment. She sure as hell kicked your ass all over the Goddamn court. Be a man and own up."

Be a man? Ouch. This was certainly not going to endear me to Carter.

Carter inhaled deeply and slowly turned to me. "Branson…" I swear to God, he looked seasick. "You were… right. You said she was lying all along, and though I'll be damned if I know how you knew…" he shook his head. "This story is the stuff of legends. I take my hat off to you."

"Oh, you're going to do more than that for her, Ellsworth. You're going to help her mold that piece until it's golden. You will see to it that she gets whatever support she needs to get it into the AM edition. I want Jennifer on the fact checking and I don't want a stock photo of Galloway or his house. I want something fresh! Ms. Branson, nose to grindstone begins now, so don't even think about going to the bathroom until we put this baby to bed. *Capisce?*"

I grinned and nodded. "Yes, sir."

"Well? What are you sitting here for? Get going!"

I quickly rose, grabbed my notes, and started for the door. Before I reached it, I turned back. "Mr. Bentley, Carter didn't really drop the ball on this. I know it looks that way, but the truth is, I went on instinct, and I cultivated some really good sources at SFPD. I had nothing concrete until a few—"

"See that, Carter? That's called *teamwork*, pal. After everything you've said and done, she's still trying to throw you a bone. She's a *class act*, buddy, and if you weren't sitting on that Pulitzer, I'd toss you out right now." To me he said, "You're a damn fine person, Ms. Branson, and I'm betting you're going to be a helluva reporter. Now, get on it."

I left his office and wasn't three steps away before I heard him light into Carter. Pulitzer or not, Carter had nearly slammed the door on a story that was as juicy as it was exclusive; and he'd done it at the potential cost of my job. That wouldn't set well with Wes Bentley, who believed people ought to work together in a cooperative environment. It was going to be a long meeting for Carter Ellsworth.

When I got back to my desk, there were a bunch of handmade and computer-printed signs that had various forms of congratulations written on them and welcome aboard. I had finally passed muster. Apparently, Carter had been bragging about what color he was going to paint Ladybug and how I better start looking for another career, blah, blah, blah. No one liked a sore loser, but I also knew people didn't appreciate a gloating winner, either, so I was gracious even in light of the fact that he'd stooped so low. Besides, it wasn't really my style. I had my first big story right out of the gate and I wasn't going to allow petty gloating to tarnish that.

I was about two hours into my writing when Carter came up behind me. "I just want to know... no... I *need* to know how you did that. How in the hell did you know? Twice!"

I didn't look up from my computer. "I know you'd like to believe it was dumb beginner's luck, but it wasn't. I had some leads you chose to ignore. I followed those leads up. End of story."

"Leads, huh? Where in the world did you *get* leads, Branson? The only thing you had was a Goddamned missing dog."

Slowly, I turned to him, choosing my words carefully. "I have a lot of connections in this city."

"Cops hate reporters, Branson, don't you know that?"

"They may hate *you,* Carter, but I have a few buddies in blue."

"Be that as it may, your *buddies* weren't the ones who told you she was lying. You knew before. I want to know how."

Ah… there was the real question. "Let's just say I have a way of reading the truth and falsities in people. It's a little game I play, but I'm done playing with you. It's not a competition, Carter. It is what it is. This time I got the story. Maybe next time, it'll be you."

We finished my first draft before two o'clock, handed it over to our trusty fact-checking department, and then headed out the door. Carter left five minutes before I did, in a slightly better mood than when we were writing. At least the tension was gone. It's not fair to an office full of people to allow your issues to cloud the entire room. I think Carter was beginning to feel that way as well. He even managed to say 'good job' before leaving.

I was just starting to unlock Ladybug when I noticed something hanging on the antennae. Leaning over, I put my hand to my mouth and gasped.

Keys.

Lexus keys and a post-it note rolled up that said, "Never say I am not a man of my word."

"Holy crap," I muttered, sliding the keys off the antennae. I had completely forgotten.

CHAPTER 28

After Danica left the bayou, it was back to work. I spent the next six months learning more blocking and shielding techniques. Melika wanted me to be able to block naturals as well as other supers.

After Tomas' intrusion into my mind, I decided that blocking was a necessary evil. I didn't like him rooting around in my brain; I was incredibly uncomfortable with the whole notion of telepathy. It was one thing to feel what people were feeling, but to hear their thoughts and then be able to project myself into their minds?

That was a little scary even for me.

So, I asked Melika about it on our daily walk. "Tomas must be a very powerful telepath, huh?"

"Oh yes. He's quite strong. I must apologize for what happened in town. I never intended for you to find out that he was watching over you. He certainly did not have my permission to do what he did. I apologize for that."

"It was a good thing, I guess. I mean, I'm glad he was skulking around..." I stopped talking. How did Melika know about what happened in town?

"Don't worry, my girl, I am well aware of Zack's little indiscretion in the shop and have already spoken to him about it."

"Oh."

"It happens to the boys… especially TKs."

"Tomas calls them movers."

"Tomas is a snob. He doesn't believe anyone's powers are as strong as his own. Who knows? He might be right. Anyway, he was charged, as he always is, with watching over you both and he did his job. If you want to be angry with anyone, be angry with me."

"I wasn't angry. I was… taken by surprise. His voice in my head felt very…"

"Disquieting? It takes some getting used to, I know."

"It might not have been so weird if it was someone else. Tomas is so intense."

"It comes with his telepathic abilities. That's one of the pieces you'll learn while you're here; other sorts of psionic powers."

"Why do I need to know any of that?"

Melika stopped and looked hard into my eyes. "Because you are no longer responsible just for yourself, Echo. We are a family, a community who need each other; who need to be understood. Some day, you might be called upon to help someone much in the same way you've been helped. You can't do that if you know nothing."

"Useful? Melika, I can barely erect a shield."

"Now, yes, but believe me, there will come a time when you can do that and so much more. We must always look beyond the moment, beyond our own distorted sense of self.

Someday, you will need to give back. You will know when that time is right, but to *do* right, you must know how."

And so, my next set of lessons began. I came to understand how Zack could do what he did. Well, no one really knew the *exact* way it was done, but I got the general idea. Melika had to work closely with him to keep his powers in check. Because he could use energy to move things about, he thought nothing about pulling something to him that was just out of reach. She had to re-teach him how to think about his way in the world. It was fascinating, really, because TKs were more of an anomaly than telepaths or empaths, and therefore, more at risk. A TK in the hands of the wrong people could be a disaster.

Then there was Jacob. Both Zack and I found him to be the oddest ball of the bunch. I did not quite understand necromancy, and wasn't sure I ever really wanted to. Most of the time, whenever Jacob seemed like he was in a daze, I wondered if he was listening to somebody's dead grandpa or something.

Suddenly, my own powers were not as strange to me.

"Oh, the majority of this sad nation believes all the animals walked on the ark and lived to tell about it." Melika continued. "They believe that a man walked on water and raised the dead, but all of that faith is constrained by the limitations of the Bible. That segment of our society believes in miracles and money, but it cannot fathom anything outside the box. Do you know that witches exist?"

"So you say…" I remembered her mentioning it once earlier to me, but we never got around to discussing it.

She grinned. "You must remember that much of what we all do is a matter of manipulating energy. It's all about energy. There are quite a few wiccans with the same ability."

"But if people found out—"

She smiled. "Only in recent history have witches decided to hide in plain sight. Now, they write books, hold open meetings, and even advertise. They can do so because the Christian segment of our country has led people to believe that they no longer exist, that they are powerless. Isn't it ironic that the very people who burned them at the stake have made it possible for them to live in the open?" Melika chuckled, a rare event.

"No longer… then you mean…"

Melika nodded. "They went underground. Now, hundreds of years later, they have been able to resurface because of the very faith that forced them underground in the first place."

I whistled and shook my head. "Hiding in plain sight. It's brilliant."

"It's what we all do. The Bishops of this world are able to do what they do because no one believes it's the truth. This will not always be the case, mind you, but for now, we are able to go about our business because the populace is a disbelieving one."

"Then you think that someday, people *will* believe?"

"Oh yes, but believing is not the same as understanding. It is incumbent upon you to understand because there is a component to your powers we have yet to discuss."

I swallowed hard. "There is?"

"Yes, my dear. You have the unique ability to read the truth about people, and once I show you how, you will be able to know the moment you meet another one of us. You will be able to look at someone and know whether or not they are telling the truth."

I nodded, not so sure that was cool.

Melika stopped and took my hand. "No, Echo, it's very cool and incredibly important. I don't want to frighten you with this, but you are far more than empathic. Your powers are like layers of an onion and we've only removed a couple so far."

"You mean… I can do more than read emotions?"

Melika nodded. "Oh yes. Much, much, more. You, my girl, are the most powerful empath I have ever met."

CHAPTER 29

I T DIDN'T TAKE long to find Shirley. She was in the same place as when we first met. I was wary when I approached her because I didn't know how long I'd have before she lapsed back into her CIA paranoia.

Fortunately, she was on an upswing today.

"Echo? Is that you?" Shirley shielded her eyes from the sun. Cotton came over, tail wagging, eyes happy to see me. "Come take a load off."

I scratched Cotton's chin and ears before taking a seat next to Shirley on the bench. I could tell she was very much her regular self. "How are you doing, Shirl?"

"Can't complain, can't complain. Old Herb told me you came by to see me, but that I was having one of my fits."

I nodded carefully. "Fits? Is that what you call them?"

"Comes and goes with the territory dear girl. I've tried all sorts of medication, but the sad truth of the matter is that I'm a loon. Certifiable. If I wasn't living on the street, I'd be in a padded cell."

No argument from me on that one.

"It's okay, dear. I know who and what I am. Sometimes I can control it… most times I can't. Yes, I am a scryer… not a very good one, mind you, but that's what I am." Shirley pushed her wild hair away from her face. "As for the who… well… who I am has never been as important as what I am."

"And you're really a scryer, huh? Wow."

"Don't be impressed, dear. We're no better than the other paranormals. I run about sixty-forty in future events, which isn't great. But you didn't come here to talk about me and my skills, did you?"

Some scryers use tea leaves to look into the future, some actual crystal balls, others use rune stones. The problem was that a scryer couldn't tell you if the event they witnessed was past or future, nor were their visions always in chronological order. It's called having the sight, but the sight was definitely one power you couldn't control.

"Do you remember coming over to my place?"

She frowned as she thought about it and then slowly nodded. "I was trying to get to you before my fit came on, but I don't know if I was successful or not. If you're here, I suppose that means I wasn't. Perhaps we should start anew. You came to me looking for something. No… someone… Bill?"

"Bob."

"Yes, that's right. Something about people missing. You wanted my help." Snapping her fingers, Shirley jumped to her feet, scaring all three animals. "Now I remember. Someone came to me about Smiley."

"Smiley?"

"Yeah. I vaguely recall someone telling me they hadn't

seen him in a few days. You've probably seen him. He's the old black guy who holds out one of those plastic Halloween pumpkins for money."

I shook my head. "I don't think I know him."

"A real sweetheart, that one. Wouldn't hurt a fly. Autism or something."

"And he's missing?"

She nodded and reached into her bag for a corn chip that she handed to Emerald. "Problem is, no one remembers the last time they saw him."

"Who can I talk to about him?"

"Here?" she chuckled. "No one. Anyone. The sane ones will keep you there just to have your ear. The *other* type will tell you anything that comes into their heads whether it's true or not. At the moment, I'm one of the sane ones, but I'm not keeping you here with idle chatter. I could go back at any second. So… here's the best I can do for you. Smiley's people live in Oakland, off MacArthur somewhere. They're street folks and he visits them at least every other week, sometimes more. If he's not with them, and I don't believe he is, bring me something of his back. Maybe I can pick something up. Don't hold your breath, though. Like my sanity, my powers come and go, but I'm willing to give it a try."

"Is Smiley his real name?"

She shrugged. "Only his people would know. They tend to hover around High Street. I've tried to see something, but that's the hard part about being semi-sane; you're never sure when an image is the real thing or not. I'm better off scrying than I am seeing. Seeing just sends me around the bend, and I'd rather not go there."

Oh, now I was getting it. Every time she uses her powers, she goes deeper into the abyss. Melika told me once a long time ago how that happens with some of us. "But... when you do tarot readings..."

"It's all hooey. By the time I realized what was happening and why, I'd lost more than I could afford. Since then, I've only used them whenever I was desperate."

"Desperate?"

"Yes, I lost Cotton once, and panicked, so I used the sight. Times like that. Otherwise, I'd rather not. Someday, I'm gonna go out and never return."

"And there's nothing you can do to get better?"

She sighed. "No. I just learned how to enjoy the good moments and suffer through the bad. Anyway, get something of Smiley's, and let's see if we can't come up with something."

"I appreciate your help on this, Shirl."

"It's been a long time since I've met anyone like me. I know we have very different powers, Echo, but it's nice to meet one as sweet as you."

"When's the last time?"

She sighed and looked away. "I met a man once, a nasty sort of guy, a telepath, if I recall correctly. He came at me wanting something... I don't remember what it was. I do remember he was a cop, I think."

"A cop?" My gut sank. "He was a cop?"

Shirley thought about it for a moment. "Something like that. Anyway, he was the last one of us I officially met until you." She fed the bird another chip.

"Are you sure there isn't anything I can get you?"

She reached over to pet Midnight. "Maybe something

for my kids?"

"You got it. See you soon." I left Shirley and her animals and returned to Ladybug. There was one message from Danica telling me the boys were staying late and wanted me to bring a pizza. I thought pizza was the very least I could do.

My second message was from Finn, who wanted to meet for coffee. Less than half an hour later, we were sitting at a small corner table in Starbucks. He looked so good in his uniform. What is it about a man in uniform?

"You look much more relaxed than the last time I saw you. I hear congrats are in order."

"I owe you, Finn. Your cousin would never have listened to me without you."

Finn grinned. "The Samoan can be a royal pain in my ass, but he's a good cop and he was impressed with your legwork. Darryl doesn't impress easily, either."

"Well, I owe you, and not just a cup of coffee. You guys saved me. I came out of this looking pretty sweet, and it's a damn good story to boot."

"When will it be out?"

"Tomorrow morning. Because I'm a rookie, it's getting the twice over by our fact checkers and editorial staff."

"So, what now? The Bermuda Triangle? Where's Jimmy Hoffa? Who built the pyramids?"

I grinned. "I'm back on the missing homeless. So far, I have a possible six guys missing."

"Is it six now?" Finn leaned forward.

I nodded. "There's some guy named Smiley whose people are in Oakland. I'll be check—"

"Please don't tell me you're going to cruise around

Oakland at night looking for this guy?"

"Oh, Finn, it's cute of you to worry about me, but I'll be fine."

"The Tenderloin is one thing, but Oakland? There's nothing tender about it."

"I grew up there, Finn. It's only dangerous in certain areas, and I have no intention of going there. I'll be fine."

"Let me go with you."

I had to laugh. "Have you looked in the mirror lately? Everything about you screams *I'm a cop!* It screams. It doesn't whisper, it doesn't even speak loudly. No one will ever speak to me with you standing there on guard. I appreciate the offer, but I think not."

"I can wear a disguise." His eyes twinkled and I knew he was kidding around. "Then take this." Flipping open his leather holder, he pulled out a can of mace. "This stuff is the real deal, not like the crap they sell to civilians. Just make sure you're far enough away that it doesn't splash back at you." Sliding it across the table, he said, "Take it."

So I did. "You worry too much."

"A woman going into the belly of the darkest place in the Bay Area is reason to worry, don't you think? Hell, Echo, if I could outfit you with Kevlar and an automatic, I would."

"I appreciate your concern, Finn, really I do, but I'll be fine. When you grow up in Oakland, you just don't look at it the way others do. Honestly it's not that bad."

"When are you going?"

"Tonight. When my story is done."

"Take a friend then and call me when you get back. Can you at least do that? I sleep better when there aren't any damsels in distress."

I laughed and nearly spilled my coffee. "Please tell me you're not serious."

"What? You don't think you qualify as a damsel?"

"Not even remotely, but I'll call, if it'll make you sleep better." Finn actually made me shake his hand and might have made me swear a blood oath if his radio hadn't beckoned.

After we both set out on our separate ways, I headed uptown to see the boys. I stopped along the way and bought their three favorite pizzas and three liters of Coke. Of course, the boys were worth lobster tail and chateaubriand, but their tastes still lingered in the high school boy section of the food aisle.

When I arrived, Danica was in a meeting and the boys were racing their remote-controlled cars.

"Princess!" Carl said, turning his attention from the race long enough to smash his hummer into the trash can. "Are those pizzas for us? Change that Princess to Goddess!"

In a nanosecond, my hands were free and they were digging into the pizza of their choice.

"This is the very least I could do considering you guys managed to pull my fat from the fire."

"Aw hell, Princess, it's what we *do,*" Franklin said, biting a piece of pizza in half.

"Yeah. It was mondo fun, man." Roger bit his slice in half as well. "It was those emails, huh?"

I grinned. "That and so much more. Electronically, you guys developed a foolproof case. It was brilliant."

"Hey, the boss was really happy. She even gave us all a bonus." Carl motioned to the remote-controlled cars with his chin. Danica really knew how to float their boats. Most people would have wanted money or time off, but the boys didn't want either. They preferred the personalized toy here and there. Their last bonus was a voice-activated robot. I think they managed to convince Jeeves to jump from a fifth story window when they got tired of him.

"When you're a big, famous reporter on Capitol Hill, we can tell everyone we knew you when you were just a cub reporter."

Before I could reply, the intercom buzzed. "Is Echo still in there with you guys?"

"Who wants to know?" Roger winked at me.

"Don't make me come in there and kick your ass, Roger."

"I'm here," I said.

"Meeting's over. Come on back."

Rising, I finger waved to the boys. "And when you're famous for developing software that makes machine learning look like an abacus, I'll tell them I knew you when you sat around playing with toys." I left them and headed back to Danica's office.

"Clark! I am so fuckin' proud of you!" Danica came over and hugged me.

I grinned and sat on the maroon leather sofa facing a huge window overlooking the city. Danica had one of the sweetest views of anyone in California. Even the Victorian she lived in had great views out of three-fourths of the windows. "Couldn't have done it without your stable of geniuses. Thanks."

"Sure you would have. That's the beauty of you. You would have found another way; you always do. You just never give yourself enough credit."

"What good are my skills if I can never *prove* what I know? It's so damn frustrating."

"Well then, how much fun would that be? You've always risen to every challenge in your life; why should this one be any different?" Danica plopped down on the sofa with me. "So, what's your next gig?"

"I'm going to look for Bob."

"Needle in a haystack. See what I mean? You dig the hard stuff. If we lived in Nepal, you'd be climbing Mt. Everest every other week. It's the nature of your spirit, Clark."

"So?" came my very mature comeback.

"So, holler if you need help. I don't know if there's anything that the boys and I can do on this one, but they'd love to try. You're their favorite person in the whole world. You know that, don't you?"

I did.

After all… I'm an empath.

CHAPTER 30

I HAD BEEN in the bayou a year when it happened. I had successfully learned how to shield and block, which delighted everyone. Finally, they could relax; I had found my comfort zone where my powers were concerned, and it felt great.

"I couldn't be more proud of you, my girl, but now, we must step up a little."

"Step up? Melika, we've been going 24-7 for a year." I smiled as I said this. You see, I wasn't just learning about my powers. Every day for three hours, the three of us were tutored in every subject from algebra to Latin. We were drilled, tested, and really put through the wringer. Our tutor was an old Cajun professor who had taught at Xavier forever. Every day, Bones delivered Professor Mathias to our dock, and every day, he rigorously demanded excellence from us.

Still, I might have preferred his lessons over some of those Melika threw at us. One day, she decided it was time to see if I had really bought into the process.

"What would you do if that alligator over there decided to make a run at us?"

I glanced at the ten-foot beast. "Climb that tree?"

"Perhaps. But you have a power, and you're not here just to understand your powers, but to make the most of them." Melika waded into the water.

"What are you—"

"Hand me that bag."

I handed her a bag that felt like it had a bowling ball in it. When she reached into it, she pulled out a whole chicken. "Let's get his attention."

Okay, to say I was scared to death would have been an understatement. There was my mentor, waist deep in the water, about fifty feet from an alligator, waving a chicken at him.

"Mel—"

"Like martial arts, there are two main styles that can be used to defend oneself. There are hard and soft shields. You erect a hard one when you need a more solid barrier."

I gasped when the alligator slid off the bank and into the water. I stepped back, knowing that if it submerged, it would eat more than the chicken.

"Hard shielding is done by extending the energy of the psychic forces into a sort of barrier around you. In an ideal situation, the barrier would be equal strength at all points around your body, thereby protecting you from harm." Melika put the chicken back in the bag and backed away from the alligator that was now gliding across the water. I gasped even louder when the alligator came to such an abrupt halt it looked as if someone had yanked his tail. "She doesn't know what hit her nose, but she doesn't want to hit it again because it's not really solid. It's energy. Animals have an aversion to unfamiliar energies, which is why so many act so strange just before a natural disaster. They sense the change in the earth's energy."

I watched in amazement as the alligator retreated back to her bank, without either the chicken or a piece of Melika. "That was… incredible."

Melika waded back to the bank and I helped her out from the water. "That was necessary. Oftentimes, when we are faced with a threat, we don't have time to do anything more than erect hard shields. The more powerful you are, the further out you can cast a hard shield. It might take you years to cast your energy as far as I did, but you *will* learn how to create one that does more than protect you emotionally and mentally."

It was at that moment I realized I did not understand a damn thing about my abilities or the energy necessary to perform them. Energy, like that used when you turn on the light, will always remain a mystery to me. I don't know how it works. I just know that touching a switch makes a light come on.

"This is what we will be working on for the next few months. It will take more energy, both mentally and physically, and you'll be exhausted at the end of every day. It's vital to get plenty of rest at night." She turned and locked eyes with me. One of the many things I had learned from Melika in my year on the Louisiana Bayou was that, like Jacob said, she knew everything.

"I just help Zack with his homework," I said. "I guess maybe I am staying up too late."

She grinned. "Now it's time for your first lesson." She

pointed in the distance, and I saw Tomas leaning against a tree. Now, I'm not one to stereotype, but that man could walk in complete silence through the swamp and never be heard. I had no idea how long he'd been standing there.

"Why Tomas?"

"We need a third person: the attacker, as it were. He also has incredible skills in energy maintenance. I found that he often succeeds with students where I fail."

And so my next big task was to learn how to create and maintain a hard shield. Every day, we went out to different areas around the house and worked until I was a sweaty, exhausted mess. This work required a level of concentration that made my first year look like a party. I would create a shield through various distractions, like Tomas tossing pebbles at the back of my head, and then I would have to shift my energy focus to strengthen the shield and make it hard.

Hard was just a term that meant it was more capable of deflecting physical properties and not just emotional energies. For the first two weeks, I couldn't stop a feather. But around week three, I was finally able to stop a pebble. Constructing and maintaining that energy wrecked me for two whole days. Although supernaturals were able to manipulate energy, there wasn't an infinite amount of it within us, so erecting barriers against physical threats meant we had to push *our own* energy away from us. It felt like someone had drained me of my life force.

By the end of week four, I thought I was getting better at it, but I was wrong. I only had a 50-50 chance of erecting a wall strong enough to stop the pebbles. This went on for two months until I became physically exhausted and I eventually got sick.

Really, really sick.

For the first two days, I stayed in bed. Poor Zack worried nonstop about me and wouldn't even go into town. We had become very close in our year together; brother and sister close. I was now sixteen and Zack was fourteen and going through those awful growth spurts boys go through. His hands and feet looked like they belonged to someone else and his voice was all over the charts.

I had been in bed about four days when Zack came by at his usual time to visit. "How are you feeling today?"

"Getting better and better. How were your lessons?"

"Not bad. I have to work with Tomas and he just bugs the crap out of me. He thinks he's so hot."

"You have to admit, he's pretty strong."

"Yeah, so what? Someday, we'll be that strong."

I sighed. "That day feels like it's a hundred years away. I just can't seem to get this hard shield thing down. I suck."

"No, you don't. Sometimes, you just don't have the right intent."

"Intent?"

Zack nodded. "Yeah. Melika calls it focus, but it was Jacob who taught me about intent."

"What's the difference?"

For the next three days, after his own lessons, Zack came in and taught me the way he was able to manipulate the energy he often used in his telekinesis. Finally, I was beginning to get it.

"Energy is energy, Echo, but you'll never reach your full potential if you don't accept who you are. *Who* you are, Echo, not *what* you are. God gives each of us a toolbox.

Some of those toolboxes are full and some are empty. Ours are full, and the first thing we have to do is figure out what tools are in our toolbox and then pick the ones that are going to be the best defense and the more perfect offense."

"Do you think Mel will mind?"

"Nothing happens in the bayou without Melika knowing about it. She's as tied to this place as one of those big-ass trees with roots that spread for half a mile. She already knows, and she's waiting for *you* to know."

AFTER A WEEK in bed, I finally found the strength to move further than the bathroom. "Show me."

And he did.

I learned about defense shields and combat shields and how to layer them on top of each other. Shields of this sort were made and maintained by concentration and energy. Some shields required less energy and more concentration and vice versa. Zack knew a great deal more than I about something he called the human energy field or HEF.

We all have a human energy field. It varies, of course, in size, shape, and color. Everything alive has energy and this energy travels in waves and bounces off objects and other living things. Sometimes it's absorbed by the object it hits, while others bounce away. As an empath, I'm capable of absorbing that energy, reading it, and even feeling it. Since energy naturally travels outward, it's possible to gather that energy and, with proper concentration, project it more forcefully. It was this shield that Zack spent days showing me how to construct. I wish I could say I was a quick learner, but the truth is, I was a sorry student. Luckily for me, he was a very patient tutor and never got angry or frustrated. He really believed in me and this made me believe in myself, which was a good thing because I soon discovered that maybe I wasn't as slow as I thought.

IT HAPPENED ONE night when I had just retired to bed after a long, intense day of learning. Melika never mentioned anything to me about my work with Zack, but kept on with my usual lessons. Slowly, but surely, I started getting the hang of it until one day, I successfully stopped a rock. I know… big deal, right?

IT WAS A *super* big deal and I found out just how big when, around 11 o'clock at night, I heard Tomas come upstairs.

Tomas never came upstairs and it freaked me out just thinking about him creeping around. Melika had gone to help the birth of one of the women on the bayou, and wasn't supposed to return until morning. That meant she'd left Tomas in charge.

Then why was he coming upstairs now?

My palms got sweaty and my heart raced as I felt his presence in the doorway. He just stood there for what seemed like forever, then he moved into the room and I panicked. I didn't know whether I should sit up and ask him what the hell he was doing, or just lie there and pretend to be asleep. By the time I decided which, Tomas was leaning over me.

"No!" I cried, pushing my combat shield out as far as I could. The strength surprised both of us as it knocked him backward. "Get out!" I ordered, reaching over and turning the light on. "What in the hell are you doing in here?"

Tomas righted himself. He was wearing a peculiar grin.

"Jesus, Echo, it took you long enough."

"Get out!"

"Take it easy, kiddo," he said, holding his hands up in surrender. "I wasn't going to do anything."

"He's telling the truth," Zack announced from the doorway. "It was time to see if you were able to put any of your lessons to good use."

"And you passed well, my dear." It was Melika standing in the doorway. She moved into the room and sat on the bed. Taking my hand, she said, "Sometimes, we just can't learn from certain people. For whatever reason, you weren't learning the offensive shield from me or Tomas very well. This happens. So I took the chance that maybe Zack would be able to teach you what I couldn't. Apparently, he was quite successful. Well done... both of you."

And so, I had learned how to turn my energies outward in order to protect myself. I could only hope that I never had to use it.

CHAPTER 31

WHEN YOU HAVE the ability to defend yourself, you tend to be less afraid. This was the attitude I took with me to Oakland. Although I had no early memories of my childhood in Oakland, I knew I liked living in such a diverse location. Bordering Berkeley, one of this country's most bizarre and colorful cities, Oakland had its own particular flavor. There was a lot to like. There was also a lot to be cautious about. A city like this didn't get its reputation without incident, and believe me, there were many incidents happening in that city on a nightly basis.

MacArthur Boulevard is over ten miles long and runs from one end of the city to the other. I knew the areas where most of the homeless hung out and aimed my little car in that direction. I knew Oakland even better than the back of my hand and knew where I could and couldn't go. To find someone connected to Smiley I would go to either.

Leaving Ladybug in a Pizza Hut parking lot, I grabbed my purse and put the strap so it hung across my chest and not just on my shoulder. Then I put my Mickey Mouse jacket on over the top so that my purse wasn't visible or accessible. I made sure to put Finn's mace in my jacket pocket. I didn't think I would need it. I'd pretty much perfected my combat shield, but knew I had only an even chance of pulling it up under extreme stress. I had managed to do so that one night, and twice more after that, but I wasn't sure I could do it outside the bayou and hoped I wouldn't have to.

I didn't have to walk for long before I found my first homeless woman. It was just smarter and safer to approach a woman, even though a woman on the streets was seldom mentally or physically healthy.

"I'm looking for Smiley's people," I said to the woman, who looked a little like Granny on the Beverly Hillbillies. She was rail thin, had her hair pulled back in a gray bun and wore glasses too small for her face. On tiptoe, she was probably four foot eleven inches at best.

She looked me up and down. "So?"

"Do you know Smiley's people or not?"

"You a cop?"

"No."

"Child support collector?"

"No."

"IRS?"

"No." I realized the questions could go on indefinitely. "Smiley has disappeared and there are folks in San Francisco who are concerned. I'm looking for his people to see if maybe he came here."

She raised an eyebrow at me and I read exactly what she wanted: money. I pulled out a ten and held out. She reached for it, but I withdrew it. "Point me in the right direction. If I end up there, I'll come back with one just like it."

She sucked her teeth with a horrible sound. "Can't trust nobody out here, eh?"

I shook my head. "Where can I find Smiley's people?"

"They don't like folks snooping around their business, so you best tell them what it is you want and fast." Her eyes never left the money. "They hang out in an alley off of High Street. Ask for Dante. I don't know what his relation is to Smiley, but I know they're family of sorts. If Smiley hasn't been to see Dante, then he *is* missing."

I left her and drove down to High Street. I knew of a decent place to park Ladybug that kept me from having to walk too far in the belly of the beast.

"Excuse me," I said, asking the first non-drunk I came to. I tell you, there were times when I thanked my lucky stars that I was an empath. "Can you tell me where Dante hangs out?"

"Why?"

"I borrowed some money from him before he hit the skids and I'd like to pay him back." Money talks, doesn't it?

"How much money?"

"None of your business." Okay, so maybe I shouldn't have bluffed with the money. I had mace. I also had combat shields. When I felt his energy change, I leaned in a little and said, "Don't make me kick your ass in front of your friends." I took a step toward him and he backed off. Ordinarily, that would be foolish for a normal woman to do, but I am neither foolish nor normal. I knew that he did not have the ability to hurt me; he was too taken aback.

"Dante'sdownthe   streetaways.   You'llknowhimby thecrowdgathered aroundtolisten."

"Listening to him? Is he a preacher?"

"You'llsee."

"Thank you." Turning, I started down the street, stepping over trash and debris along the way. When, at last, I came to a crowd, there was a short, slim black man standing at the center of it. No one spoke except him and he appeared to be telling some kind of story.

"There I was… at the very edge of a dark…" This sounded familiar. "… I stood erect, brave, unafraid of what was to come, when suddenly there he was: Phlegyas, the boat man of the river Styx. He was nothing but a skeleton racing toward me at breakneck speed. He was on fire with excitement that he was coming to collect a new soul for torment, and he howled with a rage that pierced my soul when he realized that I was not yet dead."

I imagined he would have gone on, but a cop car whooped its siren, sending creatures of the night in all directions. When the car slid silently back onto MacArthur, Dante was gathering up his things.

"Excuse me, Dante?"

"Yes?" He turned and his face fell when he saw some little white girl.

"That was wonderful," I said. "Canto eight?" His energy changed immediately. I had recognized *Dante's Inferno* from my work with Professor Mathias.

"A fellow thespian, I take it?"

I grinned as I sent out a wave of friendliness to him. He was neither drunk nor was he on any medication. Medication greatly affects one's HEF and aura color. His was very clear. "I went to Mills," I said, as if that would explain it all.

"Ah yes. Professor LaBoskey is quite the Alighierien."

I was immediately impressed. Few knew that Alighieri was Dante's last name. "Yes, she sure was. Do you know her?" I knelt down to help him pack up his things, most of which were books.

"My oldest daughter took courses from her." He finished packing and straightened up. He was very tall, probably slightly over six feet. His salt and pepper hair was cut short. "You know my name, young lady, but I'm afraid I don't know yours."

"Echo. Echo Branson."

"Well, Miss Branson, what brings you to our gritty little corner of the world?"

"Smiley. I was wondering if you've heard from him lately."

Dante shook his head. "Haven't seen him since last week. He usually comes to visit every Sunday. He in some kind of trouble?"

"According to his friends, he's missing."

"Missing? What does *that* mean?"

Inhaling deeply, I explained. "Homeless people have been missing from the Tenderloin the last few days and I was wondering—"

He held up his hand for me to stop. "How many?"

"Smiley makes six by my count."

He nodded, but said nothing.

"I was wondering if maybe you had something of his. I know this sounds weird, but…"

"But you're going to give it to a psychic?"

"Something like that."

Dante reached into his pocket and pulled out a small

key. "I think it's to a padlock, but I'm not sure. Smiley gave it to me to hold in case he lost his other one. I trust that you'll bring it back."

I nodded, taking the key.

"Good. Then come with me."

"Where are we going?"

"Someone else needs to hear this."

When we reached *someone else*, he was a six-foot-six man wearing green fatigues and a green beret. "Yo, Dante, my man!" The guy shook Dante's hand and pulled him into an embrace. "Whatcha got here?"

Dante straightened up and turned to me. "Echo, this is Sarge. Sarge, Echo."

I extended my hand and noted the dog tags around his neck. By the wrinkles and color of his fatigues, I was guessing Vietnam vet. Gulf War and Iraq War vets leaned toward the grey or tan colored fatigues, but Vietnam vets were all about the green.

"Echo? Now *that's* a street name if I ever heard one." He shook my hand; he'd been drinking, but he wasn't drunk. Not yet. "But you ain't no street gal, so, wuss up?"

"Echo here says my nephew has been missing and that he's not the only one."

"No shit? How many?"

"Six. Maybe. It's hard to tell. One is a friend of mine. Bob. He told me about the missing men one day and the next, he was one of them." I noticed the exchange of looks between the two men. "What? What is it?"

"We're missing some, too," Sarge said softly. "Thought maybe it was jus' a coincidence."

"Are you kidding me?"

Sarge shook his head. "Five in the last week. Weird thing is, no bodies, no blood, nothin'. Just poof… gone. That happened in them jungles a lot. One minute, you're sittin' next to your buddy, the next, he's gone and you find his head a hundred yards away."

I shuddered at the intensity of his emotions, but said nothing.

"And now, Smiley might be one of them," Dante uttered.

I pulled out my pad and pen. "Can you tell me anything at all about your missing people? Maybe if I had…"

"You a reporter?"

I nodded. "Busted. But I'm here because a friend of mine is missing and I owe it to him to see if I can find him. He's a good guy."

Sarge scratched his head. "Well, there's Rayban, Boston, Lemming…"

"Lemming? When did he go missing?" Dante asked.

"Week ago. Someone found his dog walking by the lake."

"Aww, man. Who would do something to old Lemming?"

"Can you describe him for me?"

"Sure. He's short, about five-six, bald, and really fit. Looks like a body builder or something. They call him Lemming because he followed his troop into a Cong village. He was the only one to make it out alive."

"Any marks or tattoos or anything?"

They both shrugged. "Never looked that close."

"Okay. Who else?"

"Montana."

Dante groaned. "He owes me ten bucks."

"When did Montana disappear?"

"The day after Lemming's dog was found. He usually gets his coffee at Dinky Donuts, but they haven't seen him, either."

"Description?"

"Does black cowboy sound like a good description? Always wears one of them beat up straw cowboy hats."

"What else?"

"He's tall and skinny. Dark guy with a loud laugh. Chews tobacco. Fancies himself a real cowboy, fucking whack job."

"From Montana?"

"Yep."

"Who else?"

"Danny Boy."

Dante began pacing back and forth. He was becoming anxious. "Not DB. He's just a kid."

Sarge removed his battered beret and ran his hand over his hair. "I'm hoping he just got tired of playing games."

"Games?"

"Sure. Danny Boy wasn't really homeless. He's choosin' to be on the street. It's trendy and hip these days among the younger, dumber set."

I'd heard that before, so I made a mental note to do a story on it. Kids who have it all just throw it away so they can be different. It made me sick. "What does he look like?"

"White kid, brown hair, goatee, skin and bones, about yea tall. Wears one of those long black trench coat thingies."

"How old?"

"Just a kid. He doesn't even shave yet. Fifteen, maybe

sixteen."

"Anything else?"

"Smokes clove cigarettes. Yuck. Anyway, that's about all. The others I only heard about."

"So what in the Sam Hill is going on?" Dante asked.

"I haven't a clue," I said, putting my pad away. "I was hoping for some leads."

"Wish we could help, but the truth is, people come and go so quickly here."

"But we'll spread the word that somethin' is definitely goin' on."

"Yeah, but none of us will change our ways. Crap happens. You're just lucky if it doesn't happen to you."

I understood that mentality from all my years in foster care. If you weren't the one getting beaten, you were just glad it wasn't you and stepped out of the line of fire. "Okay, boys, here's my card. If you see anything, hear anything, or just want to talk, please call me. Day or night, it doesn't matter."

Dante nodded. "Will do. Right, Sarge?"

Sarge nodded slowly. "Day or night."

"You wouldn't happen to know any of their real names, would you?"

Both shook their heads. Then Sarge stopped. "Wait. I'm pretty sure Danny Boy's real name *is* Danny."

"No last name?"

"No way."

"Do you think maybe you can find out? Anything. Where he went to high school. Was he a local kid? Any nugget that might help us get the ball rolling would be great."

"We'll give it our best," Dante said. "Speaking of which, it's getting late. Sarge will walk you back to your car. He's like a free pass around here. No one will mess with you."

Fifteen minutes later, I was on my way back to the city, feeling even more disheartened than ever. Before I got back, I called Finn to let him know that I'd made it back in one piece. "And... you might be surprised to hear that there are homeless people missing here as well. Do you have any connections with OPD? Something's going on, Finn. I just know it. Anyway, I'm safe and sound. Enjoy your shift." I hung up and pressed my speed dial. If you've ever been on the Bay Bridge any time other than between three and four in the morning, you know it's a parking lot.

"Thank God! I've been worried sick about you." Danica sighed. "If you make me get a gray hair..."

"Don't be dramatic. It was Oakland, not Harlem or Watts."

"How did it go?"

I told her what I knew about the guys missing in Oakland. "I need real names."

"Real names still might not bring you much. It's not like homeless guys have websites or can be Googled."

"This one might. I need something to be able to take the PD. Without real names, no one will listen to me."

"This sounds like a job for my boys. If you can get this Billy Bob's last name..."

"It's Danny Boy."

"Well, Clark, if you can get the kid's last name, I guaran-damn-tee you my boys will get a bead on him. You know, even without a last name, they'll be able to come up with a couple hundred Danny's."

"That's a start, I guess." I looked up at the darkening sky.

"Where are you off to now?"

"Back to the paper and then I need to see Shirley."

"Ah yes… more people in high places. You're just making influential friends all over the place."

"I think she can help."

"Well, good luck with that. Call me or the boys when you have more to go on. In the meantime, I'll put them on Danny Boy."

"Thanks." I hung up. I had one story that needed a rewrite and one that could be even bigger than the last. I only hoped that I had what it took to bring it all together.

WHEN I FINISHED the final rewrite of my story, I had less than ten minutes until the end of my first real deadline. It was almost midnight and I was exhausted. Carter had slashed and diced and cut it up in tiny little pieces. I'm sure he did so with glee. It'd been a really long day and it was time to put my first story to bed. In spite of my tired bones, I felt wonderful. I loved winning and I had beaten Carter to a pulp; and that pulp was now leaning against my car.

"Please tell me you're not here to bust my chops. It's been a long day and I'm beat."

"Hey, down, girl. I was wondering if you could give a loser a ride home. I kind of have car issues."

"Fine. Get in."

"How come you're still driving this heap?"

I shrugged. "It's more my style than the Lexus. I should

give it back to you."

He laughed. "Not hardly. Do you have any idea how that would look? Like I'm not only a loser, but I renege on bets. No sir, the car is yours."

I didn't know what to say, so I just looked ahead and drove.

"I appreciate this, Branson, really I do. I know I've been kind of harsh, but…"

"Kind of? To be blunt, Carter, you've been a real prick on a stick."

He sighed. "Look, let me buy you a drink and maybe we can start fresh. You know… bygones."

This bygone agreed just because I thought a drink sounded great before bed. We went to DJ's Bar because I found parking out front and it was close by. When we went in, I ordered a greyhound and he ordered a microbrew.

"To starting over," Carter said, clinking his glass to mine. "You wrote a killer story, and I tip my hat to you."

God, this was so weird, I had to lower my shield to see if he was bullshitting me. To my surprise, he wasn't. "Thank you. You were a lot of help with that damn rewrite. Are the editors always so harsh and demanding?"

"Always."

"Well, thanks."

"That was my job; to help you craft the best story we could." Carter held up his glass again. "To a job well done."

I clinked my glass to his and thought maybe he wasn't such a jerk after all. "One thing I did while hanging around the police beat was cultivate allies. I had a hell of a lot of help making that story come to life."

"Ah… allies. Good. Good move. Me and the cops… we

don't quite get along."

"That's an understatement, Carter. They *hate* your guts. What did you do?"

"Let's just say it had to do with a police cover up I wrote a story on. Cost a lot of guys their jobs."

"Ouch. Not a good move. We need those guys."

"You might. I don't. Look, I know you think I have it out for you, but the truth is, what I hate most in the world is losing. After reading your story, I realized I'd been beaten by the better reporter. I misjudged you. You have really good instincts, and your writing isn't that bad, either. Congratulations on your first."

Okay, men are weird. Now that the bet was over, he *liked* me? He even *respected* me? Too strange for words. The weirdest part was… he *meant* it.

"You look beat, Branson. I appreciate the ride. If there's anything…"

"Actually, there is. If you were on a story about a suspected serial killer and you had a list of the possible victims, how would you best utilize the list?"

Carter toyed with the cleft in his chin. "What's on the list?"

"Just their first names."

"Hmmm. Not much to go on. I guess I'd start looking for similarities in the victims. Serials like patterns and have very predictable habits. Are they all the same sex?"

I nodded.

"Okay, then line up their physical characteristics first. Look for commonalities. Then I'd use a city map and pinpoint where they lived, where they were found, etc. You have to act like a forensic profiler and get as much detailed information on each individual as you can. Then you step back and examine the whole picture. You working on a serial killer story, Branson?"

I shook my head. "I don't think so."

"Well, be careful." He sighed. "If you scoop my next story, I'm going to have to kill you."

I nodded. "Fair enough. Is this the story about Mayor Lee and illegals?"

"Maybe."

I groaned. "That's tabloid crap, Carter. Can't you do better than that?"

"It's an election year, Branson. People want to know if our city's leader is on the up-and-up before re-electing him."

I shook my head. "Dirt is dirt."

"And your story is clean?"

I grinned. "It will be."

"Well, good luck with that."

After dropping him off, I picked up the phone to call Tomas, but remembered that he was on a walk about with the Maori or something similar. I admired Tomas' dedication to extended adventures and trying to learn new things. When I was younger, I wanted to do that myself.

And here I was.

On an adventure of sorts.

And suddenly, I was missing Tomas.

CHAPTER 32

THREE YEARS HAD come and gone in the bayou and I was such a different person than the frightened little girl who first rowed into Melika's. Some of the changes were subtle, while others were quite distinctive. Physically, I was taller, now nearly five-feet-eight. I had sprouted three inches in as many years, and I'd really filled out from all of the manual labor. My hair was well beyond my shoulders, and had changed from mousy brown to a golden honey that I actually liked.

I had taken and passed my GED. It was embarrassingly easy, but Melika and Tomas had still been proud of me. I wanted Danica there with me, but the number one rule was no naturals on the bayou. It was one thing not to have Danica, but an entirely different thing to say goodbye to Jacob, who had learned all he could from Melika and Tomas and had to go back into the real world.

He had done his best to keep a stiff upper lip during our tearful goodbye, but he failed miserably… so did I. I would miss our morning boat rides, our philosophical conversations about life and death… our fun times together. Jacob would be a good man. He would probably be one of the few of us who would bury his gift deep inside himself so he could have as normal a life as possible. I could not even imagine what life would be like as a necromancer. The dead, in my opinion, ought to be left alone, in peace, to do whatever the dead do. Jacob agreed. After all, he hadn't asked for this gift and wanted nothing to do with it. He had made friends and now he was leaving them… something each of us would eventually have to do.

When we returned from taking Jacob to the bus stop, I was surprised that Tomas was gone. He remained gone for quite a few days, and this was when Zack explained that Tomas was a hunter. One of his jobs was to seek out other supers in an effort to bring them the help they needed. Sometimes, the help was not wanted, other times, it was too late. According to Zack, Tomas was one of the best hunters in the country.

This surprised me. Hell, *Tomas* surprised me. It seemed the older I got, the longer his eyes lingered over me. I had thought that Mel saw it and sent him away to cool him off.

Twice, Tomas had returned with a super who could be helped. One was Zack. The other, Leslie, came to us at the age of thirteen, and even though she had clairvoyant powers, she was simply too temperamental to learn blocking and shielding. She was hard to be around because she just didn't want to cooperate. In the end, Melika had to send her back home, where she committed suicide less than a year later. It was a tragedy, but one I had come to understand quite well. Given the choice of seeing unwanted visions or taking the long way home, Leslie opted for the latter. No one could blame her, really. Clairvoyants possess a very different power, and unless they're highly skilled, they get bombarded with visions of past, present, and often future happenings. Of course you'd go off. Most did.

Anyway, by the end of my third year, I had begun preparing for my own insertion back into reality. It was a little scary thinking about leaving the only real home I had ever known. Melika had been the only adult in my life who'd made me feel wanted. I may have had to work my ass off, but at least I knew where I belonged, if even for a moment.

So, when it came time for me to think about college, it surprised no one that Melika invited Danica to town for a conversation about where *we* wanted to go. Prior to this visit, Danica and I talked about going to a women's college on the East Coast. We both loved the idea of ivory towers and all that tradition. So, when we met up with Bishop in New Orleans, Danica and I had no clue just how off base our plans were.

"Danica," Bishop began, leaning forward. "You have proven yourself to be a very loyal and true friend to our Echo. It's not every day that a normal of such integrity and strength of character comes into our lives, but you, my dear, are such a person. That sort of loyalty and friendship should not go unrewarded." Bishop took both of her hands. When she did, I felt a cold chill go up my spine. "And you have come to trust us as well, have you not?"

Danica nodded. "Absolutely."

"And you trust what we say as well as what we can do?"

"Yes, ma'am."

"Then, please know that I share this piece of life with

you because of all the two of you have gone through. I am giving you a gift few others on this planet ever could: the gift of time."

The chills turned into something more ominous. Something was coming and Danica wasn't ready.

"Time?"

"I want you and Echo to consider Cal or Mills College back in Oakland."

"Oakland? But we wanted to go away for college."

"And you still can, if you want. But… my dear…" Bishop ripped the band-aid off as fast as she could. "Your mother will be diagnosed with cancer while you're in college."

My breath caught as I stared first at Bishop and then at Danica. Time stood still in that moment as Danica tried to swallow what she'd just heard.

"It is a vision I've had more than once since you've been coming to New Orleans. I know it comes as a shock, but I wanted you to know so that you can remain closer to home and be with her during her last years."

The gift of time. Wow.

Danica blinked back her tears and then looked at me. I could barely manage a nod. I could barely move. "So… my mother is going to die from cancer while I'm in college?"

"I do not know precisely when she will pass, my dear, but I do know that if she passes while you're in college, it will turn your life around in ways you cannot even imagine; and none of them for the better. Believe me, Danica. You are meant to do wonderful things; great things."

I reached for Danica's hand and laid mine on top of it.

"What about Echo? She can't afford a school like Mills."

Bishop grinned. "Worry not about Echo. We will get her in there and we won't have to drop one thin dime."

Danica looked at me, her eyes filled with tears.

If Bishop was giving her the gift of more time with her mother, who was I to take that away? "Then Mills it is."

And that was it.

I don't know how Melika and Bishop were able to swing it, but both Danica and I went to Mills on academic scholarships, meaning her family would have more money for her mother's care and treatment in the years to come.

It was that moment when I realized just how far reaching the supernatural world extended, because when Melika and Bishop asked people to do something, they were never turned down. Whatever they did to get Danica and me into Mills was a Godsend because life happened just like Bishop had said. Danica's mother was diagnosed with cancer in our sophomore year, and it wasn't long before she succumbed to it. Thanks to Bishop's generosity and trust of Danica, we were there with her mother when she died; a luxury Danica might not have had without intervention; intervention I had come to count on.

CHAPTER 33

I WOKE THE next morning and flew out of bed to get my paper. I couldn't wait to see my first byline, and had actually purchased a scrapbook for all my upcoming stories.

What a geek. I know.

Ripping the rubber band off the paper, I was stunned to see that my story had made the front page. The front page! I would have done the happy dance, but then I saw it. My byline actually read Echo Branson *and* Carter Ellsworth. "That bastard!" I scanned the article quickly, no longer enamored by my own writing talents. I was furious. How in the hell did this happen?

I called Wes Bentley.

"It's a little early, Echo," his secretary informed me. "Oh, wait. I see that he has a message for you. It says for you to remember that you were apprenticing this story under Carter and so, of course, you will share the byline. Then it says…" she took a deep breath, "That you'll just have to rub your sore spot and move on to the next story. He also says, and this part is all underlined, that he will *not* have this conversation with you, so consider it concluded."

"Thanks," I said, hanging up. All that work for a shared byline? No wonder we went out for a drink. *He* had something to celebrate! What a putz. "Rub my sore spot, indeed."

After showering and rubbing my sore spot, I grabbed some day-olds from Luigi and drove Ladybug to the Lexus, then switched cars. Guilt-Be-Gone. I *earned* this, but I had no intention of keeping it. I had promised myself a long time ago that if I could ever repay George for saving my life, I would. That time was now. You don't give crumbs to someone who does that while you eat the lion's share. He deserved the best that money had to offer, and right now, I was sitting in it.

Before I started across the bay, I had one very important stop to make; a lady who might be the key to finding Bob.

"Good morning!" Shirley said when she saw me. "I take it your journey through the hinterlands of Oakland was a safe one?" Shirley patted the space on the bench next to her. "So, how did it go?"

I smiled and tossed Midnight some lox. "It went well, I think." I reached into my pocket, pulled out Smiley's key and dropped it into her palm. "This was all they had."

She stared at it as it lay in her palm. "Ah, good. Metal is a good conductor for me. Not for everyone, mind you. We're all a little bit different, but metal works nicely." Shirley gently took the key from her palm. "You've done very well." She smiled as she looked at me with her one blue eye and one green eye.

Psychometry is the fancy word for scrying and generally refers to the ability to get information about a person who belongs to the object in question. The term was coined in 1842 when an American physiologist determined that students given an empty bottle of medicine had the same reaction as if they had taken the medication. He believed all things give off an emanation that carries with it a sort of record of the activities of that object. A scryer can often play back those emanations in their mind in order to get a better idea of what the object was involved in. It was an interesting process because there's no preparation or any sort of induced trance. Psychometric impressions can come in the form of emotions, sounds, scents, tastes, or images. The visions are usually very rapid in nature and are often in no logical sequence. I knew that metal worked best because Professor Mathias had taught us that we exist in an electromagnetic world, so metal maintains a better hold on the emanations.

Looking over at Shirley, I watched her "seeing" whatever history the key held. Apparently, there was a great deal because she didn't blink as she stared at it. I sat quietly and let her work. The energy around her was palpable, and both Midnight and Cotton moved away. Only Emerald and I stayed near.

When at last she turned to me, she inhaled slowly and handed the key back to me. "There is definitely trouble afoot where Smiley is concerned, but I'm afraid that I can't uncover any of it right now."

"Damn. I was hoping…"

"Don't throw in the towel yet, my dear. I may not be able to tell you *what* happened to Smiley, but I *can* tell you what he was doing just before he disappeared." Shirley wiped her hand. "He gave the key to some older man with a historical name."

"Dante."

"Yes, that's it. The key is to a bike lock."

"A bike lock."

Shirley nodded. "It's red and is locked next to a green trash can in front of a building with a blue awning. I tried to get a better bead on where the bike is, but that's the best I could do. I'm sorry."

I remembered Carter's words about commonalities. "Was he a drinker?"

"Of course." Shirley put her hand on my leg. "Who isn't out here? Probably not all he's into, either, but if his bike is near a liquor store, he'll always know where it is and if he doesn't, he'll eventually stumble upon it."

Sighing, I rose. "Thank you."

"Wait. There's one more thing. I couldn't tell what he was doing at first, but I think… yes… I'm pretty sure he… it was such an odd image, and please remember that I am unsure of the order of things, but I believe he was kneeling down next to the bike. I don't know if he was working on it or what but he stayed down there quite a while, and did so more than once. There is something… yes… there is something *on* the bike that is important to him."

I nodded. "Red bike, green trash can, blue awning. Hell, that could be anywhere in this city."

"Could be, but isn't. Homeless people have a certain territory we feel comfortable in. Unless you have family like Smiley, you'll rarely see us on a bus or on BART. No, you can rest assured that his bike is at one of two places: near his watering hole or near a BART station. I wish I could have given you more, but that's the best this foggy mind can do."

"You did really well. Thanks."

"I want to help, Echo. I don't know what's going on, but it's not good. You know, it's hard enough being a homeless, jobless, loveless person, but being friendless… well that would push those of us with a tenuous grasp on reality right over the edge."

"Hang on a sec, will you?" Running to my car, I grabbed the day-olds and a small paper bag that I had filled. "These bagels are for you and your friends." Then I handed her the bag. "But the catnip is something I snatched from my cat. There's catnip and two cans of cat food in there… as a way of appreciating all you've done."

"Aren't you sweet?"

"Just be careful with that catnip. My cat has become an addict."

"We're all addicted to something, don't you think? Where are you off to now?"

"First, I'm going to SFPD to see if I can't get somebody to make a report."

Shirley grinned. "You're not talking to a normal, sweetheart. I know that you're going there looking for a certain somebody."

I didn't bother trying to deny it. I just laughed. Can't fool a super, can you?

I LEFT SHIRLEY and her crew and called to see if Finn was in. I knew it was too early for his shift, but some cops practically live at the station. I wasn't able to reach Finn, but they did patch me over to Jardine.

"Echo Branson, famous journalist. Great article, girl. You should be proud."

"Thank you, but I *did* have help."

"We all get by with a little help from our friends."

"A Beatles fan?"

"A Ringo fan. Somebody has to like the poor guy."

I smiled as I leaned back in the luxury seat of the Lexus. God, this car was comfortable. "What's it going to take for me to get someone to pay attention to the missing homeless?"

"We're back to that again?"

"Come on, Darryl. Something is going down out here, and you know it."

"You know, Echo, the first time you asked, I didn't really know anything about you, so I sorta blew you off."

"And now?"

"Why don't you come by and fill out a report? I can't promise you anything, but at least we can get something into the system. It's the least I could do after the Galloway case. You know, you've made me look like I'm the shit."

"Aren't you?"

He laughed. "You turned crap into gold. Echo, making me look like a star lends you a couple of favors. I owe you. You come file a report and I'll make sure someone besides me reads it."

"You're a love. Thank you."

"No problem. Want me to tell Finn you called? He sorta lights up and gets all gooey when—"

"Darryl, I don't think—"

"Well, he does, but he's kind of a scaredy cat where women are concerned."

What cop uses the term scaredy cat? "What's he afraid of?"

"What are we all afraid of? Getting hurt. Putting it on

the line only to be rejected. You know, a lot of cops don't think twice about laying their lives on the line night after night for people they don't know, but when it comes to relationships? We're a little skittish."

"Has he been hurt or something?"

"Who hasn't? Look, he'd royally kick my ass if he knew I was talking to you about this, so this is strictly off the record. The guy has the hots for you."

"He thinks you have the same problem."

Jardine laughed long and hard. "Sorry, doll, but you're not my type. I just love jerking his chain that way. Always have. Always will. He's such an easy target sometimes."

I laughed, too. Men are dumb. "Gotcha."

I WENT TO the police station to fill out the police report he wanted me to file, and as I stared at my list of possible victims, I realized that I knew very little about any of them other than Bob. And even that was a little sketchy. If I was going to be a halfway decent investigative reporter, I needed better information. I made a mental note to go back to the Tenderloin to see what I could find out about the missing men.

ONCE THE REPORT was finished, I jumped in the Lexus I was quickly falling in love with and drove back across the bay. Since it was after rush hour, the bridge flowed a little bit easier and I reached the hospital in no time at all. Time is a blur when you're sitting in the comfort of a Lexus. I almost had second thoughts. Almost. I smiled to myself.

I PARKED IN one of the doctor's parking spaces only because

of the close proximity to the door. This was the first time I had been back since the night I escaped. Well… actually… Echo Branson escaped. Jane Doe was forever left behind, never to be heard from again.

George and I had seen each other in the years since I had left, but never here. He came to the bayou at least twice a year to visit Melika and his grandmother. When I was at Mills, we had dinner together once a month and I would see him at special events on campus. Hospital orderlies don't make a lot of money, so I would always give him tickets to Mills' plays, dance performances, and athletic events. George loved it, and Mills loved him. I explained his presence in my life by calling him my uncle, and Mills being what it is, didn't bat an eye.

George came to my graduation, bringing with him the best graduation present ever; Melika, Bishop, and Zack, who had left the bayou only months before. It was more fun than I could have ever imagined, as we showed them our own inner-city bayou.

I couldn't believe how incredibly excited I was. You know how it is when you've bought someone you love the perfect gift? When you know how happy it's going to make them? George drove a Plymouth Duster that looked like it was out of date before it even came off the assembly line. It was a wreck; dog poo brown with areas of rust and an interior that looked like wild tigers had had a fight in there. It needed to be put down.

When I said that orderlies don't make much money, I meant it. But George wasn't working for money. Melika's three other sons worked comparable jobs and were also spotters in different parts of the country. One's a very powerful TK, but I never met him. In my four years on the river, he had never come home. I think there were some mother issues. I'd never met her daughter, Jasmine, because she was over in Europe, painting. Little was said about Jasmine; only that she was a fine artist with extraordinary powers. I had lain in bed many nights wondering what Melika's daughter was like. If she was anything like George, she had a heart of gold.

I took the stairs up, as I usually did in the city, and went straight to the front desk. "Hi. Can you let George know that Echo is here?"

"Certainly." The receptionist picked up a phone, briefly spoke into it, and then nodded to me. "He'll be right out."

I waited less than a minute before George came out. As usual, he was all smiles. "Echo! How are you doing, Sweetpea?" He came over and gave me one of his famous bear hugs that made my ribs crack.

"I'm employed. I've lost 5 pounds, and I think I've met a guy that I might like."

George threw his head back and laughed. "Sweetpea, he must not be all that if he came in third behind weight loss."

Grinning, I took his big hand. "Come downstairs for a minute. There's something I want to show you."

"What you got up your sleeves, girl?"

When the elevator door opened, we walked out to the parking lot. "Wait till you see this." I pointed my keys at the silver Lexus and it made that fun whooping sound.

"Holy mother of Mary, Sweetpea. You done bought yourself a beautiful car!" George walked up to the car, his face lit up and he touched it like a man touching a naked woman for the first time. "It's beautiful." Stepping up to the window, he peered in. "Ah man…"

Tears came to my eyes. He was so excited about the car that my heart felt like it would burst. "You've got to sit in her, George. Those seats are like butter."

"What are they paying you at the paper? Oh, and congratulations on your story. Is this how you paid yourself for a job well done?" George slid into the driver's seat while I eased myself into the passenger side. He was in awe.

"Oh, it's repayment, to be sure. So, what do you think? You like it?"

"Like it? Girl, this is something else." George looked all over the inside, shaking his head. "This car could be somebody's mistress, she's so damn gorgeous."

I handed him the keys. "She's not *somebody's* mistress, George. She's *yours*."

He took the keys and laughed. "Yeah, right. Her and Halle Berry."

Reaching out, I touched his thick forearm. "I'm not kidding. I won this car in a bet and I'm giving it to you… for all that you've done for me."

George opened his mouth and blinked.

"I want you to have it. You saved my life. I waited all these years to find the perfect gift that could possibly convey to you how deeply I care and how much it means to me that you reached out when I needed it most. Not one day goes by that I don't think about that Rachel girl and how close I came to ending up like her. You gave me my life. My *life*, George. This car is the very least I could do to repay you for that gift."

"But Sweetpea…"

"I already have a car. And since it was the first thing I

bought with my own money, I love it too much to part with it. But you… for as long as I've known you, you've always needed a car. Now you have one befitting the kind of man you are."

"I don't know what to say."

"Say you'll drive me to BART so I can get back to work."

And that's exactly what he did, murmuring all the way there as if he was enjoying an expensive meal. When we got to the station, he turned to me with such warmth and tenderness in his eyes. "My mama… my mama told me the first time she laid eyes on you that you were special; not just because you're a super, but because of what's in here." He pointed to my heart. "You're one special Sweetpea, girl. No matter what happens in our lives, George will always have your back."

I kissed his cheek and got out, watching with a joy I didn't think I was capable of experiencing as he drove away. It may have taken nearly ten years for me to pay him back, but I was pretty sure he thought it was well worth the wait.

I know *I* did.

CHAPTER 34

WHEN THE TIME came for me to graduate away from the bayou and from Melika, I couldn't believe that four years had gone by so quickly. I had learned so much and grown-up in ways I never imagined. Suddenly, I was eighteen and had finally gained control of my powers and learned all that Melika could teach me. Of course, that knowledge didn't make it any easier to leave the bayou and my new family.

Truth was, I was petrified of leaving. I'd fallen in love with the darkness and wetness of the river. I loved everything about it, from the clean scent to the alligators floating on the water. Once I had gotten used to the harsh realities of no electricity or plumbing, it didn't even faze me. What happens in a place like the bayou when there's no television or computers are conversation and a great deal of reading. Zack and I must have read over a thousand novels between us, and I firmly believe it was all that reading that prepared me for college. By the time I got to Mills, I had read over half the books on most of the required reading lists.

Four years in one place was also a record for me, and I couldn't picture myself going back to Oakland. I hadn't been back in the years since I'd left. Other than Danica, there wasn't anything there for me. I had sunk my roots deep into the rich soil of the Louisiana Bayou and it didn't seem fair that I had to pull them out. I just couldn't imagine what life would be like not being there; not waking up to the sounds of the birds and the gentle lapping of the water as it sloshed against the bank. I'd had a taste of how rich life could be. Maybe the best lesson I'd learned was not to settle for anything less than greatness.

"Now you know what a well-lived life looks like," Tomas said to me the day before I was to go back to Oakland. I'm pretty sure that was the moment the walls around my heart began to crack where he was concerned.

"I never knew you were so poetic."

He grinned. "There's a lot you don't know about me. I may not be as bad as you like to think, but my role here was never to be anyone's friend. I do what Mel tells me to. I go where she tells me to go, and I teach what she tells me to teach. But there's a helluva lot more to me than all of that."

"I *do* know that, Tomas, but—"

"I don't think you do, Echo. Up until your eighteenth birthday, you were just a little girl who thought that I was this big, scary Indian who crept around spying on you."

"Weren't you?"

"Yeah, but that's only a fraction of who I am and what I do here. Who I am when you're here is the guy who makes sure you stay safe, who helps you with your telepathic abilities, and who's going to miss you when you go back."

"Thank you for not calling it home. I'm not going

home."

He nodded, but said nothing.

"Home is here. I feel so much like a stupid high school kid who's getting ready to go off to college and is scared to death. Does that sound dumb?"

"Not at all. You're leaving the first real home you've ever known, but college… that's where you belong. That's the one thing I never understood about you. You've got it all going on and you don't even know it."

I think this was the first real conversation we'd ever had. "Thanks. That means a lot."

When he turned, he was wearing an odd smile on his face and I wondered if he'd managed to read my thoughts. "Echo, this place has been brighter since you arrived, and it's been a helluva lot of fun having you here."

"I'm going to miss you, too."

He laughed. "No, you won't. You'll get into Mills and begin a new life, leaving the bayou and all of its memories behind. Everyone does."

"Haven't you heard? I'm not like everyone."

"Don't I know it."

I left Melika and the bayou in one of the most heart wrenching goodbyes of my life. Saying goodbye to Zack was much harder than I anticipated as well.

Tomas refused to say goodbye to me, his see *you later, kiddo* were the last words he said when I boarded a plane back to Oakland. It stung – he hadn't called me that in a while and it felt like our friendship had be dragged backwards somehow.

It was my goodbyes to Melika and Bishop that felt like someone had reached into my chest and pulled my heart through a sieve. Oh my God, if a person could actually feel their heart breaking, that's what it felt like. Melika and I took a long walk my last day on the bayou. We shared our deepest thoughts about my time there and we talked about everything for hours on end. Her last words to me I wrote on a double-size Post-it and kept on my bathroom mirror for my daily affirmation:

"Echo, my dear girl, you are a very powerful young woman, and not just because of your innate powers. You are powerful because of who you are in here. I want you to remember this very important phrase from Confucius. *To know that what we know is what we know, and what we do not know we do not know… that is true wisdom.*"

That line resonated through my spirit and was my motto all the way through college. I took more with me to Oakland than just the lessons I had learned in Louisiana; I brought with me the entire bayou.

I may have left it, but it would never leave me.

CHAPTER 35

I WAS SITTING in traffic when my cell phone rang. It was Wes Bentley.

"Echo! I can't tell you how many calls I've received about this Galloway article. No one but you saw it coming and no one has the exclusive but us. It thrills me to get the jump on that bastard in Oakland, and I've fielded calls from the Los Angeles Times, the Sacramento Bee, and even at that sodden piece of a dirty rag that shall remain nameless. You have really hit the big time, my girl."

Oh, *now* I was his girl. "It sure looks good on the front page, Wes."

"Carter says you have a new lead you're chewing on."

Inhaling deeply, I decided that honesty was the best way to go. "Homeless people are still missing in the city and now I've discovered that they're also missing in Oakland. They're vanishing without a—"

"You're still gnawing on that bone?"

"Something is going on in the Tenderloin and—"

"Let me ask you this, Miss Branson, do you think

homeless people read our paper?"

"I… uh…"

"Well, they don't. They *aren't* our audience and as hard as it is for an idealist like you to believe, no one much gives a damn if they are disappearing or not. We are in the business of writing stories that people *care* about. What else you got?"

"I don't."

"You gotta be able to juggle more than one ball. A good reporter has a bunch of stories in the air at once. You come to me with a weak story line of homeless people missing and you really think I'm going to let you run with it? Not when there are hotter issues."

"You don't think missing human beings are important because they're not our audience? You disappoint me, Wes. They're a community, and as hard as it may be for *regular folks* to believe, they deserve the same respect and legal help as any other. They know what's going on out there. They have friends. They pull together. Just because it isn't *your* community or one that *our* pristine readership doesn't care about doesn't mean we can't *make* them care."

The line was silent on the other end.

"You're telling me that Galloway's ugly domestic issues are more important, more valid than the *lives* of other people?" I shook my head. "That's as disgusting as it is sad."

Wes cleared his throat. "You say this is happening in Oakland as well?" If there was anything that motivated Wes Bentley it was scooping the Oakland Tribune. He'd had a long-standing feud with the other managing editor for years. Rumor had it, it was either over a woman or a source.

"I've done my legwork. We're talking about at least a dozen, maybe more on both sides of the bridge. No one has seen or heard a thing. No blood, no sign of a struggle, and no bodies. These people are there one night and gone the next morning. They're just gone. I think there could be a great story here."

"All right. While this story of yours unfolds, I want you to write a series of articles putting a face to the homeless. You want our readers to *care* Miss Branson? Then *make* them care. I want a story about this community on my desk before the morning. Oh… and no mention of Oakland. Stick with *our* homeless. Do interviews, get some photos of them that will grab people's hearts. Think of this as a three or four-part series before your story breaks. You need to grab interest, put a face on the issue, warm the cockles of their Goddamn hearts, and by that time you had better have something that blows the story wide open."

The news industry has no soft side, no tenderness. You're only as good as your last good story. No one cares about what you did do or are going to do. It's all about the here and now. Unless you won one of the few prizes reserved for journalists, you're humping from one story to the next. This is an unforgiving profession where precision is vital, where research must be impeccable, and the truth is supposed to be everything. In other words, there's just not much wiggle room.

"Fine."

"You might want to check out Carter's story as well."

"And what lame story would that be?"

"Mayor Lee has been accused of hiring illegals to take care of his children."

I groaned and shook my head. Mayor Lee had been a great mayor for San Francisco, bringing about many positive changes. With the mayoral election around the corner, his opponents had been busy digging for dirt and panning for gold that simply didn't exist. Why do we throw mud on the good people and let the slimy ones slime on by?

"That's not a story, Wes, that's a witch hunt. An illegal nanny? Come on."

"Well, apparently, there are other activities that are making people suspicious."

"Like what?"

"Carter seems to think there's probably a lot of dirt under the rug."

"Carter needs to go back to school. San Franciscans love this guy. He's done so much for this city that he deserves more than being muck-raked."

Wes laughed. "What is that, Echo? Journalism 101? Don't be so naive. Just because the people *like* him doesn't mean he's a good politician. I don't care if Mayor Lee is well-liked. It's our job to churn up the crystal-clear water to see what really lies beneath it. You have to get your hands dirty in the process."

"Getting your hands dirty is very different than smearing someone's good name for the sake of journalistic revenue."

"Then perhaps you were absent that day in the journalism 101 when they told you that the bottom line is about selling papers. Selling papers is about making money. Money is what we give you for a good story. If a story on your good Mayor Lee sells papers, then that is the story we'll run with. Put your philosophic side in your briefcase and try to remember the bottom line. Good day, Miss Branson."

My profession could be really ugly. My only hope was to counter some of that ugliness with a more caring angle.

Grabbing my notes and calling in for a photographer, I headed out to do just that.

CHAPTER 36

RETURNING TO THE concrete jungle of Oakland was much harder than I thought it would be. I was more than an alligator out of the water; I was rootless. And after digging my roots for the last four years into the soft earth, it was incredibly hard to find any give at all in the cement.

Mills College had all the flavor of an East Coast University, and soon I learned to love it there. I was surprised at how easy it was to fit in and to finally be able to relax and be myself. Even four years in the bayou hadn't lightened those scars seared into me for life by the foster system. For the first six months, I kept waiting for the other shoe to drop; for someone to take me out or send me away. That fear drove me to work morning, noon, and night, much to Danica's chagrin. She was on the party circuit and loved every second of it. I don't know how she ever had time to get any of her work done, but she managed to get fairly decent grades all the same.

I missed the bayou and everyone in it very much that first year away. Oakland was just so bland compared to New

Orleans. I missed the smells, the heat, the wonderful calm that fell over the bayou at dusk. I missed the color of the food, the way the sunlight streamed through the trees, and even the way the 'gators *kerplunked* into the water. Life there was to be savored. In Oakland, life was fast food; devoured without any decorum; seldom tasted and never appreciated. I had left a place that was alive and vibrant and returned to a place that felt dark and dreary. Mills College notwithstanding, I wanted to go home.

At month three, home came to me.

I was coming from an English class when I heard him. It was the first time I was actually glad Tomas could reach me.

"Hey, Echo. Feeling homesick?"

I stopped walking and sat down. *"More than you know."*

"Oh, I think I know. Melika wouldn't let me contact you sooner. She said that would only make the homesickness worse. You hungry?"

I looked around, but couldn't see him. *"I could eat."*

"I'm in the cafeteria. I'll buy you a burger."

I practically ran there. When I saw his big frame leaning against a stone pillar, I threw my arms around him and hugged him tightly. It was the closest we'd ever gotten. "God, it's good to see you."

Tomas laughed as he pulled away. "Well, that's a first. I was a little nervous that I'd get here and be sent away before I could even unpack."

"Unpack? You're staying awhile?"

"There's a possible PK running around setting things on fire and Mel wants me to reel her in before she hurts someone."

"A PK, really?" A PK was a pyrokinetic; a fire starter.

They were the rarest of all of us. Most PKs died before puberty as a result of burning themselves up in a little kid tantrum or fit of rage. Pyros who didn't understand how to control their flames were usually consumed by them. I knew why Melika wanted to get her hands on this girl; she wanted to save her before she burned herself up.

"She's been wanting confirmation on this kid ever since she heard. She wanted to send you, but she wants you to get settled in first. I need to teach you how to hunt first and then…"

"I *know* how to spot."

"Spotting is one thing; *hunting* is an entirely different ball game." He stepped back and studied me a moment. "You are getting settled in, aren't you?"

I took his hand and led him away from the cafeteria and the gawking eyes of other women. "You don't want to eat here. There's a great rib place down the road. Where's your car?"

"Over there. The guard at the gate kept giving me the evil eye." Tomas led me to his rental car, a convertible Sebring.

"A convertible? Nice touch."

"It's Cal-i-for-nia! Hop in and take me to your rib joint."

"Where's this PK?"

"Santa Cruz. I'll buzz down there in the morning to check her out."

"How long are you staying?"

Tomas looked over at me and grinned. "You missed me."

I smacked his arm. "So?"

"Being homesick is a natural response, Echo. There's no place on earth like the bayou. We haven't forgotten you. It takes a while to assimilate back into our old lives. You just have to give it time."

"How much time? I feel like a prisoner in my own life. Everywhere I turn, I see things I don't understand. I have to work daily on keeping my shield up because there are so many negative emotions around. Take that left."

"Don't look backwards. That's the kiss of death. You need to remember the lessons you learned and apply them here."

I grinned. "Take that right. You sound like Melika."

"I should. She and I have been doing this gig a long time, and she's usually one hundred percent correct one hundred percent of the time."

"That's it over there." I pointed to a small corner cafe. Tomas pulled in, turned the car off and then smiled at me. "Look, I know this is hard. Maybe it would help to know…" he reached out. In that singular moment, when his hands touched mine, he took my breath away. I never knew… never suspected… but there it was as clear as if he had said it.

Tomas loved me.

"Big."

"*Oh*," I said as he tightened his grip.

Then he smiled in a way that I had never seen before. It was warm and soft and changed the shape of his face. That smile made his eyes sparkle and it was the first time I noticed the yellow flecks in them.

"Didn't know?"

I nodded. "I… uh…" I was speechless.

His grin slipped a little. "I know. It kind of crept up on me this past year or so, then hit like a freight train. I fought it for a long time; you were seventeen and the four-year gap means a lot at our age. But also because… because I just figured it was a passing thing; that once you were gone, I'd be able to get my feelings under control. I fought it hard, Echo, and sometimes I acted like a jerk, just hoping it would go away. I had to work double time to keep you from reading me, from seeing how much I care."

I swallowed hard and pulled away. "Does Melika know?" Then I held my hands up. "Of course she does. That's why she kept sending you away."

Tomas nodded and sighed. "Nothing I've done in the last three months has been able to change how I feel. Even with new blood to work with, you're always there. Always."

His emotions were so powerful I nearly edged further away.

"Melika also thought it would dissipate in time, and when it didn't, she said I could come here and… and let you know how I felt. She said you were a big girl now, and capable of making your own decisions."

I smiled. That was so typical of Melika. "I miss her so much."

"I know. She misses you, too; more than she'd ever admit. You were one of her very favorites, Echo. Are. You still are. The place has been really quiet without you."

"This is so weird. I thought…"

"That I hated you? Yeah, I know. I had to do *something* to make you keep your distance. You were fourteen when you came to us for God's sake!"

"Then why were you so mean to Zack?"

"Because he got to spend time with you, see a side of you I never did. He *got* you in ways I never could, and I wanted to strangle him. You took my breath away, but he got to be close to you. I didn't want to feel this way, but every time I was gone, I couldn't wait to get back to you… to see you again. I knew that I was in serious trouble."

"Because of my age?"

"Because you would have to leave some day." He blinked several times. "So, I bided my time waiting for you to go back to California so I could return to my evil ways." Tomas shook his head. "You may have gone, but you never left me."

"So you came today."

He shook his head again. "I've been here a month. Mel always sends me for a check up to make sure everything goes smoothly."

"I had no idea."

"You weren't supposed to. That's not how it works. But when I saw you… I knew it wasn't over for me. I couldn't leave here without letting you know how I felt about you."

I swallowed hard, but didn't know what to say.

"It's okay, kiddo, really. I don't expect you to suddenly fall madly in love with me or gush on about your feelings. I know how I've been. I just wanted you to know…"

I had never seen him vulnerable before and my heart pounded as I absorbed some of that vulnerability. "Tomas, to be honest, I don't know *how* I feel. For so long, you were a big, scary telepath lurking around the shadows like some demon. There was one time when you stopped being so scary and that was when I looked at your ass and thought you had a great one."

We both laughed and I think that was what finally broke my shield. I *did* feel something for Tomas, but I didn't know what it was.

After all, I was nineteen and had never been in love. Hell, at nineteen, I was still a virgin. "Maybe we could just spend some time getting to know each other as people rather than as supers. You know, take some time... see where this leads us?"

His face broke into a grin. "I'd like that. I'd like that a lot."

CHAPTER 37

"WHY DON'T YOU just use stock photos of homeless people? I've got bigger fish to shoot." Jeff Simmons was one of the best photographers at the paper. He and I took a journalism course together at Cal and he had some of the best eyes in the business.

"I don't want stocks, Jeff. I need one really powerful image that will make San Franciscans care… *really* care."

"Gotcha."

"But first, I need your drawing expertise."

"Drawing? What the hell for?"

"I need something that's in someone's head. Just go with me on this."

We walked to the park and I had him wait a little behind me to make sure that Shirley wasn't having one of her moments. "Hi there," I said to Cotton as he came to greet me. "How's my favorite dog?" I reached into my pocket and pulled out a rawhide chew.

"You'll spoil that dog."

I looked over at Shirley and found her smiling. "How

are you doing today?"

"Depends. Did you happen to bring *me* any doggie treats?"

Grinning, I reached into my other pocket and pulled out a couple of candy bars. "Will these do?"

A huge smile spread across her face. "Sweets from a sweetie, eh? Have a seat next to an old girl. What about your string bean friend over there?" Shirley looked over my shoulder. "Come on over here, String Bean. If the dog barks, you can just back your skinny ass up and wait until me and Echo have finished chatting."

I looked over at Jeff, who was walking toward Cotton. "I'm a dog person, ma'am," Jeff explained, holding one hand out for Cotton to sniff. "They love me." It appeared he was right because Cotton sniffed his hand before wagging his long tail. "Cool dog. I've never seen one so white." Jeff wandered over and extended his hand to Shirley. "String Bean," he said, taking her hand.

Shirley laughed. "I'm Shirley. That's Cotton, Midnight, and Emerald. You came here to take pictures, right?"

He nodded. "And to draw."

"What I need for you to describe is the image you got of the bike and the surrounding areas," I explained to Shirley. "He'll draw a picture so that I have something better to go on."

Shirley nodded. "You just sit here next to old Shirley, String Bean, and listen carefully."

IN LESS THAN a half an hour, Jeff had drawn a great sketch of a red bike with a blue awning and a green sign. He'd been very patient with her, and together, the two of them managed to create quite a usable drawing.

"Yep, String Bean, you got it. That's exactly what I saw. Well met, young man. Are you sure you don't want a future as a police artist? You're quite good, actually. Where's your camera?"

Jeff looked over at me and I nodded. "It's back at the car. Echo wanted to make sure it was okay with you first."

"Of course it's okay. Look at these animals. Their faces were made to be photographed. Go on now and fetch your camera."

I tossed Jeff my keys as he jogged away.

"You attract good people to you, my dear. Do you have any idea what a wonderful gift that is? Do you think it's a coincidence? As you've probably learned by now, nothing that happens in this life is a coincidence. People are drawn to you; some, because of your abilities, others because of your character. Take none for granted."

"I won't."

She patted Cotton's head. "String Bean's a good one, but he doesn't know it. People misread him and therefore do not understand him. If you understand him he will be the kind of friend who always has your back. Friends like that must be cherished." Shirley closed her eyes like she was meditating. "The first favor he asks of you... be sure to fill."

"What—"

She shook her head and opened her eyes. "Just be sure to do it. That is all I can tell you right now. Just do it."

I nodded as Jeff came jogging back, camera in hand.

"Okay, I've got the black-and-white film in this dinosaur because it takes awesome shots." Jeff held up an aged Nikon. "Digital just can't touch this baby."

Midnight rose and stretched as if she was bored silly.

I watched Jeff as he clicked away, moving Cotton here and there. Cotton was easier to manipulate than Midnight, who wanted nothing to do with any of this. Typical. Cats only did whatever they wanted, but Jeff seemed to get her to do his bidding as only a great photographer can. When we were done, we said goodbye to Shirley and the animals and out of the corner of my eye, I caught Jeff handing Shirley something.

"What did you give her?" I asked, fearful he might have insulted her by giving her money.

"I gave her my card and told her if she ever wanted me to do professional portraits of her family of pets that I would do it for free."

I glanced over at him. "I didn't know you were such a softy."

"I'm not. But I know good shots when I see them and those two pets acted like they knew exactly what was going on. It was kinda spooky."

"Well, I appreciate it."

"So, what's that drawing all about?"

"It's just a place I'm trying to find."

"Want some help?"

It wasn't a matter of *wanting* help. I really *needed* help. "Sure."

"Who do you think sees everything that goes on in this city? Who has eyes everywhere?"

I grinned. "Photographers?"

"Ding! Ding! Ding! Give the girl a gold star! I'll scan this baby with one simple caption: Fifty bucks to the first shooter who can tell me where it is within the next 12 hours."

"Are you serious?"

"You got a fifty?"

"No, but I have three twenties."

"Good enough. Oh, and one more thing. Is Shirley… not all there?"

I thought long and hard before I answered. "I think we're all a little zany sometimes, don't you, String Bean?"

Jeff laughed. "I've never had a nickname before."

"Well you do now, my friend."

Jeff nodded and sighed. "I just can't get over those animals. Wait until you see the shots, Echo. They'll get somebody's attention."

And he was right.

CHAPTER 38

TOMAS AND I didn't wind up in bed together that first night, or even the second or third. He stayed for ten days and we spent the first five just getting to know each other. We stayed that first night in his hotel room laughing about all the things that happened in the bayou. We hung out in Jack London Square eating, walking, laughing, and reliving our time in the bayou. Once in a while, I'd slip my arm through his, but other than that, he made no move that might be construed as sexual or even intimate. He was the perfect gentleman, which was important to me because I was the perfect virgin and not a little intimidated by the prospect of going to bed with him.

Okay, okay, so I was a 19-year-old virgin. I'm quite sure I wasn't the only one. Not every teenage girl gets laid in high school. Besides, who was around to even be interested in me? Jacob Marley? Zack? Bones? I hardly think so. And what about time? No time plus no guys pretty much equals a big fat zero in the romance department. Even if there *had* been even a little bit of either, there was still something that stood in my way: my powers.

As an empath, I had one of two choices during a romantic interlude; I could keep my shields up and not experience any emotional exchange or I could lower them completely and feel every single emotional truth. I was afraid of Tomas' truth. Imagine, thinking that sex with a guy was this warm, loving, intimate moment, but suddenly you feel his emotions only to discover his overriding emotion was carnivorous lust? I was scared to death that that might happen to me. I mean, what then? Most women believe what's going on is a shared emotional experience. What if you could *know* what your partner was experiencing in bed and you found out it had nothing to do with love or intimacy and everything to do with getting off? See what I mean? How incredibly bummed out would you be if he was all about the physical act while you were in some emotional swoon?

Ouch.

OF COURSE, THERE was one other option: sex with another super who could block. That option was quickly becoming a reality the longer we spent time getting to know each other. I was having the time of my life… and I was beginning to feel very deeply for this man who had been both my hero and the bane of my existence rolled into one.

We were taking a walk around the lake one day when Tomas took my hands in his. "I think now is the time to be brave. Now is the time to let go of any fear and really live life on the edge. And you know why? Because you are amazing. You are bright, confident, funny, and caring. You're the complete package, Echo. Maybe now's the time for you to finally let someone in."

"That someone being you?" I said, smiling.

"In all honesty I just want you to be happy. If that happiness includes me... well... then I'm a really lucky man."

A really lucky man? Did I even *know* this guy? So much about how he had been towards me since he arrived had surprised the hell out of me. He was no longer the distant, brooding man that I had never understood or much liked. This man was displaying a kind gentleness and an insightfulness that shocked me. Clearly, there was more to him that even my powers could pick up. On one of our walks he had explained to me why he had followed me and Zack into New Orleans that day. He said he loved me even then.

"I never had a clue."

"Because Melika threatened me within an inch of my life. She would have strung me up if I so much as made a move. Besides, and more to the point, you were a girl... not a woman. No matter how much you wanted us to treat you like one. I may be powerful, but Mel..." he shook his head... "You have no idea."

"Is *she* why you don't have anyone? I mean, does she forbid it?"

"Hell no. I don't have a girlfriend because I love living in the bayou. I love helping Melika with the newbs. It's what I do best. I can't imagine giving it up... even for love."

Gulp. There was that word again.

"Don't worry. I'm not asking for a commitment or rose petals or anything lasting. I just want you to know how important you are to me. I didn't... I don't want you going out into the world not knowing how much you are loved. And I do love you."

We walked a little more in silence and I realized that this man… this man who had traveled all this way to reveal feelings he had kept under lock and key for over five years was probably the one person who understood me the most. That revelation surprised the hell out of me. I thought Danica was the only one who really got me; but I was wrong. She was my best friend, of course, but she wasn't a super. She couldn't relate to much of what I had experienced.

But Tomas could.

And did.

CHAPTER 39

I WAS MEETING Finn for dinner shortly after I finished the first installment of my series "Putting a Face on the Homeless Community." I liked the article and thought the story a good one. It would make people who had a heart care.

"Hey there," Finn said, rising when I approached the booth. And I thought chivalry was dead. "Great story. You nailed the Galloways good."

I grinned. Damn he looked good. I'd never seen him in street clothes and he was even hotter than when he was wearing his tight uniform. He had on a black turtleneck, light blue jeans, and Doc Marten boots. He used just a hint of cologne, and there was a little gel in his hair. Can you say GQ? Yummy.

"Thank you. Thanks to you and Jardine, I was able to crank out one hell of a first story. I'm practically a hero at the paper."

"I'm glad. You deserved that story, Echo. Making the department look good is not an easy task."

"Why is that?"

He shrugged. "Off the record?"

I grinned. "Let's just assume that everything between us is always off the record, okay? Unless my little pad is out, it will just be between you and me. Deal?"

"Deal. Now, where was I? Oh yeah. Look, cops make a lot of mistakes. We don't get nearly the training we really need, and it's mostly on the job training anyway. It's easy to find our faults because they're usually glaring."

"I don't see any. From where I'm sitting, you're looking pretty good." *Oh God, did I just say that?*

He grinned and there were those dimples. "Glad to hear it." He perused the menu and then we ordered. "It's nice to have the night off, but even nicer to have someone to share it with." He leaned forward. "So, let's not talk about our jobs. What is it you do when you're not being Lois Lane?"

I smiled at the reference. First I was Clark Kent and now Lois Lane. Interesting.

We spent the entire dinner talking about our hobbies, our passions, our dreams. When he asked about my childhood, I got a little jumpy, as I usually do. How much do you tell someone about a past you have virtually no memory of? My teen foster-child days were sad and pathetic, so I never spoke about those times. I couldn't very well tell him that I'd spent time in a mental hospital. *That* was a conversation stopper to be sure. And of course, what could I say about my time on the bayou?

Absolutely nothing.

So, I put as best a spin on any good parts that I could and called it a day.

Fortunately for me, Finn wasn't interested so much in

my past as he was in my present, and for that, I was grateful. He loved that I lived alone with a three-legged stoner cat. He owned a boxer named Bailey, and even carried pictures of her in his wallet.

Can you say *how damn cute is that*?

After dinner, we strolled down to Fishermen's Wharf to walk off our expensive dinner.

"Okay, I know we weren't going to talk about our jobs, but…"

Finn laughed. "Can't stand it anymore, can you?" He glanced at his watch. "I was wondering how long you'd hold out. Okay, Lois, go ahead."

I threaded my arm through his as we walked. "I still have my list of missing homeless people from both Oakland and the Tenderloin, but I don't know what to do with it to make it work for me. I mean… I have a list. I know I should be looking for similarities…"

He laughed. "And who told you that? Jardine?"

"No. Carter."

"Ellsworth? You two on good terms now?"

"Something like that. Call it an uneasy truce."

"Well… I hate to say that that cretin is right, but he is. Tell me more about your list."

"It's just street names and in each case, what little I know about each of them."

Finn nodded. "Can I see it?"

I handed it to him.

He looked at it a moment. "Pretty good. Have you found any connections other than they're all homeless men, they drink or have an addiction and some, not all, are vets?"

I shook my head. "Just that."

We walked over to a bench, sat down and he held the list up for us both to see. "Let's see what the two of us can do with this."

I sat next to him and studied the list, scooting closer. I really liked having Walt Finn in my corner. I wondered how much longer it would be before I found him in my bed.

CHAPTER 40

WHAT WE FORGET, when we leave a place, is that life there still charges ahead, and Danica was no exception. When she came to visit twice a year on the bayou, it was just the two of us on my turf on my terms. Even though I mentally understood that her life still went on, I never felt it in my heart until I saw her life in Oakland and Berkeley. It seemed like everyone knew her; everyone liked her, and her social calendar was always full. Always. I wasn't used to being fourth or fifth man on the totem pole, but what did I expect? Of course her life went on while I was in the bayou. Of course she was well-liked and popular; she was a great person. Still... to know this in the vacuum of the bayou and to see it happening were two different things. A lot had happened in my absence. A whole lot.

First off, Danica had shown an incredible aptitude in computer programming in her junior year in high school, and I was surprised to learn that she was allowed to take advanced courses in computer science at Cal. This, of course, opened doors for her and gave her ins to social circles well out of reach of most high school students.

As she got better and better at computer programming, the right people started to take notice. When computer viruses sprung up like wildfires, she started working on a piece of software that would one day make her rich and give her the freedom to start her own company.

That day came sooner than either of us expected, and so her path was determined long before we even graduated. Like Bishop had said, she was destined for great things. It was strange to see how she and her life had changed so drastically. Computer geeks are a breed apart from the rest of us. They speak a different language, they see the world through a different pair of glasses. Their world is a four foot-by-four-foot space with a flat monitor in front of their faces. It couldn't have been more different from my nature-driven world, which was why we weren't nearly as close in Oakland as we had been in the bayou. While I craved fresh air, deep conversation, and sunlight, Danica loved the solitude and isolation of a computer cubicle. Her world consisted of ones and zeros. Mine consisted of trying to fit back into a life I had left behind. And I was still feeling left behind.

I guess that was why seeing Tomas had been so important to me. As much as I loved Danica, she had her own gig going. She had no time for anyone. She and some nerds were developing a computer game that was supposed to be revolutionary, and so she ate, slept, and drank at the computer lab. Danica wasn't interested in the guys, no matter how smart, unless they had computer skills better than hers... and that was a tough row to hoe.

In the end, I was feeling left out, so having someone there who put me first was just what I needed. Maybe it just felt good to be held, to be comforted, and to be understood. Maybe somewhere deep down inside, I returned his affections more than I let myself admit, and before I could stop myself, I let everything between us get out of hand and just like that, I was no longer a virgin and no longer alone.

For the moment.

I think I was just too naive or just plain stupid to see where this was going: nowhere, fast. It was nobody's fault, really. Tomas and I were simply geographically incompatible, so I'm not sure what I was expecting: for him to stay in Oakland? Hadn't he made it crystal clear that the bayou was his home? He would have been like a fish out of water. Even with empathic powers, I had failed to actually *hear* him when he told me that not even love could move him from Louisiana.

"My powers know no distance, you know. We don't even need a phone. How cool is that?"

How cool is that? Not very, but I was a fool. In my need to reconnect with the bayou, I had made a huge mistake of hooking up with someone far more dangerous than any swamp alligator. Yes, Tomas cared for me, and maybe he did really love me, but I wasn't ready for the kind of relationship he was proposing. I didn't want long distance. I didn't want a phone relationship.

It was the iceberg approaching the Titanic.

Tomas stayed for three wonderful weeks; you know those first three crazy I-can't-get-enough-of-you weeks that every relationship experiences? The hot and sexy kind where you exist on nothing but pure adrenaline? I wonder how many women in the world get suckered into believing that there's something more beyond those three weeks.

I was one of those suckers.

At the end of three weeks Melika called him home. He didn't want to go, but when Melika calls you don't diddle around. You go. And when he left, he took a piece of my heart with him.

Unfortunately for me, one piece wasn't enough for him; long-distance wasn't enough, and my reliance on him simply wasn't enough. I eventually grew up. What had happened between me and Tomas had settled me down and given me the confidence to go on and give my new life a real shot. Before he came, I had just gone through the motions; but after he left, I turned one hundred percent of my attention to making Oakland and Mills College work for me.

It may have worked for me, but it didn't set well with Tomas. He sensed that I was so happy because there was someone else in my life… funny thing was… he was right, but it wasn't what he thought.

The someone else was me.

After being a nomadic foster child and then a 24-7-365 student of the bayou, I realized after he left that I had no idea who I was. Oh sure, I was an empath, but that was about power and skill not character and soul. I was lost because I didn't know anything about *me*. Once I started to learn who I was, my life at Mills caught fire. My grades improved, my social life opened up, and I was finally happy.

And this threatened him. I found that our mental connection was becoming more intrusive than supportive and I started resenting it. I started resenting *him* and his listening in on my life, and he resented me for being so happy without him. In the end, I had to break it off with him and bolster my shields and blocks to keep him from reading me and spying on my life.

It saddened me that this was how it ended up, but we hadn't really given ourselves any other choice. He was there and I was here and that was all she wrote. Tomas was pretty angry when I broke it off because he never saw it coming. He assumed I was completely open for him to read, but I had learned a lot more from Melika than he realized. He said some really hurtful things, but my mind was made up. I needed to learn to love myself before getting that deeply involved with anybody, least of all a telepath. I hoped he would understand.

He didn't.

It took him almost four years to get over it, and almost two years before he would speak to me again. We managed to get beyond the hurt and pain, but it was pretty obvious to us both that he was in love with me. So, we went our own ways; I dove into my studies and he dove into his, which was what took him to places like Australia; he loved learning about other people's powers. He became a student of the supernatural and I became a student of the truth. We existed under a tenuous truce and every now and then, he would pop in to check up on me and my life. We settled into an uneasy friendship that was probably less fulfilling to him than it was to me. I loved him, after all, but not with the depth and intensity that he'd loved me. It was best that we had broken up.

It just took a while to convince him, and even then, I'm not so sure he bought it.

CHAPTER 41

I WAITED UNTIL after ten in the morning before calling Danica.

"Hey, Clark. How's Metropolis' greatest reporter?"

"Good. Any plans for tonight?"

"Why? Are we super sleuthing again? You know how I love sneaking around in the dark and spying on people."

I grinned. Once I had realized that we hadn't really grown apart, I got to know Danica on her terms. Seeing her in her own environment with a fresh pair of eyes probably saved our friendship. I hate to say it, but I owed that epiphany to Tomas. Isn't it amazing what seeing clearly can do for you? One might imagine that I could see a lot about her because of my abilities, but I had promised Danica that I would never read her unless she specifically asked.

"The sad thing is I know you really dig sneaking around in the dark, but what about sneaking around in the dark Tenderloin?"

"Oh Clark, heart be still. Not another lovely junket into the underbelly of the city. Damn, are you getting any of this down? You know, I say some pretty quotable lines, you know?"

"Aren't you in a mood? What happened?"

"We sold the boys' newest computer game to Epic Studios for a butt load of money and a movie option."

"They option computer games for movies now?"

"Oh, Clark, you are a technological retard. You really need to get out more. Of course they option games. Don't you ever go to the movies? Haven't you ever heard of Lara Croft?"

"Lara who?"

"Never mind. Geez, you *are* out of the pop culture loop. Do you ever go to the movies?"

"Yes, but not to watch movies that twelve-year-old boys watch."

"Then you're missing out, Clark. Those twelve to twenty-five-year-old boys make momma money. I'll not have you denigrating my customer base."

"Fine. Congratulations on another success... momma."

She chuckled. "They're already talking about a spin-off from the original game and everything. We are going to make a bundle. But you want to know the best part? They're willing to package our educational app with it."

"Excellent."

"Yeah, it's a good start for a great product and a new market. Carl has got a great series for new readers that he's working on. Blows *Hooked on Phonics* to pieces. It's exciting. Anyway, back to you. Do you need some muscle for the trip into the dark expanse of—"

"Please... no more quotable lines. Yes, I need a backup. We're trying to find out more about these missing guys."

"Sounds like this could take all night. I'll wear my high tops and bring plenty of mace. Should I bring energy food in case we need it?"

I laughed. It was always about food with her. "Sure. Bring sweets too. Only you could make a picnic out of a job. Meet me at my place around ten."

"You'll know it's me. I'll be wearing all black and smelling of Coco Chanel."

"Nerd." I hung up, smiling. As I was feeding Tripod, the phone rang.

"Hey Echo, it's Darryl Jardine. You got a minute?"

"For you, I have ten."

"Thanks. Look, I was just thinking about what you said about nobody listening to you and I wondered if you've tried going to the Mayor about this."

"The Mayor? It never dawned on me to go that high up."

"Well, he's looking at reelection and, like it or not, he has a homeless population that needs tending to. Who knows? You might just give him a cause to hang his hat on."

"Have you ever met him?"

"Of course. He is a regular guy and I think he truly cares about this city of ours. If *he* can't get the police to care, nobody can. The brass really like him. The guy is full of integrity."

We chatted a little more before hanging up. I hadn't thought about the Mayor, but maybe he would find my information interesting enough to get the police department off its ass. At this point, I needed all the help I could get. I wanted to find Bob.

After packing up my gear and my notes, I threw another

can of tuna at the cat, who acted like I hadn't fed him in a month. Then I headed to my car. I was almost in Ladybug when I saw a white dog running toward me. I knelt down to pat Cotton, who was happy to see me.

"Lost another one last night. I thought you'd want to know," Shirley said, hobbling toward me.

"Who?"

"Name was Stinky Pete. Real sweetheart. And no witnesses. Stinky does the same routine night after night. When he didn't show up to drink and play cards with his buddies, they went looking for him. Nothing." Shirley shook her head. "He didn't show up at the shelter or any other haunt he usually hangs out in. He didn't take anything with him, either. Like the others, he just vanished."

"Anyone know his real name?"

"You got me, sweetie. About all I can tell you is that he's an old, smelly, white guy with a beard down to here. Wears this pea coat that smells, hence his name. I came as soon as I could."

"You came to the right place." I pulled out my list and added Stinky Pete to it. "Can I drop you off somewhere?"

"You're a sweetie, but I would rather you do whatever it is you're going to do to stop this. As always, I'm at your disposal if you need me. I'll keep my ear to the ground for you. Just let me know if anything comes up. People are getting nervous, starting to carry knives and pipes and stuff. The Tenderloin isn't a safe place, so you be real careful if you go out at night. Take a friend, preferably a really big one, and a gun or something. Leave your purses at home and wear really fast shoes. Don't turn your back on anyone, not even me. Where there's fear, there's danger, and the community is very afraid."

I SHARED HER thoughts with Danica that evening.

"I got all the protection we're going to need right here," Danica said, pointing to the gun she had placed in the small of her back. True to her word, she'd arrived at my house wearing a black turtleneck, a black leather jacket, black jeans, and her black high tops. The only thing missing was a black ski mask.

"Well keep it there. You know how I feel about those things."

"Don't you feel safer with one? I sure as hell do." She looked at my attire and asked, "Are you wearing *that*?"

I looked at my clothes. I was wearing blue jeans, tennis shoes, and a denim blazer. "What's wrong with what I'm wearing?"

"Look, Sweet Polly Purebred, we're going to a pretty gross place in the middle of the night and you're dressed like Mary Poppins."

"I do *not* look like—"

"We agreed on black."

"*We* did not. *You* did."

"Right. Now, unless you want to get your ass kicked, Mary, please go in there and change into something that doesn't scream *please kick my ass or rob me*."

Once I was dressed in the appropriate attire we opted for the Tenderloin first, and after nearly an hour we managed to find one person who could help us out. Just one, and even he didn't offer up much of value.

"Look, Clark, nobody down here can help you if you don't have people's real names. Without real names, we got nothing. Have you ever thought about trying the police department?"

I looked at her as if she was stupid. "Duh, I'm practically dating one of them."

"I didn't ask you about your boring and pathetic love-life; I was wondering if you had anyone look at the mug shots."

"The mug…" I threw my arms around her and hugged her tightly. "Oh my God, you really are a genius!"

"It just makes sense to me that at one time or another most of your homeless people have been arrested for being drunk and disorderly or under the influence of something. All you need now is someone who can recognize their faces and put real names to them."

Ten minutes later we found Shirley giving a Tarot reading near the park. She was more than happy to go down to the station and claim that she had been mugged by another homeless person, and she wanted to look at the books. It was a brilliant idea, really, and I was a little bummed out that I hadn't thought of it.

I watched as Shirley flipped through page after page of mug shots, nodding and pointing whenever she saw a picture that registered to her powers. About an hour into it, we had eight names, eight real names. Shirley surprised me by being far more lucid and far more powerful with her visions than I initially gauged. When she looked up from the photo of Bob, she pointed to him and said, "This is him."

When I looked at the picture I was surprised. "Under the influence? No way. Bob wasn't… isn't a drug user."

"Maybe not now, dear, but that's what they nabbed him for. Remember, everyone is addicted to something." She closed her eyes. "And his is riding the big Horse."

"Horse?"

Danica groaned. "Smack. Heroin. Are you sure you're a reporter? You need to read more." Danica put her hand on the page. "Wait. So far, all eight were or are heroin users." She turned to me. "There's your common thread."

Shirley was right about everyone being addicted to something. "Well, we've got eight names and that's a start. Whether the heroin is significant or not, we'll just have to wait and see."

We dropped Shirley off at the park, and as she got out, she turned to me and put her hand on my arm. "I can tell you this much, sweetie. They're all still alive. That's all I know. Not one of them is dead. Not one. You need to find them, Echo. You need to find them and quickly. Time is of the essence."

Danica and I drove away in silence, both nursing our own thoughts and fears.

It was Danica who broke the silence first. "If they're still alive, like she says, then where the hell are they? Who has them? And why? Why would anyone want over a dozen homeless guys?"

I started toward the office with the same questions beating at my brain. "I haven't a clue, but now that we have some names…"

"My guys are all over it." Danica pulled out the list and started texting. "They eat research for you with a spoon the size of a shovel. I think it breaks the monotony of being so creative all the time; you know, the difference between fact and fiction." She texted all the names before turning and asking me, "So what do we know?"

"Well, color or ethnicity isn't an issue. Four whites, three blacks and a Hispanic, pretty much rules that out."

"How about ages?"

"Danny Boy is in his twenties, and Stinky Pete is in his early fifties, so age doesn't seem to be a consistent factor."

"Okay, what about military service?"

"Two Vietnam vets, one Gulf War vet, other than that, nothing else. Their jail time wasn't enough to merit a look. Most of them were let go after less than twenty-four hours."

"All of them are men. I find that interesting. That probably rules out sexual assault as a motive."

"True. Then it looks like we're back to the drugs as our main ingredient." I sighed. We still couldn't find a connection. A drug dealer wouldn't kill his customers, nor would he kidnap them. "It seems the more we know the less we know."

"Hang in there, Clark. We'll get some answers."

My next stop was the office, where Danica and I pored over microfilm and had three computers going at once. None of their names produced anything online. That didn't mean they weren't out there in cyberspace, it just meant that I wasn't going to find information on them that easily. Since we knew we could leave cyberspace to the boys, we concentrated on microfilm.

THREE HOURS AND two pairs of blurry eyes later, we were still empty-handed. About the only thing I got was a headache. By the time I got home, I was exhausted and felt like I wasn't any closer to finding Bob as when I woke up this morning.

Time was of the essence, and it was running out.

I WOKE UP four hours later to the ringing of my phone. I had to reach over my drugged cat in order to get to it.

"Echo? You still asleep?"

I looked at the clock. It was 6:37. "That depends on who this is risking life and limb to call me before eight in the morning."

"It's String Bean. I was checking my email this morning and we got a hit on the drawing with the bike."

I was wide awake now. "Tell me."

"A buddy of mine is pretty sure it's a liquor store on Hyde called Fast Freddy's."

I was out of the bed now. "Way to go."

"I told you photographers are the best eyes in the city. I also got some really great shots of your street people for the story. I'll leave copies on your desk this morning."

"Thank you so much."

"That's not the best of it. The photos I took of Cotton and Midnight are awesome. I was seeing a separate story built around those photos. Echo, if you want people to care, those two animals would make even the hardest heart melt. Think about it."

"I don't have to think about it, Jeff. It's a great idea."

"Well, let me know if there's anything else I can do."

I got dressed, checked to make sure Tripod hadn't overdosed on catnip and then headed for Fast Freddy's. When I pulled around the corner and saw the blue awning, I actually gasped. There it was. And there, chained to a post just like Shirley had said, was Smiley's bike. I pulled Ladybug into the red zone next to the bike, got out, and knelt next to it. As I searched the bike, my heart thumped an extra beat when I realized what it was Shirley thought she saw. She thought he'd been working on the bike, but that wasn't what Smiley had been doing. Taped to the underside of the crossbar was a sheet of paper the size of a stick of gum. Only the ends were taped to the bike, and the rest of it had writing scribbled all over. Thank God it hadn't rained.

Carefully peeling the paper from the bike, I rose and leaned against Ladybug's bumper. I don't know what I was expecting... a note that read *here's who's taking our people?* This wasn't even close. What I got wasn't some sort of bizarre encryption; the kind that would've made Detective Jardine throw me out on my ass. On the paper was a weird list of numbers: 3, 9, 7, 30, 24, 93, 34,62 26, 86 26, 22{B}

"What in the hell?" I got into Ladybug and sat and stared at the numbers. It would have taken divine intervention for me to figure out what they stood for. Taking my lump of coal with me, I headed to the office.

When String Bean... uh... Jeff said that his photos were good, he wasn't kidding. They were incredible, made even more so by the use of the black-and-white film. Jeff had the touch of a master. One photo had Cotton and Midnight touching noses as if they were communicating with each other. Another had Midnight sitting between Cotton's paws and both were looking in opposite directions. I must have been engrossed in my conversation with Shirley because I don't remember him taking these photos.

When I finished looking at all of the pictures, I picked three that were outstanding and started writing. With photos like these, a good story writes itself. This would be a great water cooler story; the perfect dovetail into my homeless people series.

There are those people who care deeply for other people, and then there are those people who care even more deeply for pets. In a country that spends over $4 billion per year on their animal companions, this would make them sit up and take notice.

After sending Jeff an email telling him how brilliant his photos were, I called Danica and left a message for her that I was going to Oakland and for her not to worry. Then I left one for the boys saying that I had a little puzzle for them that I'd be emailing over. I didn't really have anything much to go on, but those boys made a living out of making small ideas into big realities. In the meantime, I would finish my story, and then see if Finn would put a call into OPD for me.

I was right about my story writing itself. When I finished, I emailed it to Wes Bentley and then picked up the phone and called Finn with the intention of leaving another message. I was surprised when he picked up.

"Good morning to you," he said. "Isn't caller ID a great thing? I wasn't going to answer."

"Good morning. How are you?"

"I'm wearing a big goose egg over my left eye, but other than that I'm good. And you?"

"What happened? Are you okay?"

"I'm fine. Someone clocked me with a rock. Hurt like hell, but I didn't need stitches. The goose egg is the reason I'm awake. It's telling me I need to take some Advil. And as much as I would love to think this is a personal call… something tells me otherwise. What's up?"

"I've got names for some of the homeless guys. I was

hoping…"

"That I could shake some trees and see what falls out? I've tried, Echo. Names, no names. Photos, no photos. Nothing has moved anyone of the upper brass. Nobody is interested. Let's face it, Echo, we have no proof that any crime has been committed. And even though I believe you, and I believe in your story and your instincts, I'm just a bottom feeder. If you really want action, you need to go to the top."

"And by that you mean…"

He sighed. "Haven't you talked to the big Samoan?"

"Well… yeah… but…"

"Mayor Lee would be able to put some heat on the Chief. We have a saying in law enforcement, 'shit runs downhill'. If you can get the Mayor's interest, he might lean on the Chief. The Chief would turn around and lean on the Captains until finally, someone would be assigned to investigate. Off the record, of course."

"The police department won't look good if I do it that way."

He chuckled. "What else is new? We all know the score, Echo. With all those funds being cut every year, we're short-staffed, overworked, underpaid, and have more rules to follow than a dozen jobs added together. You do what you need to do to get action. The department may initially take a hit when it becomes clear that we didn't do anything to investigate, but don't worry. We cover well."

"Then you wouldn't be mad?"

"Mad? Hell no. I'm on your side. All I ask is that you have dinner with me once this is all over. A real date. I'm your biggest fan, Echo. You can trust me."

Once I hung up, I realized that for the first time since Tomas, I actually trusted another man, and it felt really, really good.

When I handed Shirley the photographs, I included my story with them. Her hand went to her mouth and her eyes welled with tears as she looked at the pictures.

"Oh my... my babies have never looked so good. Please convey my appreciation to String Bean. These are wonderful."

"I thought so as well. I wanted you to see the story first, along with the photos."

Shirley stared at them for a very long time before looking up. "What a wonderful gift. Thank you so much."

"I'm the one who should be thanking you. I really appreciate all the help with my story. As a matter of fact, I was wondering..."

Shirley looked up from the photos. "You've got something?" She held her hand out. I had no doubt that she had probably been watching me from afar, using her sight to see if I was anywhere close. I hadn't had many encounters with clairvoyeurs, so I wasn't quite sure how they operated. I didn't mind. I know that most people would be freaked out knowing that someone could close their eyes and get a vision of where you were and what you were doing, but I'm a supernatural and it took a lot to freak me out.

"I found this on Smiley's bike, but you probably already knew that, huh?"

Shirley smiled. "Can't blame an old woman for caring. You've been so kind to me and my critters... yes I knew, and yes, I knew that you would bring it to me." She held her hand out and I put the slip of paper with the numbers in it carefully in her palm.

"So this is what I saw Smiley doing with the bike?"

I nodded. "Apparently."

She closed her eyes and stood very still for a long time. When she opened them, she shook her head. "All I can tell you is that he saw something… something that frightened him so much that he felt the need to write it down."

"But these are just numbers."

Shirley handed the paper back to me. "Maybe they are, maybe they aren't. He was a special man… special abilities. He saw the world so much differently than the rest of us and his communication style was not at all like yours and mine." Shirley sighed. "Now, can a batty old woman give you a piece of unsolicited advice?"

"Absolutely."

"Don't let this job be ivy in your life."

"Ivy?"

"Ivy looks pretty enough, but left unchecked it will kill all of the surrounding plants in an area until it is the only thing alive. From where I sit, and granted it's no palace on high, all I can see is a beautiful young girl working and working and working. Hamster on a wheel. Ivy." She reached for my hand and held it. "A yard is much prettier when it has a variety of plants. Your yard may seem fine now, but it can be a very lonely place after a while. Don't become so involved in your stories that you forget to live your own."

Smiling, I nodded. "Good advice. I just wish I knew how to take it."

"Give yourself some time. Balance, Echo. Keep your life in balance."

It was odd the way I could hear Melika's voice, and a small part of me wondered if Melika hadn't contacted her. "You sound like my mentor."

"I sound old and wise." She grinned. "It's not much of a stretch, really. You work too hard, too much, and too often. The only person you have anything to prove to is yourself. Take a step away. Take half a day for yourself and I bet you would see things more clearly. Go out with that young man who's been putting that spring in your step." She threw her head back and laughed. "What? Did you think I didn't know? Anyone with two eyes can see something has changed. Your step is a little bit lighter and there's a sparkle in your eyes... but all that ivy..." She shook her head. "You've got flowers trying to push their way through. Help them out. Step away, my dear, and clip the ivy way back. You won't be sorry." She released my hand.

I thought about our conversation as I drove to Oakland. I *did* feel driven, as if I had something to prove. It was the typical stigma of a foster care kid. I wanted to be *better* than good enough... I wanted to be the best.

When I finally found Dante, he was reading another one of his namesake's books. "Is this good news or bad news?"

I shrugged. "Maybe a little bit of both." I sat down next to him. "I can tell you this much, I don't believe he's dead."

"How..."

"That's not important. What's important is this." I handed him a copy of the paper with the numbers. "I found this taped to his bike. I was hoping you might know what it means."

Dante looked at the piece of paper and rubbed his face. "He wrote these down? That's odd. Smiley never writes."

"Then maybe they're really important."

Dante looked at them and squinted before looking back up. "You know, a bunch of us were talking the other day and the one thing we kept coming back to was the fact that these kidnappings seemed so organized."

I cocked my head at him. "And what was your thought? Gangs?"

He shook his head. "Gangs are too loud and obnoxious. Someone would certainly have heard something. Think about it. To swipe a grown man off the street without anyone saying or hearing anything would take an organized group with the proper vehicle for a quick in and out."

"What kind of large vehicle? Like a van?"

He nodded. "It's probably a large cargo van or something with double doors because they've got to be able to get a struggling man into it quickly."

I nodded again. "I guess I've spent so much time focusing on the victims, I hadn't really thought about the details of the crime itself."

He grinned. "That's because you have a heart of gold."

"But it makes sense that there's more than one guy, right?"

"Way more than one. We were thinking along the lines of three or four. For them to do a snatch and grab without being seen or heard would require at least three grown men." Dante looked down at the numbers.

"Those numbers don't mean anything to you?"

He shook his head and then proceeded to write them down on the inside cover of *Paradise Lost*. "No, but let me ruminate on them for a spell. I don't know if anyone told you much about my nephew, but he's never been right in the head. Some people call him an idiot, I prefer to call him a savant."

"So you said. Is it autism?"

He chuckled. "Something like that. Anyway, if he wrote it down it had to have meant something to him because he didn't like to write. He only trusted printed words."

"Well, if you can think of anything, anything at all that those numbers might relate to, please give me a call. And keep in touch. I mean it."

"You are welcome down here anytime, Echo. It would mean a lot to me if you could come and see my performance some night. I think you'd really enjoy it."

"Maybe I'll do that, Dante. You take care now." As I left the old man alone on the stoop, my mind was racing. I dialed Finn's number as soon as I was back at Ladybug.

"Can't get enough of me, eh?" Finn answered on the second ring. Damn that caller ID. There was no such thing as a surprise anymore.

"You know it. Will you have dinner with me tonight?"

"Tonight? Sure."

"I know a great little Italian restaurant in Moraga. Beppe and Gianni's. Is five too early?"

"That would be great. Want me to meet you over there?"

"Do you mind?"

"Is this a business dinner?"

"Do you want it to be?"

He laughed. "See you there."

When I arrived at the restaurant, Finn was already there, wearing a blue turtleneck that looked painted on his body; his very fit body. He was wearing khaki pants that looked as if they'd been ironed, and black boots spit shined to a glossy finish. Damn this guy could dress. "You look really great."

Finn stood and eyed my DKNY black jump suit. "*Really* great would be an understatement about how you look right now." He whistled.

"You're sweet."

"I can be, but don't let that get around. I have a tough guy, bad ass reputation to uphold."

We both laughed. Ivy Shmivy. I could have just as good a time as anyone.

By the time our meal came, we had discussed the various paths to our careers, what we did in high school, and some of our favorite things. I found him to be a wonderful dinner companion and an excellent conversationalist. The more I was around him the more I liked him. He told me some of the most hilarious police stories I had ever heard.

While I was laughing, Finn leaned back and smiled. "Can't say I've ever seen you laugh so hard. It's nice." Then he leaned forward. "As much as I would like to believe that you asked me to dinner as a date, what business do you need to attend to?"

Ivy, ivy, everywhere. "Maybe I just wanted to spend some time with you."

He laughed. "Oh really?" He surprised me by reaching out and taking one of my hands in his. "Oh, if that were true, I'd be a lucky, lucky man, but I'm not that lucky. What's on your mind?"

"I have a great time with you, and I would really like to go out on a real date, but it seems as if I've painted us into opposing corners for the moment. I feel like I've put you in an awkward position professionally and I apologize for that but—"

"Whoa. Wait. Slow down a sec. I'm still back on the fact that you want to go on a real date. The rest is immaterial. I would *love* to go out with you on a real date, Echo." He was grinning widely. "Opposing corners or not."

"You're missing the point."

Shaking his head, he slowly pulled his hand off mine. "Any other point is moot. I enjoy your company, you enjoy mine, and we would like to see more of each other. It doesn't have to be any more complicated than that."

I leaned away from the table. "I'm not that naive, *Sergeant* Finn. It *is* more complicated. I've decided to go to the Mayor's press conference tomorrow. After tomorrow, the police department will see me as Typhoid Mary. I don't imagine *that* will go down well with your buddies in blue to know that you're dating the enemy."

He blew out a breath. "Maybe not, but I can handle them."

"That's just it. I don't want you to *have* to handle them. I don't want them seeing me as a thorn in your side. That's not a great way to start."

He thought about it a long time before slowly shaking his head. "Shit."

"Feeling that corner now?"

He grinned a grin I was really beginning to get accustomed to seeing. "Yeah, I guess I am. As much as I don't want our jobs to keep getting in our way... they keep getting in our way, huh?"

Ivy. Goddamn ivy. "It won't always be true, but for the moment... yes."

He looked away and then back again. "Fine then. If

that's how it has to be, then I want you to be successful. I want you to find a way to make that story front-page news. Do what you need to do, Echo, just let me help. Even if I can only help from the sidelines."

I nodded. "Really?"

"Really. What have you got so far?"

"I think the missing men are being taken away in some kind of van or other cargo-like vehicle. So far, someone thinks they saw a light blue or white van. Think about it… whoever these guys are, they need a vehicle small enough to maneuver the streets of San Francisco without attracting any attention, but big enough to be able to throw a guy in and go."

"Very good, Sherlock. I'm impressed. Would you like a job?"

"I have a job. What I need to know is how we narrow down the possibilities."

"You would need a list of all van owners in the city; of course, since people are missing from Oakland as well, you need to know all of the van owners in a hundred-mile radius."

"Damn. Impossible, huh?"

He nodded. "Do you have anything else to go on?"

"I'm at my wits end here. It feels like I have a dozen different puzzle pieces I'm trying to fit into one puzzle. It's incredibly frustrating."

"Welcome to investigative work, Sherlock. You just keep your eyes on the prize and keep turning all the evidence around in your head like a Rubik's Cube. One day something will click and you'll have the whole side complete just like that." He snapped his fingers.

"And in the meantime?"

His grin slowly faded. "You take what you have to the top just like we talked about."

"And you promise you won't hate me?"

He leaned forward, eyes twinkling. "That could never happen. I told you, I'm your biggest fan. Well… me and the big Samoan."

My biggest fan and I stayed and chatted for almost two hours after dinner and dessert. When we finally left, he walked me to my car and without so much as a single hesitation or pause, he bent over and kissed me softly on the lips. It was warm and intimate and not the least bit invasive. He was a damn fine kisser and knew precisely what to do with his tongue.

When I pulled away, I couldn't feel my legs. "Umm… Sergeant Finn, is that legal?"

He laughed. "I figured I better get one in before you head to the Mayor because who knows what's going to happen when the fur starts flying."

I fumbled for my keys. "I'll try to keep the flying fur to a minimum."

Finn stepped up and put his hands on my arms. "When this story wraps and everything cools down, I will be on your doorstep with the roses in hand."

"Roses? How about purple bearded irises?" I smiled. He laughed and I kissed him quickly on the lips before getting into Ladybug. As I headed back toward the tunnel, I called Danica. "He kissed me."

"It's about bloody time! Was it good?"

"It was great."

She squealed like a 14-year-old girl. "Tell me

everything!"

"I can't. I'm getting ready to go through the tunnel."

"Tunnel?"

"Long story."

"Then make it brief. Are you going home *alone*?"

"Yes. No. I mean… I'm not going home."

"Oh, don't tell me…"

"Stopping by Oakland. There's something there to point me in the right direction. I know it. I can feel it. But I have no idea what it is."

"Damn it, Clark, please tell me Officer Love Lips is going with you."

"He's not."

"That settles it, then. Tomorrow, I am going out and buying you a nifty little revolver like the one I have. You, too, needa leetle fren'."

"I'll be fine."

"You better be. Call me when you get back. And I want all of the lurid details of that first kiss. Don't leave out one tiny thing."

"I won't." I started to hang up, but quickly said, "Danica?"

"Yeah, Clark?

"I really like him."

"I know you do. I know you do."

CHAPTER 42

I ROLLED INTO Oakland still feeling Finn on my lips. He was a much better kisser than Tomas; softer and more… present. Tomas' kisses were powerful, but Finn's was… yummy.

I had a feeling that it was Dante who kept bringing me back to Oakland. It wasn't that I was reading him as much as the situation seemed to be beckoning me. When I found him, he was standing in an alleyway with about twelve onlookers enrapt by his performance. He was very good, and though I did not know my Dante well, I did know a grand performance when I saw one; I have to say that he was truly captivating.

So, I sat down, even in my nice DKNY outfit, and listened to Dante weave his tale.

"Turn your back and keep your eyes shut tight;
for should the Gorgon come and you look at her,
never again would you return to light.

"This was my guide's command. And he turned to me about himself and would not trust my hands alone, but, with

his placed on line, held my eyes shut."

I stole a look at members of the audience and couldn't help but smile. Dante held them in the palm of his hand with his delightful theatrical flair. When he spoke, he moved with the words so that he stood there now, with both of his hands over his eyes.

...suddenly, there broke on the dirty swell of the dark Marsh a squall of terrible

sound that sent a tremor through both shores of Hell." As he spoke, his voice pitched and rose like a professional thespian. I was enthralled.

When, at last, it was time for an intermission, he accepted a small bottle of water from an older woman. "Virgil was afraid, wasn't he?" she asked, remembering the name of Dante's guide through Hell.

"Indeed he was, but Virgil tried to hide it."

She shook her head. "But Dante wasn't fooled, was he?"

Dante smiled softly at her. "What do you think, Jenny?"

She thought for a moment, like a student in class might, before finally shaking her head. "I think Dante's not so sure Virgil knows the way."

Dante grinned wider and patted her on the back. "And you would be right."

When she left, I rose and walked over to him. I sure could use a Virgil now. "This is quite a performance you put on."

"Echo! How kind of you to come." Dante took a quick drink of water. "I look at it like community service. It makes me feel like I'm giving something back to those who have nothing."

"How nice."

"We have very little to entertain us out here. There's cards, dice, and chess, but those are limited in numbers of people who could play. But a good story... well now... that can entertain as many as the voice can reach to."

If I hadn't loved this man before, I was beginning to now. "What a wonderful gift you give them. Do you do these every night?"

"Every single night. Consistency is key to the folks out here, so I'm here first and then I go down the street a bit and do a shorter version down there."

"And always *Dante's Inferno*?"

"Oh heavens, no. It's seasonal, really. I do Dante in the summer months from June to September. From September to October I do the *Legend of Sleepy Hollow*. In November and December, of course, I do *The Night Before Christmas* and other tales. And January through April I do *Paradise Lost.*"

"Wow."

"They really like *Paradise Lost,* but the *Inferno* is everyone's favorite. It's been Smiley's favorite since before he could walk. That kid knows his story like the back of his hand. I've never seen a kid love a story so much. He can recite it verse for verse. It's pretty amazing, really."

I grinned. "You still call him a kid."

"He always will be to me. It was Smiley who got me to start performing in the first place. He wanted other people to feel what he felt whenever I told a story. At the beginning, only a few folks gathered around. Most thought I was crazy. Can't say I blame them. When one of us starts orating on a corner somewhere, we usually sound quite... out there."

Something in my stomach turned. "He... *feels* the

story?"

"Well… I don't know that he really does, but that was the way he put it to me."

I blinked several times and let the thought linger a bit. "You're very entertaining. You missed your calling, to be sure."

"Thank you. I really enjoy it. It gives me something to do with my days. When I'm performing, I am at my happiest. It gives me such joy to see their faces when they listen and are all involved. It really helps pass what is a miserable time for all of us."

"Well, it's wonderful. I'll let you get back to it."

"Thank you for coming."

I stayed for the next piece, but it was getting cold and I hadn't brought a jacket. Whatever was nagging at the edges of my mind wouldn't come up, so I waved goodbye to Dante and headed for home. Nothing on my phone from the boys, nothing from Danica, nothing at all. By the time I got home, I had a headache the size of Texas. Whatever was poking at me was in a part of my brain I couldn't locate. It reminded me of when a song plays over and over in your head but you can't name it. So, I did what every other red-blooded American did when that happened… I took a shower, brushed my teeth, filed my nails, fed the cat, cleaned out my refrigerator, and did everything I could to keep my mind away from whatever it was playing hide and seek with me. When it still didn't come, I cleaned the house and surfed the internet until I could barely keep my eyes open. Then I called Danica and left a message that I'd gotten home safely.

My eyes had been closed for half a second, when the

phone rang. Checking the caller ID as well as the time, I grinned. It was Finn.

"Normal men don't call after midnight," I said, yawning.

"Who said I was normal? You've been given erroneous information if you think that. Sorry I woke you."

"I wasn't asleep."

"Liar. Look, I just wanted to call the day after to let you see what a sincere, honest guy I am."

"Aren't you sweet."

"I'm hoping you think so. That's why I called. It seems like you're ready to start a new chapter in your life and I would really like to be part of it."

"Once this story is over."

"Once the story is over. Echo, I think you're an incredible woman, and I sort of hope you feel the same way about me."

"Sergeant Finn, I think you rock. Don't you know? Can't you tell? If I wasn't so interested in finding Bob, I'd be making up other reasons to call you."

"That's good to hear. I was hoping this wasn't a one-way thing."

"It isn't. I enjoy spending time with you, too."

He laughed. "Damn, I gotta roll. I would sure like to kiss you more."

I felt a blush run over my face. "I think I can handle that. You be careful out there, Deputy Dog. This world is a better place with you in it."

"Glad you think so. Oh, and Echo? If you ever want to feel safe at night, sleep with a cop." With that, he hung up, leaving me smiling and a little tingly.

Rolling over, I sighed contentedly, feeling my eyelids get heavy again. I was exhausted. It was so nice that he'd called. He was right about this being a new chapter in my life. I was starting over emotionally and it was great that I had met such a nice guy to share it with.

New life, new chapter. Everyone needs a new chapter.

I was just about asleep when I shot up straight and turned on the light so fast, Tripod ran under the bed. "That's it!" Jumping out of bed, I ran to my bookshelves and rifled through all of my old college textbooks. "Where is it?"

When I finally found the one I needed, I pulled it out and held it to my chest. "This *has* to be it."

I was holding *Dante's Inferno:* my key to the clue kingdom.

I was sure of it.

TURNING ON MY desk lamp, I grabbed the slip of paper with numbers on it and studied it for a moment. "I *knew* there was something there. Damn." The moment Finn said the word chapter, all the doors started to unlock for me.

"Okay, Echo, calm. Calm down." My heart was pounding so I took a deep breath, grabbed a pen and pad, and then opened my copy of *The Inferno.*

Rain Man was exceptional with numbers. He couldn't hold a conversation or drive a car or even make his own meals, but he could count cards in Vegas, memorize lists, and compute almost faster than a calculator. He was a savant.

So was Smiley.

What had Dante said? Smiley knew *The Inferno* like the back of his hand? Well, we'd see about that. *Dante's Inferno* was a story about his trip to Hell, and the different people who occupied the different layers of each region. According to Dante's version of Hell, where people ended up depended on what kind of sinner they were.

I started reading from the first number 3:9. Canto III. It was called The Opportunists, people whose souls are neither good nor evil, but self-centered. It had the most famous line in the work, and though many people might not know where it was from, most of us had heard it at one time or another: *Abandon all hope, ye who enter here.* That was the sign above the gates to Hell.

But what did it mean? Why had Smiley written this down? Quickly, I flipped to the next set of numbers. It was Canto VII, which dealt with the Hoarders and Wasters, The Wrathful and Sullen. The first set, the Hoarders and Wasters lacked all moderation and thought nothing was as important as money. Turning to line 30, I read the next ten lines out loud:

Why do you hoard? Why do you waste? So back around that ring they puff and blow, each faction to its course, until they reach opposite sides, and screaming as they go, the madmen turn and start their weights again to crash against the maniacs. And I, watching, felt my heart contract of pain.

Sighing, I leaned against the back of the sofa and scratched Tripod's head. At the moment, he wasn't stoned, so he liked me a little bit. "What was Smiley trying to say?" I was beginning to think I was way off base; that I had reached too far in an effort to find an answer.

I jammed a 3 x 5 card into both cantos and moved on

Canto XXIV, which was about thieves. That was pretty self-explanatory, so I pressed on. There was one line from Smiley's notes: line 93: *In that swarm, naked and without hope, people ran terrified, not even dreaming of a hole to hide in or of heliotrope.*

Heliotrope? I flipped to the notes in the back of my translation and saw that a heliotrope was some sort of stone. A bloodstone believed to be capable of making the wearer of it invisible.

Okay…

With the exception of people running terrified, the idea that Smiley had used *The Inferno* as a way of communicating what he saw was a quantum leap, but I couldn't let go. Not yet. Canto XXXIV dealt with Satan and others. The one line, line 62 read: *That soul that suffers most, explained my guide, is Judas Iscariot, he who kicks his legs on the fiery chin and has his head inside."*

My glimmer of hope was quickly fading. "What are you trying to say? What did you see?" Flipping back to the notes in the book, I read that Judas' punishment was patterned after the Simoniacs. The who? I made a note and continued.

I looked at the last sets of numbers 26, 86; a reference to Circe. I knew that one well. Circe was a woman that Ulysses had stayed with a year when he was trying to get home.

The final set of numbers made a reference to a bridge: *by the bridge and among a shapeless crew.* Now, *that* caught my attention. Was Smiley making a reference to San Francisco's famous Golden Gate Bridge?

Standing back, I rubbed my eyes. My headache had returned. I either had a whole lot or a whole lotta nothing. The longer I stared at my pad with all my notes, the more questions I had. I was beginning to think that investigative reporting wasn't really my bag.

Feeling defeated, I decided that maybe the boys could find something, so I emailed my notes to them with an addition. *Guys – I hope you're up to this task. The numbers I sent might be sections of Smiley's favorite novel, Dante's Inferno. I've been banging my head against the wall for an hour, and I can't come up with anything. Maybe you can. Princess.*

If anyone could decode Dante's lines, those three would. I decided that after my press conference with the mayor I would see what my fellow thespian could come up with. Maybe he could sort this out. Maybe I was so far off track I could never get back on it. At least I had one thing going for me; I still had a press conference to attend.

As I lay in bed thinking of *Dante's Inferno*, I had no idea just how big that press conference was going to be or how close I was to the truth.

CHAPTER 43

"COME TO WATCH a pro in action?" Carter said when he saw me.

"Something like that."

"Why don't you sit with me? I'll lend you some much-needed credibility."

In the journalism field, there is a definite pecking order. If Carter could get me in the door, I would've sat on his shoulders if it meant getting the Mayor's attention. When we took our seats, I looked around and finger waved to a few people I knew. There were camera crews, light guys, and print media there. I didn't stand a chance in this crowd. Sure, I was with a damned Pulitzer winner, but there were also daytime Emmy winners as well as other power journalists who had been around the block long before I was born.

Carter had gotten a seat right in the center. The podium stood in the middle of the stage with three chairs on either side. When the crowd quieted down I could see everyone jockeying for space. The truth was, I was really excited to be there.

When the Mayor's press secretary came out, I got butterflies in my stomach. I know… he was just a mayor, but the energy swirling around the room swept me up.

"Just wait," Carter whispered. "His mother will be coming out in a second. Everyone thinks it's bizarre the way she goes everywhere he goes."

"Have you ever considered that it's a cultural thing, and not necessarily something bad?"

"Oh, it's bad. The old bag goes everywhere with him. It's weird. Look. There she is."

I watched the old Chinese woman walk out and sit on the chair closest to the podium. Her keen, clear eyes slowly looked over the crowd, like a mother bear surveying the territory before her cubs can play there. Her eyes made a slow, methodical pass over every face. When her eyes locked onto mine, I knew *exactly* why she was her son's greatest adviser, and why she creeped people out.

"Weird, huh?"

I said nothing, but kept my eyes on Mrs. Lee. Only when her son came out did her intense gaze shift from mine.

"Thank you for coming. I know some of you are here to help me win the re-election while others of you would love nothing more than to help me out the door. Well, I would like both sides to know that I am not bowing down to any kind of external pressure from you, my opponent, or the ugly rumor mills. I am proud of the work I've done and will continue to do so as long as this great city allows. We only just started making some of the necessary changes that will keep this city in step with the changing times. I intend to see those programs to fruition. To that end, I'm willing to answer whatever questions you may have. But let's be civil, shall we? Try to keep the mudslinging to a minimum."

"Sounds like he knows that you're gunning for him," I whispered to Carter.

"Yeah, well, watch and learn."

I did. One by one, Mayor Lee patiently answered every question thrown at him. I found it incredibly interesting that he had yet to call on Carter. Of course, I knew why.

When the mayor finished with a question about parking, I figured it was time for me to throw my hat in the ring, so up went my hand.

"What in the hell are you doing?" Carter asked under his breath. "Put your fool hand down."

"Not a chance. Why do you think I came here? To watch you?" I didn't hear his caustic response because I was too focused on Mrs. Lee. She motioned to her son, who bent down to listen to her. When he stood back at the podium, he was staring right at me and pointing. Carter stood up.

"Mr. Mayor..."

"I'm sorry, Mr. Ellsworth. I was not motioning to you. I would like to hear from your colleague in the beautiful red suit."

Oh my God, the look on Carter's face was worth my weight in gold. His head slowly turned toward me, eyes blazing.

I turned from him and smiled at the mayor as I stood up. "Mr. Mayor, are you aware that someone has been abducting our homeless people right off the street and that your police department has repeatedly refused to get involved?" My heart was banging so loudly in my ears I could barely hear myself. My mouth had that dry, I'm-too-nervous-to-speak quality, and my palms were all clammy.

"I'm sorry. I didn't get your name."

"Oh. It's Echo Branson with the Chronicle."

He frowned for a moment. "Miss Branson, you did the article on the Galloway case, correct?"

I nodded and felt a blush rise from my shoulders to the top of my head. "Yes, sir."

"Wonderful story. And what a great story you wrote about the homeless people and their pets. Fabulous photographs."

"I'll let the photographer know you thought so."

He leaned forward on the podium. "So let me get this straight. You are saying that someone is kidnapping our homeless people and that our police department has done nothing about it?"

I nodded. "I've done everything I can as a journalist and concerned citizen to get someone to help me figure out what's going on. I'm here because I'm hoping *you* can help."

He took notes and then turned to his mother. I couldn't tell if there was an exchange or not, but when he turned around she smiled politely at me. "Miss Branson, I assure you, that I will be in contact with the Chief of Police before the day is through. If what you say *is* happening, you have my word that I will do whatever I can."

Nodding my thank you, I sat down. "Thank you."

The press conference went on and I could feel the heat emanating from Carter. He could barely contain himself, he was so angry. Again and again his hand shot up, but the mayor never looked our way again.

When it was all over, Carter grabbed my elbow and pushed me through the crowd. We were practically out the door when what looked like a bodyguard stopped us.

"Excuse me, Miss Branson? Mayor Lee would like to see you right now if you have the time."

"Me? Absolutely." Turning to Carter, I shrugged before detaching myself from him. Following the bodyguard, I was surprised when he took me into a small conference room.

"He'll be right in. Can I get you a coffee or tea, or something?"

"Thank you. I'm good."

The Mayor and his mother came in shortly after I sat down. Out of deference to Mrs. Lee, I started to rise, but she waved me back down. "Sit. Sit."

I sat.

"I wanted to hear more about what's happening in the Tenderloin. I would have done this at the conference, but... well... you saw how it was. There are those journalists who would like to put me into the meat grinder."

I nodded. "I'm not one of them." I tried to remember whether or not I had mentioned the Tenderloin or if he just assumed that that was where I was talking about.

Mayor Lee started for the door. "I need some water. Can I get you anything?"

"I'm fine, thanks."

When he left, Mrs. Lee turned her chair to me. For the longest time, she didn't say anything. She just kept staring hard into my face. I didn't have to lower my shield to know what was going on.

Mrs. Lee was one of us.

"You know, don't you?"

I gazed back into her brown eyes. The wisdom in them reminded me of Melika. "Actually, I do. It's one of my gifts."

She squinted and nodded. "You're quite strong."

I didn't reply, but I did understand now why she went everywhere with him and why Carter, a Pulitzer Prize winning journalist hadn't been called on; she knew which side of the political fence he sat on and purposely avoided him.

"I haven't met an empath in many years. I noticed you right away. You were not trained in the Orient."

I shook my head. "No, I wasn't, but I was taught very well."

She continued to look in my eyes. "Yes. Yes you were. But you are not here to compare power recipes. The missing men. They mean something to you."

"Bob is a friend of mine, yes. The others, though not friends, deserve no less attention. I can't get anyone at the police station to listen to me, just because they're homeless."

"My son is very good at getting people to listen to him." She leaned forward. "But there are those who would prevent him from making this city a better place. I would like to help you. Can you help us in return?"

"Me help? How can I help?"

She grinned. "That man. Carter Ellsworth. Mr. High and Mighty. He does not like my son nor his politics. Whatever it is he is after, whatever dirt he is busy digging up, we would like stopped."

I looked at her and wondered how strong of a super *she* was. "Don't you know?"

She waved the question away. "Of course I know. Knowing and stopping his self-serving ways are two different things. That man… people listen to him. People think he is wise, but he is not. He is a little man given a big stage with a large microphone. I do not want that man's voice preventing my son's reelection."

Oh God.

"I am not asking that you silence this voice on your own. It will take more than one muzzle to silence that yipping dog."

I nodded. "He's not necessarily evil, Mrs. Lee, but he is incredibly myopic."

"He is the kind of man who will put his needs before those of the people… of *my* people. I am not asking you to do anything immoral or against your own code of ethics. I am asking that you simply keep an eye on him and inform me if he is going somewhere dark and ugly." She leaned closer. "This city needs my son, Miss Branson. It needs him more than it needs a self-absorbed journalist. Surely you understand that."

"I do, and you have my word that I will do whatever I can to make sure that Carter Ellsworth isn't given that stage."

"Good. We can help each other then."

The mayor came back with a tray of water and sodas. "I hope my mother hasn't strong armed you into anything. Sometimes, she can get carried away."

I doubted that. She was a very calculating, precise woman who did nothing without thinking about every angle and every consequence. She knew even before he called me back into this meeting how it would end up. She sat there during that press conference and picked out the reporter she felt could do the most damage and then she made sure her son steered clear of him. Then, she studied us like bugs under a microscope. In the time it took the press conference to end, Mrs. Lee knew all she needed to know.

"My mother has impeccable taste in people, and her judgment is seldom wrong. That being said, tell me more about these abductions."

I could see why this man was so well-liked. He had a smooth, polished tone like that of a trained stage actor. No hint of Ivy League snobbery, his voice was more like warm honey. He also had very gentle eyes and was gray just a bit on one side of his head. He was about forty years old, although I was terrible with ages unless my shields were down. But what really captivated me was the warmth of his spirit. This man genuinely cared about his job and the people.

About a third of the way through my story, the mayor stopped me.

"You say they're missing from Oakland as well?"

I nodded and was surprised when he pulled out of his cell phone and started dialing. "Excuse me a moment, Miss Branson." He waited a moment then pressed the speaker button before setting the phone down. "It's to Deacon Smith's private line."

Deacon Smith was the mayor of Oakland. He and Mayor Lee had put their heads together in recent years to pull off some of the most amazing fundraisers on the West Coast.

"Did you call for another golf whuppin'?" came a deep, baritone voice.

"Name the time, you lucky dog. I'm afraid this is a business call. I have a reporter here who has some disturbing news I think you'll want to hear."

"I'm all ears."

Mayor Lee nodded for me to begin. So I did, uninterrupted. I wondered if maybe the line had gone dead.

"What you think, Kai?" Deacon asked when I finished.

Mayor Lee sighed loudly. "My sources say she's reliable. She's not out to gain anything here, Deacon, other than to find her friend and maybe even save some lives."

Deacon chuckled. "Your sources, eh? You mean your mama?"

"Have you read the story about the homeless plight in the Chronicle?"

"Those her pieces?"

I answered. "Yes, sir, they are"

"Great photo of that dog and cat. Touching really. Excellent story."

"Thank you. Look, I know my colleagues and I can be hard to trust, but this stopped being about the story a long time ago. I've come to know these people well enough to care whether they're healthy and safe or not. All I'm asking is for you to put an investigator on it. That's all."

"That's it?"

"Mayor Smith, I grew up in Oakland. Graduated from Mills College. Believe it or not, I care. I'm just looking for your respective police departments to care as well."

"I'll take your lead on this, Kai. What do you think?"

"I think Miss Branson has the ability to enlist the population of both our cities with just a few strokes of her pen. For my part, I plan on speaking with the Chief this afternoon. If someone is snatching our homeless and we're seen as do-nothing politicians… well, you get the picture."

"Gotcha. I'll contact my boys, get the ball rolling on this

end. Have your men call OPD and let's set up the task force between the two cities."

My eyebrows shot up. "Task force? Really?"

"Miss Branson, other than preying on children and the elderly, victimizing the homeless is the lowest of lows. Kai and I can't afford to sit around passively uninvolved. You'll get your task force, Miss Branson..."

"And you will get the golden ink from my pen Mayor Smith."

He laughed a laugh that sounded like it was coming from the bottom of a barrel. "It looks like we've got our bases covered. Anything else, Kai?"

"We still have that sewage dumping issue, but we can discuss that later. Maybe after I kick your butt on the links. Thanks, Deacon."

"Any time. Nice meeting you, Miss Branson." Then he clicked off.

"Deacon Smith is a very good man," Mrs. Lee said softly. "He's probably on the phone to the Oakland Police Department as we speak."

I rose. "I don't know how to thank you."

Mayor Lee grinned. "Oh yes you do." He rose and shook my hand. "This time of year good press is hard to come by. Just know that I'm not just doing this because it makes me look good. As a public servant, I have discovered that few people are truly altruistic, but my mother believes that you're a woman of integrity and that you truly care about those missing people."

Handing him my card, I turned and bowed to Mrs. Lee before leaving the building. When I finally got in my car, I had three missed calls with no message left, a call from

Danica, and one from Finn. I called Finn first before heading back to work. He wasn't there, so I left a brief message saying that I didn't think the police department took a hit today; that I had effectively gotten what I needed without casting aspersions. Yes, I used the word aspersions. I grinned. He would like it, too.

Before I could even pull out of the parking lot, my phone rang.

"Yo, Princess!" Carl sounded almost relieved. "Where you been? We've been trying to call you all morning."

Ahh… my three missed calls. "Sorry, guys. They make us turn our cell phones off for press conferences. Please tell me you whiz kids have something for me."

"Well, we've come up with something for you, Princess, but we don't know if it's any good."

"I'm listening."

"We've spent all morning working on this. Puff and Blow in the Hoarders' section has a direct correlation to the Judas Iscariot line."

I uncapped my pen and rolled down my window. "What do you mean?"

"Well, Judas was a traitor, right? Well, we searched all over the place to see if there was anything else to the name. We tried anagrams, biblical references, the whole nine yards. We worked so hard on that one, our computers were smoking. Then, Roger input Judas. Just Judas. Do you know what Judas means on the street, Princess?"

"What?"

"Heroin. H. Horse. Shit. Nixon. Chick. China White. If this guy was writing in some kind of code, we think he saw something… something to do with heroin or some other drugs, maybe."

"How do you make that connection to the puff and blow section?"

"Princess, you really do gotta get out more. That's how people do smack these days. Near as we can tell, there's no order to the code. Next, we looked up heliotrope. It's also known as a bloodstone and is used by warriors to become invisible in battle. Not much there."

"Okay. I know about Circe. Anything else?"

"Well, wait a sec. Do you remember that Circe changed Ulysses' men to swine before keeping him prisoner for a year? Could be a clue. Could be nothing. I wish I had more for you, but we're still working on it. Roger thinks your little clue maker is brilliant and that we're just too dim to get it."

"He's not brilliant in the conventional way. He's a savant."

"No kidding?"

"Like Rain Man."

"Then that does make a difference. Brilliant minds are often found behind walls of autism. We'll go back to the drawing board and see if we can't figure out what he's trying to say."

"I appreciate this, Carl. Really."

"Don't count us out of the race yet, Princess. I'll call back when we get something."

I hung up and called Wes to tell him about my meeting with the mayor. Of course, he had already been informed about the first part of the press conference. Carter had apparently called up ranting and raving about how unprofessional I was and what a rookie I looked like and how I had embarrassed the paper.

"Of course he was steamed, Wes. I stole his thunder. Again. Look, we're working on two completely different stories. I'm not going to apologize for the mayor preferring to hear my question over Carter's. You think he doesn't know that Carter is out to get him?"

"Is he?"

"Come on, Wes. He's digging for dirt in a landfill. It's disgusting and I can't believe you're condoning it."

He laughed. "You either have the biggest balls on the planet or…"

"Or I'm right. Look, I happen to have the attention of the mayors on both sides of the bridge. I'm sure as hell not going to apologize for that."

"No one is asking you to, but that press conference…"

"Was Carter's? Don't be silly, Wes. Mayor Lee knows he's out for blood. He wouldn't have called on Carter if he was the only reporter in the room."

"I understand that, but how could the mayor have known?"

"He has his ways. No one has asked me, but I'm going to tell you anyway; Carter's story is bullshit and puny and the mayor deserves better."

"Duly noted. You have the go ahead on your story. Let me worry about Carter's. If you nail this story, Miss Branson, if you keep scooping the Trib, your life around here is going to get a helluva lot better. Keep me posted."

No sooner had I hung up than the phone rang again. "Hello?"

"Is this the magician?" It was Finn.

"Excuse me?"

"You must be some kind of magician to get people to

jump through the hoops they're jumping through. Hats off to you. What in the hell did you say to Mayor Lee?"

"The truth; only this time, I was able to do it behind closed doors so it never looked like I was pointing fingers at the police department. Well… initially, it may have looked that way, but he handled it with such aplomb. The guy is a winner, Finn."

"Well, guess who is in charge of the task force?"

"You?"

"I'm a beat cop. Try Jardine."

"You're kidding? That's excellent."

"I think he has a crush on you."

Poor Finn. He couldn't see what I thought was pretty obvious. "Well, I can only handle one cop at a time."

He laughed. "You think so?"

"I'm counting on it. So, tell me about the task force."

"We've got a coupla guys on it and OPD matched it. They're meeting this afternoon to see what's what. They'll be contacting you for sure. I know I'm always busting Jardine's chops, but the guy is a helluva detective. If anyone can get you where you need to go, it's him."

I didn't doubt that. "Thank you for your support. It means a lot to me."

"Well, you're beginning to mean a lot to me. I told you… if there was anything I could do…"

I grinned. We said our goodbyes and I hung up. I could only hope that the task force was in time, that the boys could dig deep enough into the notes of an autistic homeless man to find something, and that I could piece this thing together before it was too late.

I WAS FLYING across the bridge faster than I should have after I received a 911 call from George. He'd done an intake and all he would say about her was that she wouldn't talk and was afraid of him and everyone else.

"I came as soon as I could," I said when George met me at reception.

"Thanks for coming, Sweetpea. This one is a head shaker. Can't talk."

"Can't or won't?"

"Wish I knew. Hasn't said a single word since she got here. Kinda like that little gal you helped when you were here."

I was neither a spotter like George, nor a hunter like Tomas, but I *was* a very strong empath. I could possibly reach her where others couldn't. I was a communicator who hadn't yet earned my spotter's stripes. I wanted to. "I'll give it my best, George."

"I know you will."

"What was she brought in for?"

"She just stopped talking. Apparently, it was a slow progression from an outgoing, cute little girl, to this stoic, emotionless ten-year-old who says nothin' to nobody."

"She's only ten? What's she done so far?"

"She just sits there and watches the others."

The elevator dinged and we got off. "What makes you think she's one of us?"

"It's in her eyes. It's the way she looks at me; like she knows I know, but doesn't know how to confirm it for me."

I nodded. "Have they started drugging her?"

"Not yet."

"How bright is she?"

"From what I can tell, very, but that's just an old man's educated guess. Her parents brought her in, dropped her off, and haven't been back. Haven't called, haven't done a Goddamn thing."

I stepped off the elevator, looking at my watch. I had a meeting with the task force at two. "Are you sure they're her parents?"

He walked out behind me. "I'll check the paperwork and see what we've got on them."

Every time I came back to the hospital, I got the same cold chills, the same feelings in the pit of my stomach, and when the odors from the ward hit me, I was a teenager all over again. "Give me the run down." I tried shaking off the feelings and focusing on the job at hand.

"No violent tendencies, no history of seizures or depression."

"Meds?"

"Ritalin at eight. She stopped taking them just before she quit speaking."

"Depression?"

"Not that we can tell, no. She appears interested in the world around her; she's just stopped living in it."

"Sounds familiar, eh, big guy?"

"I don't think she belongs here one way *or* the other."

"I'll see what I can do."

He put his arm around me and hugged me. "By the way… I love that car. The only problem is I keep gettin' eyeballed by the cops whenever I'm in the bad part of town."

"I'm really glad you like it. It's a beautiful car."

"Here we are. I've kept her in her room in case you just want to read her through the window."

I shook my head. "You say she's not violent?"

"Not yet." He grinned. "You want in?"

Smiling, I stood in front of it. "Please."

"I figured as much. I'll be right outside. Anything you need?"

"Her name?"

"Cindy."

Nodding, I opened the door, feeling every ounce of teenage anxiety coming back at me. I hated this place, and if it was scary for a fourteen-year-old, it must be frightening as hell to a ten-year-old.

When I walked in, Cindy was sitting in a chair, her legs dangling back and forth. She was wearing red Nike high tops, jeans, and a red t-shirt. She looked much younger than ten. Maybe it was her long blonde hair and big blue eyes.

"Hi," I said softly, kneeling in front of her. I was careful to lower my shields very slowly. You never know when a newbie will pick up everything you're thinking or feeling, so I reinforced my blocks, lowered my shields, and yep, sure enough, little Cindy was one of us. She was trying to block, which explained why George hadn't been able to deduce her origin.

"My name is Echo. George is a really good friend of mine and he asked me to come talk to you. Would you mind that?" To my surprise, she shook her head. Then she turned those big blue eyes toward me and they said more than any words ever could have. There was also no fear, which surprised me. I had been very afraid when I was here, and I'd been four years older. There was also no curiosity, as if she knew exactly who I was and why I was there. Her eyes were clear, focused, and undeniably super.

"I understand you don't like to talk to people."

She didn't take her eyes off me as she shook her head.

"That's fair. There aren't many people worth talking to, huh?"

She surprised me with a grin, then shook her head.

"But you *can* talk, can't you?"

Barely a nod, then she looked away.

"Mind if I have a seat?"

She shook her head. I was picking up a lot of mixed emotions from her. She was nervous, but tentative, and far calmer than I expected her to be. Truth to tell, she was incredibly composed for a ten-year-old.

"I was in here when I was fourteen."

She cocked her head and looked at me, one eyebrow raised in question. She believed me.

"Yep, I thought I was going nuts. You see, I can feel people's emotions. It was driving me insane because I didn't know what was happening to me. I belong to a special group of people with special gifts. Some of us hear other people's thoughts, some of us can move objects without touching them. We all feel like we're going crazy until someone like George spots us and offers to help us out. He spotted you and called me to come help you. Do you want my help?"

Her blue eyes seemed to change colors as she slowly nodded.

"You know you can trust me, don't you?"

She nodded again. I read her aura clearly and it indicated trust and acceptance.

"Good. Because you can. I'm here to help. Now I need to ask you some questions. If you don't feel like answering you can just nod or shake your head, okay?"

Nod.

"Are you hearing voices?"

Shake.

"Can you move objects without touching them?"

Shake.

"Does it feel like you're being haunted, you know, like, by a ghost?"

She grinned, and then shook her head. She found that idea amusing.

"I'll bet you never knew that there are some people who can actually talk to the dead. Can you?"

She actually chuckled and then shook her head.

"Okay, I take it you're not one of those either." Leaning closer to her, I grinned. "Your parents brought you here because something happened, right?"

She shook her head.

"Something didn't happen?"

She nodded.

"Something did happen?"

Nod.

Hmm. I wondered what she was shaking her head to. "Oh. They weren't your parents."

Slow shake.

Well, this was interesting. "Okay, so people brought you in here because something happened."

She shrugged.

"Is it because you don't talk anymore?"

Shrug.

I leaned back. "Hmm… Well, let me ask you this; the food here is really bad, the company is even worse, the beds are hard, and most folks here are scary in one way or another. Would you like to get out of here?"

Her face broke into a song.

"Yeah. I thought you might say that. You know, I had to bust out of here when I was a kid. Sometimes, you gotta do what you gotta do to get by in this life."

She was still grinning as she nodded.

"Now, I doubt we'll have to bust you out, but we will find a way to get you out of here. Sound good?"

Nod.

"But there's a hitch… well… it's not really a hitch, but it is the one condition you have to agree to if I'm going to get you out of here."

The grin fell from her face and I read distrust and doubt in her.

"There's a special place and a very special woman who can teach you how to control your powers." I paused and felt her change instantly. She liked the word power. "She taught me and many others like me how to control our abilities. Would you like to do that?"

The grin reappeared and she nodded.

"I thought so. I loved it there and learned so much. You can, too."

She cocked her head in a question she didn't need to ask.

"Why did I leave? We all have to leave once we grow into our skills. But I still visit and it's still my home." Rising, I extended my hand to her. "Trust me?"

She nodded and put her little hand in mine. It was incredibly warm.

"Good. Now, let me see what I can do about getting you out of here." When I left her room, George was just returning with her file in his hands. "I thought you were going to stay by the door."

"No need. You got to her. I could see that. I take it that means…"

"Yep, but I can't tell what. Says she doesn't hear voices or feel emotions or talk to ghosts. Also says that she doesn't move things. It's weird."

"Melika will know."

"If we can get her there."

"That shouldn't be too hard." George handed me her file. "Brought in by her aunt and uncle because she would no longer talk to them. They just don't have the time to put into her because they recently had triplets. They don't really want her back."

"Then where are her parents?"

"No clue, but I think this is worth a try. If we get the okay, it saves us the hassle of getting her out of here under the cloak of darkness."

"Fine. Then let's do it right away. I'll make the call."

He nodded.

I left, mentally wiping the heebie-jeebies off of me.

That was when I jotted down my notes for my next story; the homeless weren't the only invisible ones in our society… there were thousands of unwanted, unloved, and yes, invisible children in the United States just waiting to be written about.

After making my notes, I called Melika and told her all that I knew, which wasn't much. Some spotter I would be.

"And yet, you still don't know what she is?"

"I couldn't tell, no."

"But she can talk? She is just choosing not to at the

moment."

"Apparently. I don't know why she doesn't. I suspect we'll know soon enough."

"Excellent work, my dear. I will call and make the arrangements. I can't tell you how much I appreciate your work on this, Echo. I know you have a lot on your plate right now, but you know the importance of time in these matters. I lost a twelve-year-old telepath last week. By the time we got to him, his brains were fried. It breaks my heart every time we lose one."

"Well, I think we got to this one in time. Let me know what else you need me to do."

"I will. Again, thank you my dear. Oh, and keep at it with your story. Bishop says you are on the right track. Believe in yourself, my dear. The rest of us do."

I hung up and started toward the police station for my meeting with the task force. I was excited to finally have a place for my voice; to finally have someone take me seriously. This story wasn't over by a long shot.

"THE BOYS ARE all a-flutter," Danica said when I arrived. Danica took the four boxes of pepperoni pizza from me. "You better feed them *after* they tell you whatever it is that has them all pumped up. Apparently, someone found something useful."

We walked down the hall to the Batcave. At the door, I stopped, inhaled deeply, and pushed open the door. "Hey boys!"

"Yo, Princess!" Carl said, turning from his laptop. "It's about time. We were going nuts over here."

I smiled as all three gathered around Carl's computer.

"Okay, boys, whatcha got?"

"We dug deep into every word of every line you gave us and you're gonna want to marry us when we tell you what we found. We stuck gold with the word heliotrope."

Roger nodded and waved me over to a second computer. On the screen was a flower. "What's that?"

"A heliotrope."

"I thought it was a stone."

"It is, but we're pretty sure he meant the flower."

"How come?"

Roger clicked on another window. Up popped four flowers. "Gotta give Carl his props. He never gave up."

"It just stuck out there, don't you think? *Amid that swarm…* it made me think of bees. Bees and flowers. So, I punched in heliotrope and voilà, it's a flower."

"If I said *so what,* would it hurt your feelings?"

"Be patient, Princess. There's more. A lot more. We dug for a bit, until Roger typed in Circe." Both guys grinned. Franklin nodded. I was beginning to feel their excitement even through my shields.

"The Circe line ties right in to the heliotrope line. The Dragon Circe is a heliotrope."

"Okay."

"And the Dragon Circe is only found in Colombia."

Now, they had my attention. "Keep going."

"Colombia has all the puff and blow and drugs anyone could ever want. Puff the Magic Dragon, right?"

"So, we think your guy was trying to say that the people who are taking your guys from the streets are Colombians."

I let out a huge sigh. "That's quite a stretch even for me."

The boys exchanged glances. "Oh ye of little faith." Carl punched a few things in and motioned for me to come over. "This last line," he began reading it out loud. "…*For by the bridge and on that shapeless crew I saw him point to you with a threatening gesture, and I heard him called Geri del Bello.*"

"We looked up old Geri and discovered he was a cousin of Dante's father who was murdered. When Dante wrote the story, his death had not yet been avenged."

"There are several components to this line," Carl said, inhaling deeply. "I think the bridge piece is clear. Although which bridge is anybody's guess. Could be the Golden Gate, Bay, Dumbarton, or San Mateo. The second piece, which one could completely overlook, is the word *crew.*"

I frowned.

"Don't you get it, Princess? He's talking about the crew of a boat."

I swallowed loudly. "The crew of a boat near one of the bridges?"

All three nodded and turned toward me. "Given what we have here, your savant was trying to tell you that there's a boat near a bridge with Colombians on it. Whether or not your homeless guys are still there remains to be seen. But if you believe that Smiley was trying to send a message, this is it."

"With the resurgence of the popularity of heroin among Americans, the Colombian cartels are now moving huge quantities of it to various countries. The puff and blow, which we still believe refers to heroin, is connected to the disappearances. We're just not sure how."

I rubbed my face and sighed loudly. "Why on God's green earth would anyone abduct a bunch of homeless guys and put them on a boat?"

All three guys looked at each other. "To take them back to Colombia, Princess. What else?"

Now I *knew* they were reaching. "Kidnapping rich people and using them for hostages I can understand, but abducting a bunch of homeless guys makes no sense to me."

Carl stepped closer to me and said one word that sent chills up my spine. I wasn't ready for it, I had never even considered it, but there it was, like a frozen blade to my heart.

Slavery.

"SLAVERY? COME ON, guys. This is the twenty-first century."

"We've done our homework on this, Princess." Carl opened his laptop and pulled up a schematic drawing of Central and South America. There were little red dots concentrated in various places on the map. Then, he pulled up Indonesia and Southeast Asia, where more red dots appeared.

"Every time someone is abducted in this country, we start thinking in terms of sexual deviance. We're so caught up in this sexual mindset that we forget that slavery is still very much alive and thriving in South America. Did you know that Mexico City now has more kidnappings and abductions than either Colombia or Brazil? Kids still fetch top dollar and yes, sometimes they're pimped out or adopted, but a majority of the time they're used in one of the drug-producing countries like Colombia."

I stared at the monitor. "Used for what?"

"We snagged this map off an FBI computer database

this morning. See, *they* know the truth, and the truth is that there's a steady supply of Americans sold or taken into slavery every month. Like you said, we have a huge disposable population no one will miss."

I started pacing and looked up in annoyance when Danica opened one of the laptops. "Hear them out, Clark. I can tell by the look on your face that you don't like what they're saying, but hear them out anyway. Think about it. Think of all the homeless people living up and down the West Coast, from Seattle to San Diego. They're ripe for the picking because nobody cares."

"Human cargo," Franklin said. "Human cargo would be best transported by boat because the Coast Guard is about as ineffective an organization as ever existed. Get your booty, head down the coast, and there you are. The Galloway case was a perfect example of how easy it is to get in and out of our coast without detection."

Franklin pointed to a map of the United States on another monitor. "Well over twelve thousand miles of coastline; the Coast Guard can't defend any of it."

"Boats come in, boats go out and no one is the wiser. Only two percent of the incoming boats are ever boarded and investigated. What percent of outgoing vessels do you think are ever inspected?"

"Less than that?"

"Bingo. As for the human cargo, they can sell them or put them to work doing the kind of labor even poor folks won't do. Do you realize how hard it would be to escape from a camp in the jungles or the highlands of Colombia?"

I finally had to sit down before I fell down.

"When the word Colombia came up, the Boss wouldn't

let us do anything else."

I shot a look over to Danica. "Hence the break-in to the FBI website?"

Danica grinned and shrugged. "It's not the first time. We may sell the best security system in the world, but we can also break into any security system as well. Slavery really does exist in the 21st century, Clark, and if you're thinking about taking on the cartel, you better think again. Step away from the story. Let it go. No one cares because it's too touchy a subject with a part of the world we don't own and can't control."

Carl nodded. "There's no beating these guys. They're like what the Mafia used to be: ruthless, efficient, and unstoppable. The FBI, CIA and Interpol are helpless against them. And as the American taste in drugs changes, so does the cartel's ability to fill that need. The new cocaine is heroin and the Colombians have managed to get their hands deep in that market as well."

"But I thought heroin was a Southeast Asian drug."

"If it's a drug Americans will pay top dollar for… it's anybody's drug."

"In other words, Clark, step away from the God. Damned. Story." Danica's voice was made of steel. I'd only heard her use it twice before in our lives, and it resonated just as clearly now.

I looked from one serious face to another and, one by one, they each nodded in agreement. "Even if you *are* able to convince that task force of yours what's really going on, politics would take over before justice."

"You'd see your task force disbanded right out of the starting gate. It's the way things work."

"Colombia supply eighty percent of the world's cocaine." Carl added. "Eighty percent! How come the rest of the world hasn't stopped them? How come no one has created unbearable sanctions? The answer, Princess, is politics."

"You have to ask yourself why the United States allows it. When you get an answer, you'll know it's a lost cause to take them on. People who do quite often end up floating face down in some river."

Danica walked over to me and took my hand. "No one of any significance will have your back, Clark. Nothing good can come of this."

I stared at her in disbelief.

Danica held her hand up. "And no, I haven't forgotten what we learned at Mills. I know you want to make changes in the world, but you can't do that if you're dead. Sometimes, you have to weigh the outcomes against the journey, remember? This is one fight you need to back down from." Danica held my hand in both of hers. "And if you doubt that the four of us really, really smart people are right, then ask Melika. Hell, ask Tomas. I guarantee you, both of them will tell you the same thing. This is not your fight, and it's not a fight you can win."

I heaved a huge sigh. I hated when she used Melika to back herself up. "I understand what you're all saying but…"

"But nothing, Clark. Goddamn it, you are way out of your league on this one. I'm sorry, but you really are." Releasing my hand, Danica took a folder off the desk and handed it to me. "Read this, then. If you're still set on going through with this foolishness, you need to understand that there will be *no one* who can bail you out. That file will show you all the people who have gone up against the cartel and what happened to them. Many of them are journalists."

"What happened?" I asked, taking the file and opening it.

"They were never found again. A lot of cartel enemies vanish and a lot of countries look the other way. The United States is no exception. There's a *lot* of looking the other way."

I leafed through the file, clearly stolen from somewhere in cyberspace. Photos of bloody victims made me close the folder. Apparently, not everyone simply vanished. "So what am I supposed to do? Walk away knowing what I know and then doing nothing?"

"What do you think? You think you'd get someone to hear you? You haven't been able to so far. Can you really see someone boarding a ship which, more than likely, is listed to some American or Mexican or someone above suspicion? You think anyone is going to do anything? No. No they're not. You'll end up working in the mailroom if you live through it at all. It's not *worth* it, Clark. There are thousands of stories for you to tell, but you have to be alive to tell them." Danica shook her head. "I've never asked you not to do anything, Jane, but I'm asking you now. Please walk away."

The boys were all nodding. "The Boss is right. Please walk away. It's probably too late anyway."

"But what if it isn't? What if there's a boat out there with our guys in it? What if everything you're saying is true and I do nothing? How do I live with myself?"

"The way the rest of us live with ourselves. You have to ask yourself why you're the only one willing to risk your neck on this."

I looked into Danica's eyes. I didn't have to be empathic to read her fear. Whatever they had discovered in their digging had scared the hell out of every one of them.

"Forget what they taught us at Mills and take care of yourself." Danica opened the folder and riffled through the pages. "There's a reason the cartels are still around, still powerful, still in our midst, and it's a big reason. They. Are. Killers."

"I tell you what; let me ask Melika about it. If she says—"

"Why not ask Tomas?" Danica asked.

"If he so much as thought I was going to be in danger, he would be here like that." I snapped my fingers. "Even if I didn't need his help, I don't need him in my life right now. I will, however, talk to Melika before I do anything rash."

"Fine. Hear her out, then. She's always been able to talk sense into you when no one else could."

I grinned. "We'll see." Gathering up the file, I smiled over at the guys who were now stuffing their face with pizza. "You guys are the best, you know that, don't you?"

"We're the best if we can keep you alive."

Grinning, I started out the door with Danica hot on my heels.

"Come here, Clark. I know how you get and—"

"I'm not sure what I'm going to do, but if there's a boat under a bridge, I don't know how I can turn away, cartel or no cartel."

She nodded slowly. "I realized that. I have something for you in case you simply can't stop yourself."

I followed her back to her office, where she opened her desk and pulled out the revolver she had threatened to buy for me. Then, she pulled out a gadget the size of a checkbook.

"This is your direct link to the boys' computers. It's a prototype for a machine Roger has been working on. Consider it a supped-up version of a smartphone, but stripped of bloatware and ridiculously secure. Now, it's just a prototype, mind you. We're having some problems with the embedded camera, but we're working on that."

I opened the gadget and almost dropped it. Carl's face grinned at me from the screen. "Yo Princess. Pretty cool, eh?"

Danica nodded. "The moment you open it, all of *ours* beep. They set you up with the same kind of program on your cell. This has a better frequency and longer range. Anyway, opening the monitor signals the rest of us on the same vidmeet protocol. Let's just say it's our way of keeping tabs on you."

I smiled at Carl. "Kind of like some cyber babysitter."

"Not what it was intended for, Princess, but if it will keep you safe – safer – then so be it. Take the with you and keep in touch. Regardless of how you do this, it will keep you connected to the brains of this operation… and that would be us."

I nodded. "Fine then. Are you sure you guys don't just want to put a bug up my butt?"

Carl grinned. "Don't have to. There's a GPS system built right in."

"Of course there is."

"Be careful, Princess." Carl's face disappeared from the screen as I closed it.

I WRAPPED MY arms around Danica and hugged her tightly. "Believe in me, Danica. I can do this. It's not like I'm going out there to haul them in myself."

"Right. You're an empath, Clark, not some superhero. Remember that, will you?"

"I'll try."

Funny thing was, I wasn't sure there was a difference.

"HI, MEL. IT'S me."

"Oh good. I was hoping you'd call. We've made all the arrangements to get Cindy out of there, and they are willing to release her into your custody tomorrow morning."

"Into *my* cu—"

"Just until we can get her out here. George can't come, so I bought you and the girl an open ticket. I know this is a bit of an inconvenience for you right now, but…"

"I can handle it, really."

"Good. They'll meet you at the hospital tomorrow morning at eight."

"Eight. Got it."

"As for the piece that you are struggling with at the moment, all I can tell you, all that you're *willing* to hear is that you need to do what you have always done; and that's to follow your heart."

"And if I'm in danger?"

There was a slight pause. "Echo, my dear, the world we live in is fraught with danger. Just because we have extraordinary abilities does not mean we are at all safe. We each must look into our own heart to determine whether or not we are willing to take these dangers on."

"Like the time you threw that chicken to that alligator?"

"Precisely. Remember when you first came to the bayou, how you couldn't believe we lived among them?"

"Yes. They were so big and scary, and I knew nothing about them *except* how dangerous and scary they looked."

"And Tomas explained that our 'gators were no more dangerous than the squirrels in the suburbs, remember?"

I grinned. "Like it was yesterday."

"Well, now you live in a world where danger is everywhere. You can shrink from it, attack it head-on, or walk away, but regardless of what you do there will always be danger lurking behind every corner. I understand why Danica cautions you to be careful You should be. But life is fuller when you follow your heart, and if your heart guides you to those dark places where danger lies in wait, then you must forge ahead with every bit of power the universe has given you. It's your way, my dear. It's simply who you are."

I became a reporter because truth was my religion, my honesty and my creed. I couldn't very well run from it just because it was hard or scary or dangerous. My truth now was that I just might have an opportunity to save the lives of people who deserved better than what the universe had given them.

I guess that settled it then. "Thanks Mel. You always know what to say."

SITTING AT THE table with Tripod in my lap, I pored through the file, notes and printouts that Danica and the boys had given me.

The majority of heroin *consumed* in the United States came from Mexico and Colombia. It's grown on the steep mountainsides that are harder to fumigate. A large shipment of heroin is considered about the size of a sack of flour; easily smuggled in via speedboat or other transportation. It was a cash crop, and so far, history had proven that when there was a cash crop, *someone* had to harvest it... and those someones had traditionally been slaves.

After culling through the rest of the file, I sat back, stunned. Our federal agencies were aware of the slave trade still going on in the Americas, yet because of diplomatic issues and sensitive politics, they were doing little to stop it. And by little, I mean nothing.

I called Finn.

"Hey, Echo. I was gonna call when I had a second, but I never seemed to get one. Jardine told me the task force is starting its homework."

"That's good. You're right about him being one of the good guys. He was totally cool at our meeting. I was wondering what you think I should do if I came upon information the task force might need, or if I should just back off now that they're on it."

"You got more evidence after your meeting? Busy bee. Give whatever you have to Darryl and trust that he does the right thing with it. I can't speak for the other members of the task force, but I do know he'll do everything he can to help. You give him something to work with and I guarantee you'll get some answers."

"Does he check his email? I'll just send him what I've got for now."

"Email? Anytime he has a free minute, he's got his nose in it. Go ahead and email away."

"I'll do that. Thanks."

"Dinner soon? A real date?"

"Absolutely."

"Good. Pencil me in somewhere. I've been told lately that I'm a pretty good date and a fairly decent kisser."

"Sergeant Finn, you are much better than fairly decent. If that's her highest praise, dump her and kiss someone who appreciates your moves." I laughed. "Be careful out there, Deputy Dog."

"You do the same, Lois Lane."

Opening the little computer, I watched as the tiny camera popped out and the monitor came to life. It was weird knowing that somewhere in the wide expanse of cyberspace four different people might know that I had logged onto their personal electronic universe. I had to admit that the little vidbook was pretty cool.

"Need something, Princess?"

It was Carl. Then the screen split and Roger was on as well. "Hey Princess. Taking her out for a test drive?"

I couldn't help but grin. These were my bodyguards? Three pasty-white geeks and a mixed-race woman who feared nothing? I suppose it could have been worse. "Hi guys. Yeah, I'm just learning how to use this thing. It's a neat little gadget."

"It sure is. Want me to walk through it with you?"

For the next fifteen minutes, Carl walked me through downloading my notes to Darryl Jardine. I was really proud when I hit send. It was easier than I expected, slicker than trying to sort the same thing direct from my cell, and I felt so technologically savvy. The boys congratulated me and sent me on my way, making me promise never to leave home without it. Apparently, I was worthy of my own GPS tracking device.

Despite my best efforts, I had monkey mind and couldn't sleep. My life had suddenly become very full, and now I had a 10-year-old mute girl to take care of until I could get us on an airplane to New Orleans.

New Orleans.

There were times when it pulled me like a beckoning lover. Now was one of those times. I longed to be on a boat in the bayou with the sun at my back and the alligators on the riverbanks watching with one lazy eye. I loved the bayou, with its smells and the spiritual peace it afforded me. I was already looking forward to going back with little silent Cindy. I wondered what she would think. I wondered how big the bayou must look to a little girl of ten. I remembered how big it looked to *me* at first. I hoped that she would like it.

Tossing around in bed, I thought about Smiley and Bob. Was I too late to help them even if I could? Was I putting myself in unnecessary danger by going after something no one else was willing to? Was I even on the right track?

Modern-day slavery?

The file spoke for itself. This wasn't something new in our country. Our throwaways were being snatched off our streets and no one was lifting a finger to help. Since 2002 an estimated 700,000 children had been reported missing by the National Incidents Studies of Missing and Abducted Children. Why weren't we hearing about this every day? Why wasn't someone *doing* something? The rest of the numbers were staggering as well, and it looked like the government simply passed many of them off as custodial abductions… too domestic for anyone to really go after.

Almost a million missing children. The number was mind-boggling. If children could disappear so easily, imagine how many other people were taken with no one around to monitor them or care. The homeless were the perfect choice.

So how could I just walk away? Bob was my friend. He came to me for help. What would the quality of my life be, knowing that I had turned my back like everyone else?

Pretty crappy, I thought. After all, what would the quality of my life have *been* if people hadn't risked something to help *me*?

Rolling over, I came face-to-face with Tripod. I could see him blinking at me. "Hey there, Cutie." Reaching over, I scritched him under his chin and he purred loud enough to wake the dead. Everyone had told me to put him down; that a cat with three legs couldn't get around or have a decent life.

They were all wrong.

He'd been a throwaway once. Look how much joy he had brought to my life.

Rolling back over, I closed my eyes and felt sleep calling me. Isn't it funny how the right decisions put us in a place where sleep comes more easily? I slept like a baby for the first time in a week.

CHAPTER 44

I WAS OUT of the house before seven. My first stop was to the Berkeley Marina. If there was a cargo boat by the bridge, I needed to know, and there was a man I knew who had just the boat to take me there.

"*Necromancer*," I said, reading the name of the boat.

"I like to hide in plain sight," Rupert said, leaning over the railing. "I wondered who was calling."

"You're a hard man to find."

He grinned. "Not really. You just have to be persistent."

"Nice boat." He was dressed all in white, complete with a white captain's hat. "Apparently, you're expecting me."

He grinned. Rupert was about fifty years old and had a year-round tan that went well with his silver hair. "I know you think of me as just a lowly necro, but I have many other powers as well."

"Then you *were* expecting me."

"I was expecting a super, yes, but *you* are a pleasant surprise. I got your message when I was in Catalina. I wish I'd been here to help."

"Can you help now?" I walked around the side of the boat to the plank connecting the boat to the dock. "Permission to come aboard?"

Rupert tossed his head back and laughed. "Aye, aye, matey, come aboard." He reached out and helped me across the plank. "Would you like the nickel tour?"

"Absolutely."

Rupert's boat had one of the most spectacular living spaces I had ever seen. The cherry wood adorning the walls had been polished until it practically reflected my face. Venetian tiles lay in a spacious kitchen complete with stainless steel appliances. The place was gorgeous and roomier than one might think of a yacht. Every little thing was top quality, from the doorknobs to the crown molding. If I'd come in here blindfolded I would never have guessed that I was on a boat. "Wow."

As we walked back through the kitchen, complete with black granite counters, Rupert stopped at a very high-tech looking coffee pot and poured a cup. "How about a cup of joe before we get down to business?"

"That would be great, thank you."

"Black?"

"Yes, please." I watched him pour another cup of the dark liquid into a matching mug before handing it to me. "Mind if we go topside? It's such a beautiful morning. I love the smell of the salt air. It's such a great way to wake up and start your day."

We went up to the deck, where he pushed a button and a table lowered from a wall while two chairs rose from the floor. "I don't care much for clutter, so I had this made to keep out of my way while I was dancing."

I lowered my mug. "Dancing?"

"Sure. I love to dance. Rumba, salsa, swing. Don't care much for the flamenco and tango, but the others are big fun if you have the space. Please, have a seat."

I sat down across from him and wrapped my hands around the warm mug. "You have a beautiful home."

"Thank you. It suits me." He sat down and inhaled deeply through his nose. "Now, tell me why you're really here. As much as I wish it was to engage with my scintillating and charismatic personality, I'm pretty sure this is about business." He grinned softly and looked out over his mug. "Melika business?"

"Not this time. I just want to take you up on your offer to sail the bay."

The corners of his mouth twitched as he set his mug down. "You don't beat around the bush, do you? I can see that not much has changed since your college days. What's this really about, Echo?"

"If I told you that I needed to see if there was a certain boat in the bay, would you think I was crazy?"

"Actually, I would think you're a reporter getting a story. But if you want to use my very expensive boat, you'll have to tell me the *whole* story. This is my home, Echo, and if I'm going to put it at risk I need to know what I'm risking it for."

So I told him. All of it. When I finished my explanation, he leaned back in his chair. He was wearing an expression that could only be described as a Cheshire cat grin. "So let me get this straight. You want to cruise around looking for a ship full of abducted people who may or may not have been taken by the Colombian cartel. Does that about sum it up?"

I nodded. I couldn't tell how he felt about my request. He was a great blocker; nothing leaked. "I'll know it when I see it, Rupert. I'm sure of it."

He studied me for a minute, and I couldn't tell if he was trying to read me or not, but eventually he said, "When do we leave?"

I blinked several times. "That easy?"

"Sure. You're not asking me to do anything illegal; not that it matters, of course. I've done quite a few illegal maneuvers in my life. It's a beautiful day for us to sail, E. Just tell me what time and your chariot will be ready."

"I really appreciate this, Rupert."

He reached over and laid his hand on mine. "We have to stick together, Echo. I'll never forget how wonderful you were with that boy. He was so scared, and yet you managed to calm him down enough so that we could get to the heart of the matter. I know you really wanted to be successfully inserted back into reality, but I think your skills are being wasted on the naturals. I hope that someday you realize how much our people need you."

"For now, there are a bunch of homeless guys who need me."

"Just name your time and I'll be ready."

"Well, I have to pick up a little girl, so how about eleven?"

"Eleven it is. I'll have the *Necromancer* up and at your disposal."

I quickly finished my coffee and stood up. It was a gorgeous day to be out on the water. "Thank you so much."

"So… what's with this little girl? One of Mel's new students, I take it?"

I nodded. "Not yet, but she will be."

"What is she?"

"I don't know. She doesn't speak."

He cocked his head. "So?"

"So, I'm not a telepath. Besides, it doesn't matter what she is. Melika wants her."

"You can't read her?"

I shook my head. "Not like that."

"Well then, you pick up your precious cargo and we'll show her a grand day on the bay."

Handing Rupert my empty mug, I smiled. "All we're going to do is see if we can find the boat. After that, it's up to the authorities."

"You keep trying to convince yourself of that, my dear. I'll be here ready to rock and roll."

When I got back to my car, I sat there a moment shaking my head. It had been a while since I had dealt with as many supers as I had in the past week and a half. It was weird, really. At Mills, there were a couple, but we never interacted. After I graduated and started at the paper, I was too busy to notice, so all this extra energy was beginning to kick my ass. Rupert was incredibly powerful, yes, but I still hadn't determined the extent of his powers. Now, I was on my way to pick up another whose powers I was unsure of. No wonder I had a headache.

An hour later, I was pulling out of the hospital with Cindy quietly occupying Ladybug's passenger seat. Her aunt and uncle had done their best to appear concerned about Cindy; sending her to a special school lessened their guilt, but I'm an empath and I knew better. These people were relieved and practically gleeful at the prospect of getting rid of her. It was heartbreaking, really, to see how easy it was for these two to dump her in the hands of a woman they didn't even know. Whatever Cindy had done in their home had made them very afraid of her; so afraid it was palpable.

So, after filling out numerous forms and whatnot, the family said tearless goodbyes. Not even Cindy shed a single tear. She was done. Not that I could blame her, of course. It's very difficult to see any good in a human being who could drop kick you to the curb of a mental hospital. At least with Melika, she would find a family like I had.

"You're not sorry to be leaving them, are you?" I asked, looking over at her. She shook her head. "I thought as much. Didn't like living with them, eh?"

She held her palm up and then flicked it over.

"Oh, I see. It was the other way around?"

Nod and a sigh.

"Well, don't you worry because you're going to love it where you're going. I know I did. It was where I learned about my special skills and how to use them. You'll love Melika. She's a really good teacher and a wonderful friend."

At the word friend, Cindy's head swiveled toward me, her eyes two huge question marks.

"Yes, she's now my friend and she cares about me. Even though she hasn't met you, she cares about you as well. We're like a little family who looks out for each other. I'll be like a big sister to you. Would you like that?"

Vigorous nodding.

"Okay. Now I've got some boring adult work to do, so you have to promise me one thing."

She looked at me, expressionless.

"You have to stop talking so much." I was rewarded

with a huge smile that spread across her face and her eyes lit up. "I take it that means yes?"

She stuck her hand out to me and I released the wheel to shake hers. Maybe she just reminded me of me a long time ago, but I liked the spirit in this girl.

I drove a little further until I heard a strange beeping sound. Cindy looked in my bag and pulled out the vidbook. She started to hand it to me when she realized I was driving.

"Go ahead," I said. "Open it up."

Cindy nodded and then opened it.

"Goddamn it, Clark… Oh… you're not Clark." It was Danica in all her foul-mouthed glory. "I… uh… where's Echo?"

Cindy grinned and held the vidbook so I could see it. I decided it was best to pull over so I could talk. "Hey there. What's wrong with a cell phone?"

"I'm sorry for my potty mouth. The boys wanted to test run. Where have you been?"

"Picking Cindy up. Why? Are you keeping tabs on me?"

"You know it. I know you, Clark. You don't just turn off. You wrestle. You grapple. You ruminate. And until you tell me that you're letting this story go, I'm watching you like a hawk."

"Well here I am. I've got Cindy until tomorrow night. Then we're on the redeye to NOLA."

"And your story?"

"Takes a back seat to getting her set up with Melika. Family comes first."

"Okay then. I'll stop worrying so much. How's she doing, anyway?"

I looked over at Cindy. She was smiling.

"Keeps talking my ear off. I can't get in a word edgewise." I winked at Cindy, who chuckled. "I think we'll be fine."

"Let me know if you need anything."

"Will do."

"What do you think of the vidbook?"

"It's pretty cool. Does it have games? I was sort of hoping to give Cindy something to do this afternoon."

"Games? Are you insane? Who works for me? Only the biggest gamers on the West Coast. See that red arrow button? Press it."

I did and up came the boys' names as well as Danica's, only hers said Da Boss and mine said, of course, Princess. "Okay."

"Scroll down to Carl's name and hit enter."

I did, and in less than ten seconds, the screen split and Carl was on one half of the monitor. "Yo, Princess."

I cut my eyes over to Cindy, who had her hand clamped over her mouth because she was snickering. "Hey Carl. I've got a kid with me and she would like to play some games on this thing. Would you mind walking her through it?"

"No prob."

"There's just one problem. She doesn't talk."

"Then all she has to do is listen. Can she do that?"

I looked at Cindy, who nodded. "She says yes."

"Cool. Hand her over."

"And Dani? Don't worry. I won't do anything stupid." Handing the vidbook back to Cindy, I continued to the marina. Part of me considered taking her back to my apartment, but I just didn't want to leave her alone. It didn't seem right. It was bad enough that she had been handed off to someone she barely knew; the last thing she needed was to be kicked to the curb twice in one morning. Besides, this was just a reconnaissance to see whether or not anything would pan out.

As I drove back to Berkeley, my mind wandered around in search of any clues or ideas that I might have missed. If Rupert and I found a boat and he could get us close enough, I would be able to sense any individuals inside. It was possible I could detect Bob's energy, but not if he was surrounded by a lot of others. The key, again, was Smiley.

Autistic and Down's syndrome people have a different energy field to the rest of us. When I was in the bayou, Melika taught me about the different kinds of emotional energies that different people put out. If Smiley was truly a savant, I would probably be able to pick it up… if we could get close enough.

And what then?

I figured that I would contact Jardine and the task force and maybe even the Coast Guard. Danica was right that I was no superhero. I sure as hell didn't want to get in a line of fire. All I needed was to do what I do best: feel.

Turning to Cindy, I asked if she had ever been on a yacht. She shook her head.

"Well, before we go back to my place we're going on a yacht with a friend of mine. He is… well… he's one of us. You can trust him, okay?"

She frowned a second and then pointed her finger back and forth at me and her.

"What's one of us?" I asked. She nodded. "That's a good question. One of us means that we are not like everybody else. We're special. You're special, and Melika is going to show you just how special you are."

She nodded again. As odd as it seemed, I enjoyed the company. It was nice to have someone to talk to even if she didn't talk back.

"Rupert is a really nice guy. It's his yacht and he's taking us out so I can see if a certain boat is floating around the bay. Does that sound like fun?"

Cindy gave me a thumbs up and a huge smile.

"It's a beautiful day for being on a boat. Of course, anything's better than being back in that hospital, huh?"

Nod. She closed the vidbook and dropped it in her backpack.

When we got to the *Necromancer*, Rupert was standing by the side of the boat, waving. "Well, who have we here?" He asked. "Hi there. I'm Rupert, captain of the *Necromancer*. Do you know what a necromancer is?" Rupert looked over at me. "A necromancer is someone who can communicate with the dead. Pretty cool, huh?"

Cindy nodded.

"Her name is Cindy."

"Welcome aboard the *Necromancer*, Cindy. Feel free to check it out."

Which is precisely what she did.

"Thanks, again, Rupert."

Rupert rose and helped me aboard. "It's been awhile since I've had two good-looking women on my boat, so the pleasure is all mine. Now, I've got the best equipment of any boat this size, so the chances of us finding a ship the size of what you're talking about is pretty good." Rupert pulled the ropes and released the *Necro* from the pier. "I'll get us out to the open water, Echo, if you and Cindy would bring the food up from the galley. I took the liberty of having a little spread delivered."

A little spread?

When Cindy and I went downstairs, we were treated to a buffet that included paper-thin slices of lox, creamy pâté, three different kinds of cheese, fruits and vegetables, muffins, bagels, lunchmeats, condiments, and several chocolate truffles along with chocolate-covered strawberries.

Cindy and I just stared at the food. Her eyes were as big as mine. "Oh wow. I told you he was a nice guy."

She nodded quickly.

"Well, grab a platter and let's head back up." We both took a platter and started up the stairs. When we reached the deck, we set the food down and Cindy went back for the other platters.

"Nice kid, Echo."

I grinned almost proudly. "Yes, she is. She seems pretty comfortable around me. I mean… considering everything she's been through…"

"Well, she's awfully lucky to have you to help her navigate the waters of the paranormal. No idea what her powers are?"

"None."

"How come the kid doesn't talk?"

"Melika will have to find out." I smiled at Cindy as she set the tray down and went back downstairs. "Expecting an army?"

"This is kind of like a stake out, and you have to have good food for a stake out. We will not perish."

I smiled at him. He had a boyish charm I found quite appealing. "What's our plan?"

"Well I think we should cruise by the Bay Bridge first. My equipment will locate all watercrafts within twenty miles of the *Necro*. When we spot one, we can just cruise by and let you take a look. I take it we're looking for a vessel at least forty feet long that's going to hold a minimum of twelve men. I mean, if you're carrying anywhere from one to two dozen kidnap victims, they would be best in the cargo hold of the ship."

"Preferably the kind of ship that would go unnoticed and unbothered by the Coast Guard."

Rupert turned and grinned. "Then you're looking for a ship like this one or a container vessel. Less than two percent of container vessels are searched in this country. Even after nine-eleven, our ports are our weakest link. Hell, you could back a cargo ship up to any pier in San Francisco and load it full of stolen goods and no one would be the wiser. We just don't have the security, so you're looking for either really rich or really poor."

"You find the vessel, Captain, and I'll let you know if there's energy in it that matches our missing guys."

Rupert looked at me. "Melika said you're powerful… but I never imagined…"

"I know, I know. Empaths don't get a fair shake from the rest of you. I mean… what's the benefit of knowing how someone feels?"

"Actually, I could see a huge benefit to it. And it must be very helpful in your field."

"It has its perks."

Rupert and I climbed the ladder to the Captain's loft, or whatever it's called. "And what'll we do when we find the boat?"

"Call the Coast Guard, I guess."

He laughed. "Um, I hate to break it to you, but they're not like cops, you know? The Coast Guard is seriously undermanned in this part of the country. It's not like they're lurking around the corner waiting for a crisis."

"Then I guess we call the task force… see if they have any power to get someone to check it out."

"So we're just going to recon the boat and call it a day?"

"That's the plan. I don't want any trouble, Rupert. I wouldn't put either you or Cindy in danger. Speaking of which, I need to go down and check on her."

"I'll let you know when we're in visual of any boats."

After I climbed down the ladder, I sat across the table from Cindy who was playing a game on the vidbook. With every passing moment away from the hospital, her features began to soften and she looked less and less afraid. "Having a good time?"

She nodded.

"I'm really glad. Now, I want you to know that once we get you to Louisiana you can always call me, day or night if you ever feel lonely or just want to hear my voice, okay?"

Nod. Blink.

"I would never let anything bad happen to you, and where I'm sending you is a really fun place. Do you trust me?"

She nodded, and to my surprise, pointed at me.

"What? Oh. Do I trust you? Absolutely. I think you're a really good kid."

This made her happy. I guess trust is just a hard commodity to come by when you're a ten-year-old supernatural kid whom no one understands. I wondered again what she'd done to make her aunt and uncle distrust her enough to ship her off so easily, but it must have been a whopper. That's how it usually happened with most of us; usually a display of our abilities is the straw that breaks the camel's back. I wondered what her straw was.

"Coming up on a few boats, Echo," Rupert announced.

I jumped up as we approached.

"There are rules to water navigation, just like there are rules of the road. How close do you need to be?"

"This is good. Just keep going by it. The amount of energy I'm looking for is pretty large, so I'll know it when I see it."

"Ten-four. I'll just keep cruising boats until you see one that fits the bill. Do you think Cindy would like to sail the boat?"

"Oh, Rupert, I think she'd *really* like that." I helped Cindy up the ladder. "Have a good time. Just don't crash us, okay?" She took off up the ladder as if she were born to it.

As I stood on the deck overlooking the blue-green water of the San Francisco Bay, I felt a sense of calm wash over me. I don't know if it was because I was doing what I longed to do or because I had done the right thing by Cindy and by Bob and Smiley. I just know it felt really good. I wanted this story. I wanted a happy ending for Cindy. I guess I just wanted it all.

How does that saying go? Be careful what you wish for? In less than an hour, I would see just how true that was.

WE MUST HAVE checked out a dozen or so boats before I

heard Rupert cut the engines. "Cargo ship off the port side."

I looked over at the ship, lowered my shields and was nearly knocked over by a wave of energy that had not been present on the other boats.

"Umm… Rupert?"

He came down the ladder and stood beside me. "That's it, isn't it?"

I nodded slowly. "Strong energy bundle, coupled with the kind of energy I'm looking for from a certain man."

"Would binoculars help?"

I shook my head. "Not really. Energy has a certain distance it can travel before it dissipates. This is… really strong. Strong and desperate. There's a fear that even the weakest empath would be able to pick out."

"How sure are you?" Rupert was looking through a pair of binoculars, and before I could answer, the whining sound of a speedboat could be heard as it approached us from the bow of the cargo ship. "Looks like we have company," Rupert said, motioning to the approaching boat. It was one of those super-fast ski boats and it was coming right at us. "Don't see many of those on the bay," Rupert said. "Too choppy. I think you better call in the troops."

"Maybe they're just reconning us."

Rupert looked at me sideways. "Maybe."

I concentrated harder than I had in a long time and what I picked up was not reassuring.

"What you getting, Echo?"

"Unfriendly. Curious. Suspicious. You better make the mayday call now."

The speedboat cut its engines when it was about 50 yards away. Rupert had just brought the radio to his mouth, and lowered it.

"You better go below," I said to Cindy. She nodded and then slowly went down the ladder, looking over the side of the boat at the speedboat floating closer to us.

"Put the radio down," I ordered Rupert when I was hit by their dark energy.

"Nice boat!" said the speedboat driver as he pulled alongside us. They were about 20 feet away now and had nothing but trouble on their minds. The driver was a white male of about twenty-five, heavyset, and wearing clothes that did not appear right for sailing. He had on a brown leather bomber's jacket, jeans, boots, and dark glasses. Every alarm in my body was going off, so I reached for Rupert's hand and gave him a quick squeeze. Luckily, he had replaced the radio before they saw him.

We were in trouble. We both knew it, too.

"Thank you. Is there something we can do for you?" Rupert asked. I was really, really wishing that my bag was up here with me so I had the little gun Danica had given to me. I thought about releasing Rupert's hand and making a run for my bag, but I'd never make it.

"Mind if we come aboard? Never been on a yacht like that baby, and I'm thinking of buying one." As the man moved to get onto the hood of his speedboat, I saw the shoulder holster and butt of his weapon.

"Actually, I don't let strangers aboard my boat. Terrorism and all that. Sorry, old chap."

"Aw, come on, man. We're just a bunch of guys out here partying. We don't mean any harm. I'll bet your daughter would like to see the speedboat, wouldn't you, hon?"

Rupert and I turned our heads just a fraction, and there stood Cindy. She had just come back up to the deck and was standing at the railing, staring at the speedboat with an intense gaze.

"Shit," Rupert uttered under his breath. "No," he said to the thug, "She's seen plenty, actually."

"Don't make this hard, old man," The driver said, reaching into the bomber jacket for his weapon. Everything slowed down to the slowest motion imaginable. As he pushed his right hand into his jacket and grabbed the butt of his gun, a huge ball of fire came out of nowhere and crashed into his chest, sending him sprawling back onto the deck of the speedboat. His gun hung in the mid-air for a moment before *kerplunking* into the water. The driver was completely enveloped in flames, and without a single hesitation, Rupert grabbed the *Necromancer*'s controls and pulled away from the speedboat as fast as the yacht could go. As I turned to get Cindy, I knew. I knew exactly what she was; knew what she was capable of doing, and by the looks of what was happening to her now, I knew precisely what she was going to do.

I couldn't have stopped her even if I wanted.

Already, there was a strange bluish glow around both of her hands. The air around her was like the heat from motorcycle pipes and made this crackling, staticky sound. And before the speedboat's engine could turn over, Cindy raised her hands and threw what looked like two miniature balls of sun at its bow. The speedboat, and the two men on it, blew about a hundred feet in the air, sending flaming debris everywhere. Rupert closed the controls and slid down the ladder to help me put out any of the small flaming pieces that landed on the yacht's deck.

When we had stamped them all out, Rupert looked to Cindy and then to me. "Well, I guess we know what her powers are now, don't we?"

Cindy was what was known in the supernatural world as a fire starter.

Nodding, I knelt in front of her. I was surprised by how calm she was. Of course, I had never actually seen a pyrokinetic before.

"You okay?" I asked, looking for some signs of trauma. I mean, she'd just killed two people; one of them directly from a burst of flame from her own hands.

She nodded and looked at her hands. She knew what she had done. It was no accident. She had manipulated the energy around us and created a weapon that blew the speedboat to smithereens and she felt not one drop of remorse.

"I'm going to send out a mayday, Echo, and move us away from that boat. Where one speedboat is, others are sure to follow. We've got to get the hell out of here."

I nodded, only half hearing him. "So… that's what you've done that scares people, huh?"

Cindy shook her head and then held up her index finger. Suddenly, a flame jumped from it. She blew it out and shrugged.

"Someone saw you manipulating fire once."

Nod.

"And those fireballs you just threw. You've obviously made them before, haven't you?"

Nod.

I sighed and rose. There was one last question I had to

ask. It's not that the answer mattered, but it would help me understand her a little bit better. "You've killed somebody before, haven't you?" I knew the answer before she responded. Her energy was very clear.

Slowly, she nodded, then she pointed to herself. "Cinder," she whispered softly.

I frowned as I felt the yacht picking up speed. "What?"

She pointed to me and said, "Echo." Then to herself. "CindER."

Oh crap. Her name wasn't Cindy, it was CindER... as in ashes... as in a fire... as in fire starter. "All right, then, Cinder. I suppose I should be angry with you for what you just did, but the fact is you've probably just saved all of our lives."

She nodded and held out her hand. With very little effort, she manipulated another, smaller fireball. Then, she closed her hand and the ball vanished. I have to admit, I was impressed.

"I got a distress call out, Echo, but it looks like we're about to have more company. I'm not sure blowing up their boat was such a great idea."

Cinder and I looked over the bow and saw two more speedboats. The cargo ship had pulled up anchor and was beginning to make its way out of the bay.

"Gee, you blow up one little speedboat and look what happens," Rupert said. "Think she's got any more firepower left? Because if she doesn't, we're screwed."

"Rupert! I'm not going to ask her to kill any more people." I turned and found that Cinder had already started manipulating the energy around her, so I put my hands on her shoulders and shook my head. "No more, Cinder. I appreciate what you've done, but no more. This is not your battle."

"Yeah," Rupert added. "They say killing is bad for your soul, and I should know. Well, Echo, any ideas about how to get out of this one without using the kid's power?"

"Can you outrun them?"

"In those boats? Not a chance. We're either going to have to turn and fight or…"

"Or what? Rupert, if she could just dismantle the boat, that's one thing, but she's like a baby rattler. They shoot all their venom in one bite."

"If she doesn't bite, Echo, we're gonna get creamed."

The moment I took my eyes from her, she scooted across the deck, and before I knew it, she had thrown two more fireballs at the closest speedboat. It managed to get out of the way without getting hit as one seared past.

"Cinder, stop!"

Suddenly, bullets bounced off the railing, and I ran to get her.

"Let her do her thing, Echo! We're sitting ducks out here!"

Rupert was right. We were in deep trouble, and Cinder's powers were the only ones that could save us. But how do you ask a child to blow someone to bits?

"Here comes the third one, Echo."

I looked over and saw the third speedboat drop alongside the one trailing us.

"It's now or never, kiddo. Let her kill them before they hurt you. You can't stop the inevitable."

I looked over at Rupert and knew he hadn't said that. It was Tomas from somewhere deep in my brain. *"I can't."*

"Goddamn it! I leave you alone for one minute, and you get yourself into this kind of trouble? Let the kid do it. She has the power… and the experience. If she's all you've got, use her!"

"What are you saying?"

"You know what I'm saying. Save yourselves at any cost. She'll get over it. She already has."

Before I could answer, before Cinder could fire off another couple of fireballs, there was a loud beating sound, like rotator blades. Looking up, I spotted a Coast Guard helicopter making haste for the cargo ship.

"Well, slap a diaper on me and call me Grandpa! It's the Goddamn Coast Guard!" Rupert picked up his binoculars and looked at the cargo ship. "Holy crap, Echo, people are bailing left and right out of that cargo ship. Rats jumping from a sinking ship, I guess. Where in the hell did the Coast Guard come from?"

"I thought you said…"

"They never get here that quick, unless…"

Before I could answer, Cinder pointed to the table where we had been eating. Sitting open just as she had left it was the vidbook. "Yo, Princess! Say something, man, or the Boss is gonna start throwing things!"

I turned to Cinder and grinned. "Is this what you did when we told you to go below?"

She grinned and nodded.

Picking up the vidbook, I looked at the screen. "Tell Dani that we're all okay and that her vidbook is a huge success."

"Hell, Princess, we knew that. With the GPS system, we've had you in our sights all day long. Once the kid came on with this horrified look on her face, we called the cavalry.

You sure you're okay?"

I put my hand on Cinder's head. "We are now." I turned and saw three Coast Guard ships cutting through the water like torpedoes. I mean, they were hauling and meaning business. I turned back to Carl, only it wasn't Carl, it was Danica. She was paler than I had ever seen her.

"You know I'm gonna have to kick your ass, right? I can't believe… are you okay?"

"We're fine."

"And the homeless guys?"

"From what I can tell, a lot of them are still alive, but I don't have any confirmations yet. It was pretty incredible seeing people jump ship."

"I guess it was a good job, then, Clark."

"So, how did you get the Coast Guard here so quickly?"

"Don't thank us. Thank that Detective Jardine. We made one call to him the moment we knew you were at the marina, and he was all over it. Of course, with the GPS system, we knew exactly where you were and could give perfect directions. You are in *such* big trouble!"

"From?"

"Everyone!"

I said a few more words of thanks to her and the boys before signing off. She could have my head later.

"More incoming!" Rupert announced, only this time, he meant that a Coast Guard ship was pulling alongside us. "Um, Echo, is there anything else I need to know? The girl wasn't… you know…"

"Kidnapped? Not hardly. Everything is in order, Rupert. Don't worry."

"Don't worry? Honey, you're a danger magnet walking

around with a kid who is her own army troop."

"*Attention all hands aboard the* Necromancer. *This is the Coast Guard. Cut your engines and prepare to be boarded.*"

Rupert did as he was told and then the three of us stood on deck while waiting for the Coast Guard to come aboard.

"Ready, ladies?"

I looked down into Cinder's face and grinned. "Bet you haven't had this much fun in a long time, have you?"

She grinned and shook her head.

"Well, these are the good guys, so keep your fireball hands to yourself, okay?"

Nod.

When I glanced over at the Coast Guard ship, I was stunned to see a familiar face. "Why did I know this is how it would end?" Darryl Jardine said as he stepped on board.

I couldn't help myself. I ran over and hugged him. "Boy am I glad to see you!"

Jardine backed away, a little embarrassed. "I got your email. It took me awhile to decipher where you were going with it, but once I did, I realized you were on to something. Then one of your buddies called and said they thought you might be getting a little over your head."

I looked over at the cargo ship. "Are they…"

"Alive? You betcha. We got the call that everything was okay about a minute ago. We got the perps and the vics are alive. That's a pretty damn good day in my book. Is everyone safe here?"

I nodded. "It's just the three of us."

"Good. You know, you've got a lot of friends, Echo. First, I got a call from your friend, Danielle."

"Danica."

"Yeah, her. She called me early this morning and told me you're probably out here poking around where you didn't belong. So, I called my buddies at the Coast Guard and had them on standby. We were just headed out when your computer guys contacted us and told us what was going on. You done good, girl."

Sighing, I realized how exhausted I was. "Then it's over?"

"Well… it's certainly over for the bad guys, but I'll bet it's just beginning for you. This is going to make quite a story."

"Honestly, Jardine, I just want to see my friend Bob again."

"And apparently you will, but that was quite a tale you sent me. If you'da sent it to anyone else, they'd probably think you slipped a cog. I figured the least I could do was look into some of your allegations about the Colombian cartel. Your numbers were pretty hard to ignore. You do good work."

Exhausted, I tried to erect a stronger shield, but couldn't. Jardine was pumped up, and so were the other two guardsmen standing with Rupert. Their energy was exhausting.

"Look. They're taking your guys off the ship."

"Detective," one of the Coast Guard guys said, "we need to get this yacht further away from the crime scene. Apparently, one of their speedboats blew up as well."

Jardine nodded and assumed his gruff exterior. "Right." To me, he winked. "I suppose you better get back. I mean, this is quite an exclusive you've got on your hands. If there's anything we can do to make your story better, let me know.

This is the second time you've made me look good. I owe you."

I nodded slowly. Somehow, the story just wasn't as important as seeing Bob and being able to tell Dante that Smiley was alive. The story just wasn't as important as knowing what Cinder was and that she cared enough to save our lives. In the end, the story just wasn't important.

Ivy.

I think I'd had enough for one day.

The Guardsmen came over and whispered something to Jardine, who nodded. "Time to move out. They're gonna take the victims to the ER if you want to meet them there."

"SF General?"

"Yeah. Guess I'll see you over there. Well, you and a hundred other reporters. This is gonna be huge, Echo, so I hope you're ready."

I thought I was ready.

Oh boy, was I wrong.

CHAPTER 45

THE NEXT FORTY-EIGHT hours were a complete and total whirlwind that consumed every waking hour: about forty of them. You couldn't turn on any channel without hearing about the breaking story. I was interviewed by every major newspaper on the West Coast, every television station, and even 60 Minutes. The story grabbed national attention and catapulted me into a light that was so bright it nearly blinded me. Between interviews and appearances I barely had time to write the story.

Wes was walking around like a peacock, beating his chest over having nailed such a sensational story. He was nearly beside himself with all the phone calls and back patting that came his way. Giddy would be a good way to describe how he was for the first twenty-four hours after the story broke. A story like this takes on a life of its own, and would stay on the front pages until the next story came along. Well… for three days, there were no other stories, and people in many corners murmured Pulitzer Prize in my presence. It was a boon to the Chronicle to have a reporter thrust into the cameras, and everyone was excited and happy for me… everyone except Carter.

I couldn't blame him, really. To say that I stooped to blackmail might be a little strong, but I did stoop to something. The first chance I was alone with Wes, I told him that he could only have the story if he nixed Carter's dirt about the mayor's nanny, or whatever sleaze he was working on at the moment. I explained to Wes that I had had to pull some strings, and those strings pulled back when I needed them most. My life was in danger, and had it not been for the creation of a task force, Darryl Jardine might not have been able to respond when I needed him most. Wes agreed in a heartbeat. I guess that's what semi-celebrity gets you. In the end, Carter rubbed his sore spot, bid me congratulations, and buried the hatchet somewhere else than between my shoulder blades.

For Rupert's part in all of this, he opened up the *Necromancer* to anyone who wanted a tour. He wasn't about the publicity. He just enjoyed showing off his beautiful home. And whenever any reporter tried to give him credit, he never accepted it, and instead, turned all of the credit back to me. He was very sweet when pressed, but made it perfectly clear that all he did was sail the boat. He also added, that no, we were not lovers. We were friends. I appreciated that… so did Finn.

Melika also kept in touch. She was very proud of me, but her concern was always for us as supers. She knew I couldn't up and fly to New Orleans; that would have been the very worst thing to do. We couldn't afford having any reporters following me, nor could we drag Cinder through a mob of journalists. I decided that it was best to keep Cinder out of sight, so she stayed with Danica, who took her from me the moment we got to the marina. Let's just say that Cinder spent the next three days playing with three boys who had only the coolest of toys. She dug it and so did they. They ate pizza and watched movies, and they let her play with all of their coolest techno gadgets. I loved these guys before, but after the way they were with speechless Cinder, I would have eaten hot coals for them. She was having a great time.

And so was I.

Tomas contacted me shortly after we returned to land from the bay. I thanked him for his concern and told him what happened. He was relieved to know that we were okay, and that we would be going to New Orleans in the next few days. He was happy for me, but I think he knew I was finally on my own, and that hurt him a little.

And so, what I thought would be a good story turned into something much larger and kept me running from one venue to the next until I finally collapsed from exhaustion, twenty-eight hours later. When I woke up, I made my way to the hospital to see Bob and Smiley.

Bob was dehydrated and suffered a couple of broken ribs from a scuffle he'd gotten into getting onto the cargo ship. When he saw me, he started crying and hugged me for a long, long time.

"You… you…"

"I simply did what I told you I was going to do."

"But Jane… no one knew… and yet…"

"How did they get you?"

Bob wiped his eyes and sighed. He was a bone rack and I noticed all his food was gone. I'd brought him two double bacon cheeseburgers and when I put the bag on his lap, he started crying again.

"I saw these guys cruising around Lumpy while he was sleeping. I went to wake him up so he didn't get nabbed, and they got us both. They were quick as hot snot on a greased pole. They pulled up, three big guys got out, they shoved me into a panel van, picked up Lumpy, tossed him in and were gone under fifteen seconds. It was amazing."

"Were you scared?"

"Shitless. The worst part was not knowing what they wanted. None of us understood the language, so they'd just jabber away and we'd sit and wonder what the hell they were saying. Then, they brought out the smack, and we knew we were in for it."

The idea was to collect heroin users, and that way they could control them once they got them back to Colombia. That was the thread that bound these guys together. As addicts, they would do just about anything for their fix… anything including the work *getting* the fix.

When he'd finished eating, Bob reached out and took my hand. "A lot of people claim to be your friend, but you… you really proved it. Without you, who knows what would have happened to all of us?"

"Eat. You're too thin."

"You sound like my mother."

"Or something." We visited for a little bit, and he told me that he'd already been offered several jobs from people in the East Bay; people who'd got caught up in the story. When I left, he nearly crushed my spine as he hugged me.

"Thank you, Jane," he whispered, choking back another sob.

"You're welcome."
"You're my angel. You know that, don'tcha?"
I laughed. "Hardly. You know what I am?"
"What?"
"Your friend."

CHAPTER 46

I REALLY WANTED to see Rupert before we left for Louisiana. After all, none of this would have happened had he not volunteered his now bullet-ridden yacht. When I arrived after seeing the boys in the hospital, we sat on his yacht and shared a couple of margaritas.

"What you did, Echo, was save the lives that *nobody* cared about. You wrote some great pieces before we went out, and that was a most brilliant thing to do. You made people care even before the story broke. If your boss hasn't doubled your salary already, he's a fool."

"Wes Bentley is nobody's fool. No, he's taken good care of me."

"Good. Now, how about taking care of yourself? You look like you're about to drop."

"Already did. I have a few more interviews, then I told Wes I have a family issue and need to take some time off after all of this. I've got to get Cinder to Melika."

We sat quietly for a minute before Rupert said, "Pretty wild what she did to that boat, huh?"

I closed my eyes and I could see the fireballs' path as they rocketed toward the speedboat. "Wild doesn't cover it. I never suspected she was a PK. When those fireballs hit that boat, it scared the living daylights out of me."

"Not her." Rupert turned to me. "Did you find it odd how calm she was after blasting that guy? I mean, cool as a cucumber she was. Cool enough to belt out two more of those fireballs."

Opening my eyes, I nodded. "I know what you're saying; she's done it before."

"Think that's why she doesn't talk?"

"I don't know."

"How's she doing?"

I grinned. "She's having the time of her life."

"You've done a great job of keeping her out of the press."

"Thanks, but I didn't have much choice. This wasn't her battle."

"But she fought it anyway. Have you spoken to her about it? About what she did?"

I hadn't. I didn't even know where to begin. "I've been meaning to, but I don't want to have that talk with her until we can spend some time together after. Time is something in short supply for me right now."

"Maybe in New Orleans."

"Yeah." Slowly, I rose. "What better place for me to re-energize and focus on my life? I don't know who needs it more, Cinder or me."

"Well, my offer is always standing. You ever want to take a sail down to Mexico for a couple of days, you know where to find me." Rupert rose as well.

"I'll keep that in mind."

"Call me when you get back. I'd like to know how she managed her first few days in the bayou."

"I will." Wrapping my arms around his neck, I hugged him tightly. "When this roller coaster ride is over, I would love to take you out for a thank you dinner. None of this would have been possible without you."

"It's just like Melika says: we have to stick together. She's right, you know. No matter how much you try to be normal and fit in, you never will. Not really."

I kissed his cheek, but said nothing. Rupert had always felt that way.

Leaving the marina, I was heading back to the city when my phone rang.

"Hey there hotshot." Finn and I had managed to talk to each other for only a minute here and a second there, but little beyond catching up on the latest report or interview or headline.

"Hey there Deputy Dog. How's tricks?"

"Saw you on Good Morning San Francisco. You looked great."

"Oh, Finn, even *I'm* tired of seeing my face."

He chuckled. "Celebrity bringing you down?"

"Not enough sleep. Too much bad coffee. Way too much smiling. I can't stand one more second talking about me or I'll burst. So, if you want to talk, tell me about you."

"Me? Well… after watching the big Samoan strutting around here like he owns the place; after having to constantly hear what a fine detective he is; after answering my mother why I wasn't as good as Darryl… well, gee, there's not much left to say."

I grinned. "Should I be sorry?"

"Naw. Never be sorry for a job well done. I just wish you were my girlfriend so I could tell everybody *hey look, that's my girlfriend!*"

I laughed. "Don't worry, the wave is almost over."

"So, when can you squeeze in a little beat cop like me for dinner and a movie? Dinner and dancing? Dinner and dessert?"

My stomach did a little dance. "In a week. I have family in Louisiana and I thought it would do me some good to get grounded after all of this. It's been exhausting."

"But fun?"

"It was fun for the first couple of hours, but then it took on a life of its own and, well, I'm feeling a little out of balance."

"You? Echo, you're the most grounded person I know."

"You're sweet for saying so, but I need to get the hell out of Dodge. Even if it's just for a few days."

"I understand. Will you call me when you get back?"

"Try and stop me."

When we hung up, I wondered if I was being fair to him. We were worse than two ships passing in the night… we were two ships passing on different oceans.

I wondered if we'd ever connect.

CHAPTER 47

F INN HAD MANAGED to come over in the middle of the
night to see me the night before we left for Louisiana. I
was so tired that I fell asleep against his shoulder. I don't
mean sweet, cuddly sleep in the arms of the man you love.
No, it was more like that drooling down your chin, crust in
your eyes kind of sleep that made your face all scrunched up
and ugly. Yeah, I was really quite pretty.

When I was finally tucked into my own bed, along with
a note on my nightstand that said for me to have a good
time, be careful, and call him for that date I owed him, I was
feeling like the biggest loser on the planet.

From the bayou, twelve hours later, that date seemed a
really long way away, especially when I looked up and saw
Tomas standing on the dock.

"What are you... I thought..."

Tomas smiled as he gently helped me out of Bones'
boat. "Even in a small cavern in the outback, your story,
your face was all over the news. It took me six taxi cabs, five
airplanes, and a horse to get back here quickly."

"Why quickly? You knew I was okay."

He grinned and moved a stray hair from my forehead. "I needed to make sure no one followed you here. We can't have your successes bringing riffraff and other obnoxious reporters out here. With all your newfound stardom, we didn't want to jeopardize Melika's."

"We?"

"It's good to see you again, my dear." Melika walked down off the porch and hugged me. "Oh my word, but you're barely able to stand. In all the years I've known you, I've never felt you so exhausted. Poor girl."

Pulling away, I made introductions. Cinder was at once taken in by Tomas, as most were for the first time. If the bayou hadn't captivated her, which it clearly had, Tomas most assuredly did.

"We'll talk later," Tomas whispered, taking Cinder's hand. When she balked, he stopped and turned to me. I smiled at Cinder reassuringly.

"You're okay. This is where you're going to learn how to control your power. This is the school and these people are my family. They'll take really good care of you, show you some really cool things, and keep you safe and happy. Okay?"

She thought about it a second before nodding.

"Good. Now Tomas is going to show you to your room. It might be a good idea to take a nap." I looked over at Tomas. I felt 108 years old. "It's really good to see you."

He grinned. "I know."

When they were gone, Melika took my hands in hers. "Seems you've become quite a success."

"For the moment. This, too, shall pass."

"It's good to have you back."

"It's good to be back."

"How is the girl?"

"Powerful. She needs a lot. She blew up a man and then a boat without batting an eye."

Melika nodded. "Some people can kill without much effort, nor much regret. Cinder is one of them."

"But that's awful."

"Is it? She did it for you."

"For *me*?"

She nodded. "This young girl is very aware she is different. She is also painfully aware that she is dangerous. She would have struck out at anyone threatening you because *you* are the first person in her life to acknowledge that she's different without being afraid of her or leaving her. In short, my dear, you're her hero."

Sighing, I shook my head. "I don't feel like a hero. I feel like I've just stepped out of a tornado."

"Careful what you wish, remember? You wanted to make a difference in the world. Sometimes, you can do that anonymously and sometimes you can't. You want the world to be something it never can be, but that won't stop you from trying." She smiled that gentle smile I had always loved. "Do you know what else you need?"

"Twenty-six hours of sleep?"

"You need to forgive Tomas and repair whatever rift is between you. Heaven and hell couldn't have stopped him from returning here to be here when you got back. And you know why? Because he needed to see for himself that you are all right."

"He said he came back to make sure I wasn't followed

by any of my pesky colleagues."

Melika shook her head slowly. "You still don't understand him, do you? What you have done is shine a very big spotlight on an organization that prefers to scoot around in the darker corners of the world like the cockroaches they are. What you've done, my dear, is step on the tail of a very large and vengeful snake. Whether or not that snake chooses to strike back at you remains to be seen. Tomas has returned from his journey early to make sure that it doesn't."

I blinked several times. Of course I knew I had to stop the cartel, as many interviewers tactfully pointed out to me, but I never really felt like I was in any danger.

Was I?

Were we?

"Make peace with him, Echo. Because no matter where you go or what you do in this life, he will always love you. He will *always* have your back." With that, Melika started for the house, leaving me alone with my depleted energy and weary thoughts. So much had happened so fast, I'd never really had time to catch my breath or sort through my few coherent thoughts. I knew one thing for sure: on the river was exactly where I needed to be.

SITTING NEXT TO me, in a closeness only ex-lovers share, Tomas stared out of the water. "You okay?"

"I know in my head that I am… but I just don't feel…"

"Whole?"

"Exactly."

Tomas turned to me. "That happens, I think, when a dream comes true. It's like the dream is no longer in your heart and so you feel sort of… empty. You're out of sorts."

"That is precisely how I feel."

"You have to get another dream to take its place. You always said you wanted to break a story so huge it got national attention. Well, it did. Now what?"

I ran my hands through my hair and leaned on my knees. "I think my next dream won't be so grandiose and sure as hell won't include getting shot at."

This made him chuckle. "Yeah, that last one was pretty big."

"And came entirely too fast."

Turning to me, he took my hand in his. "You were born one of those rare individuals with the capability of changing the world around you. You have *it*... only it's not a Hollywood *it* as much as it is a spiritual *it*. The problem is, while you'll acknowledge your supernatural abilities, you fail to accept the rest of your incredible personal power."

"Personal power? Don't I have enough power as it is?"

"You have personal power that can cause the kind of change you're always talking about. Accept it. You're one of the good guys."

I studied him a moment before whispering, "And you? What are you?"

"I'm one of the good guys' bodyguards."

I grinned. "You can't protect me from the world, you know."

"I know. Maybe I *can* protect you from yourself. My job is to make sure you stay in the game for a really long time." Tomas gave my hand a quick squeeze before releasing it so that he could put his arm around me. I didn't move.

"You know... I'm sorta seeing someone."

He chuckled again, but there was something soothing

about the sound. "Sort of? Echo, those are the majority of your dating experiences."

"They are not!"

"Then why hasn't anything happened? Wait. Don't tell me. Too busy. Conflicting schedules. This big story. Stop me when I'm wrong."

I took his arm and flung it back at him.

"You can't, can you? Since I've known you, you've been trying to convince yourself that you're afraid to be with me. Has it ever occurred to you that you're really afraid of being with *anybody*?"

I opened my mouth to fire one at him, but nothing came out. Could it be that he was right and that one of the reasons I was so emotionally drained was because I was fighting off any intimate feelings I was having toward Finn?

Putting his arm back around my shoulders, Tomas pulled me to him. "I don't want anything from you. I just want to be here to give you my support. And my friendship. So please relax, okay?"

I turned to him, our faces inches apart. "How can I relax when what you say is probably true? I'm an intimacy-phobe."

He grinned and his eyes danced. "Well, the good thing about fears is that they can be conquered." His eyes suddenly got serious. "You really like this guy?"

"I do."

"And he's good enough for you?"

I nodded.

"Then work with Melika to find a way past that wall you've built around your heart. And if you need someone to bounce things off of or if you just need some kneecaps broken, I'm only a thought away."

Laying my head on his shoulder, I felt the last of my energy flow from my body and into the bayou. Yes, I was an empath, and yes, Mills had taught me to be an agent of change, but no one had prepared me for how to feel or what to do once a dream comes true.

And as the dusk crept over the day, and the night sounds began replacing the day sounds, my tired spirit started to replenish itself. Yes, I had made my dreams come true. Yes, I was, in fact, an agent of change; and yes, oh yes, I *did* fear intimacy.

So maybe it was time to replace my grandiose dream with something more practical, more existential. Maybe it was time to dream that a part of my heart could actually have someone in it; maybe it was time for me to have someone to share my life with.

As my body melted into his and my eyelids turned to cement, a new dream ever so cautiously tiptoed into my heart and took residence there.

How long it would remain just a dream was anybody's guess.

Dear Reader

Thank you for reading *Shattered Echo*. If you enjoyed this book (or even if you didn't) please consider leaving a star rating or review online. Your feedback is important, and will help other readers to find the book and decide whether to read it, too.

Acknowledgements

I am a better writer because of the impact of the following fabulous females.

Chris Convissor: In the dictionary, there is a photo of you next to the words friend, loyal, and authentic. Your friendship means the world to me.

Rita Mae Brown: You opened every door the rest of us have been lucky enough to walk through. Thank you for all your words of wit and wisdom.

Tracey Fuller: When I needed a writing buddy, there you were. Now we are best of friends, and my life is better for it. Thank you for all the laughs and green bananas.

Kachita Silva: Though you're gone now, you taught me to stand on my own two feet... and boy have these feet been places. I am the woman I am because of you and in spite of you. Thanks, mom, for giving me a titanium backbone.

Sara Slack: You not only help me be better at the craft of writing, you have given me a completely new platform from which to do it. Thank you so much for all your hard work and belief in me and my characters.

Elizabeth Peters: The only writer whose novels I buy in hardback. I know you're not resting in peace... not because you don't deserve it, but because you're a doer. Thank you for the many, many hours of Amelia Peabody.

About the Author

Linda Kay Silva (aka Alex Westmore) is a 5-time award-winning author of more than 35 novels across half a dozen series.

When not writing, Alex is traveling around the world, living a wild life being an adventurer and a collector of stories.

And boy has she collected some whoppers!

Alex has lived in a haunted house, been charged by an elephant, jumped from an airplane, rode rapids in several countries, and taken many Harley trips. She has spent time with the Vodoun in New Orleans, medicine men in the Southwest, and a Shaman in the Amazon. She's been a cop, a sportswriter, an ostrich rider, and a partridge in a pear tree.

Okay, *maybe* that last one isn't true…

Alex's series include time travel, supernatural powers, police adventure, post-apocalypse, demon hunting, and historical romance.

More From This Author

To see what else this author has to offer, check out her website:

www.alexwestmore.net